# NEVER STEAL FROM DRAGONS

PIXIEPUNK #1

PATRICK DUGAN

*To all of you that are chasing down your dreams*

1

---

# GELSEY

The first rule of the Hub is never steal from dragons. The second rule is, see rule number one. Gelsey repeated this to herself, pushing her wings for every drop of speed as she dodged through the warehouse rafters, avoiding targeted EMP blasts from the Clan Caerlux guards below her. Granted, hitting a six-centimeter flying target made aiming difficult. She swerved as a blast struck close by, causing her cybernetic wings to cut out.

Gelsey's stomach lurched as she fell, tumbling toward a stack of boxes and the shouting kappa guards. She pulled her fléchette pistol from the holster and fired a spray of micro-darts at the closest guard. The kappa, a meter of slimy, mottled green reptile, ducked into its craggy shell. The darts grew as they flew, no longer affected by the magic that allowed pixies to shrink their possessions. The darts impacted the kappa's back with a multitude of explosions. A large crack appeared in the shell as the target screamed in pain. One down.

By design, the mechanical aeronautic restart on Gelsey's wings rebooted the software before she smashed into the boxes. The wings unfurled, swooping her out of the path of yet another blast. Amateurs. They should use something heavier than EMP cannons if they were trying to kill a pixie. Gelsey whizzed between two rafter supports and through a tangle of old spider webs.

Landing softly, she wiped the webs off her goggles. She needed a moment to survey the room while the guards peered into the dim recesses of the rafters for her.

Using her enhanced vision, she searched until she spotted the doorway her client had sent her to find. The air vent above the door checked out as per the plans. Clan Cerelux guards shouldn't be in a warehouse in this part of the Quad, not to protect a low-rent stash house. The whole thing smacked of a setup.

The gig had been advertised as a standard crack-and-grab job to steal a piece of nanotech that someone in the Dregs wanted. At ten thousand glint for the run, this tech was a must-have item for somebody. In Hub, everything's value came down to how much glint a customer was willing to pay for it.

The kappas below ran in circles, randomly firing into the darkness of the elevated roof. Turtlemen weren't known for brains, though they were loyal to a fault and tough to kill. She'd fly circles around them. If they got their claws on her, they'd kill her. Luckily, these were just street-level goons and not enhanced mercs, like most of the dragon clan's guards were.

Gelsey took off, once more darting between the rafters, studying her surroundings until she found a workable diversion. Across the room the electric panel came into view, solving her problem. She sighted her pistol and gently squeezed the trigger, firing a volley of darts. Shards of metal burst from the panel in a geyser of sparks, as the explosive projectiles found their mark.

The warehouse plunged into darkness and disarray. Well, for the kappa, anyway. A couple of enhanced mercs and this would have been a whole different dance.

The silicon array that had been fused to her cornea increased the existing illumination. With the power out, the darkened maze of stacked pallets glowed in a soft amber. Flying in reduced light could be challenging given the inability to pick out fine details like wires or glass panes. Ending up flattened against a window like a wayward sparrow would make her the butt of every joke in the Quad.

The warehouse was a front for the nanotech dealer they had paid her to rob. Pixies by nature had sticky fingers, and Gelsey had climbed to the upper echelon of the Quad's thieves. The wetware she rocked helped. Not only that, but other thieves couldn't match her brains or street smarts. Gelsey had learned her skills from a life spent in the worst district in Hub. The Dregs.

The kappas shouted back and forth, accompanied by loud crashes as they attempted to navigate the unlit stash house. She stifled a giggle as her wings unfurled and beat softly, floating her across the intervening space to the air vent that would let her slide into the true target of tonight's venture. The guards had been unexpected. They were more of a nuisance for an experienced thief like her. While she could have taken time to scout and avoid them entirely, it would have slowed her down.

She removed the grille from the air vent in short order. Most security consultants didn't plan for a miniature thief when they installed their systems, making Gelsey's life much easier and far more profitable. Once inside the ductwork, the crystals embedded around her goggles provided ultraviolet light that allowed her to see in pitch black. She flew through the narrow channel, nimble in the confined space. Up ahead, the damper reflected the light back to her.

Already at the air exchange. Nice.

Gelsey climbed through the opening, crossing the space to the vent that led to her score. Easy as snatching berries from a bog wraith. Her wings collapsed into a ridge along her back as she crawled over to her access point.

Through the grate, she peered down into the bright room. Somehow, they had gotten the lights back on in the warehouse. Strange. It should have taken hours to repair the panel. Below her, a kappa stood before a metal desk, hands clenched before him, beak snapping nervously. "She's gone. We drove her off, sire." The guard's voice trembled as he spoke.

"Is that so? Then I have nothing to worry about. Correct?" The sibilant voice sounded bored and rather annoyed. Rule one flashed before her eyes. If she was analyzing that voice correctly, she'd be breaking that rule in a major way.

An audible gulp reached Gelsey's ears. She stifled a giggle. This was better than the canned comedies on the holovid. The kappa, however, wouldn't see the humor in it.

"Yes, master." The kappa knelt before the desk, shaking in fear.

"Stop your groveling and get out, oaf." From where Gelsey perched, the speaker sat just out of sight. She slid around the grate until she had a better view.

*Well, shit. Why did she have to be right all the time?* Below her sat a dragon.

This wasn't a whelp or a wyrmling but a full-blown wyrm. What in Harmony was a wyrm doing in the Quad? They never left the Apex.

He sported a long, electric blue Mohawk that cascaded down his back. His deep golden eyes bulged over a full muzzle. A wide nose with horizontal slits emitted a spray of water as he huffed with impatience. The tips of his wings peeked over his massive shoulders.

Rule one echoed through Gelsey's mind again. Anyone else would have run as soon as they spotted a dragon. Since she'd taken the job, though, that meant she'd find a way to complete it. She racked her brains for a plan to finish what she'd started.

With a loud bang, the grate swung free, causing her to tumble out into the open room. Her wings snapped out, arresting her fall before she hit the floor.

"Ah, Miss Swiftwing. I've been waiting to discuss a business proposal with you," the dragon said with a touch of amusement.

Rule three in Hub, never work for dragons. She really didn't want to break that rule. Nothing good ever came from working with dragons.

Gelsey swallowed hard, forcing her stress down to a manageable level. With wings spread, she lowered herself. The room sparkled as her visual overlays picked out the surveillance gear that covered the walls and ceiling.

Without an EMP charge of her own, she'd have a hard time overcoming this many devices. The pressure plates on the floor jumped to life as she descended, though her wings meant they weren't a deterrent.

The dragon dominated the center of the room. He wore a dark, pinstriped suit with a tie in Clan Caerlux blue. His nose was wider and his teeth sharpened, marking him as an older dragon. He raised long, taloned fingers to caress the black whiskers that draped on either side of his mouth. The calculating golden eyes completed the look and left no doubt that he would not think twice about ending Gelsey where she hovered.

"Please, Miss Swiftwing, take a seat. Watching you bob in the air is unsettling. It would be easier if you used your larger form." The dragon indicated a rickety wooden chair off to her left.

Gelsey settled into the chair, feet out in front of her. She concentrated for a moment, willing herself to her larger size. Most beings on Harmony thought pixies were always small, but really, they had two sizes. Too bad the dragon was one of the few in the know. In two blinks of an eye, Gelsey sat in the chair, though even at one and a half meters, her feet still didn't reach the floor.

"You mentioned business, Lord...?" She stretched out the lord part hoping he would supply her with a name.

The dragon smirked, taking the time to straighten his tie. "You may call me Ancep, if you'd like." No one used their real names in Hub, not unless you wanted to get hacked or magicked.

She opened her mouth to call him Ancep and he held up a hand to stop her from speaking, a thing pixies tended to do a lot of. "And I don't desire the Lord or other forms of flattery. I need a useful freelancer, not another sycophant like the bumbling idiots out there."

While pretending to listen, Gelsey scanned the room. Where was the nanotech she'd been sent for? Could she still score it and escape?

The only problem was the room consisted of a beat-up metal desk, one very scary dragon, and the chair she sat in. No nanotech devices were waiting to find a place in her pouch. Gelsey rubbed at her eyes in irritation.

*No tech, no heist, no nothin'.* As the thought crossed her mind, it popped out of her mouth. "I got hired for a lot of glint to break in here only to find kappa guards decked out in Clan Caerlux blue. Those things are slimy and gross, but they can jam if you go hand-to-hand with them. Hitting small targets, they aren't so good at, or I'd be lying out there, not sitting here. You should have used djinn for guards or maybe goblins if they had the appropriate tech. Goblins are whizzes at building devices, especially weapons. Anyways, the gig offered enough glint to make it worth it. If the client knew it was owned by you, they wouldn't have hired me. They'd be blackballed so fast their jacks would fall out of their heads. So, obviously, this was a test. Did I pass?"

"I hope you can get to your target faster than you get to your point." The dragon glared meaningfully at her. "You were highly recommended by the primes in the Nefastu, even though you don't work for them. I can see why, since you deftly avoided the guards and found the weak point to the room so quickly."

The Nefastu governed the underside of Hub through glint and brawn. They'd pressured her to join, but she'd turned them down. She worked alone and meant to keep it that way. Give them twenty-five percent? No way, that wasn't gonna happen. "They know the best when they see it. I've pulled jobs nobody else would touch. One time..." She stopped when she noticed his annoyed expression. "So, what can I do for you, Ancep?"

His eyebrow quirked up. "Allow me to get straight to the point. I'd like you to fetch a few freelancers for me."

Gelsey snorted. "You've got kappa to do that kind of work." The little voice in the back of her head screamed that she should watch her mouth in front of a dragon. The louder voice in the front of her head promptly out-shouted it. "They could track down people, especially your guards, wearing Clan Caerlux colors. Of course, a group of kappa trooping through the Quad might make who you're looking for vanish. Anyhow you have a lot of others at your disposal, so you don't need me to be your gopher."

Ancep's mouth twitched into what could be called a smirk, but an annoyed one. "I've heard of your impertinence. You'd do well to curb it in my presence."

"What are you going to do? Breathe fire on me?" Gelsey was pretty sure the little voice passed out at that one. "You need me or you'd have gone with a low-tier cutter."

"Ice."

"Huh?"

Vapor rose from the dragon's nostrils. "Ice. Clan Caerlux specializes in ice. I would freeze you solid from the neck down and let you defrost over a month or so. I've heard it's an exquisitely painful way to die."

"Oh." That stopped Gelsey's mouth better than anything her ma had ever thought of. She'd always accused Gelsey of having an overabundance of personality and a lack of common sense. Right now, Gelsey agreed with her ma. Despite being well-versed in dealing with Nefastu primes, omgas, and double pops, those experiences hadn't prepared her for negotiations with a dragon lord.

Ancep's stare brought her back to the present. "Understood?" When Gelsey mutely indicated she did, he continued. "Excellent. I have a list of five professionals I'd like you to contact and arrange for them to meet us at a safe house that I'll supply for the duration of the project. You've got five days to gather the team and bring them to the indicated safe house. At that point, I'll go over the objective, the parameters of success, and of course, the pay, which I can assure you will be extremely generous."

Gelsey waited until he had finished. "Just because I find them doesn't mean they'll agree to jack."

Reaching into his breast pocket, he produced a mem stick and pushed it across the desk. Gelsey leaned forward, way forward, and snatched the stick before returning to her seat. The small polycarbonate rod was no thicker than her little finger but could hold terabytes of data. She fished a nondescript black box from her jumpsuit and inserted the stick into the port.

Ancep snorted. Using the box to verify the stick could be viewed as an insult.

Without looking up, she said, "Nobody gets a free fly. I check everything. Never know when somebody will try to slip you a nerve dance."

Muted LEDs twinkled across the face of the box until all the lights turned green. Stick was clean. Supposedly. Who knew what tech dragons had access to? Guess she'd find out the hard way. She punched the stick out and slotted it in the port behind her right ear.

Five names slid into view, each with a folder containing a bio, image, and time and place to meet them. She recognized a couple of names on the list. Aikila moved a lot of unlawful tech and assorted banned items through Hub. She'd heard of Kelthar, the mage. He had a reputation that ran toward nasty if you crossed him. These were top-of-the-food-chain types, experts in their field, much as Gelsey was in hers. She appreciated a client who didn't skimp on the crew.

"What if they don't show? I don't want to go flying around like a phoenix looking for a forest fire." Gelsey stashed the stick in a small, protective pouch. Two things warred in her mind. It's either a trap to get them all out of Hub or the job that required this kind of firepower would be legendary. She couldn't tell which idea held the most dust.

Ancep's snort filled the air with freezing mist, causing Gelsey to shiver, snapping her attention back to the matter at hand. "For what I'm paying these infernal diviners, they had better produce results."

"And if I don't take the gig?"

Ancep's smile chilled her to the core. Icy vapor rose from both nostrils. "That wouldn't lead to a long lifespan for you."

Gelsey pushed the image of her head sticking out of a solid block of ice from her speeding mind. As far as she could tell, she'd have to take the job. She could try to ditch and run back to Thornmeadow to live a normal life, helping out at the family bakery. That still might not be enough to dodge a dragon's wrath. Better to glide with the winds than fly into the storm, as her ma always said. "Fine. I'll deliver your messages. Just as long as I'm not responsible if they aren't where they should be."

"They will be there." Ancep slid a cred chip across to her. Gelsey virus-scanned this one, too. She doubted anything would be wrong, and it wasn't. She slotted it, gasping when she saw the amount of glint it contained. "There will be a second payment of equal value once the collection has been completed. If all of you agree to the full job, you'll be rewarded with ten times that amount. Each."

"Ten times the amount," echoed through her mind. Just this one gig and she could retire to the Thanas Isles and live out her life in luxury.

"What is the full job?" Any run that warranted that amount had to be dangerous, especially given the talent of the others.

"I know patience isn't a trait pixies exhibit, but you'll need to find some. You will also need these." He produced a small pouch and tossed it over to Gelsey. She plucked it out of the air with practiced ease. "Give each member their mem stick, and I'm sure they will agree to meet with me."

Gelsey flipped open the pouch and saw five identical sticks, each labeled clearly with a name from the list. She slid it into her jumpsuit pocket. Thankfully, when pixies changed size, everything touching them changed too. Every instinct told her to flee. Professional pride kept her in the chair.

"So, we have a deal?" Ancep asked over steepled fingers. His stare could have cut through solid rock. The wisps of vapor swirling out of his nostrils reinforced his earlier threats.

Gelsey shuddered internally. *Never work for dragons* auto-looped through her thoughts. She steeled herself, knowing she would regret this later. She started to speak, thought better of it, and just nodded. She wondered if the gods above would protect her from her own folly.

# 2

# SILAI

The soft melodies of the harpist followed Silai as she crossed the lavish penthouse apartment. Serving gnomes carried silver trays of every imaginable delicacy from basilisk tongue to sautéed hydra. She ignored them all, sipping on a glass of expensive elvish wine that bore a striking resemblance to the crystal blue skies of Harmony. Well, at least once you got past the smog levels of Hub.

The gods of Hub were dragons and gold, and you could dispute the order. Only the dragons dealt in gold, hoarding it in their mountain lairs, clans fighting to gain superiority. Everyone else used glint, digital gold which made transactions easier and didn't get the dragon hordes showing up at your door in gold lust. The room was abuzz with the news of Clan Caerlux molting their new Elder, Lord Helaltra, in just over a week's time.

The assorted attendees of this party represented some of the most powerful beings in Hub. They came from the Dullahan of the Northern Reaches to the Nereid of the Thanas Isles off the Southern Coast and everywhere in between on the vast continent of Tellas. Some wore outfits designed in the tradition of their people while others wore the latest designers or techno-chic that changed colors and patterns as the viewer moved around them. Holographic images of a meteor shower danced across the flowing skirt of a tall, lavender-haired elf who tittered at a joke from a stocky djinn dressed in the colorful robes of his nomadic race.

A flock of scantily clad nymphs and undine fussed over K'Pal Ree, the latest music sensation to come out of the Quad this year. Next week he'd be gone from public view, either from an overdose or lack of interest. These pseudo-celebrities never lasted long. An overabundance of glint in the hands of these fast risers from down below caused more issues than they solved.

Silai's stomach made a dull rumble as the tantalizing aroma of meat wafted past on the silver trays of the wait staff. Elves were vegetarians, refusing to destroy life to feed themselves. Another drawback of her Lady Kyerr persona. The first thing Silai would do after this job was to get a good slab of meat and eat it raw.

Ega Hul stood on one of the outer balconies watching his city. The thirteen dragon clans, each based on the color of their skin, ruled Hub, and the chromatic dragons ruled the dragon clans. Hul was a wyrm, his multi-hued wings spread out behind him. One day he would molt into an elder dragon, taking on the traditional form of his species.

As the Chromatic Sire's High Councilor, he was the most powerful being in Hub. Hul stood almost a meter taller than the two HubSec officers behind him. They had the widened nose and slightly extended muzzle of wyrmlings or maybe they were whelps like the rest of HubSec. Silai found it hard to tell the difference unless they were close. The important part was that dragons ruled and it paid to stay out of their way, which she did.

Continuing her stroll through the party, she nodded in the correct elvish fashion to those who caught her eye, never stopping to socialize. While the others partied, Silai worked, covertly checking exits and marking any guests who might cause problems. Bodyguards stood just outside their employer's earshot, though close enough to step in should trouble present itself. Two bodyguards bore the look of being vat-grown from the splicer's labs, genetically crafted to be stronger and faster than anyone could naturally be. Smart guns poked from camouflaged holsters, invisible but for a small wrinkle of fabric in a jacket or other garment. Many of the more expensive guards would have enough firepower built into their bodies to take down the entire building. In addition to the personal bodyguards, the host's private security force was also present, enhanced with everything from nanotech to the magical.

Silai stopped to admire an exquisite piece of digital art stationed at the far side of the room. The beauty of the piece was stunning, and if you were within range, each image pulled a deep emotional response from the viewer. Cathartic Art might be all the rage, but Silai preferred to keep her emotions where they belonged, buried beneath years of denial and repression.

Ambassador Q'rell from the Mangku greeted her, his presence an unfortunate aspect of attending these gatherings. The ambassador was a fixture at any event where powerful people were. His eyes never reached her face, though given the cut of the Joheim original she wore, she didn't blame him. It displayed everything quite nicely without being so form-fitting she couldn't hide a few surprises underneath it. "Ambassador, it is lovely to see you."

"My Lady Kyerr." Q'rell's fangs were visible as he smiled at her. He kissed the back of her hand gently. When the pale-haired man straightened, he didn't let go. Silai casually assessed the tattooed designs on the back of his hands. The markings grew more intricate as one climbed in power among the Mangku. "I'd been hoping to further discuss the arrangement I'd proffered at our last meeting."

Silai glanced at her sparkling rings, which hadn't darkened as they would in the presence of magic. She'd assumed that he would employ magic to soothe or sway her, making her vulnerable. The stones indicated he had not. Yet. The Mangku were renowned warlocks and feared across Hub. In order to become an ambassador for his people, Q'rell had to have power and know how to use it. She smiled demurely at the ambassador, glad that this job would be ending soon. "Ambassa--."

"Please, call me Ty."

She dipped her chin in the elvish fashion, head slightly tipped to the left as was proper. If she had her way, it would be a long time before running another grift as an elf. Too many inconvenient rules to follow. "Of course, Ty. I have business to finish with our gracious host. After-ward, I'd be pleased to join you for a drink and see what progresses from there."

A predatory smile crossed Q'rell's face, hunger reflected in his eyes. "Business can wait, my dear. I can assure you, you'll be far happier as my--"

He never finished his statement. A hand released Silai from the ambassador's grip. Lucrea stood very still, a pleasant smile on his bearded face. Candlelight flickered across the microcircuits embedded in the brown of his irises. That surgery alone must have cost more than Silai conned out of her marks in a year, though if she landed this fish, her financial future looked bright.

"Ambassador, I trust you are well?" Lucrea asked.

Anger flashed across Q'rell's face, replaced instantly by a resigned smile. "Quite well, Master Bartomi. You have excellent taste in business associates." At the last remark, he bobbed his head toward Silai, though the gesture could be considered rude in such refined circles.

Lucrea laughed softly. "Agreed. If you will excuse me, I must steal Lady Kyerr so we can conclude our business. She has procured an amazing piece of Nereid statuary for my collection. If she's as shrewd a negotiator as she is lovely, my coffers will be bare by the end of the evening, I have no doubt."

Her ring changed from a solid green to a slightly blueish cast, informing her Lucrea employed magic to get the ambassador to release her hand. Mangku were a lot of things, most of them bad, but timid wasn't one of their traits. Silai made the correct curtsy to the ambassador before turning to walk with Lucrea. "Thank you, My Lord. Q'rell can be quite..." She trailed off, unsure of the proper word to use given her companion's status.

Lucrea took this as a subtle jab at Q'rell and chuckled. "I've had to extricate many a young woman from the grasp of our predatory friends from Mangku. Rumors of Q'rell's particular pleasures have reached my ears, and I find them disturbing." He stroked his chin for a moment. "Repugnant might be a better description."

Silai blushed, for she had heard the same murmurings at the parties she'd attended over the past year. If things went well, the honorable Lady Taylin Kyerr of House Magdalyon would be another in a long line of missing women around Hub, and Silai would become a new person and move on to a new life.

If things didn't go well? She pushed the thought from her mind. No sense tempting the god of misfortune.

"I see you've heard the same as I, my lady."

A loud snarl and a crash of expensive glassware erupted behind them. They turned to see an attendant lying on the ground, blood dripping from her cut lip. The remains of the wine glasses decorated the inlaid marble floor. The attendant staggered to her feet, stammering out an apology as tears raced down her cheeks.

Lucrea stood as rigid as a statue. His olive skin darkened in anger. "What is the meaning of this affront, Q'rell? How dare you strike a member of my household?"

Q'rell pointed at Silai. "She is mine. I've paid the blood price for her."

Silai blanched. The Mangku were a secretive people who worshiped the demon lords. If he had paid blood for her, she could be in serious trouble. She racked her brain for any misstep that would have allowed him to claim her but came up empty.

"On what grounds do you claim a Lady of House Magdalyon?" Lucrea asked.

Q'rell barked a harsh, mirthless laugh. "She is no more an elf than you are. I can smell the fox on her, sure as I'm standing here."

Damn it all. How had he figured it out? It didn't matter. Lying to the ambassador about her true identity allowed Q'rell the right to claim her by blood. If Q'rell succeeded in unmasking her, Lucrea might execute her without a second thought, as kitsune, by tradition, were killed on sight.

Silai gasped. "This is an outrage! I demand satisfaction. These accusations are baseless." Her mind raced, seeking a way out, but a crowd had gathered. Gawking was beneath them of course, but most simply could not resist the urge to watch a spectacle unfold.

The ambassador grinned, fangs more pronounced than earlier. "Bring in Jartic."

A soft murmur raced through the crowd, setting Silai's nerves on edge. She didn't know what or who Jartic referred to. She maintained her composure, a bored expression on her face that befitted an elf. Two burly bodyguards escorted a short, husky woman into the room. She had dark hair pulled into a tight bun and thick spectacles perched on her nose, an affectation in this world where eyes were replaced like sheets on a bed.

Q'rell bowed to the woman. He turned and addressed the room, which hovered with pent-up excitement while simultaneously trying to feign disinterest. "This is Madam Jartic. She is a domovoi, one of the few who can break a fox's spell."

Eyebrows shot up as the crowd regarded the scene, hushed conversations increasing. Silai didn't react. The domovoi were known for their ability to destroy a kitsune's camouflage with a touch. People called Silai's race foxes since their natural form possessed a multitude of tails, nine in a mature member of the race, that merged around them to become whatever the kitsune wanted to be. Fear crept up her spine since no one should have known her true identity. For as long as Silai had been in the city, she'd been Lady Kyerr.

All pretense of indifference fled as the party guests pushed closer to see the display. Unmasking a legendary nine-tailed kitsune would be an amazing event for any party and anticipation grew to a fevered pitch.

Madame Jartic reached out to touch Silai, a smug look on her face. The crowd, silent with expectation leaned in, every eye fastened to the small domovoi's hand.

Silai stiffened. It was time to find out if her preparation and the cost of the splicer lab had paid off. If it didn't, it would cost her far more than her life.

The crowd hushed as the domovoi reached across and touched Silai's bare arm. Her stomach roiling in disgust, Silai steeled herself to be motionless, even though the touch felt like rancid oil pouring over her skin. Murmurs began as nothing happened. Madam Jartic's eyes widened as that same realization dawned on her. The smaller woman tightened her grip as if that would force the change to Silai's natural form.

Silai tilted her head, eyebrows raised in annoyance in an elvish way. "You are hurting my arm."

Jartic's mouth dropped open. "I don't understand." She looked to the ambassador for guidance. "You told me she be a kitsune. My touch has never failed."

Lucrea sighed. "As Lady Kyerr stated earlier, the ambassador's allegations are baseless. Now, if you'll excuse us, the lady and I have a deal to finalize." The host offered his arm which Silai gratefully accepted. The domovoi's presence rattled her and she couldn't afford a misstep at this stage of the con.

A scream of agony from behind them shattered the quiet of the stunned crowd. A second later, chaos reigned over the party as guests, including a very shocked Madame Jartic, ran from the center of the room where the failed unmasking had taken place.

Silai turned in time to see Q'rell's orc bodyguard hit the floor, blood oozing from the slash in his throat. Red energy flared around the warlock's bloody hands, coalescing into the form of a slavering hellhound. Q'rell locked his gaze on Lucrea. "I've paid the blood price for her, and I will take what is mine."

Quickly, Lucrea stepped between Silai and the hound. "Dismiss your pet and leave before I teach you some manners. I will see the Warlock Council strips you of your title and lands for this. No one disrespects me in my home or threatens my guests."

The hound growled, spittle dripping off its fangs and sending up wisps of smoke where the drops hit the floor. Rumor held that Lucrea was a lares, a creature of enormous magical strength once considered a god on Old Earth before the Hidden People fled to Harmony. Silai doubted it since most of the lares had stayed and died as gods rather than live with the commoners in the dimension of Harmony.

"Time to see if the rumors about you are true, Lucrea," Q'rell said, as he motioned for the hellhound to attack. The massive hound took three strides and leapt for its victim's throat. It never made it.

A blue shield sprang up before the bored Lucrea. As the hound impacted the light, it slowly disappeared as if drawn through a shredder. The few partygoers with an unhealthy amount of curiosity, or death wishes, gasped in shock. Mangku were feared for their magic, yet Lucrea hadn't moved a muscle to destroy the hound.

This fact shouldn't have been lost on Q'rell. Any good sense the warlock had when he'd arrived with had fled with the guests. A deep blue, almost black beam of light struck the shield and had no more effect than the hound had. Q'rell snarled before stomping out of the room. Lucrea didn't say a word, just watched him go.

"You aren't going to stop him?" Silai asked, disbelief clear in her tone. A sideward glance from the Lucrea changed it quickly. "No disrespect intended but we should turn him over to the authorities."

The beard hid most of his expression as he offered her his arm again, resuming their walk to the conference room where they had conducted business before. "My Lady Kyerr, one such as Q'rell would either kill anyone who attempted to apprehend him, or if HubSec managed the arrest, he'd be out and causing even more trouble in a few hours at best. I will send a message to the Warlock Council of Mangku, and they will handle any unpleasantness."

Silai needn't worry about Q'rell for long, since as soon as she received the agreed-on sum from Lord Lucrea, Lady Kyerr would vanish into the mists of Hub "So, the Council will punish him? He deserves no less for confronting you so."

Lucrea's face clouded over as he looked at her, eyes boring deep into her. "His attack worries me not, though the death of his guard troubles me much more, as I would think it would an elvish lady. Don't your people consider all life sacred?"

Damn it. She'd gotten distracted and let her character slip. The game depended on her being Kyerr. If Lucrea had any doubts, the game would go down hard and she did not fancy being on the receiving end of his wrath. She gasped in dismay, holding her hand to her breast. "Of course, we do, My Lord. My concern is for any that might cross the ambassador's path and be harmed. The gods themselves weep for the young man and will carry him to the endless lands beyond, I have no doubt."

Lucrea's mouth twisted as he studied her. They reached the conference room. Stepping through the doorway set every ring she wore dark. The conference room sported an antique table large enough for twenty. Around the table, deep, high-backed chairs waited. The rug was worth more glint than Silai could grift in ten lifetimes. It had been hand-woven and plaited with gold and platinum. The thirteen dragon clans would kill each other over that piece alone.

What was not apparent to the naked eye were the wards and tech devices stashed around the marble pillars and statuary that lined the walls. It had surprised Silai the first time that any of her rings functioned under such impressive defenses. Lucrea slid a chair out, offering it to Silai. Before it on the table stood the metal box that had been delivered earlier in the evening. He took the chair next to her.

She touched the sensor array on the top of the box, allowing it to register her as an authorized owner. A small tube popped up next to the matte silver of the box, bending toward her. She put her eye in front of it, allowing it to scan her retinal pattern. Another opening appeared and Silai placed a mem stick into the jack. A soft beep announced that the case was now properly unlocked.

Silai turned to her buyer. She'd done her research and knew that Old Earth sculptures were a weakness for him. She'd found an artist in a village on the Thanas Isles who had crafted it from a special type of marble that could only be found there. It had cost a small fortune, but Lucrea had agreed to pay her twenty times the amount. With that much glint, she'd be set for life.

Gently, she lowered the four sides of the protective case, exposing the translucent shield that kept the piece from moving during transit. She touched the switch and the barrier retracted, leaving a statue of a human male, a wreath expertly carved around his head. He held a spear in one hand and a lamb in the other. The fine details had been meticulously worn down and yellowed to make it appear to be over a thousand years old.

"The holovid doesn't do it justice," whispered Lucrea as he carefully took the figure from the case. He viewed it from every angle. Silai's heart stopped as he turned it upside down, inspecting the maker's mark on the bottom. The characters were barely visible, by design, but it should be in line with what a collector of such rare antiquities would expect. A tear slid down his cheek to be swallowed by his beard. "This is perfect. I'd not believed such a piece still existed."

"It pleases me that it meets your approval, My Lord." Silai wanted to scream with relief when it had passed inspection. She watched as he reverently put the figure back in the container before handing her a small metal case. Silai popped the latch, exposing the gleaming cred stick resting on a silk lining, before she snapped it shut and slid it into her pocket. "Thank you, Lucrea. It's been a pleasure. Shall I call again if I find another such piece?"

He nodded. "Are you not going to confirm that the payment is sufficient?"

She opened her hand before her in the elvish version of a shrug. "I would not do business with someone I feared would cheat me."

That brought a large smile to his face. "Nor would I." His eyes returned to the figure, caressing every detail of the statue. "Please, use the back entrance, just in case."

After standing, she bowed to her host and let herself out. She'd done it. She'd pulled off the con of a lifetime. Time to vanish somewhere safe and lose Kyerr forever. It might be time for a vacation away from Hub, just to be on the safe side.

Halfway to ground level, she paused the lift. The cred chip slid into the port behind her right ear. The contents opened, overlaying her normal sight. It showed a zero balance. A note pulsed in the lower corner of her vision. The words scrolled across her vision.

*My Lady Kyerr,*

*Thank you for the amusements of the past few months. For the first time in a very long time, I've had the pleasure of being the target of an amazingly detailed ruse. The statue is magnificent though I'm afraid it is no more from Old Earth than you are.*

*My sincerest regards,*

*Lucrea*

She rode the lift to the ground floor, mind spinning at the implications of the failed con. He didn't sound upset, rather amused. The elevator stopped, the door sliding open to allow her exit. Silai froze as she spotted two guards laying on the ground. Before she could move, Q'rell stepped out of the shadows.

Silai screamed, but no one heard her.

The room swayed awkwardly as Silai opened her eyes. She fought to regain her equilibrium, assuming she'd been drugged or struck, leaving her disoriented. Once her vision cleared, she peered around, taking in her surroundings. Knowing the Mangku, she'd expected a dark torture chamber or a prison cell. Her current accommodations were immaculate. A bed with a silk duvet and mounds of pillows served as her prison for now. A wooden desk occupied the other wall next to a low dresser. Each of the side walls had a door, one open, one closed. The open one would be the bath and the other would lead to freedom.

It took a moment to realize the swaying she was experiencing was not the aftereffects of her kidnapping. In fact, the room rocked back and forth in a rhythmic motion. The weapons she'd secreted on herself were gone, not that she was surprised. The warlock was cruel, not stupid. Glancing up, she noticed the portholes that gave away her location. No light came in from them, meaning it was still night. Q'rell had her on a ship of some sort.

She searched her memory, finally piecing together what happened. The shock of Lucrea knowing about the con had been so intense, she had not been paying attention to her surroundings. That failure had allowed Q'rell to ambush her. He'd touched her with a metal rod and that was the last memory she had.

She stood on the bed and checked the locks on the portholes. Bars ran on the outside of the windows, she wished she could make herself small enough to exit that way. Not much was known about the secretive kitsune. What most people "knew" had been fabricated to keep others from finding out the truth. She morphed into any shape within reason, shrinking or expanding as needed. As she matured, she would continue to grow new tails until she reached the ninth. At that point, she could mimic just about any creature on Harmony.

The good news was the sight of Hub's docks. They hadn't sailed for Mangku yet, because once that happened, she wouldn't be escaping. Ever. The bad news was the docks sat on the other side of bars and a locked door. She'd never had the interest or aptitude to be a burglar. Having people willingly hand over their possessions was so much nicer.

The door opened, causing Silai to start. She readied herself for the warlock. An opportunity would present itself if she kept her head. Q'rell entered through the doorway, stepping aside as his demon followed him in. If she was correct, that was a nightbringer, a demon who fed on blood and the agony of others. It had a large head with a mouth full of teeth like a shark. The body below looked like a drowning victim, bloated and pocked with sores. The perfect companion for the warlock.

Q'rell shut the door and pulled the chair out from its place under the desk and sat. "I tried being reasonable and that failed to accomplish my goals. I will give you one last chance before we return to Mangku soil. Show me your true form and I will bind you as my slave. Otherwise—" he indicated the nightbringer whose blazing red eyes followed her every move — "there are less pleasant ways in Mangku to get what I want, and in the end, you'll be bound to me."

She shook her head slowly, thinking through the correct response. "I am a high-ranking member—"

"Spare me your mockery. You are not elvish. You are a grifter and a petty thief and soon, my slave."

She gasped in outrage. "How dare you insult me."

Q'rell rose, shaking with anger. "I've had enough!" he roared at her, spittle flying from his mouth. He started to command his pet whose long, barbed tongue flickered in and out of its mouth.

Silai held up a hand, imperious look on her face, refusing to be frightened by the warlock or his gruesome pet. "What if you're wrong?"

The arm lowered. A shrewd look replaced the earlier mask of rage. It had been an act, as she'd guessed. "I'm not."

She opened her hands before her, head slightly tilted to the right. A subtle insult that passed by the warlock. "The domovoi didn't work, did she?" One of the few truths about the nine-tailed kitsune was that a domovoi could undo the manifestation and return them to their natural form.

His eyes narrowed. "No, she didn't, but that was a fox trick, is my guess."

"Have you ever heard of a domovoi failing before? I haven't." She ran her hand through her long hair as if to straighten it. The next part would be tricky. "Let's say that you do whatever it is to me that you've planned. What if that doesn't work? Do you think the elves will stand by and allow my death to go unanswered? After the fiasco at the party, they will know who to look to for answers in my disappearance. Mangku would be forced to hand you over or face war. Other than the dragons themselves, no nation is stronger than the elvish. Do you think the Warlock Council will accept your *guesses*?"

His eyebrows stitched together over his beady little eyes. "No. No, they wouldn't."

Silai saw the fear behind his eyes now. The Mangku were a merciless people, living in inhospitable lands where they could practice their magic and worship the demon lords away from the rest of Harmony's population. One last push and she might sway him enough to buy herself time. "As you certainly know, there is another way to unmask a fox. Allutte serum will force the truth from anyone who it is administered to, including me. I will gladly take it and answer all of your questions. Do we have a deal?"

Q'rell brows knitted together. "If I'm right, you will be an asset beyond value, but if you are indeed who you say, then the punishment would be long and painful to say the least. We have a deal. I will go get the allutte serum and you will take it without hesitation. I'm leaving my pet to guard you. Any attempt to leave and it won't matter what you are, understood?"

She dipped her chin in acknowledgment, careful to be as precise as possible. A slip here would be deadly. "I will await your return. May I use the facilities to freshen up?"

"Of course, my lady." The words dripped with scorn and sarcasm. "As long as you don't approach the outer door, you'll be unharmed." He set his hand on his pet's vile head and whispered commands to it. Q'rell stepped out of the room, shutting the door with a loud bump. The nightbringer put its back against the door. It stared at her like she was dinner. If she didn't get out of here before Q'rell returned, she would be.

She hopped off the bed and closed herself in the small bathroom. The nightbringer's snuffles sounded through the crack beneath the door. She wracked her brain for a way to distract the warlock's pet long enough to get out of the stateroom and off the boat. She rummaged through the vanity's six drawers in search of anything that could help her. A hairbrush, comb, and two small towels went on the floor. The rest of the drawers were empty. The room itself consisted of the toilet, shower, and sink set into the vanity top in front of a mirror that was affixed to the wall.

There had to be something. She picked up the hairbrush and tapped it in her hand, forcing herself to focus. The nightbringer still had its nose pressed against the bottom of the door. There had to be a way away from the infernal beast. Fighting it with makeshift weapons would be futile unless there was a bolt thrower behind the toilet.

Time would run out quickly. The dockside dealers carried anything you'd ever want. Q'rell would probably visit a known apothecary to make sure he received the real thing. She needed to be gone, and soon. She winced as the metal hairbrush smacked her palm hard enough to sting. The brush was metal. An idea occurred to her so suddenly she almost laughed. She stood up and struck the mirror with the side of the brush. A loud crack rewarded her. It would break. Another few strikes and a piece of glass fell free from the shattered mirror.

She retrieved the shard and sat on the toilet seat facing the vanity. She sliced her arm open enough to draw blood, which she rubbed on the vanity and the wall. The snuffling outside intensified to a whine. The door shook as the nightbringer banged its head against the surface, seeking entry. She tossed the shard on the floor while a towel wrapped around the wound controlled the bleeding. She'd have one shot at this, so it had to work.

She reached out and unlatched the door before she jumped back into the shower stall. The thing slammed against the door, throwing it open, and its claws scrambled over the tile floor to gain purchase. It leapt to the vanity, its tongue cleaning the blood from every surface. Silai slid behind the beast and pulled the door shut. Loud, furious scratching started on the other side. After allowing herself a quick breath of relief, she ran.

Surprisingly, the rest of the ship sat unguarded. Q'rell must not have wanted any witnesses to her kidnapping. Once on the deck, she got her bearings. She didn't know the harbor south of the Quad well, though she was familiar enough with the landmarks to understand where to go. Abandoning all caution, she ran for the ladder and climbed to the pier.

Pleasure crafts of the very wealthy docked in this section of the port. She glimpsed a figure at the pier's entrance trotting toward her at a brisk pace. Was it the ambassador returning with the allutte serum? She hastened down a connecting pier, stepping behind a small supply building.

Changing to a new person quickly wouldn't pass close inspection. In the dark, it would have to be enough. She concentrated, unbinding from her current form. Her seven tails swirled around her, leaving her true self visible for a moment. The cool air on her skin felt like heaven but she had no time to linger. Pulling the image of an orc she'd known growing up, Silai pushed herself into its image. Her tails helixed around her, forming the cocoon that protected her from the world. Moments later a greenish-skinned orc woman stood in Lady Kyerr's place.

Silai pressed herself against the back of the supply hut, out of Q'rell's sight as he passed by. Once the sound of his steps on the metal ladder reached her, she fled. Screams of frustration echoed across the still waters.

The harbor walls lay ahead, but she couldn't chance leaving through the guarded exits. If Q'rell had tipped them off, they might hold anyone they didn't recognize until he arrived. Glint bought a lot of favors in Hub. She forced herself to increase her pace, searching for a hiding place that would keep her from the warlock's clutches. She spotted a door to a gear shed that hadn't been fully closed. It would have to do.

As she tugged at the door, a soft murmur of beating wings announced that she wasn't alone. Silai stopped. A small pixie floated down in front of her. "Wow. That was amazing!"

What had the pixie seen? Silai decided to stay in character on the off chance she hadn't witnessed her transformation. "What you mean?"

The pixie applauded theatrically. "No worries, I'm a friend. I've been hired—well, really forced—to come get you to attend a meeting for a client who'd like to hire you. Anyway, I've got something for you after we get you out of here. You know—"

The pixie stopped as Q'rell screamed, "Kyerr!"

Silai's head dropped in defeat. After everything, the con had failed and the psychotic Q'rell would capture her. Silai turned to run.

"I've got a plan, well, sort of a plan, or at least an idea. You should follow me and then--"

Silai cut her off. "How do I know you aren't working for Q'rell?"

Gelsey's eyes widened in shock. "Me? Work for a psychopath Mangku after they murdered half my people?"

"Good point." She followed the young woman as she flew off down the pier.

3

GELSEY

Gelsey looked back using her enhanced vision to spot their pursuer. The warlock ran behind a nightbringer, its nose pressed to the pier as it tracked Silai. An idea formed in Gelsey's head, pulling a giggle from her in the process. Nightbringers relied on smell, and the pier had a wide variety of awful scents to choose from.

They ran past ships of all sizes, Gelsey searching for an odor that would mask Silai's scent. The promenade, where the rich kept their yachts, was crafted into a gaudy showpiece, all ornate light posts, inlaid tile patterns, and shiny new tie-offs. You'd never see that kind of excess on the east side where the merchants unloaded their goods.

Gelsey's nose wrinkled as a horrible stench assaulted her nose. If the disgusting smell that rose from the surrounding water was any indicator, a pleasure barge had recently emptied its bilges. Nothing could track its prey with that odor around. She flew down to Silai's eye level, pointing to the edge of the pier. "Jump in."

The orc wrinkled her nose. Under other circumstances, Gelsey would have rolled with laughter. "Yes, princess. Jump in and stay still if you want to get out of here. Make sure you dunk your head and swim under the pier. Stay behind one of the supports."

A horrified expression crossed the orc's face as the sounds of pursuit increased. Silai jumped. She submerged herself under the filth before

23

bobbing up. Technically speaking, the dunking hadn't been necessary, but after seeing how beautiful the fox was, Gelsey figured she deserved it. Gelsey willed herself to grow to her larger size, pulling her pistol and concealing it in her lap as she slumped down by the barge.

Two figures approached, the man from earlier and a nightbringer, a horror composed of all teeth and rotting flesh. Gelsey had seen warlocks and how their unnatural minions hunted prey for fun. Fear rose like bile as she forced herself to immobility. The fléchette pistol in her lap would perforate the snarling creature no matter what level of hell it had come from. She swallowed hard and prayed to Iraos that it would do the job.

The warlock caught sight of her as the monster charged toward Gelsey. "I knew I'd find you!" he screamed in victory. "You thought you could get away from me."

Gelsey clenched her teeth to keep them from chattering. The thing slowed, sniffing furiously as it bypassed Gelsey. The nightbringer still had Silai's scent. It ended at the edge of the dock where Silai had leapt from. The thing mewed and paced uncertainly.

She'd waited as long as she could stand it. Gelsey forced a frantic giggle. Dusters got high on a powdered fungus that made them very happy right up until their hearts stopped. She giggled again louder. "Man, you got any dust on you?" Another laugh, this time a little shriller. "I really need a hit."

The warlock ignored her to go look into the water where his pet whined, its nose trailing snot over where Silai had been just moments earlier. He pointed at Gelsey. "She's changed forms. That must be her. Smell her."

His pet snuffled over to Gelsey, nose against her leg. She cringed back involuntarily, but they either didn't notice or took it to be her coming off a trip. "Man, get your pig away from me. I need that magic dust now."

"I have no dust, you wretch. Do everyone a favor and drown yourself." He turned his back and peered into the water intently.

This needed to end, and soon. How long could Silai stay in that filth without making a noise? Time for act two. "Get your pig away from me!" she shrieked in horror, curling into a ball. She continued to scream until the warlock stepped away from the edge.

"Kill her." He waved at the nightbringer.

The pistol snapped up, fléchette darts striking the beast straight in its giant mouth. The back of its head exploded, covering the warlock with brains and gore. "I gashing need dust. Give it to me!" She leveled the pistol at him. He fled. She fired a few shots over his head, screaming about bringing her dust until he was out of sight. She moved to the side of the pier. "Come up. There's a ladder over here."

A very dirty, smelly orc emerged from the water. "You enjoyed that," she accused Gelsey, who shrugged before leading the way off the docks. They made it off the pier and Gelsey took Silai to a safe house in the Anchors. Silai showered and returned looking like one of the dryad maidens who worked at the bars all over the Quad. Great disguise down here.

Silai sat on a chair across from Gelsey, who perched on the edge of a table. "Why did you help me?"

Gelsey didn't answer. Instead, she tossed her the mem stick. Silai regarded it for a moment before slotting it. Her face twisted with emotion. Whatever Ancep had on these people was serious. All it had taken to convince Gelsey was glint and the imminent threat of being frozen solid. She had already lost everything and had nothing left to exploit.

Tears welled in Silai's eyes as she accessed the data on the stick. Gelsey floated across the room and returned to her larger form to strip down her fléchette pistols and reload the empty chambers. She included a set of darts laced with demon's bane, just in case she ran into the warlock again. She worked until Silai set the stick on the table in front of her. "Why did you bother saving me if this is what you'd planned?"

Gelsey shook her head. "Don't know what's on those. All I know is we are supposed to meet in three nights' time at the address he told me. He's got a job for us."

Silai nodded slowly. "I'll be there."

"Good. I've got more work to do." Gelsey shrank before speeding out into the night to find her next target.

# KELTHAR

"Don't you think you should go home?" the bartender asked for the third time. Her long blond hair looked out of place against the gray of her skin. "Kelthar, are you listening to me?"

He listened enough to ignore her. Women spent all their time either trying to save him or nagging him into submission. Neither worked. The night had fallen and the first moon, Reatrix, had just made her appearance in the sky.

"I'll have another, Mystic. It's early yet." He took a long drag off his Talhut, enjoying the sensation as the fine particles of spiv drifted into his lungs. A mild euphoric feeling blanketed both his mind and his problems.

Mystic frowned at him before fetching him another of the dark ales. Erinye produced two exports—fierce woman and great beer. Not the mass-produced piss with no flavor that most of Hub drank. No, might as well drink from the harbor, it had more taste. She slid the glass of dark goodness to him.

"Put it on my tab."

The frown deepened. "Your tab is already over three hundred glint. Mox will cut you off if you don't pay up soon."

Kelthar waved her away. "Mox will whine about it until he needs the hoodu put on someone, then all is forgiven. Just been longer than usual, is all." He wiped his hand over his bald head, pushing nonexistent hair out of his face, an old habit. Tennin men progressed toward portly and bald in their middle years, though he'd had no lack of company for all that.

Kelthar sat at the polycarb bar, perched on a barely tolerable stool, enjoying the beer and the spiv, zoning on the edge. Too much and you got sloppy, not enough and why bother? Mystic prowled behind the bar, handing out drinks, Talhuts, and advice in equal measure. Regulars knew to keep their hands to themselves since she kept a bolt thrower under the bar and wasn't afraid to use it.

The zone beckoned Kelthar, whispering to him of peace and the unconsciousness he craved. He pushed it aside for now. It would always be there. Voices rose from the far end of the bar, not unusual for the Shifting Shadows. If things progressed too far, HubSec, or the squids as they were known on the street, would be called in to arrest people. They continued, getting angrier as the argument progressed. He didn't usually pay attention to such things, but curiosity won out over solitude.

He should have known better. Thrante, Mystic's insane ex-whatever-they-were, stood at the bar shouting. He ran a small-time gang called the Onyx Slash. Why she put up with him, he'd never understand.

He should just return to his diversions and enjoy his evening.

Or, he could entertain himself with a bit of fun. Given how many favors Mystic had done for him, he made his decision. Kelthar gulped down his beer and adjusted the bag that held the implements of his profession before stumbling down the bar toward the commotion.

Thrante stood a meter taller than Kelthar and weighed half as much. The Svartan people were tall, thin, and nice to look at with purple eyes and flowing locks. This wouldn't be the first pretty boy he'd tangled with. He muttered a spell under his breath as he fell into the taller man. "'Scuse me, son," he said, slurring his speech as if drunk. "You should leave the nice lady alone."

A hard shove answered Kelthar's words. Not that he'd expected anything different from the arrogant punk. He noticed two of his Onyx Slash toughs by the door. *This was gonna be fun.* He released the spell on the unwitting Thrante.

"You need to leave before I call the squids on you, Thrante. You've no business being in my bar." Mystic's voice trembled, perhaps with fear. Her ex had a rep in the Quad as a badass.

The dark elf puffed himself up. "I have every right..." A loud, wet-sounding fart burst forth from him. A stench rose like a miasma from behind the Svartan. His hand shot to his stomach as his eyes grew larger.

He dashed for the jakes. A second later, the two thugs went after him. Once they were out of earshot, Kelthar allowed himself a good laugh.

"What did you do?" she asked, annoyed beyond belief. "He's dangerous. He will hurt you."

Kelthar chuckled. "Myst, he's a trumped-up gryphon. All squawk." He plopped down on a stool where he had a good view of the jakes. Mystic didn't respond. Instead, she brought him a beer, on the house no less.

He'd finished his beer and was pondering another when Thrante returned. Was the dark elf walking differently or maybe he just imagined it? Kelthar grinned from ear to ear, noting that Thrante's Slashers were still otherwise occupied.

Thrante adjusted his belt. "What did you do, runt?"

Kelthar feigned a shocked expression. "Me? I did nothing. What could a short, fat man do to such a mighty Slasher like yourself?" Out of the corner of his eye, Mystic stood next to the hiding place of the slug thrower. It wouldn't come to that, but he always appreciated backup.

Thrante's eyes narrowed as he grabbed a handful of Kelthar's blue and black striped shirt. "Get out of here before I beat you." He pulled Kelthar out of his seat and shoved him toward the door. Kelthar struck a table, knocking drinks all over two of Cal's girls, marring the lovely outfits they barely wore while on the job. He fell to the floor with a dull thump.

Kelthar had spent a lifetime meting out aggression for a goodly amount of glint. Tonight, he had broken his cardinal rule and used his magic for personal satisfaction.

Thrante laughed as Kelthar pulled himself off the floor. The Svartan stalked down the bar toward Mystic.

Kelthar recited his next spell just as quietly as the first, feeling the energy gather around him. Some schools of magic taught pentagrams and runes to build spells of massive power. Other schools used devices, emblems, or representations to ply their craft. In his trade, mages worked with a bit of everything. Kelthar liked somatic spells because of the ease with which he cast them. No preparation, just results. He finished his spell and waited.

Mystic recoiled as the spell took hold of the dark elf. Warts and tumors grew from every inch of exposed skin. Thrante caught his reflection in the polished chrome of the bottle racks. He panicked, scrubbing his face with both hands, his polished nails leaving furrows that bled. Kelthar broke the spell, and Thrante's skin affliction vanished, leaving the Svartan's face a tangle of scratches and reddened skin.

Thrante stopped digging up his skin as the spell faded.

Kelthar, wearing a malicious grin, waited for him to turn to him then said, "You want to keep going, pretty boy?"

A primal scream answered his question. Kelthar ducked the initial charge and headed for the door as fast as his stubby legs would carry him. Thrante yelled. "Get him!"

The two Slashers, who'd finished in the jakes, flanked the door to intercept him.

Kelthar had a rigid set of self-imposed rules. These rules usually appeared after experiencing painful situations he'd decide to avoid forevermore. New rules would come into existence to handle bad situations. This exact thing was why he had a non-interference rule in the first place. The two Slashers cut off his exit.

Luckily for him, tennin were one of the few species inhabiting Hub that could still fly. Not very far or high, but a properly motivated tennin can move quite fast. Kelthar, being extremely motivated, leapt into the air and soared just over the thugs' heads through the expanding iris of the bar's entrance. He hit the night air at full speed, banking to the left before landing on the walkway.

Thrante bellowed in rage as Kelthar escaped the Shifting Shadows. The smart thing would have been to duck into the crowds of slummers, wireheads, and assorted riffraff who descended on the Shade district's bars at night and lose Thrante in the process.

He liked drinking at the Shifting Shadows and he especially liked Mystic, so he did the dumb thing instead.

"Yo, Lord Farter of the running shite. You look better that way. You should thank me!" he declared before dashing away with the three Slashers in pursuit.

Shouts followed Kelthar as he ran through the crowds of the Shades. He tossed hasty excuses over his shoulder to the passersby he bumped, nudged, or otherwise collided with. Being just over a meter tall had its advantages, but when you wanted to make sure the Slashers followed you, not so much. Kelthar fired insults at Thrante like a first-year mage practicing magic missiles. Pretty boy's fragile ego made sure he'd keep up the chase.

Kelthar ran headfirst into a HubSec security officer, bounced off him, and landed firmly on his ass. Fear shot through his system at the thought of being arrested, leaving Thrante free to return to the Shifting Shadows.

The squid revolved to face the prone mage. The officer's long pointed ears flattened against his head. His slightly elongated snout wore an irritated expression that showed off his fangs and the tip of his forked tongue. He wasn't mature enough to have wings or a tail yet. Didn't matter. Any dragon, even a lowly whelpling, could tear apart a full-grown troll. The patroller's partner snickered behind him. "You in a hurry tonight?"

Squids were touchy under the best of circumstances. HubSec employed the lower castes of dragons to guard and protect the city. Kelthar chose his words carefully. "No, sir. Having some fun with my friends and wasn't watching my step. Won't happen again."

"You are correct on that count. Drunk and disorderly. I think a good long sit in the hole will make you more careful." The squid's partner tapped him, and they held a whispered conversation.

The mage saw the Slashers pacing behind the squids, waiting to see what happened. Kelthar could have magicked his way out of this if they weren't dragons. Only the most powerful spells affected the winged monsters or their kin. These two weren't exactly wyvern food, but patrolling the Shade district, with its clubs, dollhouses, and tourists, isn't prime duty.

The squids finished their conversation and turned their attention to Kelthar. The first one said, "Get out of here. You aren't worth the time to fill out the forms."

Kelthar bobbed his head in agreement. "Thank you, sirs." As he climbed to his feet, an idea tickled the back of his brain, taking shape as he moved around the officers and down the walkway. A quick gesture and a spurt of magical energy, and a small explosion provided enough of a distraction to get past Thrante and his boys.

He waited until he had a fair distance between them before he yelled, "Yo, turf muncher." All three heads snapped around, their puzzled expressions making Kelthar laugh. "See you later!" He resumed his more subdued rate of speed and headed down the walk toward the Flow. The squids watched him for a moment before resuming their patrol.

The Slashers followed but not at a rushed pace. They hung back, and laughed, acting like they were out on the town to party. Thrante didn't exhibit much in the way of patience or, for that matter, brains. Of course, he'd landed Mystic for a while, so he had something going for him. Kelthar left that thought alone.

Passing the Dollhouse, one of the Shade District of Hub's most popular brothels, he decided to fight this battle another night. He cast a shield at his back, rendering him invisible to Thrante and his boys. When he didn't hear them shouting, he looked over his shoulder. Thrante was strolling along, smirking, and Kelthar bumped directly into the reason Thrante didn't seem concerned. A slasher stood in front of him. No, he corrected himself, five pissed-off Slashers. He could take out five Slashers, though it would be a challenge. The Slashers hoisted him by his arms and dragged him into an alley on the far side of the Dollhouse.

Open dumpsters smelling of rotting food and decaying metal greeted them as they force-marched Kelthar into the dim alley between the buildings. Behind the entertainment venues of the Shade district ran a series of roads that maintenance and garbage removal vehicles used so as to not interrupt the flow of glint into the pockets of the Nef crime lords. As long as the money poured in, the squids and Nef ignored everything else. The day a citizen's activities interfered with profit, they'd be found floating under the docks.

The two Slashers holding his arms threw him against the alley wall. Kelthar caught himself but fell to the ground dramatically to the harsh laughter of the thugs. Thrante sauntered up and kicked him casually in the ribs. More laughter.

Kelthar sighed. Let Thrante restore face in front of the Slashers, then it would be over. This was why he created rules about meddling in the affairs of others unless it was making him glint. He took another kick, groaning loudly. "Please, what did I do?"

Two of the toughs flipped him into a sitting position against the rough wall. Since it was after dark, the access road was empty. Only stim dealers and fleshers would stray back here to do business. Not that they would be any help.

Thrante grabbed the skin under Kelthar's chin. He locked eyes with the mage. "You embarrassed me, and we both know it."

Kelthar tried to shake his head, but the elf's iron grip prevented movement. He forced his eyes open as if in terror. "I didn't, I sw—"

The grip tightened until it became painful. "Don't bother, mage. I know you cast that spell. I'm gonna off you and then I'll make sure Myst learns an important lesson about trusting lowlifes like you."

Until now, this had been a lark to pass the time. In a matter of minutes, it had gotten out of hand. With Myst's safety at stake instead of just his own, fear descended on Kelthar in a sudden downpour. "She knew nothing. I did it as a joke."

Thrante's smile was so cold, icicles should have been hanging from the

Svartan's lips. "I know. She'll think twice about being nice to lowlifes after tonight." He stood up, pulling a knife from the sheath on his thigh. "This is gonna hurt."

So much for the easy way. While Pretty Boy preened for the Slashers, they cheered him on. Kelthar made a series of hand gestures. A burst of light exploded from him. The Slashers reeled away, temporarily blinded. Kelthar climbed to his feet. Svartans had amazing night vision, which made a flash-bang extremely effective as a defense.

Kelthar pulled a rune-encrusted rod from his emergency pouch. Mages tinkered in all the branches of magic, making them strong but not extremely powerful in any one path like the sorcerers or warlocks. He danced into the fray and tapped each of the reeling Slashers with the rod, activating it with a word. They slumped into unconsciousness. He'd have to recharge the dang thing later, but in emergencies it helped greatly.

Thrante stumbled around, cursing loudly. "I'll slit you open, you gashing dwarf." He kept rubbing at his eyes, which did his bleeding face no favors. "What did you do to me?"

He would need to remove the threat to Mystic permanently. The Slashers would pick a new leader and go on as they always had.

"I didn't like the odds, so I evened them," Kelthar said, staying out of the large man's reach. It didn't stop the enraged Svartan from lunging at him. What should he do with the Slasher's leader? While he'd killed many during his years as a professional, he didn't enjoy it. Sometimes you had to do what was right, not what was easy.

Kelthar retrieved his ceremonial knife from his satchel. He'd make it quick and as painless as possible. With a spell, Thrante froze in place. He readied the knife to end the slasher's life.

A light female voice interrupted. "I thought I'd have to pull your ass out of the fire." Kelthar spun, seeking the owner of said voice, and saw no one. Many of the races could camouflage themselves, though, which would explain it.

"Do any of you mudders ever look up?" the voice continued above him. He peered up to see a lovely, tiny lady, wings a blur as she hovered. Her bright blue hair and pointed ears spoke to her pixie heritage.

Kelthar grunted, lowering the knife. Pixies weren't known to be violent. "No, I guess we don't. Who the hell are you and why are you interfering?"

"Who in the name of Iraos are you talking to? I'll kill you both once I can see," Thrante yelled, but since he couldn't move, Kelthar ignored him.

The pixie sighed. "A client paid me to bring you in for a meeting. He wants to hire you to do a job."

"And if I don't want to be hired?"

She shrugged. "That's up to you. My client is very direct. Not sure it would go well turning him down."

A new plan popped into his head, drawing a chuckle. "Tell ya what. If you'll help me with a job I need to finish, I'll go to your meeting, no questions asked."

"Deal. What do you need me to do?"

Kelthar turned to Thrante. "We're leaving. Next time I see you, I'll kill you. You can thank Mystic for your life."

"Gash you, runt." Thrante's head thrashed back and forth as he tried to break the spell. "Mystic will bleed for what you've done to me.",

Kelthar waved for the pixie to follow. Once out of earshot, he whispered "Svartan are so friggin' proud, bites 'em in the ass every time. I have a plan to deal with the peacock back there."

A huge smile broke out across her face. "Will it be fun?"

"Fun? Maybe. It will be interesting either way."

Her eyes lit up with glee. "What do you need?"

Kelthar explained the plan as they walked. On second thought, he decided it would be a lot of fun.

---

Mystic stood behind the bar at the Shifting Shadows, drying a glass that had been dry for at least five minutes. The business with Thrante had unnerved her far more than she would like to admit. The fact that Kelthar had stuck his overabundant nose into things had only made it worse, not that he'd known how things would go. The mage always had a smile on his face and a quick joke at the ready. Mox, the owner of the Shifting Shadows, had trusted him with a lot of problems over the years, and now he was embroiled in her mess.

The bar had closed an hour ago; the customers had left and the neon that lit the front had been extinguished. She should have gone home already. Mox had a service that would transport her safely, but she knew what was coming. Better to deal with it here than out in the Quad. She took a moment to move the bolt thrower into easy reach in case it came to that. At least Mox would find her in the morning in whatever state Thrante left her.

As if thinking his name summoned him, Thrante strolled through the unlocked entry. He keyed it to lock before walking toward the bar. Mystic used the highly polished glass to pour a draft of Svartan black ale. Her customers complained about the stench of rotted moss when she served it. Tonight, there was no one to complain. She set it on the bar in front of her, grabbed another glass, and dried it.

Thrante strode across the bar, eyes fixed on her the way a hawk stared down a rabbit before the kill. He deftly avoided the tables with a grace innate to their people.

She gasped as he stepped into the light of the bar. His face bore deep scratches and bruising. Any hope he'd leave her alive fled. He glared at her before sitting on a barstool and picking up the beer. He raised it in a salute. "Chra Na Thal."

May your enemies die in pain. Not really a heartwarming toast. She put the glass upside down on the rack and took the next one, repeating the process as Thrante drank his beer in silence. He'd never been a thinker, something she had loved in the early days of their time together. The Svartan warrior, tribal head, leading the Slashers against the filth they'd been forced to share Harmony with. He'd even killed a dragon, albeit one newly morphed from a hatchling into a whelp.

Thrante had set her up with Mox so she could tag easy targets for the Slashers. It'd been fun at first, until she got to know the regulars and realized that most were nice beings, working to get by in the Quad, dreaming of the day they'd leave Hub and live free.

That was what had torn them apart. There was no place for a soft Svartan in his world, so she'd rejected all vestiges of that harsh life. She tired of hurting others when they should be trying to achieve their dreams, not be someone else's nightmare. He might just beat her instead of killing her outright. She never knew what he might do when enraged.

"You know you could walk away and leave me. I'm an outcast. There is no honor involved." She didn't look up from drying the glass as she spoke.

He stared into the darkness of the beer for a few moments, turning the glass back and forth, watching it intensely. "I must. The mage made a fool of me, and I must avenge my honor. I will be sorry after."

Her cheeks darkened with rage. "Honor? You are the leader of a street gang that steals from old women and drunk tourists. You aren't K'threal, the mighty Svartan warrior."

He struck so quickly that she didn't have time to prepare for the blow. His fist caught her in the side of the face, snapping her head around. The glass slipped from her grasp, shattering on the floor. She could taste blood from the gash in her mouth. A savage sneer crossed his twisted face. "You've no right to even speak his name. I should have killed you when you left the clan. I won't make that same mistake again."

She touched her cheek where he'd struck her. He might kill her, send her soul to be judged by the immortal goddess of her people, but she'd not lie down and let him. She eyed the resin stock of the bolt thrower, glad she had thought to move it earlier.

He returned to the seat, pushing the near-empty glass across to her. She reluctantly filled the glass with the dark beer. She slid it over to him, took a new glass, and poured herself one. Mox forbade employees from drinking on the job. He could scold her corpse in the morning for the infraction. She lifted her glass and downed a large amount of the pungent ale. The flavors burst forth as the liquid surged over her tongue, leaving a lingering warmth behind.

Thrante drank from his glass, eyes never leaving her. He pulled a gleaming silver dagger from the sheath and set it on the bar, point facing her. The mono-filament edge would cut through just about anything. He'd taken it off the dragon he'd killed in their early years together. Most would have sold it. Knives of that quality fetched over a thousand glint in the Flow markets. He'd never even considered it.

He swallowed the last of the beer. It was time. "Will you allow me to offer you an easy death?"

She set her glass down on the bar and shook her head. Her hand opened slightly, readying for the fight.

The blade leapt into his hand in a flash as she grabbed the rifle, pivoting to dodge the knife and take her shot.

To her surprise, a force pressed down on them both, freezing each exactly as they'd been. She could see, though movement was impossible. The dagger would have pierced her before she had fired.

She tried to move but her muscles wouldn't obey. Her senses worked still. *What is going on?*

Kelthar strolled into the bar from the storage rooms. He unlocked the front door before he approached the bar. He wrinkled his nose in disgust as he walked toward them. "That beer smells worse than your farts, pretty boy. I can't believe you drink that stuff."

He removed the knife from Thrante's hand, throwing it across the room. It stuck in the far wall, quivering from the impact. He climbed up a stool onto the bar and went to where Mystic still held the bolt thrower.

He eased her fingers off the weapon, set the safety, and dropped the gun on the floor behind the bar.

Mystic's eyes darted around like a trapped animal. She saw that Thrante was doing the same. They were completely at the mage's mercy.

"Seems like you two were just about to do some really stupid shit." He sat cross-legged on the bar and eyed Thrante with distaste. "I told you, boy, next time I saw you I'd kill you, but I have a better idea. Gelsey!"

The entry door irised as a tall man dressed head to toe in black and a small woman flying just off his shoulder entered. The pixie zipped across the intervening space, landing next to Kelthar. "Whoa! What is that stench?"

The mage glanced at Thrante before he grinned at Mystic. "Told ya. It's the blight-laden beer the Svartans drink. Smells awful." He nodded to the man as he stepped up to the bar. "Dr. Laah."

The pale-skinned man inclined his head. "Your associate requested my presence. This is very unusual, sir." He studied Thrante carefully. "Is this the specimen?"

"It is." The mage's face didn't betray any emotion. Mox had called him a stone-cold killer before, but Mystic had never seen it, until now. "I'm sure he's up to standard."

The man produced a scanner, running it up and down the length of the Svartan's body. "Hmmm, some nice neural enhancements. His organs are in excellent shape. I can give you twenty-five thousand glint for him."

Kelthar tilted his head in agreement. The doctor slid a cred chip across the bar that the mage didn't touch. The doctor raised his eyebrows. "Would you like to verify the amount?"

"No, your lab is reputable. I know where to find you."

Two large men entered and put straps around the immobile Thrante. Mystic felt tears course down her immobile face as she watched them truss him up and carry him out. The spell released as he reached the door.

"I swear I will kill the both of you! I swear I—" A swift cuff to the head ended his tirade.

Mystic glared at the mage. "Why?"

The mage shrugged. "Could have killed him in cold blood. It seemed a waste of a healthy body. He'd have never stopped trying to kill you to appease his misguided honor. Take the chip, sell the knife, and open your own place."

She stiffened. "I'll not profit from his murder."

The mage reached out and took one of her hands. "You've paid for that with years of pain and fear. You've earned it a hundred times over. Open a place of your own. Just make sure I have a comfortable stool to sit on and a hefty tab."

As she imagined being able to walk without fear that Thrante would pull some twisted stunt to prove he still owned her, relief she'd never hoped to feel surged through her. She took the chip. "I'll think on it."

"That went well!" Gelsey said gleefully. "Now we have business to discuss." She extracted a stick and tossed it to the mage who caught it as it grew.

"What's this?"

"Information. Man wants to hire you for a job." Gelsey ran down the specifics on when and where to meet. "The stick he gave me for you to review. Guess it explains why you'll come."

The mage slid the stick into his bag before jumping off the table. "No reason not to come. You'll be there?"

Gelsey nodded vigorously. "You betcha!"

"Wouldn't miss it for the world then."

5

GELSEY

Gelsey studied the mage as he hopped off the bar and strode toward the entry. He had weird notions about duty and junk you never heard in the Quad. Mystic came out and stopped him.

"Thank you," she said to him. The warrior nation had strange notions of honor and sacrifice and 'Thank you' was virtually unheard of from a Svartan. "I was sure that Thrante would kill me tonight, but now I have my whole life ahead of me. It is all due to you."

Kelthar bowed his head. It looked like a sign of respect, though reading people wasn't Gelsey's strong suit.

"I wanted him to leave while he could. Everyone deserves the chance to walk away from a bad situation, so I let it go until the last possible moment."

Kelthar winked at Gelsey as he went out the exit and into the Hub night.

Gelsey watched the mage go, wondering why he hadn't just killed Thrante like most mages would have. With a shrug, she slotted the stick with the profiles and flipped through the dossier on Kelthar. As before, there wasn't much there. Lots of guesses and innuendo but no facts to speak of. Seeing how he gave Thrante enough rope to hang himself spoke volumes about his character. Even bringing in the chop shop man to

38

make sure the parts didn't go to waste indicated efficiency in the face of a no-win situation.

Mystic returned to the bar, picked up her beer, and drank it in a single gulp. Gelsey floated over to sit on the tap handle next to her. "This is a really cool bar. You probably don't get many pixies in here, I bet. In fact, I may be the first. Pixies are lightweights when it comes to drinking." Gelsey laughed gleefully at her own joke. "A thimbleful will do ya, as my ma always said. One time, my pa got so drunk . . ." She noticed Mystic's raised eyebrow. People did that a lot around her, especially when she was talking. Better ask her question before the Svartan ignored her like most other mudders. "What can you tell me about Kelthar?"

She thought for a second. "Not much. He's been a friend of Mox's for years. He drinks for free until Mox needs something done. Kelthar handles whatever it is and never discusses it." She poured another pint of the "fragrant" beer and downed half. The stench hit Gelsey like a shot from a bolt thrower.

"What the hell happened here?" Mox's shrill voice cut through the silence of the empty bar. "Kelthar said there had been an issue. This place is a disaster." The goblin studied the room, a scowl plastered on his face. "There's a gashing knife in the wall."

"Sorry, that's mine." Mystic finished the beer, leapt over the bar, and retrieved the knife. She studied the blade for a minute.

Mox, a half-goblin of some sort, stomped to the bar. "Are you drinking on the job?" The goblin's voice hit a new note of anger.

Mystic headed for the exit, stopped, and said over her shoulder, "I was, and I quit." She held the knife by her side and stepped out into the night. Gelsey figured a new bar would open in the Shades sometime soon. She would avoid it if they served that smelly stuff Mystic drank.

"WHAT!" Mox screamed, but it was too late, she was gone. "Gashin' wonderful. She ups and quits." He stomped around behind the bar, swearing profusely. He glared at Gelsey. "Who are you and why are you in my place?"

Gelsey sighed. The reassuring weight of her fléchette gun hung on her hip, and right now using it was highly tempting. Instead, she asked, "How well do you know Kelthar?"

Mox stopped cold. "The mage? What's to know? He's extremely useful, always does what he says, doesn't gouge me on the contracts, and mostly takes his pay in beer. Nobody knows him."

It seemed that Kelthar would stay a mystery for longer than Gelsey would have liked. She leapt into the air and flew out into the night. She had more work to do before she could sleep.

# 6

# NYX

The hiss of the pneumatic locks alerted Nyx that he had company. He stared at the metal wall of his cell, waiting. The door slid open before the dull thud of boots announced the guards. Tonight would determine if his hastily constructed plan would work or if he'd be dead.

"Get up. Warden wants you." The voice behind him held a deep grumbly quality to it. Tel-ko wasn't a bad sort for a guard. The ebu came up to his shoulder but outweighed him by at least forty kilos.

Nyx rolled over. Tel-ko held a heavy stun baton across his armored chest. The guard had large eyes, stubby ears, and an abundance of coarse brown fur. His numerous scars attested to the years he'd worked as a guard at Demon's Gate. The guard behind Tel-ko made Nyx clench with anxiety. R'gar, a massive orc, contained more muscle grafts than Nix had ever seen outside of prison. The implanted stim packs pumped a cocktail of anti-rejection drugs mixed with a psychotic agent that, once triggered, turned the orc into a buzz saw. The fact the warden had sent R'gar to fetch him put into question the wisdom of this plan.

Wrath, wanting to take over as the leader of Memory Crash, an elite group of phantoms who could hack any target, had set him up. The bastard had betrayed Nyx and handed him to the squids. Nyx had only a few minutes to plan before he was arrested and set into motion an escape from prison. He'd been in for over a month. Tonight, he'd see if he could escape or not.

R'gar's face cracked with an evil grin, his metal-capped tusks gleaming. "Warden really pissed. You should know better than to steal from kthor."

Nyx fought not to roll his eyes at the orc. Phantoms like Nyx saw the world as ones and zeros. R'gar was definitely a zero. Kthor meant leader, and the warden wasn't one by any definition of the word. Corrupt, stupid, and cruel would describe the ogre well. He wouldn't last ten minutes in the Quad, but he was predictable when it came to how he treated the inmates who crossed him. It never worked out well for them.

"Time to go to Boom-Boom Room, big ears," R'gar shouted with malicious glee. Tel-ko snapped the restraints around Nyx's wrists before pulling him to his feet and propelling him through the oval hatchway and into the hallway.

The ebu didn't harm him as they walked, which Nyx appreciated. Of course, they would use the Boom-Boom Room. The unofficial torture chamber would more than make up for the lack of abuse on the way there. Even in Hub, torture was frowned upon, though the warden did it without consequence. As long as the warden kept the inmates from disrupting the flow of gold, the dragons didn't care what else happened.

"Gonna cut yer ears off and sell 'em down in Quad," R'gar grunted out a laugh. "Alchemist say eat them, they make you hard as rock."

Nyx ignored the brute, concentrating on his goal of getting the stashed deck in the med lab. The sealed lights cast a constant blueish glow as Tel-ko led Nyx through the sterile halls of the penitentiary. The other inmates went about their daily rituals of nothing through the translucent doors of the inmate quarters. Their ten-by-ten cell would be the last thing most of them saw before they rolled off into Axana's realm.

Before long, Nyx stood outside the Boom-Boom Room's entrance. The door held no windows, no cameras, no record of what happened on the inside. Nyx's breath caught. As he'd sat in the confines of his cell, the plan had made perfect sense; standing on the brink of death, though, he longed for the solitude they had taken him from.

Tel-ko noticed the change in him. "Should have thought about crossing him before you did it. Give the glint back and he'll probably let you live."

Nyx nodded, eyes transfixed on the door as it opened. R'gar shoved him so hard that he fell to the floor in the middle of the room. His bound hands did nothing to break his fall, so he face-planted, drawing a round of laughter from the guards who lined the walls of the Boom-Boom Room. A trickle of blood dripped from his left nostril as the guards hoisted him to his feet. The room fuzzed at the edges until his vision cleared.

Oot Smashammer, Gol Carceran's prison warden, had been an ogre chieftain until his tribe had crossed Clan Luteus. Rumor had it that Oot's reward for turning over traitors was this prized post. The execution of every last member of his tribe was a small price to pay for a lowlife like Oot Smashammer.

The warden dwarfed the custom-made "throne" that he lolled on. At well over two meters tall and two hundred kilos, scars crisscrossed his tan skin, attesting to his brutal nature. Intelligence and fury shone in his eyes as he stared down Nyx.

"You stole from me, leaf eater," the warden said in a menacing growl. The onlooker guards who gathered in the darkness around the room laughed. Not a raucous laugh like in the stim dens or the needle shops of the Quad, but a nervous titter from people who weren't sure if they should laugh or not.

"Good one, Kthor," R'gar blurted.

"Shut up, runt." Oot turned his attention back to Nyx. He pulled a bolt-thrower pistol out from behind him. The slug projectile tore through anything it hit, making it a popular weapon with thieves and drug runners. In Oot's massive hands, it resembled a toy. He lifted his chin to R'gar. The orc's smile widened before he slammed his fist into Nyx's exposed abdomen. Nyx dropped to his knees in agony. R'gar grabbed a fist of hair and pulled Nyx's head back.

Oot shoved the muzzle of the thrower into Nyx's gaping mouth. "I want my glint back, but I'll be happy with blowing your brains all over the room. Understand?"

A subdued nod would have to do since a massive pistol currently resided in his mouth. A trickle of sweat ran down his spine. He had reached the dangerous part of the scenario.

The pistol slid back, still pointed at his forehead. "I want the account number and access codes." The warden waved, and a small creature with goat's legs and a humanoid upper body ran up with an old manual interface device. There'd be no way they'd let a phantom like Nyx use a deck to access anything. He was capable of massive amounts of damage in the blink of an eye. Given his reputation, he wouldn't even be allowed to touch a manual interface.

"Can't. I—" Nyx said, waiting for the gun to go off.

A beefy hand struck his head before he could get anything else out. "Wrong answer." Nyx's blood dotted the ogre's fist. The metallic taste lingered in his mouth even after he spit it on the floor.

"The glint moves between accounts randomly. I need a deck to get into the core to put it back." Nyx held his breath. They'd never go for it. He'd prepared for this scenario long before the ill-fated run.

The ogre bellowed a laugh. "You think I'm stupid." The warden slumped his shoulders, pushing his belly out. "Oh, me give thing, you give glint." He straightened himself. "I'm not some backwoods hick, chasing after virgins to eat. I want my glint, and since you've got it, you will give it back now."

Tel-ko, who'd been somewhere off to the side, handed the warden a black box with a digital readout and deck hook-up. Nyx feigned fear but had figured this was how it would go down. He'd heard that the warden used the device on prisoners. The Personal Emergency Device allowed wireheads to back up data.

But there was another, unofficial use for PEDs. It allowed the operator to duplicate a person and store them for future use. The rich did this so they could move between bodies. In the Quad, you bought and sold people this way. Phantoms were always in demand for extremely high prices. A phantom like Nyx would fetch enough to triple Oot's glint.

"Ah, you know what that is." Oot laughed harshly. "Hook him up." He returned to his seat while the ebu pushed the plug into the jack that sat behind Nyx's ear.

The ogre slid the pistol back to its hiding place. "I gave you the option. You'll reroute my glint from a sim, and then I'll sell you as a virtual slave on the fastware market. Downside for you is I'm letting R'gar have some fun with you before you die. Need to discourage others from stealing from me."

A low whine from the machine quieted the room. The red flashing light didn't make Oot happy. "What is going on?"

Tel-ko flipped switches, muttering to himself. He sighed heavily before facing the warden. "Says the connector is malfunctioning."

"What!" The ogre rose, his face turning a deep shade of red.

The ebu stared at his feet. "You may have broken his socket when you hit him, sir."

Oot flew into a rage, slapping Tel-ko into the far wall with one blow. Next, he punched Nyx in the shoulder. Something made an audible snapping noise as pain flooded his system, dimming his vision. Nyx curled on the floor as the ogre raged.

"What game are you playing, elf?" Oot screamed.

A long time later, at least it seemed that way to Nyx, Oot's rage died off. "Take him to the infirmary."

R'gar stepped over Nyx, who had stayed down, intent on not being a target. "I get to kill him. You says so."

A sharp cuff to the head that would have sent anyone else sprawling was his answer. Nyx held on to consciousness, barely. "When I've got my glint, you can have him. Anything happens to him before then and I'll be selling your parts down at Doc Water's. Got it?"

The orc grunted his agreement before hoisting Nyx over his shoulder. None of them knew Nyx had just accomplished his mission.

R'gar's delivery service needed a few tweaks. Nyx feigned unconsciousness while upside down over the massive orc's shoulder. His head bobbled along with the odd gait of the guard, pushing his sense of equilibrium to the breaking point. He managed not to vomit down R'gar's back, though it was a close deal. His left arm hung toward the ground like a pendulum. From the pain and lack of movement, Nyx guessed Oot's fist had broken his shoulder.

A sudden stop bounced Nyx's head off R'gar's massive back. A series of beeps sounded before the automated locking system announced, "R'gar Othar, you are cleared for entry." A quick hiss of the pressurized door, and they were moving again. "Put him in the examination room," someone ordered. Nyx narrowly opened an eye but didn't see who had spoken. "Leave him on the table and you can go."

"No, he has kthor glint. I stay."

"He's not going anywhere," the person replied. "Oot wants me to get him back in working order and I can't do that with you hovering over me. So put him on the table in exam one and go."

A rumbling grunt was R'gar's response before he clomped down the hall to the examination room. A door slid open. The trip ended abruptly when Nyx was slung onto a table.

"I sell you ears, runt." R'gar stomped out of the room, shaking everything not bolted down in his wake. Nyx just needed to play dead for a few more minutes before he made his move to free himself.

7

# GELSEY

The instructions clearly stated the coordinates for picking up Nyx. It was time for him to arrive. Gelsey leapt into the air so she could survey the hovercraft yard of Demon's Gate. No movement, nothing. Ancep guaranteed that the intel from the diviners would be accurate. True, she'd found Kelthar exactly where they'd said, though she'd had to help him clear Mystic before he agreed to the meeting. The odd little mage still befuddled Gelsey. She'd been in the Quad for a long time and had met no one like him.

She buzzed the yard, looking for Nyx, and didn't spot him. Motion sensors relied on full-sized people triggering them, so she flew around without issue. *Where are you?* Ancep wouldn't be pleased if the hacker didn't make it out in one piece. The thought of telling him that one of his chosen couldn't be delivered caused her stomach to ache. She'd never seen, let alone worked for, a dragon before, but she doubted they were overly understanding.

Moving in closer to the back of the prison, she finally found signs of life. Three guards stood at the employee exit, arguing intensely. She couldn't hear the words, but the tone definitely sounded angry. Whatever had happened, Nyx had to be involved, and since he wasn't there it didn't concern her. Yet.

The loading dock bay doors were open with hovercrafts backed up against the concrete platform, waiting to be unloaded. She floated down, landing on the metal roof of the first trailer. Slowly, she moved to the end where she had a view into the warehouse. Nothing. She waited a few minutes, hopping from trailer to trailer. Still nothing.

*What do I do?* She reversed her course and headed to the first hover-craft. The commotion had died down after the guards who'd been arguing left. Silence reigned over the yard. *Maybe there's another exit, like from the sewers, back where the coordinates are.* Her heartbeat raced and her palms sweated at the thought of failing Ancep. She had reached the first hover-craft again, readying herself to fly back to the coordinates.

"I told you I handle it." A deep, gruff voice came from below her. "Now leave me alone."

Gelsey tiptoed to the edge of the hovercraft, peering down between the rows of crates. A massive orc stood there, cracking his knuckles. She jumped back as he strode toward the loading dock stairs and entered the warehouse.

*I'll wait until twenty then follow him.* She didn't make it past eight before leaping into the air and following. The warehouse contained towers of pallets that made ideal cover for the miniature pixie. The orc stepped behind a stack of crates and waited for something.

Gelsey flew to the top of the wall of pallets across from where the orc stood in silence. She flattened herself at the edge so she could see him. As usual, the fact that mudders didn't look up worked in her favor. In fact, she'd made an entire career out of that tendency. The larger species of Harmony forgot that a six-centimeter thief fit places that larger thieves didn't. Sometimes being small gave her a skewed perspective of the overall world, but Gelsey felt certain that the orc waiting below her was the largest she'd ever seen.

His muscle grafts weren't well done, bunching in places and uneven across his body. With orcs, it might have been intentional in an effort to mimic the great warriors of the early ages of Harmony, when the Hidden People had declared Old Earth lost to them. The first host of exiles died fighting against the jotur who had lived on Harmony pre-exile. The orcs, ogres, elves, and the other warrior races bound together and drove the jotur out.

That cooperation ended with the war.

Gelsey didn't care for orcs. Her intuition tingled as she studied him. Something was up and this orc was involved. She settled in to watch and wait for Nyx.

# 8

## NYX

After ten minutes of silence, Nyx popped his eyes open and took a quick look around the room. Alone. He used his good arm to pull himself to a seated position, hoping nothing besides his shoulder was broken, fractured, or otherwise damaged enough to require an expensive repair. It might heal on its own, though it would take weeks. The clinics in the Flow would patch you up overnight if given enough glint.

As soon as his fingers touched his left shoulder, he confirmed the break. Escaping a maximum-security pen with one arm? Child's play. He finished checking for broken bones in his torso. Deep purple bruises had formed on his bare ribcage. Luckily nothing else appeared damaged beyond repair.

Listening closely for any sounds, Nyx forced his battered body to push his legs out until they touched the floor. He probed his damaged face, wincing as he touched the place where Oot had struck him. His fingers came away sticky with drying blood he rubbed onto his grimy prison pants. Gingerly, he prodded his cheek, not feeling anything out of place. He checked his teeth. One wobbled but that could be taken care of later.

What he needed, he'd stashed behind his last molar. Implanted into his gums lurked a small metal stud that activated the port behind his ear. The phantoms told stories of the transfer device goons like Oot used on people who pissed them off, so he'd taken precautions long before Wrath had set him up. The gods smile on those who are prepared, the old saying said.

With his good arm, he wrestled himself to his feet, holding the edge of the table for support while the room spun. A concussion would interfere with jacking into his deck, which would trap him here for the short remainder of his life. He knew exactly where Oot's stolen glint sat, so he'd return it if his plan failed. The warden might let him live, but R'gar would hound him until he was dead. The only way out was to follow the plan and escape. Then he'd deal with Wrath.

Nyx wobbled as the room came to equilibrium with his head. The table he used for balance had synth-hide padding over a metal framework and large straps to restrain overactive guests. On either side of the room sat hulking metal counters with storage bays. The ceiling had arrays of sensors and retractable arms that allowed a healer to perform remote surgery as well as other basic medical functions. No sense in getting their hands dirty on the Hub trash locked up here.

Nyx's contact had given him the code to open the left storage bay. It was the last message he'd received before the Squids crashed his deck. As he squatted in front of the cabinet, his hand trembled, causing him to enter it incorrectly the first time. The lock bleated in protest. He glanced over his shoulder, hoping no one had heard his failed attempt and would come investigate. After a few silent moments, he forced the pain back and concentrated on the sequence of numbers. As he entered the last digit, a green light popped on, and the audible click of the lock disengaging sent his spirits soaring. He'd be out in a flash.

The door swung open to reveal a black body bag and a small air respirator. The Sparlow deck that he was expecting to find wasn't there. He pulled out the supplies, but the deck wasn't under the bag or in it. He broke out in a cold sweat as the implications of the missing deck hit home. The top of the bay held a drawer. Forcing himself to slow down, he opened the drawer to find a surgical tool set.

Nyx's heart raced. The deck had been moved, or worse, taken. Without the deck, he couldn't free himself, and he'd most likely be killed once the warden had his glint back. Nyx froze as he heard the outer door of the infirmary open.

There was one last, desperate option and Nyx prepared to take it. He pulled the scalpel from the set and crept to the side of the door, prepared to kill whoever walked in.

Nyx tensed as the door slid open. *Any second now.* The door fully opened. Nothing happened. No one walked through, no sounds of foot-falls running down the hallway. The door stayed open, meaning someone had to be there.

"I'll take it you are waiting to attack me since you are no longer on the table?" The voice that had told R'gar where to put him asked, his tone plaintive. "Piper asked me to do her a favor and I have the equipment with me, though I'd hate to drop such a nice deck on the floor. Might damage the inner workings."

He'd paid Piper a lot of glint to place that deck in here so he could hack the prison systems to get him out in a body bag. Chances were it was legit, but it didn't ease Nyx's tension. He tossed the scalpel to the floor with a clink and stumbled over to lean against the table. A short person, either a gnome or a halfling—Nyx could never tell them apart—walked in carrying the Sparlow deck in one arm and a hypodermic gun in the other.

Nyx started at the gun, causing the little person to pause. "Relax, friend. I noticed Oot worked you over pretty good. This will amp you until you can get out. You can call me Bevo."

"Bevo it is, and my thanks."

Bevo raised a bushy eyebrow at him. "No thanks needed. Glint makes a lot of temporary friends." Bevo placed the deck on the table next to Nyx. He placed the gun against Nyx's leg and pulled the trigger. The cocktail flooded his system, deadening the pain and filling him with buzz of energy.

"Hi-Lo?"

Bevo nodded. "Hold you for about half a day. Better be near a bed when you crash. It's all I could get on short notice."

Nyx titled his head in the traditional elvish manner. "Agno."

"Never expected elvish manners from a wirehead," the halfling said with a smirk. "So down to grit?"

In the Quad, grit meant business and not of the above-board kind. If Bevo worked with Piper, he came from the Flow district or at least the merc markets. "No ca? Piper paid you. I've got my way out."

"No ca? Huh." Ca was street for understanding or knowledge. The halfling shrugged. "Guess you didn't hear Oot's having all the cadavers scavenged for pieces. Well, good luck."

"What? When did that start?" Nyx shook, though he couldn't tell if from the drugs or the thought he'd come close to being dismembered. "My source guaranteed the information."

The halfling barked out a vicious laugh. "You just in from fairyland?

Snitches lie to get paid. Climb in that body bag and I'll call it in for you. See how that works out for you." Bevo turned to leave.

Nyx sighed. Either Bevo was playing him or wanted something or both. It didn't matter; he'd have to make good. "How much is your help going to cost me?"

He turned toward him, a satisfied smile on his long, thin face. "Oot's glint." Before Nyx protested, he held up his hand. "Look, phantom, I know you didn't get put here to snatch the Warden's glint. My guess is you got screwed and this is your backup plan." He flipped a folded piece of paper to Nyx. "Transfer the glint to that account and I'll show you the easy way out."

*The shorter they are, the meaner they get.* Out loud he said, "Fine." He pulled the deck across to him. For a simple transfer he could use the embedded display screen. He pushed the jack into the port behind his ear and read in the account information along with a return code. The glint would revert back to Nyx's account in the morning. He pulled the cord free and glared at the halfling.

Bevo pulled out a handheld display and nodded when the numbers changed on his screen. "Come on, we have little time." He set off through the door, forcing Nyx to grab the deck and stumble after. The drugs had taken away the pain, but he felt unbalanced as he followed along.

The halfling trotted down the hall going away from the entrance. Unlike the high security doors, the nondescript entry Bevo chose had a standard keypad that any apartment would have used. Heavy pipes and conduits ran along the ceiling and walls of the dimly lit service tunnel. The air stank of garbage and bodily waste as they went deeper into the inner workings of the prison. After a series of turns, Bevo stood holding his device out in front as if he were lost.

Shouts rang out from back the way they had come. "Gash it all," Bevo swore under his breath. "We have to move or we're both going down."

Luckily, Nyx's longer legs made up for his unsteadiness as he followed the running man. Heavy footfalls grew louder as the pair went, losing ground to their pursuers. Bevo skidded to a halt in front of an air grate set into the concrete even with the floor. He reached down and opened the large metal frame. A slight metallic squeal couldn't be avoided. Nyx climbed into the pipe, pushing the deck ahead of him, wishing he had use of both arms. He slid along the metal until his feet were inside the duct a ways. The halfling entered, carefully closing the grate behind him.

The footfalls grew louder as the guards chased their prey through the service corridors. Both men sat stock still as the guards ran past their hiding place. The noise decreased as their pursuers went down the tunnel in the direction they had been headed. Bevo blew out a deep breath. "We can follow this down to another exit, though it will be harder on you."

Nyx grunted as he shifted. His shoulder didn't hurt per se, but it was damned inconvenient. "Being dead would be even harder. I need to get out of the void soon."

The halfling rolled his eyes. "You phantoms and your void this, cyber-space that. You'd not be in this jam if you'd been any good at it."

Pushing past Nyx turned out to be harder than expected. Bevo grabbed the deck and headed out. His handheld gave off enough light to by without throwing shadows when they crossed other junctions. "We're almost to the loading docks. I'll set off a diversion and you run for it."

Nyx was injured, drugged, and in a bad part of the Quad, and the halfling's plan was "run for it." Nyx's other option consisted of a slow, painful death, especially since Bevo now owned the warden's glint, well, for 24 hours. He needed to escape, hole up, and wait until morning to find a better place to heal. With the deck, he could get a hovercraft to pick him up and return him to his place in the Flow sector. After that, his shoulder would need to be repaired and he could figure out how Wrath had set him up on his last job.

The last twenty meters of the duct rose gradually, making it harder for Nyx to push himself along. Sweat beaded on his brow and ran down his back in equal measures. Bevo sat inside the grate, waiting on the exhausted elf to arrive. After he'd checked to make sure they were alone, he opened the cover and motioned Nyx out. It took some effort to extract himself from the ductwork, but he made it.

Crates, boxes, and containers of all shapes and sizes sat in a row out to the open delivery entrance. Bevo handed over the deck and, before Nyx could do anything, he swung himself into the duct and let the grate slam into place. The sound echoed across the empty warehouse and Nyx forced himself into motion, knowing he only had a few minutes to get away.

He walked down between the pallets of boxes that formed a path through the warehouse and out to the dock. Hands reached out, grabbed his injured arm and slammed him into the wall of supplies. A groan escaped his lips as he hit the heavy wooden crates. Without thinking, he dropped to his knees, just in time for a great gnarled, greenish fist to slam into the box where his head had been moments ago. R'gar pulled his fist out of the broken box, blue syrup clinging to it as he turned.

Nyx pushed himself onto his back and tried to move away from the angry giant, one arm holding the deck cradled against his chest and the other dangling uselessly by his side. "I'll give Oot his glint, R'gar."

A loud snort erupted from the orc. "No care. Me take you to meat shop. Get good glint for elf."

Nyx's brain raced through options, looking for the one that would keep R'gar from killing him on the spot. His ideas were as empty as the void he would die in. Nyx couldn't bear the thought that his last great plan would end in his death. He'd be the tragic tale people told their kids to keep them away from the phantoms and the decks. Worse yet, he'd have proved his parents right when they'd called him a failure and disinherited him from the family.

R'gar raised his overly large arm, flexing the massive grafted muscles. "Bye, elf."

Nyx closed his eyes and waited but nothing happened. A loud thud and a large, wet weight dropped across the lower half of his body. He opened his eyes and saw R'gar's body lying on top of him. The back of the orc's head had been torn open as blood spurted across both the floor and Nyx in equal measure.

"Bigger they are, the more fléchette you need to drop 'em," a tiny voice said from where it hovered over Nyx. "Name is Gelsey and I've been sent to retrieve you. Come on, before the rest of the brute squad shows up."

Nyx's brain flatlined for a moment. Pixie. She was a pixie with a fléchette pistol in her hand. It took a bit but he managed to get out from under the massive orc whose blood now covered his prison uniform. He stumbled along, half dazed, after the small, winged fairy.

Nobody had warned Nyx that there would be days like this.

9

GELSEY

Gelsey led the way to the loading dock and halted. As soon as Nyx cleared the dock, the motion detectors would notify the guards, and they'd be hunted. She flew near his face. "Wait until I yell, then run straight ahead until you reach the fence."

Nyx nodded dumbly at her. She shook her head, exasperated. This was the amazing hacker who'd skimmed the Nefastu accounts and gotten away with it? He seemed like a flatline rider who didn't know he'd died. Gelsey punched her wings up and soared to the roof where the motion sensors were housed. She repositioned the sensor until it pointed out of the hovercraft yard. "Go!"

Nyx did as he was told, running in a fairly straight line toward the fence. The alarm went off a moment later. "Gash it!" Gelsey yelled in frustration. She took off at full speed, passing the guards who came after them. Pistol in hand, she reached Nyx before them, though not by much. Unfortunately, she didn't carry enough ammo to take down all the pursuers.

"Gelsey, over here!" a voice yelled to her. Without a second thought, she flew toward it at full speed. Nyx lumbered along behind her, sweat pouring off the injured elf. Magically, Kelthar stood by a hole in the chain-link fence that surrounded the hovercraft yard. "This way." The mage dove through the hole, followed by Nyx, then Gelsey.

Kelthar whispered, "Sit perfectly still."

Gelsey landed, shutting down her wings. They all held their breath as the guards searched where they'd seen the fugitive. After what seemed like an hour, they moved on.

Kelthar grinned at Gelsey. "I looked up. I saw you enter the prison hovercraft yard and figured it pertained to our upcoming joint mission. I thought I'd see if you needed a hand."

Gelsey nodded. "Good thing you did, or I'm not sure we'd have made it." She glanced over a Nyx, who still clutched the deck even though he had passed out cold. She keyed her comm device and called in a favor.

With the use of a levitation spell, they moved Nyx to a safer place to wait for their pickup. "I'll see you in three days, Gelsey." Kelthar bowed and vanished into the Quad. Gelsey felt more tired than at any time in her life. Gashing Ancep sending her after all these people. Her head dropped as she realized she still had two more to recruit.

# AIKILA

The Dragon's Throat gate stood off in the distance, traffic barely existent at this time of the morning. Animasor, the second moon, had risen, and Reatrix, the larger of the two moons, reached its zenith. Aikila studied the gate through her holoviewer, waiting for the signal it was safe to cross. The three hovercrafts behind her held enough merchandise to fund her for a period of time, though not as long as it should have. Trips outside of Hub were profitable, but since the dragons started cracking down on smugglers, the bribes for entry had increased exponentially. Until whichever dragon lord got bored with making everyone's life miserable, the increased security and costs would keep going up.

After thirty minutes, the signal rose from above the gate. *Finally.* Her irritation seethed below her calm exterior. These bribes were eating into both her profit and her patience. If it hadn't been for the antique firearm and three bins worth of skin grafts, she would have marked this trip a failure. Without a proper storage system, the skin would be ruined soon, so it could still be a waste.

Signals passed between the hovercrafts alerting the drivers to make ready. Aikila always drove the lead vehicle, and her men brought up the rear. Superstitions ran deep in the naddaha clans when it came to commerce. All the best dealers in Hub were naddaha. Some thought the puny leprechauns to be more formidable deal makers, though most hoarded gold like a dragon. You had to spend glint to make it.

Aikila jumped into the driver's seat and started down the road to the gate. The largest amount of the trade for Hub came in by ship, but ships sank, or pirates seized them, or the HubSec boarded looking for contraband. Too many factors and costs to make it worthwhile. The hovercrafts picked up speed as they came down the last hill before the gate. They hit level ground and Aikila slowed her vehicle. The all-clear signal was gone, which struck her as unusual. They'd passed the point of no return by the low wall of HubSec turrets that protected the gate from nothing. The last giant uprising to reach Hub had ended in dragon fire as the thirteen clans of dragons unleashed their elders to finish the invaders. Since then, wars broke out between countries, but they never impacted Hub. Dragons had a long memory and a longer lifespan.

The checkpoint glowed under the floodlights, which gave Aikila a good look at the guards. Crron, the gargoyle inspector, stood to the side, a portable resting in his gnarled hands. As the hovercrafts parked next to him, he strode to the lead vehicle's door. Aikila stepped out, adjusting the holster of her pistol. She nodded politely to the inspector. In reality, Crron wasn't a bad sort for an inspector. He only raised rates when he needed to and would look the other way from a whole host of offenses that others charged extra for.

"Aikila, there's a problem." The gargoyle started to say more. He stopped as his eyes focused on an approaching figure.

Gash it all, she couldn't afford any more "problems." She turned to see a tall, lanky squid headed their way. The twisted blue cord around his shoulder announced him to be a member of the Caerlux. As he closed in on them, it became apparent that this wasn't a dragon-born but a bastard mix. A cut-rate, body-mod lab had obviously done the widespread nose at a discount rate. Scars lingered from the bungling modder. They had docked his ears to the appropriate style with the same lack of finesse. Most of the bastards underwent genetic surgery when the house accepted them into their ranks. This one must've screwed up bad to be out here, and that meant horrible news for Aikila. Ladder climbers looking to make a name for themselves created a mess of everything they touched. She groaned quietly.

"What is the meaning of this, Inspector?" The squid asked. His haughty tone and rigid military stance set every nerve in Aikila's body on edge. "Why have your men not searched these vehicles?"

"Magistrate, they just arrived. I haven't even scanned their permits." The Gargoyle's low, rumbling voice sounded annoyed. The lack of bribes would make any guard surly.

"Then get to it!" The squid's eyes flew up and down Aikila hungrily. She shifted her long coat to display her pistol. HubSec were referred to as squid on the street given the passing resemblance young whelplings had to their water neighbor. Aikila preferred the nastier nickname of pods, a reference to the insect eggs that were common in Hub. She had glint enough to buy her way out of a murder charge of an unhoused bastard. From the way he stepped back, he suspected as much. "I'm sure there is contraband here. Find it!"

Crron rolled his eyes as he made a show of reviewing her trading permits. "Everything is in order with your paperwork. No need to search the vehicles, they are properly licensed."

The pod flushed with anger. "I said search them. You will do as I tell you." The fact that the pod didn't try to loom over the inspector spoke volumes for just how low he was. The Gargoyle didn't move. "Fine." He spoke in low tones over whatever hardware he'd had stashed in his empty head. Three burly orcs came through the gate, each carrying a rifle and a vibro-knife strapped to their hips. These were jacked up street toughs, not HubSec units.

Aikila cleared her throat. "Those aren't HubSec or customs officers. You've no right to search my vehicles."

The pod snorted. "Being dragon-born is the only right I need."

The voice in the back of her head screamed not to do it. Her mouth couldn't help it. "Dragon-born? You? Next time you might want to go someplace that doesn't give you a toy with your surgery."

His eyes widened with rage. For a moment Aikila thought he might strike her. Instead, he turned to the goons. "Search these vehicles. You may shoot anyone who tries to stop you."

Crron put a jagged hand over hers as it clutched her pistol. "He killed Archea during the last search. You can replace anything he takes."

She knew he spoke sense, but this trumped-up pod had no right. She should have kept her mouth shut and not pissed off the pod. Crron's people would have overlooked most of the expensive pieces and grabbed a couple of low value things to satisfy the buffoon. She could hear the thugs tearing into cargo that cost more than the worthless orcs ever would be.

"Uggg, smelly!" came from the middle hovercraft followed by a stasis container full of harvested troll skin that shattered on the pavement, spilling its now ruined contents all over.

She bit her tongue to keep from screaming. Those skins were worth more than a year's salary to most of the Quad. This trip wouldn't bankrupt her, though it would certainly put a dent in her business for a long while.

A happy yell rang out from Aikila's vehicle. The orc with the broken tusks emerged with the antique pistol in his grubby paw. "Look, gun!"

A self-satisfied smirk appeared on the pod's face. He took the revolver from his henchmen, examining it carefully. "I'm confiscating this. We do not allow traders to bring unregistered weapons into Hub."

"What?" she shrieked. "That is an Old Earth artifact. It's a relic that doesn't even fire." She reached for the weapon. A collector would pay a small fortune for such a prize.

The pod batted her hand away. "Seize her. I'm charging you with gun smuggling. You'll stand trial before the magistrate's courts."

"You can't do this!" Aikila placed her hand on her pistol but froze when the orc shoved the barrel of his slug thrower into her face.

The pod smiled at her. "I can. Make sure you get a lawyer that doesn't offer a toy with your defense. Take her away."

1 1

# GELSEY

"Gashing Ancep," Gelsey swore as she clung to the cargo box. Said box being strapped to a hovercraft transport had made getting to Dragon's Throat a bit more challenging. "He could have provided better accommodations."

It had been a long ride for the wind-battered pixie. She hadn't thought to bring a harness to secure her between the hovercraft and the trailer it pulled, which would have freed up her hands for more important things like pretending to strangle Ancep.

Hub had been built to withstand any assault from outside. The Canoware Sea contained a single passageway in, bordered by the western side of the city with mountain ranges bracketing in the other three sides. The only land route into Hub ran through the Dragon's Throat.

As they approached the gate, she wondered what this Aikila was doing there. The list of options was all bad. The guards searched vehicles, confiscated contraband, and sent you on your way, either into or out of the city. You'd have to do something really awful or stupid to get stuck at the inspection point.

She glanced up at the sky, noting the slight orange tint, a byproduct of the shield that kept all fliers out of Hub. Gelsey, of course, had firsthand experience with the spell shield and exactly how painful it was to cross. Experience taught powerful lessons, and she had had to relearn some of them many times.

60

When it appeared they wouldn't be moving for a while, Gelsey decided to stretch her wings and scout out the area.

"Ahhh, the air is so clean. How wonderful." She shot upward, spinning as she flew. To a pixie, freedom was the ultimate drug and Gelsey bordered on overdosing.

"Squawk!"

Gelsey snapped out of her daze, diving sharply to avoid the hawk's outstretched talons. The bird screamed with rage as it missed. It circled, readying for another pass. The angry hawk tracked its prey as it spread its wings to line up with its next meal.

Being small made you a target for a lot of things, but the raptors were the worst for the pixies. They were relentless, and fast as all get out. Even Gelsey's enhanced wing rig couldn't outdistance a determined hawk. The cry from above warned her that her attacker had her dead to rights.

The hawk folded its wings and plummeted from the sky, talons extended, the very essence of death. It approached at an alarming rate on the fleeing pixie, who pushed her wings at full velocity as she darted for cover. Closer and closer the razor-sharp claws stretched to grasp its prey.

Gelsey flew faster, her escape would be a near thing. The hawk dove faster than she thought possible. The dull metal of the hovercraft loomed as she sped down toward it. She felt the presence behind her. At this speed, she couldn't afford to look. She'd make it or not. The side of the vehicle filled her view. She went into freefall, dropped below the hawk, and gunned her wings to life before she fell more than a meter. The upward jolt wrenched every part of her.

Going far too fast to pull up, the hawk barreled into the side of the hovercraft with a dull thud. The bird rebounded, sailing across to tumble in the dirt, stunned. Gelsey allowed herself to laugh as the hawk shook itself before taking off in the opposite direction. Pixies were attuned to the cycle of life, but she had no plans of being eaten to continue it. The hawk could go find something less challenging for dinner.

# AIKILA

All things considered, the orcs weren't as bad as they could have been. Aikila landed in her cell minus her pistol and her dignity. In all the years she'd been brokering goods, she'd never been jailed. There had been confiscations, harassment, and downright intimidation. The slug had sunk to an all-time low for dragons. The gashing lowborn pod would pay for this. That antique pistol, in the right hands, would have paid handsomely. This trip had pushed her to the brink of collapse, physically and financially.

The cell had a bed and a toilet, both built into the walls. The front wall contained an old pneumatic steel door that was operated by a switch placed on the far side of the hall. A small circular window with bars sat unlocked so the guards could speak to the prisoner from outside. They had left it open on purpose, so she heard the rough treatment her men received from the thugs who'd brought them in.

"Aikila, you okay?" Crron's craggy voice came from through the barred window. She got off the bed and went over. The Gargoyle looked a hundred years older than before. "I shut down the all-clear as soon as I saw the magistrate show up. I'm sorry you got caught up in this mess."

She shook her head slowly. "Not your fault, Crron. I should have kept my mouth shut for a change. If I hadn't tweaked his bad nose job, he'd have stolen from me and I'd be in Hub already. Who is he, anyhow?"

Crron shrugged his shoulders. "The slug whose sire wants him to prove himself before he'll house him. From the looks of it, he's been sent out here to rot. Won't even tell us his name, just that he's a magistrate."

Aikila chucked at the use of the term slug for the half-dragon. Enforcing the searches made little sense. Everyone knew illicit goods came through the Dragon's Throat, but what came in over the water dwarfed it. Why send flunkies down here to stir up trouble? If it got bad enough, the smugglers would find other means to gain entry to Hub's markets. "Why send him here? The dragons make far more from goods moving through the city than from cracking down on the traders."

Crron glanced over his shoulder to make sure they were alone. "They're looking for something. A few days ago, word came down that we were to take any magic item we found. Funny part is they sent more inspectors for inside the gates than out."

"Interesting." Covering up a search for a stolen piece of magic by enforcing stronger security checks. "Does the pod out there know what's going on?"

"Yeah. Power went to his head when he realized he could do what he wanted." Crron pushed a small metallic case through the bars on the window. She quickly placed it in a hidden pouch of her coat. Unless they scanned her, they wouldn't find it. "Got my hands on your data sticks. At least he won't rob you blind. Gotta go."

"Thanks, owe you a beer." Aikila watched as the Gargoyle scurried down the hall and out of sight. The hallway stood empty. Raising her voice a bit, she called. "You boys all right?"

Saltmane's raspy voice responded. "Aye, Aikila. I'd certainly like a rematch with those gashers when I have me rifle."

She'd have chuckled under different circumstances. They'd humiliated her and injured her men. One way or the other she'd get even with that bastard. "I'll find a way out of here."

The Dwarf grunted. "Know ya' will."

She returned to the bed, the situation over. With a loud clang of the locks being undone, the door opened with a groan. The magistrate strode into the room as if he owned the place. Aikila swore she wouldn't goad the gasher and maybe he'd let them go. She inclined her head respectfully. "Magistrate, to what do I owe this unexpected visit?"

"Learned to control your tongue, have you?" He almost beamed with pride at her subservient words.

Her stomach roiled in disgust at the thought of bowing before this slug. She focused on her men and getting them out of there alive. "I regret my earlier . . ." She searched for the correct word. "Remarks. They were uncalled for and I apologize for them."

He sniffed at her. Puffs of air came out of the bad incisions from the sloppy surgery. She fought down a laugh.

"Something amusing?" he asked, his tone frosty. His face went stiff with suppressed anger. Dragons were a prickly lot with more etiquette rules than even the elves. The fact that his behavior smacked of non-dragon rudeness was lost on him.

"No, sire." His ego swelled at being referred to by a term reserved for the eldest of dragons. "I'd like to discuss the release of me and my men."

He studied her for a moment. "I can't place your race. What are you?" His eyes stayed on her, probing for information.

Aikila's mouth dropped open at the sheer rudeness of the question. She closed her mouth and thought rapidly. It wouldn't do to tell him and tip her hand. "I'm of Xana descent. My family still lives in the mountains north of the capital."

His eyes narrowed and leaned against the wall of the cell, lost in thought. He sighed loudly before speaking. "I have a proposition for you. If you agree, I will drop all charges and release you."

"How about my goods? Your men destroyed a precious ..." She clamped her mouth shut. "Forgive me. As you were saying?"

"You are a vexing woman." He, too, composed himself before continuing. "If you will agree to fulfill my needs, I will allow you to go with your men and your wares. If you satisfy me, I will add in enough glint to cover the losses you incurred."

And Aikila thought the rudest thing to come out of the bastard's mouth was the race crack. "So, you want me to sleep with you, and if I do a good enough job, you'll pay me? Do I have that right?"

The magistrate nodded, ignoring the fact that not only was he forcing himself on her but compensating her like a prostitute. "Exactly, do you agree?"

"I'm going to need some time to consider your offer." She bit her lip to keep from saying more. The idea of laying with that repulsive reptile turned her stomach. There had to be another way to get out of the situation without prostituting herself to do it.

"This is a one-time offer for today only. I'll return in a few hours to accept your agreement. I warn you, do not disappoint me." He strode out of the cell, leaving Aikila alone. Rage and embarrassment warred within her. The fact that the overgrown salamander thought she'd willingly sleep with him was ludicrous. She took his warning seriously, though, because alone she couldn't fight him off.

Aikila didn't believe in a no-win situation. She heard her father's voice in the back of her head. *There is always a loophole if you know where to look.*

She had a couple hours to find that loophole.

# GELSEY

Gelsey opened the folder and browsed the contents as she traveled. Aikila Dziuban dealt in, well, everything. Exoskeletons, weapons, genestock, muscle grafts. The document looked like the contraband list the squids published. The odd part was that her race was listed as indeterminable. Was that a race? Gelsey shook her head, wondering if she'd be better off just starting a new life out of Hub. The thought, however, of stealing turnips from farmers didn't thrill her. She knew she'd see this mission through; Ancep did as well.

The real worry wasn't in the dossiers or the people she recruited. Ancep shouldn't have been in the Quad doing this kind of business. The clans lived to "one up" each other, and a full wyrm hanging around the Quad would have been fodder for months. What kind of risk would be worth the loss of social and clan standing? The number of fully molted wyrms couldn't be over five percent of the dragon population, though who knew what happened underground in the lairs.

She searched the files again, looking for any clue about what the team would be doing. Nyx had had a golden track record until recently. Nobody had ever heard of Silai. Rumors floated around Hub about Kelthar. The nagualan merc would be the muscle. Aikila traded in contraband. No common thread, no easy way to piece them together. Gelsey pondered the mysteries as she found a nook where the view gave her a better lay of the land.

# AIKILA

An hour had gone by and Aikila didn't have a plan, idea, or inkling. She might be able to delay the inevitable using her naddahan skills, but that wouldn't get her out of the predicament she found herself entrenched in. Her mother had warned her that her mouth would be her undoing.

She flung herself off the bed and paced the three meters of open floor space. When she turned, her coat flared out and something thumped on her leg. She ignored it. There had to be a way out. Turn. Thump. Pace. Turn. Thump. Aikila stopped to pull the case out of her coat, tossing it on the bed while she thought things through.

Pacing back and forth, ideas popped up only to be shot down due to lack of resources or danger level. Even if she dropped the bastard, she'd need to get her men out. Any old-school naddahan merchant would have sold any of them to the highest bidder. Aikila didn't prescribe to that way of thinking. She didn't abandon men who'd stuck with her.

Frustrated, she dropped on the mattress, landing on the case. She grabbed it angrily to throw it, then realized that might be the last glint she had to her name until she could get back to Hub.

Aikila opened the case Crron had given her. Seeing the stick made her feel slightly better. She had enough funds to pay the bribes and get her men out, at least. Well, once the magistrate handed them over to the regular pods, that is. Bribing the bastard would be useless. She slotted the chip to be sure it still contained her glint and was relieved to see it did. She unseated the stick and slid it back into the case.

The case had a fold-out compartment that held twelve sticks. She flipped through each one, hoping she'd find something, anything, that might help. Payroll records, inventory, and transaction receipts wouldn't be of any use unless they bored the magistrate to sleep. Next, she popped open the false back and took out three sticks. The first contained implantable heavy armament training that turned anyone into an expert in moments. Hard to get but it was of no use. The second had an ISS cracker that in the right hands got you access to anything military-grade and highly illegal. A wirehead would pay through the nose for that stick. Unfortunately, the bastard wanted wetware, not hardware. Gallows humor. She laughed at the joke even though her time was running out.

The third stick. She'd gotten it off a kappa a couple of months ago. He'd needed glint in a hurry and had come to her as a last resort. He swore it contained data of a plan that Clan Koxalan had been crafting. Dragon politics consisted of besting the other clans for power and prestige, often at the expense of the inhabitants of Hub. Still, if you wanted to get rich, you had to go where the glint was. She should have been a prosperous trader like her father and his father, until they married her off, after which her husband would run the business. Instead of following the rules of her homeland, she'd moved to Hub with its lack of rules to pursue her own destiny.

In the end, she'd given the kappa a couple of thousand glint to go away. She had no idea of what the stick actually contained. Her SecOps pal warned her it pulsed with viruses and wouldn't touch it. If the stick contained Clan Koxalan secrets and the bastard needed a win to get housed, it just might work. She slotted the stick without engaging it. The last thing she needed was a nova logic bomb going off in her brain. She didn't pack wetware but who knew what could happen.

Doubt filled her. Would the data free her? He might just take the stick and force her to submit to him. She needed to make him want the stick more than he wanted her. She wouldn't rely on chance—it had to be a sure thing.

She examined the cell. She hadn't noticed anything to indicate that the cell had any cameras, but you were never sure with a scanner. Lowering her head so she couldn't be seen, she popped the contact lenses out of her eyes and set them inside the case. One peculiarity of Naddahan biology gave them away: the lack of a colored iris. The Naddahan had solid white eyes which held their power of mesmerization, or so the legends said. Either way, Aikila needed to make sure the magistrate took the stick and not her.

She closed her eyes and waited. Anyone who saw her would assume that she had accessed the socketed stick and was immersed in its contents. She didn't have to wait long before the lock announced the bastard's return. Aikila jumped as he entered, pulling the stick and trying to hide it away.

"What do you have there?" the magistrate asked. He stomped toward her. "Show me now or I'll take it from you."

She cowered against the wall, head down so he couldn't glimpse her eyes. She held the stick out from her so that he'd be forced to reach across her to get it. With a great huff, the magistrate bent over her and grasped the stick. Aikila faced him, locking her eyes on his. "The data stick has secret information from Clan Koxalan on it. Your sire will reward you for turning it in."

The magistrate's face slackened as the power of hypnosis took him fully. You couldn't hypnotize a person to do something contrary to strongly held beliefs, but this played directly into his greatest desires. "We are in a dispute with Koxalan and my sire will reward me for helping to best them," he agreed in a dreamy tone.

She cooed at him. "Yes, you will be given a place of great power and privilege. Women will fall at your feet awaiting your pleasure."

A lopsided grin crossed his face, showing off the extent of the bad grafting he'd endured. "They will. I will have my choice."

"Yes, you must take the stick to your sire before it's too late. You will be a hero."

He shook his head slightly, trying to clear it. Dragons were immune to her charms, but he barely qualified as a dragon. "You are wasting time. Koxalan will have moved against you and you'll have lost your chance. You must go now."

"Now. You are correct." He straightened and stepped through the door. The door boomed shut. "If this contains what I believe, I will free you and your men. If not..." He walked away, the sound of his bootheels echoing down the hall. The implied threat lingered behind.

Aikila replaced her contacts and waited for her fate. Had she done enough? Was the data what she'd been promised? She dozed off with a million questions circling through her mind.

She sat up with a start when the door unlocked and the magistrate entered. "You are free to go. The data is more than adequate for an exchange."

The news stunned her. The Kappa had been telling her the truth. "Thank you."

The magistrate nodded. The harsh report of a gauss pistol discharged outside her cell. Blood sprayed through the open door as the lifeless head of the bastard fell into view. Aikila froze, not knowing what to do next.

A moment later, a figure stepped through the doorway over the dead body. The assassin carried the full dragon pedigree. Unlike the bastard, he showed all the sigils of his clan. He carried a pistol she could tell he used quite well. "You are free to go, trader, with Clan Koxalan apologies for any inconvenience the Caerlux low-born has caused you."

She bowed her head in respect. "Thank you." She kept her head down as was proper. From the pointed nose and the scale ridge on his forehead, she sat before a wyrmling. Everyone knew wyrms never left the Apex. This one might be high up in Clan Koxalan one day.

"You saw nothing here. Be on your way. Your men are in their vehicles." He left the room. Aikila shook with adrenaline. She took a few deep breaths, steadying her nerves.

"Nice play there."

Aikila jumped at the voice, head whipping around. She sat alone.

"You mudders never look up," the voice stated firmly. "I'm up here."

She followed the voice until she spotted a pixie hovering just shy of the ceiling. Wings blurred silently behind her as she floated to eye level with Aikila. She sported blue hair pulled back into a tail. She had the softness of a child, even with her tilted eyes and pointed ears, but the pistols on her hips and the zap gun on her wrist told a different story.

"Who are you and what can I do for you?" Aikila asked. It had been a long day and the pixie's appearance didn't bode well for it ending soon.

Gelsey tossed a data stick to Aikila. "Name's Gelsey. I've got a job offer from an important suit."

Of course, she did. Aikila pocketed the stick and stood to follow the pixie. She was ready to quit this place and return to Hub. There'd be time to review the job soon enough. "It never pays to keep the customer waiting, but we need to get out of here first."

Gelsey nodded.

"You need a ride back?" Aikila asked.

"Sure! It beats riding on the roof."

Aikila gave her a sideways glance, wondering if that was a pixie expression of some sort.

They joined her men and set out for Hub. Aikila shuddered as they drove out away from the guard station. That had been far too close for comfort. Now Gelsey appeared with a mysterious job offer.

The day became stranger as it went.

# 15

# LORCAN

The dimly lit entrance tunnel of the Slaughterhouse Arena boomed with the pounding of the crowd above. The Quad contained members of all races, each with their own quirks, rivalries, and abilities. Tonight, they all agreed that watching others battle and die was good entertainment.

Lorcan had fought in enough wars, skirmishes, and border disputes that he had little liking for blood sports. The assembled grafters, skin merchants, and others who could afford the tickets gathered for a night of blood, pain, gambling, and drinking.

Lorcan's tail lashed in time with his rising anger. The ogre's pale skin was the opposite of Lorcan's spotted hide. He had strong, bulky fists, which were formidable, but not as lethal as his retractable claws. Lorcan needed every advantage his heritage had provided if he were to beat this foe. The fates had conspired against him when his daughter Jaana had been diagnosed with a brain tumor, forcing him into the ring to clear his debts. At least merc pay could be lucrative . . . when the job ended well. Being on the losing side of his latest job had hurt him financially. The clients had been slaughtered, leaving the mercs they hired unpaid and without the promised bonus he'd signed on for.

Since his wife's death, there was no one else to help care for their daughter, so he couldn't take on contracts that required him to travel. Without glint, legitimate surgeons wouldn't touch her, so he'd headed into the Flow sector, with its low-end wetwork shops and cheap gear warehouses, to find a clinic that specialized in repair jobs. They'd done the work on her tumor and then placed his daughter into cryo until he paid the bill. According to the agreement he'd signed, if he defaulted after ninety days, they would sell his kitten to the highest bidder.

With no other choice, he entered the Slaughterhouse. If he emerged victorious, he'd clear enough to get his child out of the clinic and to safety.

Today he faced Vikog, the perennial champion of the Slaughterhouse, an ogre who'd won every contest he'd ever been in. He had no choice but to beat the monster. To do so would take all the skill and luck he could muster. Ogres' ability to withstand a lot of damage was legendary, though they were slow. After years of being a successful merc, Lorcan had military-grade neurostim and grafted muscle built into him. He also had an embedded targeting system to link up to his weapon. Not that it helped in unarmed combat.

Vikog claimed to be fully organic, and the Slaughterhouse showed the scans that "proved" it. With no rules against enhancements of any kind, the statement was more for show than anything. He'd seen the big man fight, and he suspected he packed low-grade upgrades. Maybe a pain dampener or a minor neurostim implant. Nothing anywhere near what Lorcan was wired with. Lorcan's other matches had been close calls—on purpose. He didn't want to give his opponents any idea of what a fully enhanced nagual could do. And if things turned out well, the audience would never know.

The match currently underway between Vikog and his opponent, a scrappy acuna fighter, wouldn't last long. Unlike the opponents Lorcan had fought, the competitors the ogre faced weren't serious challenges. The odds were stacked in the champion's favor. So far, Lorcan hadn't had to kill anyone; he'd just disabled them, giving himself a reputation for weakness. Killings, of course, were encouraged in the ring. Even when that didn't happen, a lot of the losers died from lack of medical attention. The Slaughterhouse had earned its name.

Screams and cheers rained down on the arena as Vikog finished off his opponent, much to the delight of the audience. Gore rose in his throat at the thought of having to support this barbaric spectacle, but hard times required hard decisions. If it saved Jaana, it was all worth it. He prayed to the gods that he could finish there and be done with Hub once and for all. The cesspool had taken its toll on him, and he would return to nagual with his tail between his legs and beg his parents' forgiveness. He'd find work and raise his daughter in the town he'd grown up in.

The fantasy dissolved as the Slaughterhouse promoter came toward him from the arena gate. Lorcan hated the green-skinned Goblin on sight, knowing he made glint off the pain and death of others. He had an old hardwire out of the back of his head linked to an oversized prosthetic eye. The tech had to be twenty years out of date. He sported a dusty black vest and maroon pants that hung over his combat boots.

"There's my guy," the promoter barked as he came down the hall. "Vikog had a hell of a fight. Just about tore the poor bastard's head clean off. The crowd loved it."

Lorcan swallowed a low growl. He'd shunned his parent's teaching of nonviolence, though glorifying murder turned his stomach. "I'm sure they did."

The promoter stopped short as if deciding some personal space might be wise. "You've done a great job in the ring, but really you aren't a match for Vikog. You barely beat that guy from Xana and he was still limping from his last bout."

The promoter lied, as did all goblins did. Give them a bit of power and they thought people were too stupid to see through their falsehoods. The Xanan had fought well and admirably until he'd slipped in the blood that coated the floor of the arena. Lorcan grunted instead of answering.

"Riiiiiight," the promoter said. "I have a deal for ya. Take a dive and I'll pay you half the amount you'd win. In a few weeks, come back for a rematch. Crowd loves a good revenge story."

"No."

"What?" the promoter whined. "Kid, Vikog will tear your arms out and beat you with them. You can make a lot more if you play ball."

"It's not enough. I have to win." Lorcan stared at the Goblin.

The promoter backed away slowly, hands up in a placating gesture. "Your funeral. Don't say I didn't warn you." He turned and scurried down the hallway to the arena.

Lorcan grunted in frustration. Dealing with Hub scum didn't sit well with him. He'd worked for his share of unsavory employers. His day-to-day consisted of other professionals who at least understood the soldier's code, even if they didn't follow it. In Hub, everything revolved around glint and the pursuit of it. He'd never understand these people.

The green light above the arena door glowed and Lorcan steeled himself for the fight. He said a quick prayer to the gods that he'd prevail for his daughter. He reached the door and entered the chaos.

The speaker above blared, ". . .<u>and his opponent, Lorcan the Mighty!</u>" Boos and insults flew at him, as did trash that landed at his feet. Lorcan stood in the challenger's spot and waited for the signal.

The reigning champion of the Slaughterhouse paced back and forth, throwing his arms up to encourage the crowd. The ogre stood well over two meters tall. His gray-green skin held the scars of many fights, as did his switchback nose and a mouth full of broken teeth. He fought bare-chested wearing cut-off pants that hung low due to an expansive gut. He glared at Lorcan as, <u>"And fight!"</u> came over the speakers.

Vikog stepped toward Lorcan, hands down in disrespect to his foe. Lorcan feinted left then struck to the right, avoiding the ogre's grasp. His claws sliced into the giant's arm with a satisfying ripping noise. He hadn't needed to use his claws in earlier bouts, so Vikog hadn't known to watch for them. The ogre closed the distance, fast for such a large man, and attempted to grapple his smaller opponent. That would be the end of the fight.

Vikog's grab collapsed on air as Lorcan spun to the side, slicing into the giant's ribs, leaving ribbons of torn skin and blood behind. The only way to win would be to wear the ogre down until he passed out—unless Lorcan was forced to kill him to save himself. The crowd screamed in frustration as Lorcan landed another vicious swipe across the ogre's shoulder, splattering blood over the metal floor. He ducked under the ham-fisted attempt at an answering blow. Another overhead smash came close to landing, but his enhanced reflexes kicked into overdrive, saving him from a crushed skull. He snarled in frustration at the ogre.

"Come here, kitty," the ogre yelled over the noise. The crowd laughed and screamed in approval as the two circled each other, looking for an opening. "You fast, no hurt Vikog." As he finished, he swung a backhand at Lorcan.

Dodging the blow, Lorcan raced in, full up on neurostim. Two light-ning-fast hits, both drawing more blood and cheers, before he whipped out of the range of the ogre's massive fists.

His opponent roared and charged, once again faster than Lorcan had expected. He darted to the left. The brute's shoulder clipped his ribs and spun him into the thick bars of the cage. His head impacted the metal hard, sending him sprawling across the blood-soaked floor. Vikog's fans went wild.

Lorcan shook his head to clear it. With so much crowd noise, he almost missed the heavy footfalls of the ogre. Rolling to his right, he slipped past a double-handed hammer. The ogre howled in pain and rage as he struck the solid floor instead of a squishy body.

Lorcan spun, still on his back, lashing out with his foot, his toe claws slashing across the back of the ogre's heel. The leg buckled under the massive weight, sending the gigantic warrior to the floor. Lorcan bounced to his feet immediately, catapulting himself high into the air, and delivered a devastating blow to his foe.

The hit never landed. A blurry arm struck Lorcan full in the chest, sending him flying across the arena.

Neither regained their feet easily. A loud horn sounded, indicating the end of the round.

Lorcan's chances were quickly running out as the fight drained his strength. Neurostim didn't last forever.

Slaughterhouse's goons ran out and pulled Vikog to his feet, not an easy task. Trash fell from the stands around Lorcan, along with insults and curses. The room twisted slightly as Lorcan stood, back straight, head high. He strode to the entrance tunnel and stepped inside, out of sight of the crowd. He glanced over where the ogre was being injected and stitched up. Knowing the scum that ran the Slaughterhouse, they weren't injecting him with vitamins. He knew the next round would start once Vikog had been doctored to withstand another bout. *At least he'd held his own before the staff interfered.*

And the ogre for sure sported a couple of mods. Striking Lorcan out of mid-air should have been well beyond his capabilities. So much for the "organic" label.

The promoter stood off to the side of the entrance, two large, well-armed mercs in full riot gear and assault rifles at the ready. Their earlier meeting had obviously upset the Goblin who'd brought back-up this time. "You put on one hell of a fight. I'm willing to pay you seventy-five percent of the winner's purse if you'll take a dive."

"No. I have to win." Lorcan leaned his head against the wall, trying to get his vertigo under control. He'd had head wounds before, but the force of hitting the cage bars topped any of them.

The Goblin waved his hands emphatically. "I'm not done. I've got a contract here that guarantees you two matches a month in the new series we are starting. Pays twice what this one does. Whatdoyathink?"

Lorcan held back the snarl that threatened to come out. "I can't. I must win today."

One of the guards chambered a round. Lorcan's head shot up. "Whoa!" the Goblin protested. "Nobody's doin' nuthin' here but talkin'." He punched the offending guard in the chest plate. "Got it?"

The guard's helmeted head bobbed its agreement.

Lorcan turned to face the promoter. "I must win because I need the glint today. I'm sorry I can't take your offer, as generous as it is."

The promoter walked past his guards who still watched Lorcan. "It's your funeral, bub." He sulked back down the hall with the two guards backing away after him. The promoter was up to something.

"Hey!" A small voice came from deeper in the tunnel. Lorcan's nagualan vision allowed him to see well in the dark, but the owner of the voice eluded him. "Up here."

Lorcan lifted his gaze until a pixie, dressed in a chameleon fight suit, appeared before him. "Little sister, it's not safe for you here."

"Really?" she asked sarcastically. "Thanks for the heads up, Leo. I'm here on business. I brought this to help." She dropped a small plastic disc that grew as it fell.

He snatched it out of the air, keeping his back to the ring and prying eyes. The disc turned out to be a field syringe from a military med kit. The lightweight, nearly unbreakable plastic made transporting lifesaving drugs easier on the med staff. He flipped it over, not seeing any markings on the package. "What is this?"

"Your ticket to the dance. What do you think it is? Use it before big and ugly is ready to rumble." Her wings increased their speed, and she floated up and away from him. "I'll see you after the match. We've got business to discuss."

He shook his head. "I'm leaving Hub as soon as I win."

Her delicate laugh reached him. "Somebody paid a lot of glint for that. You'll want to talk after." She flew off into the darkness.

Lorcan studied the field syringe, wondering what it contained. Behind him, the crowd chanted Vikog's name, and the champion bellowed in return. It could be a setup by the Slaughterhouse. Why would a stranger provide him with a way to beat the champion? The odds were heavily against him. Possibly a gambler looking to cash in?

Vikog paraded around the ring, throwing his arms up, getting the crowd into it. From the lack of a limp, the trainers must have turned him into a walking pharmacy.

If he had any chance, he'd need to take the risk and hope for the best. If he didn't find a way to win, Janna was lost. He sighed and did the inevitable, placing the disc against his forearm and delivering the payload into his system. He tossed the empty container on the ground where it smoked and curled into a charred ball. Someone wanted no one to know what had been administered from that device. Right now, if it helped him win, he didn't care what it was they'd sent him.

Nothing happened. Lorcan saw where the microneedles had pierced his skin, but he felt the same. His head had ceased to swim, though that could have been from the rest. His body still ached. So it didn't help, but also didn't appear to be sabotage. He'd have to rely on what he'd brought with him tonight.

Lorcan pushed the pixie and the mysterious drug from his mind. Once he'd underestimated the ogre and wouldn't make the same mistake twice.

The horn sounded, calling the fighters to the center of the ring. "Kitty gonna scratch me again?" Vikog asked, showing off the lack of wounds. They'd pumped him up with healing agents. The ogre beat his chest, roaring as the crowd matched him.

Vikog favored his right foot where Lorcan had sliced the tendons. You could speed up healing only so much.

"Fight!" came over the speakers, setting the fighters to circling. Vikog definitely limped a bit, even though he strove to disguise the weakness. Lorcan launched a series of quick feints, forcing the ogre to step back on his right leg. If the grunts were any indication, Vikog couldn't keep it up forever. Sooner or later the tendons in the ogre's leg would snap under the stress.

Vikog knew it as well. He advanced toward Lorcan, forcing him to give ground or get pummeled by the flailing fists. Lorcan danced to the side. He avoided being driven into the cage where the brute could use his greater mass as a weapon. The tendon injury had affected his speed. This made it easier for Lorcan to dodge the charge when the ogre threw himself into a rage.

This time, as he slid passed the ogre's massive body, Lorcan set to do as much damage as possible. Lorcan felt his heart rate accelerate as the world slowed down around him. The drug the pixie had given worked. Each attack moved faster, delivering more damage as his neurostim flew into overdrive. He continued his onslaught on Vikog's undefended flank.

The ogre bellowed in pain, throwing a massive backhand at Lorcan that he noticed too late. Lorcan crossed his arms in front of him to absorb the blow. The arm struck with the force of a rocket, but he didn't budge. In fact, his arms barely flinched from the impact. Vikog turned toward him, and Lorcan could see fear in his eyes, for possibly the first time ever.

Lorcan pulled away and punched the ogre as hard as he could. Blood spurted from his opponent's nose as he fell backward, clutching his face. Lorcan retreated as the ogre rolled on the floor. "He's down. Stop the fight," Lorcan shouted only to be drowned out by the frenzied crowd.

Once again, his combat neurostim saved him. Vikog slammed a metal pole at least five centimeters in diameter with a wicked-looking curved hook where Lorcan had been standing seconds before. He dove to the right, rolling up to his feet. The promoter stood behind Vikog with a wicked grin on his face. He'd given their champion a weapon to ensure his win. The audience intensified their chanting as the ogre swung the massive weapon at Lorcan time after time. Weapons weren't allowed, according to the rules, but the Slaughterhouse followed the rule of convenience.

He dodged the first few blows until he slipped in the ogre's blood. The hook pierced through his unprotected abdomen and out the back. With a quick pull, the ogre swung his fist straight into Lorcan's stomach, knocking him off the hook and onto the ground. Blood flowed from the puncture wound. Vikog stood over his downed opponent as he raised the blade over his head. "Bye, bye, kitty!"

Lorcan knew he had no other options. The neurostim fueled him as he rolled to his feet and leapt onto the giant. His fangs sunk into the ogre's neck, tearing it open. This wasn't a repairable injury. It was a death blow, and they both knew it. Gouts of blood sprayed from the wound, and the brute collapsed in the center of the ring, dead.

Lorcan stood over the fallen behemoth, still in shock that in a final, desperate attack he'd taken the ogre's life. The crowd cheered wildly as he was crowned the new champion of the Slaughterhouse. If there was a title Lorcan wanted less in this world, he didn't know what it was.

The Slaughterhouse team who had stitched up Vikog ran to assist him out of the ring. They rushed him down the champion's tunnel, a broad, brightly lit, and well-decorated affair, to a large room. Comfortable couches sat off to one side next to a kitchen where chefs prepared a meal of some sort. Lorcan wondered dumbly if he would eat anything that an ogre would. He doubted it. They propelled him through an archway that led to a small medical facility and lowered him onto the table and began to work. The drug the pixie had given him had left his system completely exhausted in the aftermath. The team worked to repair the various injuries he'd taken during the match. At some point, he passed out.

He awoke, a bit groggy. The promoter and his guards from earlier stood at the end of the bed in which he'd been placed. He still wore the blood-soaked clothes from the fight, but the puncture from Vikog's blade had been stitched up and looked to be in good shape.

The promoter grinned at him, gold tooth gleaming in the brightly lit room. "That was amazin'! I haven't seen anything like that since Thunder Max got himself cut up with a chain blade. The crowds screamed themselves raw."

Lorcan pushed himself up, grimacing at the pull of the stitches. He'd won. Now to grab his glint, pay off his debts, and get his daughter as far from Hub as possible. The shame of returning to his people would be well worth having his kitten protected. "Can I get my pay now?"

"We have business to discuss, you and me." The promoter pulled a datapad from his vest. "I've got a year contract here. Ten times what the purse is and you'll never fight anyone like Vikog, you can be sure."

"Thank you, no. I must pay off the men I owe." He forced himself to his feet. Nothing leaked as he straightened, always a good sign after a wound. "Can I get my glint?"

"Seriously?" The promoter eyed him, calculating for a moment before he continued. "Never would have expected you to be a haggler but you got me. I can increase it to fourteen times the winner's purse. One hundred and forty thousand glint. Plus, you can live here for free, and food is on the house. We have a five-star chef on staff. You're gonna love it." He shoved the datapad at him. "Sign here." He pulled the device back. "Just don't use the claw, you'll scratch the screen."

Lorcan growled. Injured, tired, and wanting his daughter, he'd run out of patience. Both guards pointed their rifles at him. Even on neurostim he'd never live through that exchange. "All I want is what I'm owed, and I'll leave peacefully."

"And what am I supposed to do without a champion? You killed Vikog. What good is a gentlemen's retreat without a champion for the ring?"

"I don't know, and I don't care. I tried to not kill him. You forced me to. Find a new champion, I'm done." Lorcan leaned back, clutching his side. If the guards relaxed, he might stand a chance, but without the promised glint, he'd lose his daughter to the slavers or the chop shops.

The promoter pouted. "Fine. I'll get the stick for you." He left the room, the guards on either side of the archway, guns ready to fire if the need arose. The time dragged on until Lorcan feared the man was doing something underhanded. Voices reached his ears as the Goblin returned with a small woman who wore her hair in a bun and a simple, orange dress. She carried a mem stick in one hand and a manual reader in the other. Her eyes grew wide as they approached Lorcan.

"Miss Buttleband has your glint on the cred chip for you," the promoter said, gesturing to the woman. "She's my accountant."

Lorcan inclined his head respectfully to her and she yelped in surprise. No doubt she had witnessed the earlier fight. Her hand shook as she passed over the mem stick and the reader. "Thank you," he said as he took them. The stick went in the slot and the display lit with the figures. The stick only contained two thousand glint, not the ten thousand that he'd been promised. "What is this? The agreement was for ten thousand, not two."

Miss Buttleband swallowed hard. The guards hoisted their weapons so they were pointed in his direction. "If you review the itemized bill, you were paid ten thousand glint. The medical staff had to repair your wound. You'd have died otherwise. All of the procedures and equipment prices are listed and are correct."

Lorcan lowered the reader. "I did not agree to this."

The promoter barked a harsh laugh. "You did when you agreed to fight. Maybe you should read your contract, huh?"

Miss Buttleband tsked him. "All of the charges are lower than any of the surrounding clinics would treat you for. It is quite fair."

Lorcan pulled the stick free and set the reader on the bed. He'd gone through all of that and failed. He refused to accept he'd lost his daughter.

"Get him outta here." The promoter told the guards. "I don't wanna see your stupid cat face around here ever." He motioned for the accountant to follow and they left. The guards grabbed him by the arms and shoved him down a back hall and out into an alleyway behind the Slaughterhouse. One tripped him as he went through the door, and he fell into a heaping pile of garbage.

His side burned from the hard landing. His hand probed to see if the stitches had pulled loose, but they appeared to be intact. He grunted as he forced himself to his feet and followed the sidewalk away from the Slaughterhouse, mind racing with how he would rescue Jaana.

Ever since his wife had died, he'd been on the losing end of life. His only link to his beloved was their daughter, and he'd put her in extreme danger. Now, Jaana's only chance was her beaten-down father. She deserved so much better.

He straightened up to his full height. Whatever the outcome, he'd proceed as a strong, nagualan warrior and not some common street tough who played at being a merc. No one was going to show up to save him, not this time.

# 16

# GELSEY

G lad you survived. It's time to talk business," Gelsey said from her vantage point over the warrior.

Lorcan stopped to regard her. He didn't speak, merely scowled.

She tried again. "I take it that stuff worked since you're walking out and not in a body bag."

Lorcan snarled. "It did, but it didn't solve my problem." The merc moved past her, headed for the main street of the Shade. "I've got to go finish some business and I don't need company."

Gelsey sped around, confronting the merc at eye level. "Listen, I don't care what you've got to do or where you have to do it. I've got to deliver this offer of employment from my client. Believe me, I'd rather have a Kobold hump me than put up with a grumpy cat, but here we are."

Lorcan stopped, examining the pixie as she hovered in front of him. "Get out of my way before you get hurt."

She pulled her fléchette pistol, aiming directly into the merc's left eye. "Go ahead and try, kitty." Lorcan didn't budge. "I hand you the stick, you review it, and then you come with me or go. I get paid either way. What's your choice?"

Pixies tended to be major nuisances, and this one was a pro at it. Still, if he could get the rest of the glint he needed up front, he could rescue

Jaana and disappear before anyone missed him. The big merc didn't say anything, just held out his paw.

Gelsey dropped lower to settle on his outstretched paw. She set the stick down at her feet. It grew to normal size.

Lorcan retrieved the stick with his other paw and slotted it. His brow furrowed as he reviewed the offer.

A low growl came from the big warrior. Gelsey tried to launch herself away. She didn't make it. His paw collapsed around her, crushing her into the pads. The armature of her wings snapped under the pressure of his grip. She tried to scream, but she had no air. Tears streamed down her face as obvious pain racked her body.

17

LORCAN

He opened his hand. "You tell your master I'll not bow to his demands," Lorcan growled out. "Now go."

Gelsey's battered body protested as she tried to straighten. Her knees buckled, causing her to fall back sobbing. She'd had her wings surgically replaced and now they were ruined. Everything she'd stolen had been boosted to afford the wings and the neural upgrades to use them. Flying home wasn't even an option now.

Lorcan shook his hand. "Go tell your master, sprite."

"I can't, you gashing idiot." She turned to show the mangled wings up close. "You've destroyed my wings. I can't fly."

"I barely touched you. Save your tricks, I'll not fall for them. Be gone."

"Look!" she screamed. "Look at what you've done."

Gelsey felt Lorcan touch the wings gently. The broken structure and torn webbing from his attack were plainly visible.

"Oh." Lorcan's voice dropped in intensity. "I'm sorry, little one."

"I should have let you die. You're all honor this and that until you're angry, and then it's too bad." She cried into her hands, not caring if he thought her weak. Without her wings, she was a cripple. Hub didn't treat the injured well.

Lorcan's paw cupped under her knees as he began to walk. "We will go to the meeting and I will make your master repair your wings."

Gelsey had had it. She stood awkwardly in his paw. "He's a flaming

85

dragon and not a baby one, a fully molted wyrm, one step from becoming an elder dragon. He'll eat your gashing liver if you mouth off to him."

Lorcan kept walking. Gelsey directed him resentfully, guiding him to the meeting. What would Ancep do to her now that she couldn't fly? The diviners would have told him that she'd be crushed, her wings broken beyond repair. He'd known all along, and he didn't care. He'd sacrificed her for his stupid games.

Lorcan stopped in front of a nondescript gray building that bordered the Flow. Gelsey glanced around for signs of trouble. The Slashers ran this section of town or had. Without a body and HubSec not looking into it, the other gangs wouldn't know for a while.

Lorcan grunted. "We go up. I've got a bone to pick with a dragon."

# 18

## SILAI

Silai arrived, hidden within her dryad form, at the address to find a worn, gray building with The Regal in script over the entry. The building lacked any indication that the name had ever fit. Emotions warred within her. How the client had gained so much information about her was unnerving. She could flee but had no doubt that anyone who uncovered this level of intel had the resources to carry out the threats the sticks contained. Even if the threats were empty, she would not chance the release of so much sensitive material. The kitsune had been hunted to near extinction, and she'd not risk their lives or hers.

She entered the building, still disguised as a dryad, right down to the server outfit. Anyone seeing her would think she'd gotten off work at one of the better establishments in the Shade Sector. She called herself Breeze, in the dryad fashion, so she could make inquiries into the place. Nothing turned up, as she expected. Whoever they would be working for had covered their tracks well.

The foyer reeked of disuse, a faint musty odor that tickled her nose, though she considered it pleasant after being in the bilge water at the pier. It had taken two days to get the odor off her skin and longer from her tails. She swore the taste still lingered in her mouth. Three silver elevator doors waited across a floor of cracked beige tile.

From the looks of it, the foyer had been recently cleaned, though not well. A door to the far left was labeled stairs. Three boards had been affixed to the frame to bar entry. She wondered if the whole place had been created to force them into a fixed pattern. She crossed to the elevators and pressed the up key. The center door jerked across the track to the open position. Stepping in, the security camera mounted in the corner whirred as she entered, and she ignored it. The real deal sat in the bank of buttons, a miniature lens that would be able to scan for cyber and weapons. She had neither and pressed the button for the top level.

As the elevator ascended, she examined the interior, noting that it appeared the floor had been tampered with. She guessed anyone not on the list would find a very rude welcome awaiting them. She pushed her bangs out of her face as the door slid open far more smoothly than it had closed. Exiting the elevator placed her in a cavernous space. Silai found herself impressed despite her feigned indifference. An elegant table stood in the center of the room, gunmetal legs holding up a glass top. Expensive sofas and handcrafted wingback chairs sat in conversation clusters around the room. At the far end stood a door that led into a kitchen area. The room was clad in a techno-chic vibe of random metal and glass panels of various colors and thicknesses. No expense had been spared.

"Please take a seat at the table."

The voice came from a speaker, not a person. Crossing to the table, she selected a seat facing the elevator and to the side of the kitchen entry. You learned early to always know what was behind you. The leather chair slid smoothly away from the table. Silai lowered herself into to it, feeling how the seat adjusted itself to fit her perfectly. Lucrea didn't have this kind of luxury in his palatial loft on the Bluffs. You'd never know you were in the Quad sitting in this room.

The gentle hiss of the elevator door caught Silai's attention. A tall Elven gentleman entered the room. He carried a bag over one shoulder. Unless she missed her mark, he'd be a wirehead of some sort. He wore all gray, including his shoes. The jacket had a high collar that fastened in front. He sauntered across to the table, a slight, silvery pattern playing across the surfaces of his outfit. *Interesting, a chameleon blending suit.* Obviously, there was more to the elf than he let on.

The man nodded to her before taking a seat at the far end of the table. He dropped into a chair and ran his hands over the tabletop as if caressing a lover. "This is a Nanyo sixty series." He leaned back, inspecting the metal supports under the table. His hands slid under the table where he pressed something, and a panel rotated up to sit in front of him. He whistled softly.

As he examined the table, she studied him. Closer up, she saw bruising around his face, noticed how he winced occasionally as he used his left arm. She stored it away for later. Cyber-jockeys didn't normally interact with the physical world, or *the void* as they called it.

The elevator opened again and a striking woman stepped out. Rainbow dreads flowed down her back, offsetting her bronze skin and dark suit. She didn't move toward the table but strolled around the perimeter of the room, contemplating each piece of art or decor as she went. Her hands stayed behind her as if strolling through a museum. She wore a fashionable suit jacket with the high collar that was in style this year. The center revealed a striking leather blouse that showed numerous metal clasps. Whoever she was, she knew how to dress for effect.

After surveying the room, she sat across from the Decker. With her back to the door? A confident woman. When she noticed Silai regarding her, she stared back, one eyebrow raised. Something about her eyes made Silai uncomfortable. The elevator door opening broke their standoff as the latest member of the team arrived.

"I heard there was a party here tonight," the little man with large ears said as he approached the group. His complexion was a soft tan and his eyes twinkled with an untold humor that it seemed only he saw. He stopped short of the table and addressed the wirehead. "Did somebody shoot your best friend?"

He strolled over and took the seat next to the Decker. The seat lowered to allow him to sit, then rose so he could see over the table. He unslung a brown leather bag and set it behind him in the chair. The "invite" said no weapons, so what did the bag contain? "You look far better than the last time I saw you, boyo."

The Decker stared at the man, who swung his legs like a child sitting in his parent's chair. "I'm sorry." He tilted his head in the proper elvish fashion. A slight scowl crossed the elf's face, a serious breach in protocol. "I don't recall making your acquaintance."

*Too much time in Grid would do that to you. Deckers held a fairly tenuous grip on reality and Nyx seemed to be a prime example.* Silai thought while listening to the conversation.

"No worries. You were a bit . . .err . . . under the weather at that point in the evening."

The elevator door opened again and an imposing nagual warrior entered. He stood well over two meters with the head of a jaguar and the body of a humanoid. Thick ropes of muscle shone through a huge hole in his shirt, blood encrusting the torn fabric. Bruises fought with his natural patterning for dominance. He held his paw against his chest with very deliberate motions. He stepped to the table and opened his paw.

The group fell silent as they beheld the broken form of the pixie. Silai noticed the stunned looks and realized the young woman had contacted each of them, in turn, to recruit them for this job. "What happened to her?" Silai asked, cursing herself for opening her mouth before she knew the score.

"A momentary inconvenience, I'm afraid."

Silai looked at the wall across from her. There stood a wyrm, dressed in a pinstriped gray suit, a Clan Caerlux blue tie, and custom-fit shoes. Long, electric-blue hair stood from the center of his skull and ran down between his wings, which were spread out from his sides as he entered. Silai had never seen a wyrm up close. Her brain screamed at her to run. She glanced around the table. Even the little man sat stock still. Dragons were universally feared by all races. A fully molted wyrm technically could be killed, but she'd never heard of it happening in her lifetime.

The nagual came to his senses first. He pointed a claw at the pixie. "You did this to her. I have delivered her to you, so you fix her. I am leaving now."

"No, you did this to her. Before you run out, I have your daughter. If you'd care to see her alive again, you will sit and listen," the dragon snapped, and the large warrior obeyed instantly. "You've all met Gelsey. Unfortunately, our rather large friend hurt her when she proffered the generous offer I had instructed her to deliver. I've made arrangements to have her wings replaced as part of her service fee. You will need her skills to complete the job for which I am hiring you."

"Who says we've agreed to the terms?" the well-dressed woman asked him pointedly. "I don't take too kindly to being blackmailed."

The dragon smiled, showing the long razor-sharp teeth of his kind. "We can banter all night. Until we are agreed, Miss Gelsey will lay there suffering. She's helped all of you over the past few days. I think it a poor way to return her kindness to you."

Silai caught each person's eye and they nodded in turn. "We are agreed, dragon."

"Excellent, we'll see to Gelsey in a moment. She will want to hear this," Ancep said with a toothy grin.

Silai's heart sank. They'd all broken Hub's third rule, never work for dragons. Time would tell if they'd regret taking the deal.

The dragon grinned, knowing full well that none of them would refuse him. Taking a seat at the center of the table, he pulled up the interface on the sixty series. "Let us discuss why you're all here."

Silai wanted to flee, but it was the long con that brought the most glint. She settled in to listen.

# NYX

*The void totally sucks.* Nyx sat listening to the jacked-up rant of the dragon. In the Grid, he could have taken the bastard down a notch or two. Given the data on the stick, doing so would end up with the Nefastu hunting him down. He'd erased every ghost from the PAE job he did on them last year. No one should have been able to trace anything back to him. He'd even EMPed the deck he'd run the DISCS from. He'd written it himself and had cut the Nef ICE without issue.

Yet somehow the dragon had found his ghost and located the assets he stole. One word and he'd be cooked. The Nefastu killed any decker stupid enough to cross them, and Nyx had done a lot more than cross them. It had been stupid, but he'd proved who the top phantom in Hub was, even if only to himself.

The beautiful dryad at the end of the table caught his eye. She tilted her head, an elvish form of inquiry which, coming from a tree hugger, caught Nyx off guard. Only elves used nonverbal forms in public. Why would the dragon hire a bubbly airhead for a job? None of this made sense.

"Let us begin with introductions," the dragon said to start the meeting. "You may call me Ancep. To my left, the proud nagualan warrior is Lorcan. He's to be the muscle on this job."

Muscle was right. The nagualans had a nasty rep in the Quad. This zero had all the wetware installed. Grafts, nerostim, probably some splicetech. His kit must have cost some serious glint. Nyx had only seen a couple of nagulans in the years he'd been in Hub. This job kept getting more and more intense.

"To his left is Silai, though she's going by Breeze today. She'll be our master of disguise." Ancep indicated the dryad. "She's had surgical modifications to be able to assume other's facial features so she can blend in with the target."

Nyx frowned, but let it go. What these zeros did in the void didn't affect him. He'd be riding the electronic surf to get what they needed.

"Next is our mage, Kelthar." The little man bounced to his feet and bowed to the dragon, who looked annoyed at having the attention diverted from him. He cleared his throat and the mage flopped back into his seat. "As I was saying, Kelthar will be dealing with the magical challenges you'll face on this job."

Ancep indicated Nyx. He stilled, wondering what the dragon would disclose about him. In order to walk away clean, the rest needed to learn nothing about him or what he'd done. "Nyx is our decker or, in his terms, our phantom. He'll be dealing with the target's electronic counter-measures."

*Phew, nothing of any use.* At least he didn't drop anything important about Nyx.

"Aikila will be responsible for acquiring and outfitting the team with the equipment you will want once the job starts. She will also be our explosives expert, if required." That raised eyebrows around the table. Aikila must have an interesting history to be able to do demolitions.

"And that leaves Gelsey," Ancep said, nodding to where she lay on the table. "Once she's back to her normal self, she will be our reconnaissance and physical security expert. Our pixie friend will get the rest of you access to the target site. We should take care of her needs so we can set our date."

Two women clad in blue surgical scrubs entered from where Ancep had come in from earlier. One gently picked up the injured pixie, and the other bent to whisper in the dragon's ear. Nyx didn't envy Gelsey at all. The dragon nodded twice and then dismissed them both.

He turned his attention back to the group who sat watching the receding backs of the staff. The personal table displays lit up in front of each of the team. "I have taken the liberty of employing one of the top genesplicers and nerostim experts in Harmony. Before you is the first part of your payment. She will be on-site throughout the job to assist Silai in adapting to the appearances she feels necessary to complete her portion of the job."

Aikila looked up from her screen. "You keep mentioning this job, but we still don't know what we're after."

The dragon sighed. "Very well, I will keep the full briefing for after your enhancements are complete." He tapped his display and the center of the table lit up.

Nyx grinned. He'd never seen a live sixty series work. It projected the images so that wherever you sat at the table it appeared in the correct orientation. It was an amazing piece of tech.

A paper scroll spun in the center of the screen. "This is a scroll containing a spell that Clan Caerlux spent over a century developing." Kelthar whistled, earning another glare from Ancep. "The purpose of the scroll is to detect gold. We had planned to teach our mages how to use the spell to find naturally occurring veins so we could then sell the location information to the dwarves, trauco, or gnomes for a percentage of the load. The influx of gold would have moved Caerlux higher in the council."

"So, we are to retrieve this stolen scroll for you?" Lorcan asked, his face a mask of concern. "Under the law, shouldn't HubSec be brought in to take care of this?"

Ancep laughed. "Ah, the nagual are always so refreshing. Lorcan, exposing the existence of the spell would allow the other clans access to it while the courts took forever to resolve it." He glanced around the table before continuing. "Plus, you know the first rule of Hub?"

"Never steal from dragons." Lorcan didn't appear to be any happier. "There has to be another way to gain justice."

Without saying a word, Ancep touched his display. The image in front of Lorcan flickered and the big man gasped, clutching the edge of the table. "You can leave the team and I will return her to the clinic if you'd prefer?"

"No! I will do as you ask without question, sire." Lorcan's head bent over the screen as if he wanted to climb through it.

"Excellent. You six will retrieve my property and make sure the message is delivered." He tapped his display again and Lorcan eased away from the screen. "Does that satisfy your curiosity?" He directed his comments to Aikila who nodded. "Can we resume the discussion?"

"Of course, I meant no offense." Aikila bowed her head, but Nyx saw a smirk she hid from the dragon. *She's dangerous.*

"On your display are the kits my expert has suggested. Kelthar, your screen contains some implements I think you'll find helpful since you aren't enhanced."

Kelthar grinned as he examined the items on his list. Nyx heard happy murmurs from the mage. *Must be some good gear on there.*

Nyx read over his list and his heart just about stopped. Avijo Neural Network was at the top. That piece alone would have been worth doing ten jobs for. The sockets that were standard to even go to public school interfaced with a very small section of the sensory systems. It was what allowed the user to view images, hear sounds, smell or taste or touch in the construct the socket produced. Zeros used it for shopping, watching sims, virtual relationships and a lot of stuff meat puppets got off on. The Avijo increased connections to a much higher percentage of the user's brain. Hub SecOps used it for combat troops to enhance training and combat performance. Phantoms drifted through the Grid at a speed factor of ten.

Next on his list were Vivize Mark VI eye replacements, Bovor BioChip storage, and enhancements to his reflex nerostim. He'd built a name for himself despite his lack of enhancements and gear. This would push him far beyond most phantoms. He could go up against the true hacker legends. He'd have made a deal with the prince of the underworld himself to get this kind of edge.

Nyx swallowed hard, wondering if he had done exactly that today.

2 0

KELTHAR

The surgical staff came in turn to collect each of the members for their enhancements. Ancep sat in an oversize armchair where its curved back allowed his wings to hang behind his seat. He could have been an emperor from an earlier time. Kelthar trusted no one, but that went double for the dragons. Their motives never lined up with that of mortals. Even the elves who lived for centuries didn't understand the levels of complexity of the dragon clans' plots.

"Kelthar, you have been left out, I'm afraid," the dragon said lazily. "You mages don't much like technology."

"Magic flows through us, and changing your body inhibits that flow. The farther you get away from your true self, the less magic you can wield. It would be nice to be able to watch sims without a viewer, though." Kelthar sat on the floor cross-legged. He ran a hand over his bald head, a tic when he got stressed.

"Interesting. You'll have your work cut out for you. I hope your reputation is based in fact, not lore." The dragon slid his talons against each other, making a scraping noise that set Kelthar's teeth on edge. Ancep was digging for something, and the mage couldn't determine what it was yet.

Pretending nonchalance, he shrugged. "I do fine. The toys you've gotten me will help. I wouldn't think a spell of that nature would be so important." He resettled his bag next to him on the floor. No sense spilling his gear.

96

Instead of answering, Ancep again slid his talons against each other again, filling the room with the annoying sound.

Kelthar sat patiently waiting for the sound to end.

With a huff, Ancep answered, "Dragons covet gold. It is one of the ways the houses keep score against each other. A spell that guaranteed the influx of gold would increase our standing amongst the great clans."

Anytime a dragon made something sound that simple, they were lying. Kelthar had been around enough of them to have a clue into their minds. Ancep had a deeper game in play, and until he knew what it was, all six of them were in serious danger—and perhaps more than just the six of them. "You spoke of Lorcan's daughter earlier. Will she be joining us here?"

"No. She is a child." Ancep tilted his head to regard Kelthar. "Does it bother you that a child is being used as a bargaining chip?"

It did down to his core, but he said, "No. Just trying to connect how she fits into all this. Will she be a liability? Will Lorcan bolt mid-run if something happens to her? Nagual are a proud and loyal people. Great attributes for a warrior, not so much for a smash-and-grab job."

"She had a disease and Lorcan didn't have the glint to afford the treatment. One clinic in the Flow restored her to health. Instead of returning the girl, they placed her in a cryogenic pod and gave him ninety days to pay before they sold her for parts or to one of the doll houses. Unseemly business."

The fact that Ancep thought something to be "unseemly" almost made the mage laugh. "Won't he be upset you told us?"

The dragon shook his head. "No, it's been public knowledge since he attempted to get the glint at the Slaughterhouse earlier this evening."

Kelthar frowned. "Did he lose?"

"He won, but the house cheated, and he didn't get enough to buy her back. I, however, persuaded the clinic to give her over to me. She is a healthy, noisy child, and my people are keeping her safe."

*Interesting.* So Lorcan was being controlled by his daughter's safety. Each piece of information drew Kelthar closer to the truth of the job

Ancep stood. "As exhilarating as our conversation has been, I must attend to other matters. Your associates will be under the care of the surgical staff for a week if all goes well. The staff will provide anything you need, but please do not attempt to leave. Secrecy is paramount to the success of this endeavor."

Kelthar bowed his head in respect. "As you wish, Lord Ancep."

The dragon's eyes narrowed as though trying to decide if the impertinent mage was mocking him. He appeared to take it at face value, for now. He left the room through the doorway he'd arrived through earlier. Kelthar had a lot to think about and a week in which to do it.

A woman in an ankle-length black dress with a white apron tied around her waist entered the room. Two horns rose between her pointed ears. "I am Estril, head of the house staff. Master has requested I show you to your quarters."

"Why, thank you, Estril. I will gladly follow you." Kikomora servants were common among the upper classes. They made excellent maids or nannies even though their protruding snouts couldn't form some consonants well, giving them a slight slur to their speech.

She led him across the room to a doorway across from the one Ancep used. To the right was a door marked STAIRS. She turned to the left, down a short hallway to Kelthar's quarters. "These are your rooms for your stay. If there is anything you need, we will provide it." She turned and left.

Kelthar opened the door and entered his room. A huge bed dominated the far wall. The opposite wall had a bank of windows that displayed a beach scene. On another wall stood a desk and armoire. The entrance to the bathroom shared the wall with the entry.

He shut the door before remarking. "Welcome to our very comfortable prison."

# 21

# SILAI

Authority figures were a source of constant irritation for Silai. Kitsune were free spirits and loathed being confined. The gods had given them the ultimate gift of flexibility in all aspects of their life. The other races on Harmony feared that freedom, forcing all kitsune to hide.

Silai paced around the room, ready to be gone from the Regal. They had designed the room to function as both a surgical recovery suite and a well-appointed bedroom such as you'd find in any upscale hotel on the Bluffs. Regardless of the surroundings, Silai chafed at being stuck there.

A knock at the door interrupted her from her brooding. One of the staff must be checking on her. "Come."

The door opened and Ancep stepped in, closing the door behind him. "Are your accommodations to your liking?"

She bit back a scathing response, as being rude to her host would not do well in the long run. "They are lovely but why have I been assigned a surgical team? My display had no enhancements listed, and other than my socket, I don't use wetware."

"You pose a very interesting dilemma for me. I realize you are protective of your abilities, but to be useful you have to be able to assume different forms." He ran a hand down his tie, straightening it. "My only valid choice comprised of you having reconstructive surgery to change your appearance. Of course, we both know you don't need it. The important fact is the others will buy it."

She thought it over and agreed with his logic. Only one race on Harmony could change their form, and the others knowing her true identity wouldn't do. She sat on the end of the bed, facing Ancep. "Gelsey saw me transform on the pier. What about that?"

"Gelsey is a true professional and you have no worries with her."

Silai didn't buy it. "She's a thief. She trades in goods and information. How much do you think it would take to flip her? A hundred glint, a thousand?"

Ancep shook his head. "Your lack of trust is disturbing but understandable. Once this job is complete, take your payment and disappear into the crowds of Hub. Even knowing you are a kitsune is of no use unless you understand how to find one."

"And how did you find me?"

"When you are as old as I am, certain patterns are plainly obvious." He huffed out a blast of frosty air that Silai could feel from where she sat. He stepped over and handed her a black stick. "That has two identities I'd like you to familiarize yourself with. All the proper steps have been taken to ensure a thorough examination will not breach your cover. Over the next week, you will need to compromise the target contained within. You'll find a suitable wardrobe on the fourth floor."

"Is this for the job we're about to do?"

Ancep huffed. "No, this is a personal matter I'd like your assistance with."

"And what if the others come looking for me?"

"They won't. All but Kelthar will be recovering from their upgrades. A surgical outfit is in the bathroom. That stick will unlock all of the entries, so you can come and go as you please."

No more confinement and a job to keep her occupied. "I'll take care of it."

Ancep smiled, though it didn't reassure Silai any. "I knew you would." He turned and exited the room.

She slotted the stick and got to work. Things were looking up for a change.

## 22

### GELSEY

*Beep.*
*Beep.*
*Beep.*

Gelsey reached out to silence her alarm. There was no way she was getting up today. Something tugged on her arm. Cracking her eyes took effort, but she accomplished it. A tube ran out of her arm and into a drip bag. "Where am I?"

"Ah, you're awake." A face appeared above, startling her. Well, she assumed there was a face behind the contamination suit faceplate. "You were injured."

Images came flooding back. The Slaughterhouse, the nagual, Lorcan beating the ogre, his paws smashing her wings. "My wings!" She tried to sit up. Restraints held her down.

"Please, don't move. You'll disturb the integration factors." The tech checked the readout by the bed. "Everything looks good. Your wings were beyond repair. Your employer instructed our team to replace them with Metafy Sky Sharks. Far better than the Lunescent set you had before."

She'd been through the surgery and interfacing with a pair of wings in the past, but never had it made things so fuzzy. "I'm having trouble focusing. What did you give me?"

The tech tapped the read-out twice. "Standard load. Pain, anti-coagu-

101

lant, and such. You've been outfitted with new eyes and an increased neural net and stims." The beeping sound grew more rapid. "We'll give you the full rundown, but you need more time under for the interfacing to complete."

The derm injected into her arm, and that was the last thing she'd remember for a while.

# 23

# SILAI

Silai had been provided Vazzrivi Hingri, a PsycheDoll, as her cover for this job. She cringed as she read through the "services" she provided her customers. Vazzrivi, being a uselan, needed pain, theirs or another's, in order to thrive. They covered themselves with tattoos, piercings, and anything else that sated their cravings. They fed on others' pain, which made them well-suited for numerous careers that most found distasteful.

Curelum Ri turned out to be the mark's name, an explosives expert for Xtron Corp. He had a lot of bad addictions, Dwarf Crystal, Lo-Down, and smoking Talhuts by the box as well as an expensive habit in the Shade District's seedier Doll Houses. It amazed her he still lived.

The plan had a certain simplicity to it. Gather up Ri, get him to a state of unconsciousness, then switch to a HubSec officer, crash the party, and convince him if he didn't do as she said, he'd be taking a trip to prison. Ri frequented a lovely establishment in the Dregs called the Body Shop. They catered to more "discriminating" clientele.

No sense in wasting time. Silai spent the night fashioning her appearance to match the Doll's. Changing her hair and adding the vestigial wings only took an hour, but the tattoos took most of the day. They were intricate and often overlapped, making them difficult to perfect. She practiced shifting from dryad to uselan until she could do it in under a minute. She then mastered the uselan to HubSec transformation. By the end, she lay on her bed, exhausted, and fell into a restless sleep.

She checked the time and decided to get moving. After donning the surgical staff garb, she left her room and took the stairs to level four. She stepped into a hallway like the one above. She followed it as if she were going to her room. The door opened for her and she found the promised wardroom. She required three outfits for this job. Something a dryad would wear in the Shade District, an outfit for the PsycheDoll, and a HubSec officer's uniform.

A bag sat on a small bench before the racks of clothing. Next to the bag sat the IDs and implements that she'd need for the con to work. She examined each before putting them into the bag. She could have created her own outfits, but physical clothing made each facade easier to maintain. The racks of garments would cover just about any con she'd be forced to run for this job. The dryad and HubSec's outfits were standard for her, but the PsycheDoll's wardrobe had less fabric than an eyepatch. Internally, Silai knew people weren't seeing her body. Still, she flushed with embarrassment as she selected the most modest outfit that barely covered her top and bottom. She added a chameleon pouch that affixed to her thigh and blended in with the tattoos so she could carry her gear on her person.

Dressed in a Dollhouse server's outfit, bag over her shoulder, she descended the stairs and opened a door into the Quad night. The moon Reatrix stood near the horizon while its twin, Animasor, had climbed to dominate the sky. The clubs down in the Dregs would be hopping by now, filling with patrons who wanted a more "intense" experience. Almost anything went in Hub, but the Dregs offered pleasures that most found distasteful or dangerous. For the people who lived there, life tended to be short and mean.

Catching the tram, she debarked down the street from the Sin Palace to give herself a moment to case the establishment. A group of Daemons stood in the alley, toking on grubweed, hassling the people on the street. She lowered her eyes as she passed them, trying to ignore the toughs and avoid any trouble.

"Hey, tree girl, I got some wood fer ya!" one of them yelled as she walked by. Silai feigned offense and hurried to pass them. One started to follow. "Did you hear me? Come here, I'm talkin' to you."

She turned to face the Daemon. His cracked red skin and muddy-colored horns were all she needed to see to know he was a street-level grunt. She had to hurry to catch the target before he got bored and hired a different girl. "I just got off work. I got to find my guy and hope he hasn't blown the rent money."

The tough came up to her shoulder. His long, matted black hair hung in braids along his face. "You too good for the likes of me?" His hoof clacked on the sidewalk impatiently. "You don't say hello when you're spoken to?"

"Hello," she said with a sigh. "Can I go now? I really need to find my man and get my glint."

A semblance of a smile creased his ugly face, all fangs and no mirth. "You come back with us and you'll get all sorts of glint, I promise." He barked a harsh laugh as he grabbed her by the arm. He yelped as her knife pierced his bicep.

Silai pulled him close enough that she smelled the grubweed and whatever offal Daemons ate, which she really didn't want to know. "Let go of me," she said between gritted teeth. "I said I was busy. Now, I'm going to retract my blade and you're going to leave. Understood?" A twist of the handle elicited a grunt of pain.

"Was just havin' some fun." His tone reminded her of a child denied his favorite toy.

The blade snapped back into the handle, but she didn't slide it back into its arm holster. "We bona?"

His head snapped up, eyes widening. In the Quad, bona meant you were connected with the Nefastu. Street toughs like the Daemons knew better than to cross the primes who ran the city. Using the code when you weren't got you killed, fast. He nodded rapidly. "Sure. Don't want any trouble."

"Go." She turned on her heel and headed up the steps to the Sin Palace. The bouncer glanced at her, noticed the server's garb, and gestured for her to go in. With how she was dressed, it should have tipped off the Daemon to leave her alone and look for tourists to prey on. Music enveloped her as she entered the club. The upper levels rocked with the DJ working the crowd into a frenzy. A heavy bass line and synthetic chords wove together to keep the patrons dancing and spending the night away. Ri would be at the back bar where the dolls hung out. Silai headed for the back slowly, checking out the scene, making sure the real Psyche-Doll wasn't on the premises. The crowd covered the spectrum from tourists looking for fresh kicks to dealers, dolls, and dead ends. Silai scanned the area for a few minutes before she spotted her target, drinking while twirling a cred stick in his fingers.

She slid into the bathroom to change into the PsycheDoll. The room had been designed to look high-end, but years of neglect left it a sad ghost of what it had been. Four sinks lined one wall, tarnished mirrors in dirty frames hanging over each. Four floor-to-ceiling doors made up the back wall. Silai chose the farthest one and entered, closing and locking the door behind her. While she could make clothing during her metamorphosis, it was far easier to create the body then slide into the appropriate clothing, especially if she might need to remove anything. She stripped out of her current clothing. The outfit she'd chosen replaced the dryad's server garb. Her tails helixed around her as they unwound from the dryad form before shifting to the tattoo-covered uselan doll.

Heavy footsteps sounded outside the door. She didn't care who could be out there, being it was mid-shift. Her tails formed around her, adopting the shape and coloration of the PsycheDoll.

Someone pounded on the door. "TyLynne, are you in there?"

Silai ignored it as the hair, eyes, and teeth changed as she'd practiced. Black wings sprouted from her back, poking past her shoulders. Uselan couldn't fly, but they prized their wings. The tattoos shimmered as she concentrated on the image she'd so carefully crafted.

Another rough pounding at the door. "Woman, get out here."

A high-pitched voice screeched outside the door. "What the hell are you doing?"

A solid slap rang out. "Get out of here, you perv!" the woman shouted again. "I'm getting the bouncer!"

"No! I'm leavin'," the man said frantically before she heard his feet pounding out of the bathroom.

Silai shook her head as she finished the transformation. It only took a second to pull on the clothes she'd picked out. In the chameleon pouch, she confirmed that three derms of drugs, her mem sticks, and a collapsed stiletto blade were still there. She adhered the pouch to her upper thigh, in easy reach for emergencies. She folded her other outfit and placed it in the bag. The false bottom held the HubSec uniform she'd need soon enough.

She opened the stall door to an empty room. She slung the bag over her shoulder, avoiding her wing at the last second, and checked her appearance in the mirror. Gray skin peeked out from between the multitude of ink images that covered her body. The bones were prominent given that there wasn't any body fat on the PsycheDoll. Pushing her pitch-black hair out of her eyes, she headed for the door.

The music attacked her as she left the quiet of the bathroom, emerging into the club. She turned toward the back bar, intent on finding Ri and getting the job done as fast as possible.

A hand grabbed her arm, yanking her around to face the last person she wanted to see.

## 24

# LORCAN

Forced inactivity chaffed at a nagualan warrior under the best of circumstances. Lorcan seethed at being restrained. The muscle grafts, neurostim upgrades, and sensory enhancements all took time to heal and calibrate with his nervous system. Word from the surgical staff was to expect a ten percent boost in speed and strength, which was unheard of from the clinics in Hub. People in the Bluffs might be able to achieve such spectacular results, but the cost would be unbelievable.

Lorcan had spent little time in nice establishments. Being a merc meant being in the field, fighting for whoever paid you. Occasionally he'd done bodyguard work, mostly in the outer reaches of Harmony, which meant the accommodations were much worse than where he found himself now. The bed, or prison, depending on your viewpoint, sat against the wall. They had placed a stool, instrument tray, and monitoring equipment next to the bed for the surgical team to feed him and run tests on how his body handled the new material. A bathroom he couldn't use yet was through a door next to the desk and bureau which were the only other furniture in the room. The wall of faux windows showed images of the plains of the nagual, but that didn't give him any idea what time it was.

The door swung open, admitting the bald mage instead of the polite surgical staff who never answered questions.

"What are you doing here?" Lorcan asked

Kelthar paused as he closed the door. "Nagual tempers are legendary. I thought I'd see for myself." He finished shutting the door, approached the bed, and hopped up on the stool left by the staff for feeding time. He took in the restraints and smiled. "Tried to get up without permission?"

Lorcan growled. "Yes." Two small attendants had forced him down to restrain him. Time to change the direction of this conversation. "How are you not confined to your room?"

The mage spun the chair, pointing behind his right ear. No ports of any kind pierced his tanned skin. "No tech in this head. Messes up my flow of universal forces and all that." The stool swiveled until Kelthar faced Lorcan again. "Old, mean, and scaly won't let me leave, not that he could stop me."

"Then why not leave and return when it's time to plan the job? He wouldn't even realize you were gone," Lorcan said.

"He'd find out, I assure you." The mage grinned like a delighted child. "No sense screwing up the job just to tweak the dragon's nose."

"I'd leave. I'd get my kitten and make a run for Nagual. The pride would hide her from anyone who came around." Lorcan hadn't meant to say that. The drugs they used on him left him light-headed and talkative. At least that was what he told himself.

Kelthar nodded gravely. "While I can't get you out of here, I may be able to set your mind at ease."

"Doubtful. I don't trust that dragon's word one bit," Lorcan said with a laugh.

"Nor should you. The dragons rule because they are ruthless and will remove any who stand in their way. You were wise not to make an issue of him holding your daughter." Kelthar reached over, grasped a piece of Lorcan's hair, and tugged.

"Now why would you do that?" he asked tersely.

No answer came from Kelthar as he dug through his bag, setting a host of junk on the silver tray. He took the hair he'd pulled from the nagual's arm and placed it in a triangular device. He muttered under his breath, making gestures with his free hand. This continued for several minutes as Lorcan watched, transfixed. "What is your daughter's name?"

"I don't see what…"

"Spare me. I'm trying to help you. Her name, *NOW!*"

"Jaana," he said quietly. He hated to divulge anything to these people, but mages were an odd lot who ran counter to most others in Hub.

Kelthar moved his hand as if coaxing something from nothing. "Jaana, avail yourself to me." The mage continued until he abruptly broke the device in half. A lazy ball of haze rose from the ruins of the device. Lorcan leaned forward to peer into the roiling mass of whatever it was. The heat in the desert sun could make the air ripple in a similar way, though the room felt cool.

The hazy area grew as it rose to eye level "Jaana, show yourself. Your papa worries about your safety."

The air shimmered as the boiling increased until the center cleared. A small figure centered in the area, vague and indistinct to Lorcan's view. As the image expanded to fill the air before Kelthar, it became apparent that it was indeed Jaana. She sat in a room, playing with dolls. Piles of books and toys covered the floor behind her. She reached over and grabbed a snack that she popped into her mouth. She looked perfect. Her color had returned as well as the sheen to her fur. Behind her sat a woman dressed in a Clan Caerlux uniform. A slug thrower rested under her arm as she leaned back against the wall. Ancep hadn't lied about rescuing her from the clinic.

Lorcan studied every feature of his kitten as she played. She turned to speak with the woman, who nodded and gave the child a friendly smile. He couldn't hear them, but Jaana wasn't afraid. The weight lifted off his shoulders as the image slowly dissolved.

"Thank you."

Kelthar slumped on the stool, exhausted. He glanced up and caught the big cat's eye. "This has to stay between us."

Lorcan nodded his agreement. "Of course. May I ask why?"

"Many reasons, some of which are simple, others most complex. For now, let me answer with a question." Kelthar rolled his shoulders back before picking up the pieces he'd laid out, placing each in his bag. "Given the chance, would you have gone looking for Jaana?"

He realized that the mage knew the answer as plainly as Lorcan himself did. "Yes."

Kelthar smiled weakly at him. "The dragon lord didn't bring us here to steal a data stick off a blind man. Everyone here is an expert in their field. We need you. Will that suffice for an answer for now?"

"Of course. I appreciate you showing me, regardless of why. Curious, I guess."

The mage snorted. "It's the old adage about cats and curiosity?"

Lorcan groaned. "Do you know how many times I've heard that?" Nagual hated that saying more than anything.

"As many times as I've listened to bad egg insults, I'm sure." Kelthar's face grew serious. "There may come a time that we need each other if we are to survive this job."

The door opened as a surgical tech brought in a food tray. They all wore the same blue suit that covered every inch of them. It made it hard to tell anything about them, which was the point. "Who were you talking to?"

Lorcan barely moved his head but he was alone in the room. He thought quickly. "My uncle. He came to visit." He slurred his voice as he spoke.

"Well, I hope you had a good visit." The food went on the tray. "Let me check your dosing schedule."

Lorcan laid his head back, closing his eyes. "It was a very good visit. Yes, it was." He looked forward to being able to discuss things with the mage soon. First things first. He needed to get ready for the job.

Then he'd see what this deal with the dragon really meant.

# AIKILA

ikila, what are you doing?" the voice said from behind her. She knew the voice as well as she knew her own. Her father, Djar, stood off her right shoulder as she tied down the cargo net that held their goods on top of the hovercraft transport.

"Papa, I want to make sure we don't have an issue. We will ascend to the Apex to deliver these goods. It would not do for the cargo to be damaged. Clan Nivladai's payment will clear our debts. The antiques from Old Earth are too valuable to take chances with."

He chuckled. "Just like your mother. More so every day." He placed his hand on her shoulder and squeezed gently. "I will get ready to leave."

He strode across the compound to speak with the warehouse manager. She double-checked all the connectors, replacing two that showed wear along the service pins. They'd sold off the rest of their vehicles in an attempt to pay the debt collectors from the Nefastu primes. The interest rates ensured that it was virtually impossible.

The cargo was ready to go. A well-paid phantom had cracked the Dullahan encrypted data stores and emerged with the location of the crates of antiques. Long ago, one of the warlords had stashed his treasures and killed everyone who knew where they were and then promptly died himself. Until now, they had been lost.

She climbed into the passenger seat and buckled the harnesses into place. Anything from Old Earth fetched a fortune, but these relics were from a place called Japan where the dragon clan had originated, long before most of the races on Harmony. The humans had destroyed the planet, forcing the hidden people of Old Earth to flee through nexus portals to Harmony. The races had stolen technology from the humans and learned the price of depleting every resource the planet provides.

Djar pulled himself into the driver's seat and started the engine, lifting the hovercraft a meter into the air. He grinned at his daughter, enjoying the thrill of the sale. "Today we will resume our place among the Naddahan elite traders. No more stands in remote villages or haggling over bits of glint."

Aikila hadn't seen her father so animated since her mother had passed into the next realm. Today was a big day, which made her nerves jangle like a wind chime in a gale. Hub sat at the end of their ten-hour drive. The road up to the Apex held more security than the whole of the trip had.

With a wink, Djar drove out of the loading zone and off toward their destination. More than anything she wished she could have stopped her father, but once he made his mind up, there was no changing it. <u>Never deal with dragons</u> echoed through her mind as she watched the scenery fly by.

They passed through security without issue. The mem stick the Nivladai had sent opened the way before them. The Dragon's Throat held vehicles of all shapes and sizes as they headed deeper into the civilized world. Naddaha's capital could fit inside Hub's Apex level four or five times with room to spare, according to her father. She didn't believe him since he constantly exaggerated, in the way all good traders do.

They took a turn that led up and away from what the locals called the Quad. They passed the Terrace and its plain but orderly adornments, the buildings appeared more industrial and less slum. Signs for businesses floated alongside the road as it climbed, the images changing to suit the inhabitants of the vehicles that passed.

Another security checkpoint stopped them. "Is this the Apex, Father?" HubSec officers strode around the vehicle with devices to ensure they weren't a danger to anyone.

"No, child. This is the Bluffs where the elite hide from the rest of the inhabitants. If we turn enough profit, one day we could live up in the sky."

She grinned. "Why not the Apex? Wouldn't the richest merchants live there?" She thought of the Council of Elders who ruled Naddaha. They were all former merchants known for their cunning and riches. Those would be the type who lived at the Apex.

"Do not say such things." Her father looked around to see if any of the officers had taken notice even though they were outside the vehicle. "Only the dragons live on the Apex. We won't be allowed past the Prismatic Gates. Dragons are a touchy race, and it is best not to anger them."

<u>Or deal with them</u>, a tiny voice said in the deep recesses of her mind. "I am sorry. I should have thought before I spoke." She lowered her head, embarrassed by the slip.

"Not to worry," he said, as he patted her knee reassuringly. "Just keep quiet while I do business."

"Yes, Papa."

The HubSec officer waved them on, pointing to the ramp on the far right that led ascended the mountain that Hub had been carved from. The incline wound its way up until leveling out before another security gate. They were forced to exit the vehicle, and a much more thorough inspection took place. The Nivladai stick was verified as they waited. Soon a wyrmling approached on a scooter of some type. He wore a fashionable yellow suit with ruffles cascading down the front of his shirt. Aikila didn't miss the fact that he carried a pistol on his hip that looked like it had been used before. "Master Dziuban?" he asked.

"That am I," her father said as he nodded his head in a slight bow. "We have brought the merchandise as agreed."

"Excellent."

The young man held out a cred chip that her father took hesitantly. "What is this?"

"Your payment. After we offload your cargo, you'll be free to go." His clipped tone indicated he was well ready to be done with this whole business. His gaze ran over Aikila in her brown vest and tan work clothes. The grimace on his face told her what he thought of her.

Her father slotted the stick in a portable reader he carried for business and gasped. "This is only two hundred thousand. It should be five hundred."

With a massive eye roll, the wyrmling answered. "The Lord Reglath has decided that market prices have fallen. He sends his condolences that your profits may not live up to expectations. Business is business. Good day."

The pretentious lizard turned to go but her father grabbed his arm, thrusting the stick back at him. "Deal's off. I'll take my wares down to the

Terrace and sell them there for a fair price." He pushed the stick into the man's front coat pocket. "Come on, we'll be going now."

He hadn't made it five steps before the crack of the pistol sounded and her father dropped face-first on the ground. The HubSec guards looked on from where they surrounded the hovercraft, but none moved to help. She ran to her father, falling on the hard concrete beside him, unconcerned about the tearing fabric and skin of her knees. He wasn't breathing. The shot had gone straight through his heart. Blood oozed from under his corpse.

The sound of boot heels announced the dragon. He dropped the chip next to her as she hugged her father's lifeless body. "I'll assume that you will take the offer, or do I need to repeat myself?"

So wracked with sobs that she couldn't speak, she settled for nodding to her father's murderer. She studied his face through her tears. It was a face she'd not forget.

"Excellent. At least one of you has brains." He stepped over her father's splayed legs. "Unload that and bring it to the Clan Nivladai warehouse at once. Send the girl on her way and make sure this mess gets cleaned up."

The nearest officer saluted. "Yes, Lord Y'sser."

Y'sser. Aikilia burned the name into her memory. Y'sser of Clan Nivladai would pay for his crime one day. She swore the vengeance oath of her people upon the lizard.

***

"Aikila, we are going to change your bandages," a voice said from a distance. Bandages? She hadn't been injured. A tug at her hair pulled her away from the scene where she cradled her murdered father. The scene slipped away as she returned to a foggy consciousness.

"Father, I will avenge you."

"Did you say something, Aikila?" the voice asked. Aikila tried to open her eyes but failed. "You can't open your eyes for two more days while the implants calibrate to your nervous system. We'll keep you comfortable in the interim."

Sparks exploded across her sight as the bandages came off and clean ones were wound around her head again. Her memory faded away like her father's ghost. "What did you do?" she croaked out of her overly dry mouth.

"The surgeon neurospliced improved sensory pathways. Don't worry, he didn't touch those beautiful eyes of yours, though the days of using contacts to hide them are over. You'll be extremely happy." Aikila's head was gently lowered onto a pillow. "I'm going to put you into a coma state for two more days."

Aikila started to raise an objection, but the sedatives pulled her back into the darkness and her own personal hell.

## 26

### SILAI

Ty Q'rell, warlock and ambassador of the Mangku, held her arm. It must be his signature move. *Had he tracked me here? Did he have my scent?* Silai fought the urge to flee and instead dropped into character and sighed. "Can I do something for you?"

The warlock appeared offended. "I got glint and I showered like you told me last time. I had a bad night and I require a diversion."

"Sorry, I have a scheduled session." Silai removed his hand from her arm. "I'll see you later."

A confused look crossed his face. "Session? Here? You think this is a high-end establishment?"

Her training kicked in. "Look, if I call it a session, I can talk up the price, or are you too stupid to get that?" She bared her fangs at him, pushed her wings into an aggressive pose. "Do you need me to explain it to you?"

The warlock held up his hands in surrender. "Sorry, you know I like it when you explain things, Mistress."

When she saw the dragon, she was going to kill him. Of all the things to force her to be, a low-brow doll. "You keep it frosty or I got nuthin' fer you. You ca?"

He nodded, though he glared at her. "Yes, Mistress."

She pivoted on her heel and swayed her way across the bar to where the dolls worked. Hungry eyes followed her as she walked, bag over her shoulder, into the doll house.

A burly orc sat on a stool at the entrance. "What's the bag for, Vazz? Should be stored in your locker."

A slow smile crossed her face, showing the tips of her fangs. The effect on the orc became apparent as he adjusted his position on the stool. "Special props for a show tonight. Big spender, you ca?" She raked her nails across the massive arm, drawing a bit of blood in the process. Her eyes rolled up into her head as if she feasted on his pain. "Oh, delightful." The orc shivered as she passed. A uselan's idea of a good time usually involved a trip to the hospital or the morgue afterward.

The driving bass of the dance floor receded as she entered the private portion of the Sin Palace. Burly bouncers dotted the walls like statues carved from rock to protect a temple. These, however, had wetware that ancient warriors would have thought of as magic from the gods. Silai knew there were no gods in Hub, only glint.

Silai strolled between the secluded booths, most of which contained groups intent on drugs and drinking before the real party got going in the secluded rooms downstairs, away from prying eyes. The Sin Palace took its security seriously.

Ri sat at the end of the bar, laughing with one of the girls, a seelian with purple hair, large breasts, and obviously a good sense of self-preservation, the last becoming apparent when the girl fled at the sight of the fake Vazz. Ri's head swiveled to check her out, eyes already glassy with too much partying.

"Vazz, I've been waiting for you, my pretty doll." His words slurred slightly. Silai sank her nails into his shoulder, feeling them pierce the skin. Ri's alabaster flesh bore the raised scars from earlier dates with the real Vazz. His breath shuttered; his eyes rolled up in pleasure.

"Let's go," she purred in his ear, releasing her grip on his shoulder. A derm of Down-Lo spun between her long fingers. "I brought something to help the party." She pulled him behind her, past the desk clerk who waved them on. Ri was a regular who paid weekly, according to the files she'd been provided. They descended the stairs and went into the third door on the left, just like the mission plan showed.

A horror holovid might have been shot in the dungeon setting of Vazz's room. The gray walls had black manacles hanging at various heights. A bed dominated the center of the room with blood-red linens and a headboard to which several metal rings were fixed. A chain with a dog collar dangled from one. The concrete floor had been painted black, but discolored patches could be seen around the room. Silai tried unsuccessfully to dispel images of how those had gotten there. An old barber-style chair had been bolted into the floor in the corner next to the bathroom. She keyed the locks on the soundproof outer door before tossing her bag into the bathroom. She pondered how to proceed. She sure as hell wasn't having sex with Ri just to finish the con.

He threw his clothes on the ground, revealing the pure white skin of the haltijan, covered by scars, some old, some still sporting scabs. "Mistress, I am unworthy of you!" Dropping to his knees, Ri pressed his forehead to the floor.

Silai pulled the derm tab and put it on Ri's forearm. The drug should knock him out, but considering how many other chemicals swam through his system, who knew? She waited, hoping the drug would work before anything else would be required.

"Mistress, have I displeased you? I will do anything to gain your favor." Here was a man who worked with explosives, kneeling before her, begging. She vowed again to kill the dragon for sending her into this demeaning situation. She'd never stooped this low to do a job.

The drug wasn't working fast enough. "Get on the bed and tell me what I did to you last time."

He scrambled up onto the bed and began to describe in lurid detail the events of their last meeting. All the soap in Hub wouldn't get the taint off her skin. Midway through, he swooned*/*and fell back, unconscious.

*Finally.* She made sure he was truly out before heading into the bathroom to transform into the HubSec officer for the last part of the setup. She shoved the disgusting excuse for an outfit in her bag and retrieved the uniform she's hidden in the concealed portion of her kit. Concentrating on the officer's form, her tails unwound, losing the shape of the uselan doll to reveal her true appearance. In a way, this form was the most alien to her. She'd spend months as a person, learning everything about them, as she worked a con. Kyerr had taken almost a year of her life.

She refocused on the job at hand. Pushing herself into the HubSec officer's form took a few minutes, though this shape required less precision than the Doll with all her tattoos. The mirror confirmed that she had been successful, given the dragon who peered back at her. The uniform slid on easily as did the weapon she hung from her hip. A white mark of Clan Nivladai decorated her left shoulder. HubSec officers from that clan tended to be smaller than most of the other clans. She hadn't matured enough to grow more tails to pull off a larger frame, like say Ancep.

Hearing a noise from the bedroom, Silai cracked the door, and a sharp tang assaulted her. Pushing the door the rest of the way brought her up short. The real Vazz lay on the bed next to Ri, who held a bloody vibro-knife in his hand. She'd been sliced open from her collarbone to her crotch.

The outer door's locks clacked. Only a patron with a key card could access those locks. The door swung inward to allow Ancep entry into the room. He carried a portable holovid player and an energy pistol.

"What are you doing?" Silai demanded, her voice sounding odd coming from the officer's mouth. A slip that would be deadly under normal circumstances. "This wasn't part of the job."

Ancep snorted. "Not the part you were given. You may leave."

Silai should have walked away. Should have run, truth be told, but the discovery of a corpse had her unnerved. She didn't work with a body count. No one got hurt from her cons, just lost glint that her targets had too much of anyhow. "The game was to blackmail him into doing your dirty work, not killing an innocent woman. The plan would have succeeded without her dying."

Before she knew he'd moved, Ancep had the pulsar pushed up under her chin. "You would be extremely difficult to replace. There are other options. Do not question me. Go do what you need to and return in four days to be briefed on the job."

Courage wasn't an attribute that anyone in Harmony would claim the kitsune possessed, especially not Silai, who was stunned at her sudden burst of bravery. "And if I don't return?"

Ancep considered her for a moment before removing the pistol. "You will. This is the biggest game in town, and you know it."

She stormed out, knowing he was right and hating herself all the more because of it.

# 2 7

## NYX

Day seven finally arrived. The surgical technician entered Nyx's room with his Nanyo deck in hand. "The splicer said to take it easy, give your jack time to recalibrate with the input."

Nyx only half listened. He took the deck, thumped the power node, and pushed the connector into his improved jack, wincing slightly at the jab of pain. He set the deck in his lap, fingers running through a series of exercises that in the origin would execute a series of offensive and defensive maneuvers. No runs today. Phantoms were a superstitious lot, and the ritual centered him. He flicked the silver stud on the board and dove into cyberspace. His demon avatar pixelated into being with the nameplate Cargo123 over his head. The associated account would lead anyone dumb enough to try to pierce it on a wild goose chase across Harmony before dead-ending in a cafe in the Thanas Isles. He hot-keyed into a virtual arcade where a lot of the phantoms hung. They'd not be expecting him since his capture had made all the news feeds.

He dropped his v-coin into Aerial Assault, taking on the role of a dragon fighting off humans as they tried to invade Harmony. Everyone knew that humans existed, but only the dragons had been alive when the inhabitants of Harmony had fled the dying Earth. These games reminded the nulls that humanity existed and would destroy our world just like they had Earth. It was gashing nonsense.

As he played, he sensed the world around him. The zeros loved this place with its shopping, games, hangouts, and every imaginable sex act you'd ever want to find without ever meeting the other person. Once you'd been in the origin, worked with the raw data, you saw what this place really was, an illusion.

He dropped the game and left the arcade. Since none of the major players were present, it was a waste of time. In the physical world, his fingers flicked the stud again and his vision swam as he entered the origin. The illuminated grid that built out the conceptual visual interface expanded before him. A pain shot through his temples that he ignored, though the surgical tech's warning rang in his ears.

It was beautiful. The data structure of every business and personal entity in Harmony was here, linked across all the kilometers. In seconds he'd hacked into his mother's household controls and flicked the heat off. She hated being cold.

With a laugh at the juvenile prank, he skimmed past banks, huge corporations, and a myriad of organizations. DISCS protection shields flared as he got too close to the WeSee holovid corps structures. Pipes of data flowed in and out as they delivered content to the people all over Harmony. It would be child's play to inject his own code into the streams to mess with the feeds. Couldn't make glint off that kind of attack, though.

The pain in his brain intensified the longer he rode through the digital domain. Abruptly, he was booted out of the constructs and back into the void. The tech stood facing him, her hand retreating from the power switch. "Told you to take it easy. You fry your receptors and you'll be a null in the void."

Nyx grimaced. Not only did it sound ridiculous coming from a null, but that would be the end of his career as a phantom. Once you lived outside yourself, the physical world became a burden. The hackers who fried killed themselves shortly after or became dust addicts. He shook his head, wondering which fate was worse.

The tech pulled a derm out and pressed it against his wrist. Within seconds the pain subsided as warmth flowed over him. "Splicer said you all push too hard the first time. You won't be able to jack in for a couple of hours, but that will help stabilize your new wetware."

"Thanks."

"Don't mention it. The dragon is back and asked me to have you join the rest after your test run."

*Wonderful.* He detached the connector, slotting it back into the holder on the Nanyo deck. He pushed off the bed before a wave of vertigo and nausea crashed over him. The room spun and darkened.

The technician caught him. "Take it easy. The neuro-boost will mess with your equilibrium for a bit."

He swayed as the room slowed to an undulating wave of disconcerting fuzziness. Slowly, he returned to solid ground as the world subsided back into void norm. A stumble like that in the origin could have thrown him into a hostile DISCS that would have flat-lined him in an instant. "I've got it now."

The tech didn't release his arm. They crossed the room to the door, his balance improving with each step. He pulled the door open and the tech finally let go, hovering over him while he staggered down the hallway to where the meeting would take place at the series sixty table.

Nyx stepped into the main room, his eyes twitching from the brighter lights. Everyone else sat around the table, including Gelsey. Surprisingly, he felt better seeing the diminutive pixie, wings opened out behind her. They flickered as she ran them through the color cycling.

"They can even switch to full night mode that mimics the nighttime sky based on your coordinates," Gelsey said gleefully.

He smiled as he dropped, harder than he meant to, into the chair he'd been in at the last meeting. He checked each of his team, looking for their upgrades. Kelthar hadn't changed. Magic and tech didn't always mix well. Silai also hadn't changed. Her subdermal implants wouldn't be in use while she wasn't working a job. Aikila caught his eye and held it. He hadn't noticed the gold flecking in her brown eyes when they'd met or realized how attractive she was.

Lorcan almost shook with contained energy. The upgrades to his neurostim must be in overdrive like his improved processing was for him. He'd been huge before. Now he seemed leaner and faster, not bulky like that R'gar had. The difference between the Dregs' chop shops and the grafters from the Bluffs.

"Nyx, are you well?" Ancep said, forcing him to stop gawking at Aikila's beauty.

He nodded. "They had to give me a stabilizer, zoned me out a bit. I'm ready to roll." He glanced at Aikila again and decided she was attractive but not overly so. Strange. Drugs were messing with his perceptions

"Excellent," the dragon announced, tapping on the display in front of him. A structure appeared before Nyx, a long rectangular building with curved ends. Metal grates covered the exposed glass fronts of the sides. The ends were solid.

Lorcan scratched his chin. "Is the only way in through the center structure?"

Nyx got why the nagualan asked. The ends were supported by columns with only a concrete base and a large, fortified door set into it. A single entrance made it extremely difficult to penetrate—and escape. He grinned at their reaction since he could control any of the lockdown systems from the origin.

"Yes," Ancep said, his hands steepled in front of his muzzle. "This is the Insulvend secure housing facility that is a bastion for Clan Koxalan. They call it the Fortress, claim that it is impregnable, and multiple teams have failed to penetrate it. Attempts to determine what systems they've employed have hit dead ends. Plans are non-existent; anyone associated with its construction has been removed from Hub. Your team will need to access the building, retrieve the scroll, and return it to me."

"It must be running some serious DISCS to keep the phantoms out. All that intel has to be on their core systems." Nyx studied the architecture, looking for the service ports that would tell him what kind of cabling they used. In that new of a building, it probably would be silicone fiber which could be compromised, if necessary.

Ancep smirked at him. "There are no external systems."

"*What?*" A sharp pain shot through Nyx's head, causing him to wince. "There has to be. Power, water, sewage. Those systems need to be run from the core."

"None. Everything is internal to the building. My guess is contractors are brought in from around Harmony and don't leave until their service is finished." Ancep stood, nodding to them. "I need the scroll retrieved within a week."

A chorus of protests arose from the team. Ancep held up his taloned hand. "You have everything I have in front of you. This team can either crack it or not. In eight days, the dragon Council meets and Clan Koxalan will unveil their stolen spell, and this endeavor and the six of you become worthless to me. Good day." The dragon lord strolled across the room toward the elevator.

Nyx groaned. "Well, that was a kick in the balls."

# 28

# AIKILA

Aikila stared at the dragon lord's back as he left the room. The arrogance reminded her of Y'sser, who she'd seen in the drug-induced hallucinations. One day the dragons wouldn't be all-powerful, and the races of Harmony would topple them, but that day was a long way off. She studied the building, wondering what other treasures the fortress held. She'd lost every bit of glint she'd invested in her last trip to the trumped-up slug. For all his haughtiness, Ancep hadn't skimped on the gear for the team. She now possessed a cred chip with enough to outfit a small army.

Yes, the dragons had it coming. She just hoped she'd be alive to see it.

"A military-type strike is out of the question," Lorcan said as he scowled at the structure. "A cub with a slingshot could hold that doorway against a squad of troops." He spun the image, zooming in on places before gnashing his teeth in frustration.

Nyx regarded it. "Without cyber access to the internal systems, you'll never be able to drop the security and get through the front door."

"Any ideas on which system they are running?" Gelsey asked. She flew up and down repeatedly, though Aikila wasn't sure if it was nerves or excitement over her new wings. Sky Sharks were about the best wings on the market according to their resident pixie. She'd repeated this at least twenty times today

The glare Nyx shot Gelsey should have knocked her out of the air.

"No, but they are running top-grade DISCS if they are as hardened as they appear."

Aikila cleared her throat. "DISCS?"

"Sorry. Directed Intelligence Synchronized Combinatorial Systems. These systems use ICE, or Intrusion Countermeasures Electronics, to block phantoms from entering their systems. It used to be that a company would buy a package, install it, and hope that it defended the core from hacks. Now, they use DISCS, which monitors the ICE and then launches new counterattacks or even flatlines a decker mid-run. Stuff sends feedback that shuts your heart off. Nasty."

"And you do this for what reason?" Aikila asked, wondering why anyone would risk their life for data. She'd traveled all of Harmony searching out deals to make glint in Hub, but she avoided danger most of the time by being careful and clever. To die at a machine's command seemed ludicrous.

The light returned to his eyes. "To be the best, to show my pare—, err, everyone that Nyx is the best phantom on the planet. To become a legend."

"In his own mind," Kelthar quipped. The mage slapped his knee as he laughed at his own joke. "Now, boyo, just a bit of harmless fun. We need to keep our wits if we're going to crack this egg."

Interesting way to look at it. Aikila studied her teammates as they pondered, launched ill-fated ideas, and stewed at the hopelessness of the situation. "If we were going to 'crack this egg,' what do we need to start?"

Kelthar grinned. "A huge hammer."

"Not helpful." Aikila moved on. They had seven days to finish the mission. This was as close to getting intel on Y'sser as she'd ever been. One way or the other she would avenge her poor father. "Nyx how do we shut down the security systems?"

He scratched his chin. "First, we need to understand what is deployed around the building and what protects the internal systems."

"The physical security can be obtained easily," Silai said. She hadn't spoken much since she'd arrived for the meeting. Ancep had kept the rest of the team in the Regal, yet she had been on the outside. From the lack of a rebuke, the dragon knew about it. The layers kept building faster than she could peel them away.

"How is that, Silai?" Lorcan's deep voice echoed around the small space. Everything about the man screamed danger. He would be a good ally to fight alongside.

She smiled at him. "Set it off, of course. Once you see it in action, you'll understand the nature of the systems we face."

"That only gets us one node of data." Nyx stood, leaning toward the holovid of the facility. "We need to ascertain all the layers they have in place. A security threat would have to trigger a full-scale response. We need a total lockdown to repel whatever it was."

Silai put her hands on the display, going through the files instead of the building configuration. She murmured to herself as she flipped through the data. "We could hire a small team to try to get in, see what happens."

Kelthar shook his head, setting his ears to swinging. "We'd have to get them to the Bluffs and once they saw that place, they'd turn tail and bolt. Part of the place's security is just looking at it. When you can't see a way in, you assume there isn't one."

"We can't tip our hand, either." Everyone's eyes locked on Aikila with varying expressions. Silai contemplated. Kelthar grinned, nodding his head in agreement. Lorcan's brow knitted together, not sure of what she meant. Gelsey's eyebrows had risen in surprise. Nyx rubbed his temples, trying to ease his stress. Being a smuggler and merchant, you learned to read people well, knowing more about what they'd do than they did in most cases. These were professionals, but they all had their tics and it was Aikila's mission to find them. "If we attack, they'll go into defensive mode, and it will be much harder to break in. If we trigger the defense systems, they'll have to assume it was a mistake, not an attack."

Understanding crossed Lorcan's face. "Good point, Aikila. I agree with your logic. We need a diversion, not an attack."

Nyx hadn't bought in yet. The decker would be the lynchpin who held the others back. "A diversion is fine, but we need to scan what is there so we can find the holes. Kelthar, how do you find what magical defenses are in place?"

Now it was Kelthar's turn to look anxious. The inner workings of magic were a closely guarded secret among the practitioners of the craft. They didn't share much information, if any at all.

"There are ways to divine what is in place, though that takes weeks of preparation that we don't have. I can construct a toy that will let me read the outer layer of spells that have been used." Beads of sweat dripped off his earlobes. He dabbed at them with the sleeve of his blue and red patterned shirt. "Best I can do on short notice."

"But what happens once we are in?" Gelsey asked. "How do you get us through spells you don't know about?"

The grin returned as he patted the ever-present leather bag at his hip. "I'll have what I need to handle anything they can throw at us."

Aikila didn't express her doubt over that statement. She'd seen too many tricksters with a bit of talent bilk honest people all over Harmony. "What do you need to build this 'toy' of yours?"

"I have everything I need. It will take me a couple of hours."

Nyx chimed in. "We could build a remote terminal entry port."

"Why didn't I think of that!" Gelsey said, slapping her forehead with her palm. "What are you talking about?"

He shot her another glare before he continued. "If Aikila can get the parts, I can build a device that would be able to detect an open port inside the building, tunnel in from there, and remote hack the system."

The inkling of a plan tickled her brain. "I can get you anything you need. How close does it need to be?"

"On the building. The roof should be within range of the network. I can remote from here, but the device has to be within thirty meters of the open port, given the construction of the building."

"Great plan, genius. How are you going to get it there? Walk up and ask them to put it on somebody's desk?" Gelsey said in her snottiest tone. "Did you think of that all on your own or did you have to write a program to do it for you?" She stopped, realizing the other five were staring at her, smiling. "Oh, no. I am not flying near that place."

Aikila grinned. It would take a while but the pixie would be doing exactly that, and before the morning if Aikila played her chips right.

# 29

# GELSEY

Gelsey knew the job well, but that didn't mean she liked it any better. The mudders thought because they didn't notice her, that surveillance systems didn't, either. No matter the arguments she presented, they claimed to have faith in her abilities and really needed to know what they were up against.

In the end, she'd taken the port sniffing device that Nyx provided and the necklace Kelthar had given her and set off to buzz the target. She'd suited up in an enhanced full-body chameleon suit. Not only would the suit blend into the surroundings, but the design confused tracking systems, making her harder to target. It synced with her wings, reducing visual anomalies that might give her away. Mesh over her face let her see and breathe normally, which was far better than the old suit that Lorcan had trashed.

Her first pass took her well out of the range of any counter-intrusion measures the Fortress had set up, and when she'd returned, no data had been collected. The second pass fared slightly better. Since nothing tried to kill her and she got hits on the building's systems, she considered it a win. Unfortunately, though magic and technology registered, she hadn't been close enough to deposit the device within thirty meters. To top it off, Nyx had built the hardware out of pieces from Aikila's sources that would only transmit data if—and this was a huge if—she could stash it on the roof. Nothing like a suicide run to brighten your day, or middle of the night, as the case may be.

She flew in low over the top of the nearest building, which sat over a hundred meters away from the Fortress. The designers were ingenious, which pissed her off to no end. They had a garden surrounding the building on all sides, a civic improvement project donated by the builder. People took their kids there to picnic and read. All the boring stuff the mudders wallowed in. No wonder they spent their lives in a trance. Pixies lived for the thrill, flying through a world not built to suit them. They danced on the edge every day and loved it. The pixies who grew to their larger size and stayed that way found their wings atrophied from lack of use until they fell off. Gelsey had replaced her natural wings with synthetic ones, but she still had her wings. She'd rather die making this run than watch her life ebb away.

Time to give these Sky Sharks a workout. Switching her wings to stealth mode, she dove off the neighboring building's roof, speeding to the nearest garden. She blew past ornamental shrubs and carefully crafted flowerbeds. The speed gave her a heady sensation, having never gone this fast before. These new wings were better than she'd ever hoped. Her best chance would be to reach the top of the Fortress without dying, drop the box, and beat it. She wouldn't have time to find the spot Nyx had described in his condescending, elvish manner. With all the heat, this place would be packed. Drop-and-run was the only avenue open to her.

She flipped her eyes into spectral mode, seeing a composite image of ultraviolet, heat, electromagnetic, and whatever else all at once. Flying this way was tricky since a lack of detail lent itself to spectacular, and painful, crashes. A burst of an EMP cannon, for example, would be blinding. She headed toward the nearest solid end-cap of the building without windows or bars protecting it; the ride should be easier. She'd attained the twenty-meter mark when the building lit up like a dragon fire celebration. Security weapon nodes came alive as she darted toward the Fortress's forbidding walls. She took evasive maneuvers to make her harder to target.

The first burst of energy shot through where she'd been moments before, leaving an afterimage scorched onto her retinas. She switched her eyes back to night vision and banked sharply up, doing a full roll to the side. Her old wings would have folded under the exertion, but the Sky Sharks kept up, nowhere near their limits.

The hair stood up on her arms as unseen energy beams flowed around her. She flipped the zapper on her wrist open and dropped a series of small, intensely hot ball bearings, fanning them out below her. She switched to thermal vision and saw the energy weapons reducing them in rapid succession. All this and she hadn't even reached the building. She punched her wings to the max and flew straight for the roof.

Around six meters from the building, the firing stopped, as the systems adapted to the perceived threat. Small drones, approximately four centimeters in diameter with two articulated arms, launched from bays in the wall in front of her as she passed. A wonderful new addition to the tale of Gelsey the suicidal pixie. It would sell millions, and be an amazing holovid shown in the best theaters the Bluffs offered. But the death of our plucky pixie would have to change. Nobody liked a depressing ending.

She banked hard to the left and cut her wings, falling past the swarm that chased her, twisting to change direction. Nothing happened. Her wings hadn't kicked back on. According to the surgical tech, the wings could reboot in under a second in case of a failure. Still nothing. More drones were coming up from below to eliminate the falling pixie. *Gash it all. I'm going to splat on the ground. How embarrassing.*

As the drones closed in, one got near enough to shoot out an arm with a nasty pincher to grab her. Pulling a somersault, she flipped over the drone's arm, landing on the back of the machine. It dropped but regained altitude even with the additional load. Once again, the security engineers who'd built the system had thought of everything. Well, almost everything. She grasped the edges of the drone and rolled, veering the drone head-on into its brothers. Passing through the swarm, she kicked any that got close, spiraling them into the others. The system hadn't been designed to cover a full-scale collision. Some of the drones plummeted to the ground as they lost connection with the controller.

With a whirr, her wings sprang back to life, lifting her and the drone in the direction of the roof. To the internal cameras and trackers, the drone would look like another malfunctioning bot. She might actually pull this off. The roof raced closer and her heart sank. Hunter-seeker drones were rising from small hatches on the rooftop. The ten-centimeter bots carried a serious arsenal of weapons and enough gear to spot a speck of dust at twenty meters. For a six-centimeter-tall pixie, this was the equivalent of Lorcan taking on a Kraken with a toothpick.

*Gash it all.* She and her unwilling mount dove as the first hunter-seekers cleared the roof line. Nyx specifically said that the device must be placed on the roof. Not that it mattered, accessing any part of the building would be just as hard if not worse. Especially since the drone she'd hijacked had died. The extra weight slowed her down but it might still be of use. Sweeping toward the adjoining park, she dropped it in a bush with a homing device she'd activate when she was ready.

Above her, the hunter-seekers were canvassing the area in a grid pattern. Nothing like a rigid protocol to handle a chaotic situation. She rose straight in the air, far enough away from the Fortress that she didn't risk detection, and then flew far above the building. From that angle, she pinpointed the openings in the sweep. She counted them out, and each hole in the grid occurred for three seconds before closing. They repeated every thirty seconds. Her eyes traced the pattern around the spot on the roof closest to her. It would be a tight fit, but she could do it.

Her route would take six seconds for the full run, so at twenty-seven seconds she dove, wings pushed to their full capacity. Three, two, one. She sped through the dead space in the pattern. *Woohooo! Made it!*

The celebration ended abruptly as her wings cut out. Her forward momentum carried her through the dead spot, but her sight scrambled and her limbs twitched as she fell. *What is going on?* She struck the roof edge, bouncing along the concrete. The world stopped as she skidded to a halt. *Well, I got to the roof.* Her vision flashed in and out as tremors shook her body. Her body was in full system failure.

The concrete made a lousy bed. Gelsey pushed herself to her knees. She removed Nyx's device from the pouch at her waist. The damage was obvious even to a half-blind pixie. The switch had broken off at some point, but she got it turned on. Well, at least she thought it was on. She crawled to the edge, placing it under the overhang. As she removed her hand, the device returned to its normal size. *Well, I did what I set out to do.*

Her vision came back online first, and moments later her wings and neurostim systems. The hunter-seekers had changed patterns and were circling in an ever-collapsing circle around her. The chameleon suit had kept them fooled. Her time was running out. She stood, said a quick prayer to Iraos, the god of thieves, and launched into the air.

She skimmed along the roof, hoping her proximity would cover her escape, knowing it wouldn't when it happened. The hunter-seeker closest to her reeled as if had been struck, spinning sideways into its neighbor. Both crumpled before dropping like stones. Pieces of drone scattered across the rooftop. Some were the matte gray of the hunter-seekers, while other pieces were bright colors. It didn't matter. Gelsey punched it, speeding away from the death trap and from the building.

Thank you, Iraos. I owe you one, but please wait a long time before you ask for the favor in return.

# KELTHAR

Kelthar grinned ear to ear when the Pixie returned. It had been a close call.

Gelsey sat on the table, a bit worse for wear. She'd delivered Nyx's box and brought back a Fortress drone. In his hands, it looked like a child's toy. Gelsey obviously didn't see it as anything so innocuous, by how ardently she complained after delivering it to the team.

"The box took a beating. I don't think it's working," Gelsey said, still rubbing at her face where she'd hit the concrete. "My gashing wings shut down twice. They are supposed to be top of the line. At the prices they charge for these things, they should never have issues. Gash it, for what they charge they could cook your freaking dinner and fu--"

A shadow crossed Aikila's face. "They did glitch. We'll get the techs to run diagnostics on them." She turned to Nyx. "Can you connect to the box?"

Nyx's fingers were already flying across the keys of his deck. He didn't respond to Aikila's question, but judging by the scowl on his face it wasn't good news. Aikila sighed. "I'm going to go with Gelsey's assessment of the situation and say it doesn't work."

Gelsey snorted. "Thanks. It's nice to know I can spot junk when I see it. Speaking of junk, what's up with the drones? I'm grateful for the hunter-seekers being distracted so I could get away, mind you. I hate those things. Who in the name of Poanke builds a drone to kill off an adorable pixie just out for a quick bit of air? Can somebody tell me what happened at the end there?"

Kelthar made note that everyone turned to Aikila whenever a question needed to be answered. Strength flowed through her, along with an unhealthy dose of anger, unless he missed his guess.

Not for the first time the mage wondered at the true intent of Ancep's game. This mission was reckless. Dragons lived for a long time. The same held true for mages, especially the careful ones. Kelthar understood the virtue of caution, though his outward appearance never hinted at it. Something didn't add up.

Silai paced back and forth in conversation with someone over the wireless. A smile crossed her face as she reached for the plug and jacked into the table. The projector created a face over the series sixty, the green, scaly face of the person on the other end. A trog of some sort. The veins in the fins that ran down the center of his skull pulsed with anger. "I am Scolalmos, the head of security for Insulvend. What is the meaning of your attack on our facility?"

"Attack? My dear Scolly, may I call you Scolly? We have all the proper permits in place." She glanced at Nyx, who had removed the plug from his jack. He nodded to her. "Drone Battles will be WeSee's newest holovid hit and rating darling of this year."

"My name is Scolalmos. I've never heard of Drone Battles." The jutting crocodile maw of the Trog gnashed in irritation. Kelthar was glad he would not be on the receiving end when they finished this discussion.

"Thank you, Scolly," Silai continued as if he hadn't spoken. "Of course not, it hasn't been released yet, and now you've destroyed my racers. Do you know how many weeks you've cost WeSee? My production schedule is in ruins, and you want to argue about a few cheap drones?"

Scolly's eyes flashed red. "Cheap drones? Those were state-of-the-art Plagen Industries advanced security AI…" His jaw snapped shut, realizing he'd said too much.

"You can keep speaking gibberish all day, but your company was given warning of the race. We sent out the required electronic notices three days ago."

"I never got…" His eyes widened as he found the aforementioned directive. "Um, Miss…"

"Yvivra Barkskin, head of new media at WeSee Holovids." She huffed as if dealing with an unruly child. "The reason I contacted you is one of your micro drones was retrieved in the recovery of our racers. My tech is replacing the locater modulator thingamajig and it will return shortly."

"Thank you, Miss Barkskin. Please accept my apology. Is there anything I can do for you?"

She huffed again. "No, you people have done enough damage for one evening." She disconnected the link and removed her jack.

Nyx laughed. "That was quite the performance."

Silai curled into her chair. "Good work on getting the documents in place. He verified everything."

Lorcan scowled. "Deceiving people is not honorable." Everyone ignored him.

Aikila picked up the drone. "Nyx, can we use this to gain access?" She twirled it on one finger like a display carousel.

He stood, setting his deck on the table. Aikila deposited it in his hand. He held it up to examine it. "I believe so. It's a bit small, but I may be able to rig up something."

"Could you build another of the devices that broke earlier?" Kelthar asked from where he sat cross-legged in his chair. The look on Nyx's face morphed from "Are you serious?" to "Are you stupid?"

"No, the device is too heavy for this type of drone to carry."

Kelthar's impish grin sprang to life. "Pixies haven't cornered the market on making things shrink. You've got an hour, boyo, to get this thing flyin'."

Aikila didn't even wait for Nyx to respond. "Lorcan and I will get the parts in twenty minutes. Fix whatever you can while we're gone."

Nyx retrieved a black cloth kit and unrolled it, pulling out all manner of tools, and set to it. Within minutes the drone was in pieces as the elf worked his magic on the device.

Kelthar approached Gelsey. "Do you have the amulet that I gave you earlier?" Up close, the bruising stood out against her creamy skin even more. Her electric blue hair dimmed as if her energy had been diminished. "I'm curious as to why your wings failed."

"Me too." She flew over to where the mage sat, landed, and grew to her larger size. The amulet came off over her head before she tossed it to Kelthar. "Leave it to me to get a dud set of wings. I'm getting a drink. Maybe two." She walked to the bar and poured a glass of amber liquid that Kelthar didn't recognize and tossed it back. A second followed. A surgical tech approached her, and they left together. Kelthar flipped the amulet over. He knew the answers within would lend him the ability to help crack the egg in question.

Without a sound, Lorcan appeared next to him. Kelthar started, unused to being surprised. The giant cat warrior moved with as much sound as sunshine. "Kelthar, you seem troubled. Are you well?"

"I'm fine." He wondered if that was true but continued anyhow. "Things about this job don't make sense. I'd like to know Ancep's mind better before we retrieve the item he has requested."

Lorcan grunted. "Who can understand the mind of a dragon? They manipulate people in their sleep." He glanced around the room to make sure they weren't overheard. "Could you take me to see my daughter?"

Kelthar looked into the face of a father who felt he'd failed his child. It tore at the warrior more than any physical weapon ever would. "No, it wouldn't be wise. Ancep has her guarded, from you as much as from the clinic she was stolen from. If we were to go there, we'd be compromising her safety."

A low growl came from the nagual. "Do you think the dragon would harm her?"

Kelthar thought for a moment about how to best answer the question. In the long run, it would be better if the big cat understood the situation. "I do. The dragon will do anything to acquire what he wants. That is part of the puzzle. The value of the prize doesn't match the effort to get it."

"Thank you, Kelthar," Lorcan said with a nod of respect before he resumed his pacing. "You are an honorable man. I will bide my time."

"Lorcan, there will come a time that you will have to leave your honor behind to accomplish this job. What will you do?" Kelthar studied the big man as he paced.

Lorcan stopped and regarded Kelthar, his eyes reflecting the fear and aggravation that the merc had to be feeling. The proud nagualan warrior returned to his seat, head bowed. "I will do whatever it takes to save my kitten."

Kelthar wondered if he really could. Nagualans were high-strung and rigid in their beliefs, but being away from the rigors of his people's code may have softened him. When the time came, Kelthar hoped he would make the correct choice.

The energy flowing from the amulet beckoned to him, wanting to be unleashed from its binding. Better to do it out of sight of the others.

His bedroom lacked all the features a mage required. It worked for the short term. Really, he missed his alchemical lab and all of the implements that he needed to craft his magic. Sitting on the floor was not as comfortable as the overstuffed chair he'd been provided, but it felt wrong to him, so he used the floor.

"No time like the present," he said to the empty room. After selecting a small, enchanted black pine bough, he spoke the word to release the information the amulet had gathered. Energy exploded out of the amulet like fireworks at the Emperor of Japan's feast days of his youth. Power shot in all directions as he invoked the spell on the bough. The essence coalesced around the pine branch, shimmering as it took shape. Iconographs of the spells the amulet had encountered rose before him. He spat a curse as he realized that Gelsey's wings hadn't failed. She'd been hexed by a powerful ward. The amount of power in those wards astonished him. Only a few practitioners had the strength and talent to pull off conjurings of this magnitude. Inferior equipment would have failed completely, leaving Gelsey dead outside the Fortress.

That was bad, but the next piece of information was what really upset him.

All magic carried a "fingerprint" from the caster, but nothing gave away who had created these wards. A few moments of consideration led him to a small, onyx with a spell of revealing. The orb levitated off his palm, spinning counterclockwise as it floated into the energy of the amulet. Sparks erupted as the two met. The orb cracked, falling to the floor in a shower of jagged stone pieces.

Whoever built these wards had known that they would be tested. Most practitioners wouldn't have the know-how to best these defenses. Kelthar did, though his suspicions as to who the caster was left him with a cold chill. Choosing the correct talisman would be crucial here. If his hunch held water, he'd need something to offset a sorcerer's power. He retrieved the old, very discolored finger bone from his pouch. The thing made his skin itch. Sorcery demanded blood as the energy to fuel the magic, a practice Kelthar found abhorrent. Sometimes you had to fight fire with fire.

The bone floated on the same trajectory the orb had taken moments earlier. When the magical fields touched, there was no reaction. The bone twirled over the amulet as if dancing with excitement. The iconographs changed slightly, revealing a symbol that made Kelthar blanch. He knew who the sorcerer was. In fact, knew her far better than he should ever have. The caster was Litri, his ex-wife.

This job had just gotten very personal.

31

LORCAN

Lorcan watched as the mage left the room, carrying the device he'd given Gelsey before her near disastrous run. Mages and their secrets had never sat well with him. In his experience, secrets always came out at the worst possible time and ruined whatever the mission was.

The warrior thought he'd run the team, but Aikila had become the leader by some unofficial consensus. He valued Kelthar more than the others, but he'd been burned in the past by those he'd depended on and his trust only went so far. The people who lived in the Quad would sell you out if the price was right. What would Kelthar's price be? Could he force the mage to take him to Jaana? That was the last resort. Better to finish the job than risk losing his daughter forever.

While Lorcan dwelled on the fate of his daughter, the elf worked at fixing the drone. Silai studied his every move. The dryad was beautiful, as were all her kind. The ones he'd met hadn't been the brightest of creatures. Silai didn't exhibit a joyful abandon as his mother would have called it. His squadmates called them party-time girls. Her participation in such a deadly mission didn't add up, but as long as she did her job, those were idle thoughts to pass the time.

Aikila motioned for him to follow her. He didn't question, just did as she asked, which felt normal to the merc. People didn't pay him to think, he protected whoever he was told to keep safe. They entered the elevator

139

and she pressed the lobby panel. The doors slid shut soundlessly, unlike the way they'd creaked and shuddered when they'd arrived the previous week.

"My contact, Gipes, will meet us at the Rusted Ratchet. Not the worst place in the Quad, though you might have to break a few heads." She watched him closely. Lorcan knew they all held reservations about him being on the team. Nagualans had a reputation for strictness in their beliefs and not budging from them. Given the situation, he would have the same worries.

He reached over and pressed stop. The elevator slid to a halt as he turned to face the leader. "I'm going to be upfront with you."

She grinned at him. "I thought all nagualans were upright and forthcoming. I'd expect no less."

He caught the sarcasm and bit off a hasty reply. Instead, he continued. "Ancep has my daughter. I will do anything…" He locked eyes with her, slightly baring his teeth as he loomed over the smaller woman. "….anything to get her back. There is no rule I won't break, nothing I won't do to make this job successful. Understood?"

A nod was the only answer he received as she pressed the lobby button, resuming their descent.

"Thank you for telling me. I have my own reasons to want this job done," Aikila said. The door slid open, and she left the elevator, not checking to see if he followed. She exited the faded lobby, pulling the black hood of her jacket over her head.

Lorcan stayed beside her, surveying the few vagrants who wandered around the area. His enhanced vision ran over each of them, looking for anything out of place. Both men and the woman appeared to be dust addicts from the way they twitched as they walked. It might have been a mercy to end them, but the only thing that mattered was the job and getting Jaana back.

"Let's go. We don't have much time left." Aikila strode down the concrete walkway toward the borders of the Dregs and the Flow districts. Most of the inhabitants here worked in the factories on the Terrace or freelanced at fixing or building illegal devices. Ethics rarely came into play in the Quad and only if you could make glint off it.

Lorcan strode two paces back and to the left of Aikila. She carried a pulsar under her jacket, so being on her off-hand side made sense. Lorcan hadn't chosen a weapon from the stores that Aikila had brought in after the meeting yesterday. He preferred his claws to a weapon that could break. Weapons had their time and place, but tonight he wouldn't need them.

The buildings started to look better maintained as they left the Dregs. Men and women dressed in workers' overalls or specialized gear for the more dangerous factories walked together in twos and threes. Some laughed, some swayed, and a couple argued over who was the hotter between two holovid starlets. Lorcan would never understand these people.

A dirty LED light over a sign with a Goblin sporting a huge ratchet over his shoulder announced they had arrived at their destination. Lorcan stepped past Aikila, pulling the door open, keeping her in front of him as she entered. He ducked his head and followed her into the dimly lit space. A ghastly odor of stale beer, vomit, and urine assaulted his sensitive nose as they wound their way around tables and drunk patrons to a room in the rear of the bar. A large female Troll sat on a beat-up stool in front of a metallic fabric that concealed the entry behind her. Her long blue hair hung in a braid at the back of her head, exposing her green-tinged skin and small tusks that curved up past her upper lip. She banged on a hand-held device, attention totally fixed on the flashing screen.

Aikila stopped, waiting for the troll to acknowledge her. Grunts and harsh laughs continued as she played her game. Aikila cleared her throat. Still no reaction. Lorcan reached over and snatched the game out of the startled troll's hands. She reached for the pistol on her belt before her eyes focused on the very large, very angry nagual that stood before her. "We're here to see Gipes," he snarled at her.

Trolls weren't always the fastest learners, but she jumped off the stool and pulled the covering to the side. Aikila entered, and Lorcan did likewise, tossing the game back to the troll, who caught it deftly. "Aw, man. You wrecked my level." Lorcan smiled as the curtain swung closed behind him.

Gipes sat behind a counter, smoking a Talhut as he rebuilt an ancient bolt thrower. His long, hooked nose was the only thing that kept his beady red eyes from touching each other. He glanced up, stubbed out his smoke in an old can, and wiped his nose on a grimy sleeve. "Aikila, I got what you want. Gonna cost, though."

"When has anything ever not cost me an arm and a leg, Gipes?"

The goblin cackled, a sound that reminded Lorcan of metal scraping down concrete. "Never!" He pulled out a new Talhut and lit it on a soldering iron. He puffed the acrid smoke into circles that collapsed as they rose through the stagnant air. "The remote controller, breakaway handles, and signal generator will set you back twenty thousand glint."

"What?" Aikila gasped. "Altogether that shouldn't cost more than five. I have no issue with making a profit but this is an insult." She moved closer, glaring at the Goblin who puffed more smoke at her.

Gipes looked at his Talhut, considering for a moment. Lorcan had no patience for squabbling, but he stood behind his leader, ready to lend a claw if necessary. "Tell him to back off or I'll call Unda in and have him removed."

Lorcan stepped closer into the stench of the smoke. "You mean the girl playing her game outside the door?"

His eyes widened as Lorcan's lowered himself to the goblin's eye level. Gipes swallowed hard. "Right. We're good." Lorcan withdrew. "I tell you, finding guards worth the glint is impossible." He gestured with both arms, sending ashes all over the floor behind the counter. "Since we're friends, fifteen. You convince big and furry to work for me and you can have it for free."

Lorcan snorted, earning a glare from Aikila. "I'll do eight and not have my associate rip your arms out of the sockets."

Gipes' eyes shot straight to Lorcan, who smiled as he flicked his claws out.

"Deal." The Goblin slid the chip reader over to her for payment. Once the glint had been received, he slid a small sack across to Aikila. Quickly, she pulled each piece out, checked to make sure it worked, then redeposited them all in the bag.

"Pleasure as always, Gipes." They exited out through the fabric, again startling Unda, who dropped her game on the floor. The sound of cracking polymer could be heard across the bar.

"Gash it all," she yelled as she picked up the shattered device. Aikila headed for the front door, but Lorcan paused to speak with the young woman. "You might want to consider a new line of employment before you get more than a broken game."

Unda nodded, her mouth hanging open. "My mother wanted me to be an actuary."

Lorcan grinned at her. "Do that. It's good to listen to your mother."

# NYX

"Done." Nyx glanced at the timer and saw fifty-six minutes had passed. The repaired microdrone and new remote network access controller which, thanks to Kelthar's magic, was a centimeter long, sat on the table ready to go. The controller's handles snapped over the drone's arms, and the tiny piece of tech could be detached remotely once the drone returned to its base.

Gelsey swooped in, grabbed the package, and took off at full speed. "Thanks for all the extra time," she said over her shoulder, heading out of the Regal. The drone contained a tracker that reported its location at all times, and no one wanted the Fortress to know where the team was. She might not get too far, but any distance was better than in their laps when the drone activated.

Nyx pulled the plug from his Nanyo deck and jacked in. He dropped into cyberspace and shot through to the origin. He keyed the loc code for the Hub Transportation Authority. Every camera and drone surveillance bot across Hub could be accessed through their systems, except for those in the Apex. Dragons liked their privacy, and since they ran Hub, they got it. A faint yellow sheen surrounded the small blue disk that represented the server.

A glowing list of code snippets and injectors flashed into view on the left side of his vision. He pulled up the Puck injector and loaded a basic impersonation snippet. The Nanyo's processor compiled the code and fired a missile at the yellow shield. A nano-second later the shield pulsed and dropped for him. Internally, the server provided the correct credentials that gave Nyx access to the system and would ignore him afterward. The origin visualization core translated all of this for his optic nerves to process.

The cyberdefenses at HTA were notoriously lax. Nyx wondered if they'd given up on trying to block phantoms but bought enough security to keep the pranksters and the script kiddies out. Those groups would damage systems, deface digital property, and generally screw up everything. The professional phantoms got in, took what they needed, and most times cleaned up after themselves so nothing remained of their passage. Nyx added to the security grid on the occasion when a new script hit the forums, just to make sure the anarchists couldn't mess it up for the rest of them.

Nanyo systems built an excellent deck which Nyx admired more the more he used it. The keys were extremely quiet and sensitive, and the graphical processing flowed smoothly, not giving the user the experience of riding down a bumpy road like the cheaper decks did. His old Sparlow had been top of the line two years ago which made it ancient in tech terms.

A few keystrokes later, the interface formed a list of options. The layout and usability astounded Nyx as he flipped to the drone list, locating one near the Regal. A few more commands and a window opened with the view from the HTA bot's camera. A virtual control appeared before him, allowing him to drive the drone through the skies over Hub, though not high enough that he'd hit the shield. The Nanyo fed Gelsey's coordinates to him as he maneuvered, so he could track Gelsey and the Fortress's micro drone.

Nyx set the autopilot and jumped back into cyberspace. He gathered a couple of scripts and fired them off to destinations. These would establish routes for later on. He hadn't taken the time yet to pull together all the back doors and escape routes he'd need if the job spiraled sideways.

A beep sounded, and he jumped back into the drone control SIM. It took a minute to locate the floating micro drone since the pixie had engaged her chameleon suit. The Fortress sent the activation signal moments after she deposited it on the top of a nondescript building a kilometer from the Regal. The drone lifted off, heading toward its home base. Nyx followed at a safe distance, not wanting to give the Fortress anything to be concerned about.

The return trip took about ten minutes for the drone to reach its destination. As it crossed over the Fortress, the handles automatically released, dropping the controller onto the roof, where it bounced, coming to rest near the original, broken one. The HTA drone hovered out of range, and cameras zoomed in on the returned drone. A block rose out of the featureless rooftop. A door slid open, revealing four highly armed and armored guards. They moved out, taking up ordinal positions around the prone microdrone. Nyx recorded the scene; Lorcan would know more about the gear the troops wore. Scolly followed them out, carrying a clear box. When he reached the drone, he pulled a handheld scanner out and ran it over the drone. Nothing there, Scolly. He hadn't tampered with their precious bot.

It must have passed inspection since he placed it in the clear box. The guards fell into a diamond formation as they returned to the elevator. Once the rooftop emptied of the security goons, Nyx released the HTA drone and punched out.

Nyx grinned. "They took the drone. My guess is they'll sweep the area, looking for any anomalies, before returning to their standard security levels. In the morning I can try getting into the system." Nyx pulled the camera feed over to the Series Sixty for the team to review. "Lorcan, see what you can figure out, based on the guards' gear."

Silai stood up, startling Nyx as he ran through the data he'd scooped from the drone. "Scolly is pinging the connection you set up for Yvivra."

Aikila tapped on her controls. "I'll run it through here. Nyx, monitor the vid feed for anything useful."

"On it."

Silai faced the camera and collected herself before she said, "Yvivra Barkskin speaking."

"Miss Barkskin. I just wanted to thank you for returning our property intact. Your technician did an excellent job of repairing the antenna."

"I'll pass along the compliment."

Scolly's bared his teeth in a frightening approximation of a smile. "Please do. I see you are at the WeSee studios. I'd like to send over a small gift."

Silai tipped her head gently, a very Elven gesture that Nyx found odd in a dryad. Her face hadn't changed, but he felt like he'd missed something in the conversation. "Your thanks are gift enough. Is there anything else I can do for you? I'm trying to get a handle on the earlier situation."

The scary grin widened. "Yes, you can." The smile dropped. "You can die."

# GELSEY

With the run complete, Gelsey decided to survey the Fortress just in case Scolly and his boys came back up looking for the access device they'd left behind. She probably should find a place to perch and watch what Scolly did, but pixies fly, that's what they do.

The Sky Sharks ran perfectly. Gelsey was glad to know the Fortress' magic had messed them up and not some screw-up by the surgical teams. Pixies loved their wings, and removing her natural wings for cybernetic replacements had been a difficult decision. These new wings made all the sacrifices worth it. Even if Ancep never followed through on the rest of her payment, she'd be happy.

In full chameleon mode, she put the wings through their paces, diving, climbing, dropping, twisting, and an assortment of aerial stunts as she followed the slow-moving bot back to its base.

Could they do this heist with only a week to prepare and pull off the job? The whole area, not just the building, had been constructed to stop incursions. She admitted that they had gotten farther than she thought possible in such a short time. Silai pushed every button Mr. Scaly had and invented a few more to irritate him. The device Nyx needed sat in place, ready to exploit the internal systems. Lorcan had smashed her wings accidentally even before his upgrades, so there was no telling how strong he was now. Aikila could find just about any gear they needed, and Kelthar beat the Thrante at his own game. His organs sold off at the local chop shop for sure.

"Well, time to return to the roost." Gelsey popped up, zipping into the air. She paused when she spotted a larger drone emerge to hover over the Fortress, a black box affixed underneath. Four propellers, each larger than her, whirled as it gained altitude. "Interesting. What are we shipping out, shark face?"

The machine moved along, gaining speed. Curiosity killed many a pixie, but if they shipped out packages, there might be an opening that she could exploit. That drone could hide a diminutive thief for sure. *It's too good of an opportunity to pass up checking it out. I'm not curious at all.* No one answered, which at her current elevation, was to be expected.

She sped along in the machine's wake. Based on the current trajectory, it looked like it would lead out of the Terrace or to one of the lower levels, including the Quad and the Regal.

Nonsense. Hub was enormous, and the odds that old scaly had found them and dispatched a drone to their hideout defied logic. The drone increased its speed as it crossed into the Terrace before veering to the east, toward the Regal and, as she reminded herself, more than half of Hub. The drone rose higher, speed increasing again. Gelsey closed the distance, dread rising as she realized the box wasn't a delivery strapped to the bot; it was a bomb.

Once the drone hit its peak altitude, it dove, using gravity to increase its velocity. As soon as Gelsey pulled the area map up, she knew the target. WeSee Holovid Studio lay at the end of the run. She sped after the drone, unsure of what to do. If she disabled the drone, it would drop into the center of the Terrace. A hit to a refinery or a chemical shop would magnify the explosion by a factor of ten. An idea popped into her head as she sped to catch the racing bomb.

She matched its speed, realizing she only had a few seconds before she'd be too close to the blast. Gelsey aimed her zap gun at the straps that kept the bomb in place. The flare setting would deliver a burning hot cinder that might cut the straps. She fired a series of shots, forming a line across the first strap. The line glowed as the fire started, only to flicker out a moment later. It hadn't even scratched the surface. She flew up and over the drone, landing on its back, looking for a release. Nothing. The straps went into the carapace. If she couldn't cut them, she'd have to dismantle the drone to remove them.

The insistent beep of her proximity warning system chimed in her eardrum, alerting her that she was rapidly approaching the ground. She'd tried and failed. Her wings caught the wind and propelled her away from the impending blast. She turned and faced the building, setting her optics to record. The team needed to see what Scolly had done in response to them intruding on his domain.

The drone streaked downwards, its speed maximizing as it hit the windows on the western side of the building. A second later, all the windows in the five-story building blew out. Fire shot erupted in plumes before the building collapsed. Tears blurred the end of the recording as Gelsey wept for the people in the building. Hopefully, it was early enough that not many had shown up for work, but even one death was too many.

Time to make that damned trog pay for the lives he'd taken.

# AIKILA

Aikila watched the playback from Gelsey's feed, horror and dread mingling into a cocktail she'd not wish on anyone but her worst enemies. The same question repeated itself over and over. What were they hiding that they'd kill innocents to protect? All the local holovid had streams of the fire that "officials" claimed resulted from an underground gas leak. Powerful forces were at play that went deeper than protecting a gold-finding spell. Dragons never told you the whole truth, and figuring out which parts were lies was the real game.

The emergency crews used water and magic to contain the fire. Nyx sat cross-legged on the floor, deck in his lap, ignoring the situation. In one way, it irritated her to no end that he discounted the void, as he called it. On the other hand, he'd done his job so well that their target had destroyed a holovid studio instead of tracing the intrusion back to its actual source. They all owed Nyx their lives, not that she'd ever say so.

As if summoned, Nyx pulled the plug from his jack, carefully storing it in his deck. His eyes focused on the news stream over the table. "Wow, it's worse than I thought."

Gelsey flew toward him, her face so red Aikila worried she would burst into flames. "What the hell do you care? You checked out as soon as I told you what happened. All those people died because of us."

Nyx leaned away from the angry woman who, while small, had killed

R'gar, the orc prison guard. His eyes flashed around the room as if gauging the rest of the team.

Aikila noticed none of the others were as openly hostile as the pixie, but their body language echoed a similar sentiment. In a hurt tone, he replied. "I didn't 'check out,' I jacked into the holovid systems and entered Yvivra Barkskin's credentials into the logs so it looked like she was in the building and had been in the systems working on replacing the drone racers. I left a rabbit behind."

Lorcan looked puzzled. "A rabbit? Why would you be using animals while you're in cyberspace?"

With a roll of his eyes, he continued. "It refers to a rabbit snare that Old Earth hunters used to catch food. Can I continue?"

His arms across his chest, knees up, and with a surly tone, he'd slipped into full defense mode. Aikila couldn't leave it this way. "Nyx, please go on. We'll be quiet as you explain." She shot Gelsey a stern look, telling her to keep her mouth shut.

Gelsey pouted as she dropped down to sit on Lorcan's shoulder.

His eyes shifted between the two before he continued. "I left the rabbit to see if Scolly would send a phantom to verify Yvivra had been onsite. Right after I finished, the snare forwarded me an alert it had been triggered. I've got enough data to help me figure out what kind of tech staff he's got access to. The good news, if there is any, is that whoever he sent triggered the trap without knowing it."

Silai's expression was one of the hopelessly lost. "That's good because?"

"An experienced phantom would have found the trap and avoided it. I have an access scan running on the--"

Kelthar groaned. "Boyo, none of us are wireheads or phantoms or the like. You're losing us in the details."

"Oh, sorry." Nyx relaxed a bit, took a deep breath, and finished. "Whoever he sent isn't talented. Should make getting in a bit easier."

Aikila nodded. "We all have different skills and ways of doing our job. Let's not turn on each other. This is hard enough as it is." Agreement came from all of them, though Gelsey's blood was still up, and it took her longer. "So where do we stand?"

Gelsey buzzed over and perched on the edge of the Nanyo sixty series table. The backdrop of the burning building made it an odd sight. Lorcan moved to shadow the diminutive thief. "Well, we know they are ruthless bastards."

Silai walked to the bar on the other side of the room. She returned with a bottle of elvish wine and a tall spiral glass. She poured a measure, taking a long drink. "I hate to sound callous about the death of innocents, but we can use that in our favor. Scolly will overreact and that makes him vulnerable. I need to think on how to best to provoke him."

"Does that help you think?" Lorcan asked her, indicating the drink.

Aikila took note of how the warrior stood between Gelsey and Silai as if he expected the wine glass to attack her. Ever since he'd injured Gelsey, he'd become more…protective. Aikila stored that away for later, returning her focus to the events at hand.

Silai arched an eyebrow at him. "Why, yes, it does." She took another pull before refilling the glass and setting the bottle on the table next to Gelsey. She returned to her chair that she curled up in.

Aikila cut off any more judgmental comments from Lorcan. "What about the guards? Anything from their gear?"

"Yes." He leaned forward, tapping on his display. The images from earlier replaced the raging fire, and he zoomed in on the lead. "The insignia on his shoulder is the 12th Legion from Dulla."

"Aren't those the freaks that take their heads off?" Gelsey's high-pitched voice hit a new painful range of the sound spectrum. Lorcan and Aikila both winced, their new sensory network making it far shriller than it needed to be.

"Gelsey, please." Aikila rubbed her face in frustration. The stress of the night was taking its toll, but they had to push through. With only six days left, delays weren't an option.

Gelsey flushed with embarrassment. "Sorry."

Lorcan sighed. "That is a tale from Old Earth. It's not true." He rotated the image so the subjects' faces could be seen. "The dulla all have a gray pattern over their skin, not unlike my spots. They believe that they are born with their fates determined by the pattern. These are lesser warriors or they'd have not left their countrymen." He rotated the image so all four could be seen. "Two men and two women."

Kelthar approached the table, squinting. "Lad, how can you tell they are women?"

Gelsey giggled. "Been that long, Kelthar, that you can't remember?"

He laughed along with her. The mage had a talent for lightening the mood.

Aikila thanked the gods above for a break.

"I think I remember all right, but in all that armor, how can you tell?" Kelthar asked.

Lorcan enhanced the image until one took up the full view. "See the throat? The males cut the skin across their throats. Even though their heads are not removed, they like to perpetuate the myth."

The gray and white skin didn't have any scarring. "So, the women are smart enough to not mutilate themselves?"

Lorcan smirked at her. "You can look at it that way. I've found the women to be the more dangerous fighters among the dullahans." He pushed the focus back to include all four of them. "Gelsey, would you say it was hot last night?"

She kicked her legs back and forth, rocking on the edge of the table. "No. In fact, it was a bit chilly last night."

Silai cocked her head. "Why would that matter?" She took another drink as she watched Lorcan.

He didn't mention the drink again. "They are sweating. They don't do well in the heat."

*Interesting.* Aikila felt the beginnings of a plan forming in her head. "Kelthar, what do the magical defenses look like?"

Kelthar stood in front of his chair, which lowered, allowing him to sit. Aikila wondered if the tennin mage could fly or was that another myth left over from the folklore of Old Earth? Only in Hub did the various races mingle to any degree. You never knew what abilities your opponent actually had.

Kelthar's ears wiggled as he collected his thoughts. "Quite a bit and that's only on the outside. I spoke of the hex spell that interrupted Gelsey's wings. The amulet detected a lot more, though fortunately, she didn't trip those wards." He took a deep breath and plunged in. "There is something else I need to bring up. I know the Sorceress who crafted these spells, and she is formidable."

Aikila didn't like the sound of that, not at all. "How well do you know her?"

"Far too well. She's my ex-wife."

# NYX

It was early morning by the time the team had reviewed the system crash and news of Kelthar's ex-wife working for the Fortress. Nyx needed to escape the void. After the lengthy discussion on the impact that these realities had on their job, everyone dispersed to get some sleep. The others thought he'd jacked in, so they left him sitting in the living area. The dragon had searched their rooms while they were unconscious, so Nyx had stashed his goods out here. Once he was sure he was alone, he went to the bar, and reached under the counter to where he'd affixed his stash. Nothing. He moved his hand around frantically searching for the drugs he's secured there.

"Looking for these?" Gelsey asked, holding up a strip of derms Nyx had acquired before coming to the first meeting.

"Those are mine." They contained Diethylpropion Hydrochloride, what they called Zombie Rush on the street. Phantoms used it to stay awake for days on end so they could pull off major hacks. Most claimed it made them more responsive in the origin. You crashed hard, but it was the price you paid to be a legend. "It helps me ride the cyber better."

Gelsey, floating in midair, tapped her foot as if she stood on something solid. "I would think your upgraded neural system would be enough. This will rot the few brains you've got left."

His anger flared, causing his face to flush. "What's it to you? As long as we get this job done, who cares what I do?"

"In case you forgot, I saved your broken ass from the grafted gorilla before he sold you for parts." She hovered near him but still safely out of arm's reach. "You don't need this, but we need you. If you don't crack the security, we all die."

Nyx slammed the drawer shut. "It's none of your business."

Aikila's voice came from across the room. "It's *all* of our business." She stepped out from the hallway wearing a form-hugging sleep suit. Nyx found his temper dropping as his eyes fought to stay focused on her face. Aikila closed the distance between them, her mesmerizing eyes locked on his. "Nyx, you don't need the derms. They are a crutch that holds you back. Without them, you'll be a legend."

"No, I need them," Nyx whispered.

"You don't. Listen to me and understand they are killing you," Aikila said.

Nyx tried to fight; tell her she was wrong. All the reasons slipped away as he stared into her eyes.

"You don't need the drugs, Nyx," Aikila said again.

She made sense. He didn't need the drugs messing up his system, especially with the new wetware installed. "You're right." Her eyes were a beautiful white and filled his vision. "I don't need them. Thank you, Aikila."

"You need to sleep. Go to bed. I need you to access the Fortress's systems in the morning."

Nyx tried to make it to his room, but it was too far away. His brain lay under the soft blanket of Aikila's words. He settled on the floor and slept.

⸻ ⋅◈⋅ ⸻

"Nyx, you awake?"

No, he wasn't. Why was there someone in his room? He cracked his eyes and sat straight up. Silai had a cup of tea in her hands. They were in the main room of the Regal. How had he fallen asleep out here?

Silai handed him the warm mug. "Here, drink this. Aikila wants you to see if you can access the Fortress's systems. Lorcan is out with her now."

Aikila. She'd spoken to him last night. Gelsey had taken the derms. It didn't matter anymore. He'd done his last hit of Zombie Rush. Didn't need it. He must have dozed off after his talk with Aikila. Everything around that time felt unfocused. He drank some tea, the warmth rejuvenated his tired mind.

Silai came through the kitchen doors. The only thing that mattered was the run against the Fortress. They'd have a military-grade DISCS running the anti-intrusion systems. Today he'd cross the line into legend, the only phantom to ever breach an unconnected AI. Finishing off the tea, he showered and put on clean clothes. For some reason, he didn't want Aikila to see him looking sleep-rumpled with jacked-up hair.

After retrieving his deck, he settled into one of the large chairs near the bar. He jacked into cyberspace, heading for the Black Carbon. He switched his profile to anonymous, throwing up a series of baffle programs that would defend him from probes and viruses that other phantoms used to steal from the unprepared.

The outside of the Black Carbon resembled an ancient stone temple. Carved lions stood sentry by the door, their mouths open. A quick twitch and his credentials fell into the waiting mouth. The eyes flashed green and the doorway spun with colored lights. He stepped through into an infinite warehouse. He keyed the address. The first priority was to obtain a cracker and some additional tools for the run.

The room blurred and he appeared inside an old-time pawn shop. Oddities of all shapes and sizes sat in glass cases waiting to be purchased. A wave of the hand brought up the details of each piece and the price. The last of Oot's glint, stolen back from that damn halfling, would cover today's run. He should have gotten glint from Aikila but he took perverse pleasure knowing that he used the ogre's stash instead.

The first case held a wide variety of cutters: programs to disable a range of ICE and DISCS bots. He'd written his own cutters that far outpaced the garden variety that the Black Carbon carried. He moved down the line past rows of ICE breakers, line tracers, rabbits, skunks, and other miscellaneous hacker tricks. The back counter held what he'd been looking for.

His system registered layers of interwoven security protocols around the case. A Nova bomb hung overhead as a warning not to tamper with the security. The bomb would flatline anyone in the immediate vicinity, killing the phantom as well as protecting the goods. Nasty stuff, but necessary when you dealt with the hacker community.

The display case held a bunch of one-of-a-kind tricks. A seashell read as a proxy overwrite control that could be configured to rewrite an entire network. Useful, though not for this run. The next piece resembled a toy drum painted in garish day-glow orange and red stripes. Details popped up in front of Nyx: a Maxalin level-five virus guaranteed to penetrate any DISCS, with Directed Intelligence Synchronized Combinatorial Systems in parenthesis so the noobs would know what it was. Maxalin gave the user control of the host systems which was a useful tool to have. He clicked it and saw half of Oot's glint vanish from the account. The last piece resembled a toy hovercraft. The Castor Logic bomb it held would decimate an entire system. He started to pass when the image of the fire at WeSee flared in front of his eyes. He accepted the purchase and exited the Black Carbon to the confines of the digital arcade.

The flashing lights and noise hit him like a hammer after the dim confines of the store. A few clicks and he transferred to the origin. He keyed the address of the controller he'd activated on his last run. The glowing green circle hovered over nothing, as he'd expected. He launched a scan that returned four open ports. A probe ran down, opening a door into the Fortress's systems.

Nyx sent off a series of probes to query the attached systems, collecting authentication details from the various nodes and logging them for later review. *Goldmine!* One of the nodes had the data that ran the DISCS. He threw baffles up and sped across the network to the node. The door held a series of locks which, in reality, were authentication gates, but the deck used everyday items to represent abstracts in the origin. He released the code-breaker software that ran against the locks, retrieving the passwords without triggering the security protocols. Within a second, he'd entered the room which housed the data store. A bot appeared and started downloading data as he ran scripts to keep the DISCS unaware of his presence.

At fifty-two percent complete, a red skull, representing an elimination program, entered the room from the other side, headed directly for Nyx's phantom form. If it touched him, he'd be detained or possibly flatlined depending on the system parameters. After the WeSee bombing, he guessed the later. A series of delay-command scripts turned it slightly but didn't deter it like it should have.

Another skull arrived and Nyx realized he couldn't wait on the bot to finish. He collapsed it, dropped a virus that would eliminate his ghost, and forwarded the security admin a report that an abnormality in the data had been corrected. Nyx backed out the way he'd come in, set the rooftop controller to sleep, and re-entered his body in the Regal. He'd been gone less than five minutes and had sixty-eight percent of the data from the Fortress stored on his deck.

Now the fun began—looking for a hole in the Fortress's defenses.

3 6

# KELTHAR

Kelthar sat in his usual seat at the table. Nyx, having penetrated the Fortress, had the team buzzing with excitement. He wished he shared their confidence. Knowing Litri had designed the spell defenses made him wary. He'd trained with her and their skills were comparable, though she'd traveled the path of the sorcerers, whereas he had gone down the mage path. She would be stronger in specific areas, while he had a wider array to pick from.

He wouldn't tell the team that the easiest way to defeat her would be to kill her outright. Anchored spells would still function, but any active spells would fail once she died. While he didn't much care for her or the choices she'd made over the long years since their divorce, he wouldn't harm her directly.

Aikila cleared her throat. "We have five days to pull off this job and I intend to complete it and get the hell out of here."

The others indicated their agreement.

She continued. "Without an entry point, we are as good as done."

Gelsey's wings twitched with nervous energy. She'd been on surveillance of the Fortress since Nyx had hacked into the systems that morning. Reatrix reached its zenith, marking the passage of one day into the next. "The Fortress's security goons found the controller, so Nyx can't hack back in."

Lorcan stood off to the side, next to Gelsey. His tail swished back and

159

forth as if pacing, though the rest of him stayed still. "They will be expecting us. The security will be much higher."

"No, they won't," Nyx said from his seat on the floor. He leaned against the wood-paneled wall as he worked his deck. "The controller had a proximity sensor. As soon as scaly boy got close to it, the internals melted. All he found was a collapsed polymer casing which happens to be the same material as the drones we crashed into them."

Aikila smirked. She'd made sure that all the parts from round one of her plan would be useless to determine what they'd been up to. "He's right. They can examine it carefully, and the best they'll find are parts consistent with a racing drone."

Kelthar glanced over at Silai, who sat in the corner, wine glass in one hand, empty bottle in the other. The dryad seemed to have retreated into her shell since the bombing of the WeSee building. He'd known con artists over his years and they, to a fault, didn't want a body count. He'd keep an eye on her, and from the way Aikila kept glancing at her, she would as well.

Gelsey chortled, doing a little flip. "Serves the bastards right." She spun around in the air, obviously enjoying her new wings. "We'll pay them back tenfold."

Silai took another drink from her glass.

"You aren't going to find an answer at the bottom of that glass, Silai," Kelthar said as gently as possible. "What happened wasn't our fault. The best thing will be to steal that scroll and let Clan Koxalan punish the head of security for his failure."

Silai's stare could have frozen water at fifty meters. "Even more blood on my hands."

"The problem is we need you. If you can't get past this, you'll have to leave," Aikila said as she caught Kelthar's eye, and he caught on that he would be the kind squid, while she was the hard-assed squid. "All of us have to be all in. In or out?"

Kelthar sighed. "Give her a couple of days, Aikila." Kelthar's gaze swept the room but the others were staying out of it. "Dryads are a sensitive race. She'll get it together."

Aikila rounded on the mage. "We don't have time. You have to choose now. Anyone wants out, go! Ancep can do what he wants with you later."

Kelthar groaned, putting his hand over his mouth, to cover the grin he couldn't squelch. Aikila played her role well.

"I'm in," Silai said, standing up. "Gelsey's right, we need to pay them back. There isn't any other way."

Whatever Ancep had on Silai had to be extremely significant. You didn't come around that fast unless she'd been faking her grief, which he didn't believe to be true. The people in this room were hostages to the dragon, and nothing would change that.

Would finishing the job be enough for Ancep to release them? He dropped that line of thought for now. No sense in borrowing trouble that might not come to pass.

Aikila nodded. "Anyone else have an issue?" When no one spoke, she continued. "Nyx, anything interesting in the data you pulled?"

The display over the table lit with a video feed. "This is one of the few camera feeds I managed to get."

A DelvSafe transport approached the building on the road that led through the gardens to the back of the building. From the camera's vantage, the transport disappeared behind the building. The time-lapse jumped forty-five minutes, and the transport drove out again.

"So they do get deliveries," Lorcan said absently as he studied the scene. "How often do those deliveries get made?"

"I didn't get any data from the Fortress on it." The elf punched up a new window next to the loop of the transport delivery. "DelvSafe's systems, however, could be cracked by a hopped-up korrigan with a spoon."

Kelthar chuckled. For a wirehead, Nyx had a streak of a showman, or maybe show off. He'd have made a good street mage.

"I pulled their delivery schedule and the transport in the holovid isn't on it. Imagine that." He tapped the keys again and a red screen appeared under the original schedule. "That transport is used only to deliver to the Fortress."

"Handy to have your own vehicle to ensure proper service," Aikila said as she read down the list. "The next delivery is in three days. That means we can start the job, return, and meet the dragon, with two days to spare."

"Does it have specific drivers assigned?" Silai asked. Her energy had changed now that they were planning the job. The gleam in her eye as she worked through what she'd need to do to pull it off.

Nyx beamed. "Great question, Silai. There are two." With a few clicks, two pictures floated above the table. One, a squid in uniform, red cording to indicate his allegiance to Clan Koxalan. The other was a woman who looked similar to Mystic. Kelthar spared a second to wonder how Mystic fared before pushing it aside to listen to Nyx.

"The squid is named Madorius of Clan Koxalan; the other is a Svartan woman named Elra. They are the only two allowed into the Fortress."

Silai studied the images. "I'll need full backgrounds, documents, and sound samples of their voices, if possible." Her hand reached out, rotating the figures back and forth. She turned to Aikila. "You'll need to be the Svartan woman."

Aikila smirked. "You're going to impersonate a male squid?"

Silai didn't appear to be listening. "I'll need to make some purchases, but it can be done."

Kelthar arched an eyebrow, but he'd seen stranger things than a dryad impersonating a squid. Working with the elemental forces changed your perspective on what was possible. He rather liked Silai and figured she'd not take on something she couldn't handle.

"I've sent what I have to your display." Nyx pulled the schematics of the transport up. "This thing is a rolling sensor array. The Fortress has nearly every monitoring system available installed so they can verify the shipment contents. I've never seen anything like it."

Neither had Kelthar. All of this security to protect a spell to seek gold felt wrong. Ancep had something up his sleeve and the more they dug into this job, the more convinced he was of it. He'd unsuccessfully tried a divination spell to find the truth of the situation. His auguries portended indeterminate lies and despair, but anyone with eyes could see that much.

Gelsey spun around the display. "What are they delivering? Anything we can steal?"

Nyx grunted. "Looks like crates of food and some equipment. The transport will be full."

Aikila had a smile on her face. "We've got our opening. Nyx, how many guards are in the Fortress?"

"From the records I got, six. I didn't get the full shot, so there might be more. I wish I'd had another second to finish the transfer."

The scowl on the elf's face betrayed how upset he was that he'd had to cut and run. Nyx hated that the system had bested him. Kelthar wondered if the second match would go better for Nyx. If he couldn't shut down the security systems, it would be a very short trip.

"Gelsey, I sent the building's physical plans to your display. It's current as of last month. Lorcan, you've got the manifests for supplies. You or Aikila will know better what is important." Nyx looked at Kelthar. "I have no gashing idea what you need, Sir Mage."

Kelthar laughed uneasily. Neither did he.

# LORCAN

The next few days flew by in a whirlwind of activity as the members of the team prepared for their parts of the job. Lorcan took over as the tactical lead for the run. His combat experience made him the natural choice. They practiced the steps, over and over, until everyone knew everyone else's parts as well as their own. Everyone switched roles and ran through it to ensure they could seamlessly implement it.

All the planning and practice had led to this morning. The DelvSafe hovercraft would be here in three minutes. The team had to be back on the road within eight minutes to ensure they arrived at the prescribed time. For a seasoned squad of soldiers, it would be an aggressive timetable. For six strangers with three days to plan, it was nearly impossible, but it had to work. He would save his daughter at any cost.

Gelsey flew through the upper window of the warehouse where the team waited. Aikila had rigged explosives on the road outside to force the transport to stop. Lorcan hoped she was up to the task. An experienced heavy ordinance expert would have a tough time stopping a moving vehicle without damage.

Gelsey landed on Lorcan's shoulder. "The transport will be here in about twenty seconds."

"Get to your places." Silai and Aikila moved to the back of the room.

The dryad delivered on her promise; both women were exact duplicates of the drivers. Their own mothers couldn't have told them apart.

Lorcan readied the stun cannon he'd gotten from Gipes. The goblin was obnoxious, but his selection was outstanding. Nyx and Kelthar held the handles of the bay doors ready to slide them apart once the explosives detonated. Lorcan counted it down for the others.

The explosion went off and the warehouse doors slid open. The squid had just climbed out of the passenger door when the blast from the stunner hit him in the sternum. He crumpled to the ground. The Svartan woman rolled under the second blast, making a break for it. Kelthar stepped out, gestured sharply, and said an unintelligible word. The woman fell to the ground as if poleaxed.

Aikila ran for the transport as Lorcan pulled the debris out from under the hovercraft's front grill. The explosives had fired rods into the underside fans, immobilizing them. The sudden loss of the front-end lift stopped the vehicle without visible damage. A pair of bolt cutters freed the transport so that Aikila could pilot it into the waiting bay.

Kelthar pulled the unconscious woman in behind him after levitating her a few centimeters off the ground, making his job easier than Lorcan who pulled the heavy squid into the small room that they'd set up to hold the drivers. Gelsey removed all their possessions before she slapped sleeping derms on both of them that should wear off in twelve hours. Lorcan cuffed the squid just to make sure he wouldn't go anywhere.

Aikila parked the transport next to the loading dock where a specially prepared container sat waiting to be put in the hovercraft. Lorcan tugged the freight lift over and moved enough crates to make room for theirs. He settled the massive box into its new location and then packed around it. The front of the crate opened to allow enough room for the team to sit, though it was a tight fit.

Nyx unbolted the transport's panel to replace the sensory chip that he'd built. Everything was perfect with the hovercraft as far as the Fortress would be able to tell.

"Two minutes!" Silai yelled as she stood at the warehouse door. "We've got to go."

Lorcan climbed into the container while Nyx battened down the panel hatch. Gelsey zipped in. Kelthar sat on a small box. Nyx got in last, giving Aikila the thumbs up as she closed the container's false front before pulling down the transport's cargo door. Nyx settled himself on the floor before the transport lurched forward.

They stopped again while Silai closed the warehouse doors and engaged the locks. No sense in having someone stumble upon the unconscious guards before they completed their job. "Thirty seconds to spare," Aikila's voice came over their comms. The micro-pore tape kept the comms hidden behind the ear. "Silai called in a delay per plan. We are on target for arrival."

Lorcan let out his breath. The first steps of a plan were always the most stressful. Too many variables to account for, but they'd held together and were on the way. A good sign if there was one in this job. He forced the image of his Jaana out of his head. No distractions today.

Kelthar chuckled. "This sounds like a bad joke. An elf, a nagual, a pixie, and a tennin walk into a box." They'd installed a small light so as to not ride in complete darkness. The mage's grin was plainly visible. Lorcan wondered if he was that relaxed or that crazy. His glint was on crazy; magic tended to fry the brains of the user.

Gelsey giggled as she perched next to Nyx. Lorcan kept his eyes on her. Since he'd crushed her wings, he'd become her defacto bodyguard, though Gelsey could handle herself. His shame wouldn't allow him to stop. In another life, she'd be a good companion to have. The pixie's indomitable spirit and independent streak a kilometer wide were a welcome diversion from brooding over his circumstances. She flew headlong into danger and came out the other end smiling.

Deck propped on his lap, Nyx jacked in, erasing any trail that would lead back to where the transport had been taken. His fingers flew across the board as he worked. Kelthar pulled items from his bag, laying them out as he spoke soft words over them. Of all the pieces of this job, Lorcan worried the most about the mage's ability to handle the magic that protected the treasures of the Fortress. A facility that big and heavily guarded hadn't been constructed to defend a single scroll. The fact that they'd killed all those WeSee employees to protect the secrets within spoke volumes.

"Lorcan, I've got a bad feeling about all this," Gelsey said, as she settled on his shoulder. "Do you think we can do this?"

He considered the question for a second before answering. "There are things being kept from us about why we're doing the job, but if anyone could pull it off it's the six of us."

Lorcan couldn't see her though he heard the sigh of relief. "Thanks. I hate working for dragons. They never tell you the whole truth and what they leave out can get you killed."

He snorted in amusement. "You aren't wrong, little one. If we stick together, we should make it through." Lorcan didn't have friends. After his wife had died, taking care of his daughter had become his whole life. Would having friends have helped him come up with a better way to pay off the clinic than the one that got Jaana taken hostage? The past casts shadows that no one can see through, his father always said. "If things go bad, you get yourself to safety. No coming back for me. Understood?"

She lightly punched his neck. "You aren't getting away from me that easily, kitty."

The mage gathered his gear, taking his time to pack everything away. He caught Lorcan's eye as he looked up. "Lots of bad juju in this bag if things go sideways. I'm hoping we don't need to resort to drastic measures."

"You and me both," Lorcan agreed. "Since Nyx found the bay the scroll is housed in, we won't have to waste time looking for it. Hopefully, that means less chance of setting off the alarms."

"Let's hope so. I'd rather be on a warm beach than in the ground. As soon as we're done, I'm headed south to the tropics. This old body's been in Hub for far too long. Will you return to the pride?"

Lorcan suppressed everything besides the job. His carefully constructed screen broke with the question. "Maybe. Might be time to settle down and raise my daughter among our people. I thought leaving to be the better choice, but now I just don't know. I feel like I need to settle the score with the scum that held her for ransom. I'll think on it if we survive the day."

"Fair enough."

For once, Kelthar didn't have a smile on his face. The pressure had everyone on edge. Sitting idle grated on the merc's nerves, and he longed for action since that would mean they were that much closer to finishing the mission.

Nyx's head came up sharply. "We're there."

Lorcan grunted. "Good. Get ready to move."

The elf's eyes were wide. "Our arrival has triggered an alarm with the Fortress guards. Do we abort?"

"No. We'll deal with the trouble we've got." He cracked his neck, loosening up. "Stay close."

Lorcan heard the cargo door open. It was go time.

# 38

## SILAI

**B**uildings flew by as Silai stared out the window. Aikila deftly piloted the hovercraft through the busy streets. All the paperwork was in order, so they passed through the checkpoint at the base of the Bluffs without issue. This level of Hub held the mansions and high rises of the rich and powerful. After years of working the system, this section felt more like home than the Quad ever would. Silai belonged more to the thieves, whores, and delinquents than the upper echelon who lived here. In reality, the residents up here were just better thieves with more glint.

Their route drove past Lucrea's building where he'd uncovered the fake statue. He had had every right to be angry, but she was profoundly glad he hadn't been. Especially after seeing him handle the warlock. The truly powerful didn't need to make examples or torment those below them to convince themselves that they are worthy.

Aikila steered through the last turn toward the Fortress. "Does my makeup look right?" The skin-darkening pigment would take a couple of days to fully leave her system. The ears, nose, and brows could be removed with a bit of rubbing alcohol.

"You are Elra's twin. Her mother couldn't tell it wasn't her." She smiled at Aikila until she realized what a grotesque sight that would be since she'd transformed into a squid. The expression on the other woman's face confirmed her suspicions. "Sorry, forgot my current appearance."

Aikila laughed. "I'd never have believed that you could make yourself into a squid, but you certainly did. No wonder Ancep wanted you on the job."

She looked away, not wanting to lie. The team had treated her as an equal, though they thought her a dryad. If they knew the truth, things would be different. Gelsey was aware, and that hadn't caused any issues, but the pixie floated through life without many cares. Keeping her true identity secret was necessary. Funny how she lied to her rich marks with ease but worried about being honest with thieves.

The Fortress came into view. The hulking menace of the place set her nerves twitching with anxiety. What she wouldn't give for a straight-up con with no one's life in the balance.

"You ready, Madorius?" Aikila asked, forcing her voice into the lower registers, trying and failing to mimic the Svartan guard. If the guards questioned Aikila, it might go bad.

"Let's go. I'll do the talking, just follow my lead." She depressed the button that signaled their arrival at the facility. The interior alarm started to go off, a blaring siren as they pulled up to the blast door that housed the loading dock. The door rose and four guards emerged, rifles leveled at the transport. They moved in tandem until two guards covered each of the drivers.

"Get out!" the lead guard yelled, his gun never wavering as it pointed at Silai.

This wasn't part of the plan. Both women stepped out of the hovercraft and away from the vehicle, Aikila effecting a severe limp. A squat Dwarf with a long beard ran in shortly after they had been moved far enough away. He carried a deck that looked similar to Nyx's rig. The security lead left Silai alone with the Dullan guard. She was unsure if this was a man or a woman because she couldn't see its neck with the long blast shield down. According to Lorcan, the males ritually cut the skin on their throats.

The dwarf climbed into the transport and opened the panel that Nyx had rigged. Silai's heart stopped. When he found the new chip, he'd guess they were up to something and the crew in the back wouldn't stand a chance against the assembled guards.

"Found it!" the dwarf yelled as he emerged, holding a piece of something white in his hand. "Shorted out the thermoelectric cooler. Whole panel overheated. Put a new one in and scanned the rig. She's clean."

Taking the piece from the tech, the leader studied it. "You sure that nothing's been tampered with?"

"As sure as I know you wouldn't have any idea which end of that to plug in." He took the piece, muttering about working with idiots while he returned to the Fortress.

Weapons lowered as the all-clear sounded. One of the guards on Aikila's side motioned for her to back the transport into the loading dock. She climbed in, a scowl on her face as befitting the nature of the driver she impersonated. Nothing out of the ordinary here.

Aikila backed the transport in without incident while Silai stood, arms crossed, an irritated scowl plastered on her dragon face. The Fortress guards gave her a wide birth; nobody ever worried when a dryad scowled. This form might be useful in another job, a piece of information she stashed away for later. She followed the guards to the dock, watching for subtle cues about what they expected. They paused at the cargo door, glancing at her.

Silai strode to the rear of the hovercraft, unlatched the locks, and opened the back, exposing the crates within. Aikila had stayed in the driver's seat per the plan.

"Why isn't Elra unloading?" the lead guard asked, blast rifle raising slightly as he waited for an answer.

Silai growled, causing the guards to step away from her. Upsetting squids didn't tend to extend your life expectancy. "Stupid bitch dropped a crate on her leg while she loaded the transport. Doubt she'd be much use."

The lead guard motioned for one of the others to go check. He found the patched-up wound under a torn pants leg. Silai had included a small air bladder filled with blood that would squirt if they yanked the covering off.

"Ugh, that's disgusting," came from the driver's side of the hovercraft. The guard returned with blood splattered over his armor. He'd had his blast shield up from the looks of the blood dripping from under it. "Torn up good, sir. A wonder she can walk on it."

"She doesn't need to walk, just pilot the damn transport. Get your guards and unload it yourself."

A new voice came from behind her. "Madorius, if your partner can't work, you'll have to do it. My guards aren't hired labor."

Scolly joined the party. Silai straightened, turning to face the troglodyte head of security. She kept her face still, betraying no emotion.

"You presume to tell me to unload cargo?" When in doubt, play it arrogant with dragons.

Scolly scoffed and pulled a strip of derms out of his pocket. "You talk tough but without your Nitro, you'll be mewling around on the floor licking my boots. Get the cargo unloaded before I 'lose' your payment."

Wonderful. The files hadn't mentioned Madorius was an addict. "Fine," she snarled at him. Scolly laughed, his guards joining in. She gathered this wasn't the first time they'd tormented the squid by threatening to withhold his drugs. Silai spotted a pneumatic pallet jack off to the side. She released the locks, raised the tines, and rolled it over to remove the first box off the transport.

"Now, Madorius, you know the cargo goes in the green area. Let's not get sloppy." Peals of laughter rang out as she turned the jack and took it to the indicated area. Reversing the controls, she returned for the next load.

"Oh, I'm so forgetful. You had it in the right place before."

This was getting old. She returned to the first load and returned it back to the dock. The second crate contained the team. Moving the jack into place, she froze as she realized it didn't have the raised bed that allowed the tines to fit under to lift it. She maneuvered to the left and took the next stack.

"What is in that large crate?" Scolly asked as he walked over and banged on it. "This isn't from our usual vendor." The guard's rifles pointed at the container, fingers hovering over triggers.

Silai reached into her pocket, praying to every god she could think of that Nyx had covered this eventuality. "How would I know?" She tossed the stick containing the shipping manifest to the troglodyte. "Check the document and let me unload."

Scolly caught the stick, inserting it into a pocket viewer on his belt. "Hmmm. Pixombu Security Server. Freaking wirehead spends more than any ten people combined. Unload the rest."

He focused on the manifest as Silai rolled up to the container she couldn't unload, placing the jack in front of the oversized crate. If she was really a squid, she'd have been able to lift the crate through brute force, but just because she looked like someone didn't mean she got their abilities. She stepped into the transport and moved behind the container. "I could use some help."

Putting her shoulder into the container, she pushed with all her might and it didn't budge. She really wished she had a weapon as a last resort if she couldn't get the crate into the green-marked area. Slowly, the crate rose a couple of millimeters off the metal transport floor. She silently thanked Kelthar. With apparent effort, she slid the crate onto the jack. Quickly, she placed it next to the rest of the supplies, with the door facing a computer access port Nyx needed.

The rest of the cargo unloaded far faster and she finished. Scolly stood to the side, arms crossed. "I should hold on to this to make sure you understand who's boss around here."

"Sorry, won't happen again," she said, stammering out the last word as if her Nitro was wearing off. Scolly cocked his head, clearly waiting for something. "Sco--Sir." Silai caught herself before she called him Scolly.

The crocodile mouth approximated a smile as he tossed the derms to her.

He hadn't noticed the slip; the derms disappeared into her pocket. "Thank you, sir."

"See that you don't forget it." Scolly waved his hand, dismissing her. Turning on her heel, Silai crossed to the transport and closed the cargo door before getting into the hovercraft.

Aikila started the engine, and the craft lifted smoothly off the floor. They drove out and back the way they had come. "How did it go?"

"It's done. I just hope the rest have better luck than I did. Almost called him Scolly."

Aikila whistled. "That would have been a disaster."

She hoped that was the worst thing to happen, but deep down she knew it wouldn't be.

# 39

# GELSEY

Lorcan sat next to where Gelsey floated. The big cat had followed her around like her pet since her wings had been repaired. That bothered her, as she always worked alone. Did he think she needed his protection? Gelsey had been on her own in a world where everyone was larger and yet she still came out on top.

This whole job stretched what little patience she had. What did these mudders know about breaking and entering, avoiding motion detectors, and disarming needle traps? The list went on and on. Still with the security systems, guards, and magic wards, she'd probably be glad to have them along.

Nyx had wired a nanolead on the outside of the container so he could see and hear what happened while they sat in what might end up being their coffin if things went bad. The guards did what was expected, though Scolly showing up hadn't been part of the plan. At least he'd left once the van had.

Nyx smiled. "She did great. I can jack into the port and get to breaking their security."

Time dragged as the guards tallied the inventory. Gelsey buzzed around, nerves fraying around the edges. Lorcan looked like he might explode from the forced inactivity.

Kelthar had repacked his bag before closing his eyes and softly humming to himself. Gelsey had seen him do this before, mostly after using his magic. She thought of it as his recharging time, like a battery that had to be plugged in to recharge. Of course, Kelthar said he was very old, so maybe it worked well enough for him.

The guards left via the reinforced security door that was the only entry into the Fortress. This was farther than anyone else had ever penetrated before. That they knew of. If they pulled this off two days ahead of Ancep's schedule, it would be truly impressive.

"You ready?" Lorcan asked her.

She nodded. "Piece of cake." Gelsey pulled the hood of her chameleon suit over her head, putting her wings into silent mode. She opened the tiny door they'd concealed in the side of the crate. No guards had stayed behind, which was good. She flew over to the port and set the miniature jack in the socket. Once the device was out of her hands and returned to its normal size, she retreated to the container.

"Nyx, you should be good to go."

He nodded, fired up his deck, and punched the silver stud. His fingers tapped at the board. A minute later he said, "I'm in. The cameras are cycling a clean loop. Time for you to go get the scroll."

Lorcan opened the front of the crate, hoisting his stunner. Why he wouldn't use a Pulsar or a bolt thrower or something lethal Gelsey didn't know. He was a merc, for Zuldione's sake. The big cat stood up and stretched, warily scanning the area, rifle at the ready.

Gelsey followed him out with Kelthar right behind her. The mage held two small glowing orbs the size of marbles. He closed the door, leaving Nyx to his assignment. They had twenty minutes to get in, grab the scroll, and get back here. Aikila and Silai would wait nearby to drive them to the hideout. *If* they got out, she amended in her head.

She punched the acceleration on her wings and headed toward the door at full speed. She hovered by the locking mechanism. Most doors in secure facilities had both a mechanical and an electronic portion to stop people like Nyx from popping all the locks. The mudders relied too heavily on electronic gadgets to keep them safe when quality physical hardware deterred thieves of lesser skill. Anyone could buy an EMP charge, fry the security devices, and open the door, but it took a professional to open a lock and leave it intact. She grew to her normal size, making it easier to pick it.

Kelthar chuckled. "Never seen you at your larger size before. Good thing that suit grows with you."

She ignored him as she got her tools out and set to work. She affixed a 'trode to the door, watching the meter set in the face of the scanner. After a couple of seconds, the meter dropped to zero, and the alarms were off. Nyx had gotten in. One more win in their column. She inserted a lever and pick, fishing for the tumblers on the inside of the lock.

"Damn," she swore. These were hardened locks; the picks didn't move the internals. Sliding the picks back into the case, she pulled out a torque pick and tried it next. Solid metal pins extended and retracted until the sequence matched correctly. It was worth every glint she'd paid for it. Aikila had bought everyone else's gear, but Gelsey already had everything she needed to do her job, though she'd let Aikila buy her a new fléchette pistol. The lights on the torque's handle strobed until they all showed green, interrupting her vision of shooting Ancep with the pistol he'd paid for. A quick twist and the lock popped, but the door didn't budge.

"Why isn't it opening?" Lorcan asked as he glanced about the loading dock. The odds of anyone coming through the reinforced blast doors that served as the entry into the Fortress were minuscule until it happened. Better to be prepared for the worst than experience it.

"It's got a floor lock." She grabbed a cylinder, coaxing an ultra-thin wire from it. The wire slid under the door smoothly until it reached the restraining bolt. She moved the wire back and forth, cutting through the bolt until the wire came free. Gelsey placed the tools in their proper spots before she resumed her smaller size.

Lorcan pushed the door open, checking for guards as they snuck down the hall. Gelsey shot off ahead to scout, staying near the ceilings where the chance of being detected would be minimal. "Hang back. Let me see what's ahead."

His voice came back strong and clear. "No risks. I need you safe. We do this by the numbers."

Leave it to the merc to ruin all her fun. Nyx hadn't triggered the comms yet, so as far as they knew, the security systems were still active. Guards might not see her with the chameleon suit on, but infrared and heat sensors would, even with the dampening effects of the suit. The hall remained clear of guards and devices. She reached the corner and froze, spotting a full array of sensors and another locked door. She backtracked to avoid detection.

"We've got eyes down here, and from the looks of it, all the security is still up. I'm headed back." How long did it take to drop the security systems? Every second that ticked away was one less that they had to get the scroll and get out. This would have been easier if she could have used the ventilation ducts to access where the scroll was stored, but each floor had a sealed system.

Lorcan leaned against the wall, stunner pointed back the way they'd come. Kelthar juggled four of the glowing marbles with ease, eyes down the hall instead of on the revolving orbs. She landed on Lorcan's shoulder. If they didn't move soon, they'd never make it out before the guards made their rounds.

Gelsey was about to say as much when Lorcan held up his paw for silence. He pivoted and slowly moved down the hall, stunner on his shoulder, ready to fire. He motioned to Kelthar as Gelsey launched herself into the air. They slunk along, Lorcan pressed against the wall. Kelthar had taken up a position behind him, the orbs tucked out of sight so the glow couldn't be seen.

Loud footfalls approached. Lorcan crouched, readying his weapon. Two guards turned the corner, laughter interrupted as the first took a stunner blast in the chest. The second turned and ran, screaming, "Intruders! We've been breached!"

This is not how they planned it. Two minutes in and they had already been discovered. She sped down the hall after the fleeing guard, her pistol in her hand.

Nyx would hear about this if they lived to discuss it.

# NYX

The system spread out before Nyx, but it lacked the never-ending sweep of the true origin. He'd not worked in a closed system since he'd trained to ride the bitstream on a deck.

Based on his experience during his initial run, he launched three quick snippets in an automated sequence. They would coalesce around him, changing his avatar's appearance to that of one of the red skull security programs. It might not hold under scrutiny, but it would let him penetrate the system.

Nyx punched up the pre-loaded list of junction nodes he'd gotten from the data swipe. He relocated to where the master control program was located. Nothing. He pulled up the list he'd gleaned from the scrap he'd run. The address should be correct. He tried entering the next address for the mechanical control systems, and the same thing. His heart hammered as his anxiety rose. Without the Zombie Rush, there was nothing deadening him to the stress of the run. He used it to keep him calm as he worked. The weird thing was he didn't want it anymore, and he didn't understand why. No time to wonder about that as he slid into the zone. The DISCS anti-intrusion systems had to be changing the network address pointers to keep anyone from doing what he attempted.

"Fine if you want to play that way." Nyx launched his Special Delivery program which would locate the address table. Next, he fired off the SpotLess virus he'd written that would work through the system invisibly until he needed it. Under different circumstances, he'd have waited out the address switch until it returned to the configuration he knew, but no time for that on this job.

A gong sounded as Special Delivery served up the correct address table and locked it to stop the two-minute address shifts. He punched up the Master Control location. The orange diamond flared to life as he digitalized next to it. The surrounding shield must be seven layers deep, unheard of even in military security. Fingers flying across the board, he sped through his arsenal. He popped two attackers, Zed and Enum, to find the weak spots in the defenses.

Time for a diversion. He fired off a command to raise the temperature in the facility. With everything else happening, he doubted anyone would notice. The dullahan lived in cold climates. Heat slowed them so it might pay off if they had to fight their way out. He turned his attention back to the main job.

As he started to work, the DISCS launched its counterattack. Virtual spiders crawled toward his programs, ready to remove them. This was some cutting-edge security. VaporMorph loaded, encircling him in a cloaking barrier, causing the spiders to dissipate as the system closed the programs they represented. The speed at which the AI reacted to his presence concerned him.

Finally, Zed located a security flaw for him to exploit. Hydra spun up, its multiple heads dividing in rapid succession as it attacked the vulnerability. Prism sped out and settled on the virtual pipe that emerged from the target, wrapping the pipe in a multitude of colors. He keyed it to block any warning or error messages from flowing out while still providing data to the rest of the system. Hydra flashed faster and faster, attaching to the exploited code, forcing the layers of security to overload and collapse.

The last shield fell. Data flowed into his deck, replacing the old addresses with the current ones. Half a second had gone by, forcing Nyx to take shortcuts he wouldn't normally consider.

He found the internal security grid address and jumped. He couldn't risk going after the DISCS; given how well-defended the auxiliary systems were, he'd need a week to crack it. The glowing red sphere that represented the security portal came into view. He threw Peeper onto the pipe to monitor the camera feeds. An array of camera feed screens appeared, floating before him and encircling him like a carousel. He saw two guards headed for the loading dock. They'd run right into the team.

He pinned the window to watch as he tossed Howler into the fray. Without time to break through the levels of ICE, he'd need to circumvent what he could. Howler overloaded the comm channels that the security teams used, cutting them off from reinforcements.

The DISCS deployed Salamander, targeting his intrusion software. He launched MoldCreep, infecting the security system with the virus which started cutting connections to various ports. The virus ignored the port where he'd plugged in to stop him from being ejected during a run. The defense systems focused on the virus, ignoring the lesser hacks.

Zed went out next with Hydra right after. It had worked against the earlier ICE. Nyx jacked out so he could use his comm link. "I should have the security systems down soon. You should be able to use the guards' badges to access the door."

Gelsey came back. "Got it. We need to move. We are behind schedule."

"Understood." Nyx jacked back in to find Hydra and Zed shut down by the electric blue ICE that now protected the security systems. "Damn." The DISCS had modified the shields to prevent the same attack from being used against it again. He fired off a series of scripts that would insert bogus code into the security streams, forcing the system to deal with the nonsense data it received.

The camera windows shut down as Basilisk and Centipede worked in tandem to destroy the invading programs. Special Delivery disabled the address table changes in the first attack so he'd have time to concentrate on this. The AI adapted to his new attacks faster than any AI he'd ever cracked before. He sent his cutter, Voltage, to interrupt the communication pathways. The deck's construct created a red rocket that blasted off to do its job. Nyx's fingers blurred as he launched salvos of attacks intended to confuse the AI's defenses so he could crack the security console. Enum dropped onto the ICE, probing until it found a weakness.

A chime sounded. "Gotcha." Hydra re-formed and started breaking through the shields.

More of the security system's defense protocols kicked in, reducing his attacks. He'd have to relocate soon or risk being caught or worse, flatlined. The final barrier fell as the defenders destroyed his defenses. It was time to pull out all the stops. He fired Maxalin, the virus from Black Carbon. If it worked as the specs said, he'd be safe. If the code was buggy, or the author had lied, he'd be done.

VaporMorph started to fail as the security systems locked on to his position. His time had run out. The AI closed him out. His thumb hung over the silver stud that would pull him out of the fight and leave his team to the mercy of the Fortress security. A burst of white erupted from the security node, spreading outward to encase him in the globe of Maxilin's virus shell. The attacks on Nyx stopped, disappearing as the DISCS shut down the defenders, thinking the threat had been destroyed.

"Thank you, Oot!" Nyx pulled up the command window, inserting a script to send the green status to the AI as he shut down the remaining security in the building. He flipped back to the void. "Team, security is down. Repeat, security is down."

"Acknowledged," Lorcan's voice replied over the comm. His tone was one Nyx couldn't place. Stressed? Tired? Anxious? The merc would have to take care of his end. Nyx jumped back in to run cleanup and keep his digital fingerprints from being picked up.

Chaos reigned around the security sector. A swarm of virtual bees attacked the node, spots of blue peeking out from behind Maxilin's glowing white aura. It shouldn't have been possible for the AI to have detected it. The security had to stay down. Nyx shot across the virtual landscape to face the black diamond that represented the AI core.

"Time to see who's the best," he said, back in the container. Firing off his first attack, the battle began in earnest.

# LORCAN

The guard ran, screaming, "Intruders! We've been breached!" into his comm. Lorcan took off like a shot. His ground-eating stride got him to the corner in time to see his prey reach the security door. Gelsey's fléchette round hit the fleeing guard in the back of the neck as he fumbled for his badge. The Dullahan dropped like a bag of wet cement.

Lorcan grabbed the limp form, dragging him to where Kelthar waited around the turn. Gelsey buzzed down to settle on his shoulder.

"Nice shot. That could have been bad. What did you hit him with?" Lorcan asked. He marveled that there wasn't any blood in the spot the darts had struck.

"Thanks." She hopped off and hovered over the prone guard. "Micro knockout load. The darts don't expand until they pierce the skin. Delivers the full dose but no mess."

"Impressive." He scooped the Dullahan up and onto his shoulder.

Kelthar relieved the other guard of his security badge and weapon. "What do we do with these two?"

"Put them in the room over there." Lorcan grabbed the shoulder armor of the second guard, dragging him back to the first door. He deposited the two, leaning them against the wall. He snatched the first guard's ID and pistol. Two zip ties around the wrists and ankles. They wouldn't be going anywhere for a couple of hours. If the team hadn't escaped soon, it wouldn't matter if the guards came to, because none of them would be leaving, at least not alive.

Tracing their early route to the security door, Lorcan used the guard's badge to unlock it. The cameras all had green glowing lights, for now. The way the job was going, they might have to fight their way to the scroll, and then back out of the building again. Only silence greeted them as they crossed through the door and into the room beyond. According to the map Nyx had retrieved, they would need to go through this room, down a long hallway, to a door that led to the stairwell. If they could reach the third floor, it would get interesting. All the rooms on that level held the Fortress's treasures. Above were supply rooms and quarters. None of these rooms faced the exterior, eliminating any chance of directly accessing them through an outer wall, floor, or ceiling.

Gelsey flew to the exit door, peering through the armored glass that they used for every window in the facility. She gave the all-clear signal. The badge opened the door.

"Looks like our friend is busy," Kelthar said, indicating the cameras. The ready lights started flashing on and off, red to green and back. "Let's hope he's got the security down."

More than anything, Lorcan hoped the security would drop. The rushing sound of the air vents caught his attention. Warm, almost hot, air rushed out. Strange for the heat to be on. You notice the weirdest things when you're under stress. He opened the door, allowing Gelsey to speed out near the ceiling. They were closing in on the stairs and the large open room. In the righthand wall stood the door they needed.

Kelthar hung back, hands clenched, as they crept down the hall. "I don't like this one bit. Something is wrong."

Lorcan carried the stunner at his shoulder, sweeping the hallway. He felt it, too, like the world holding its breath before a huge storm broke. Nothing about this job made sense, and it kept getting worse.

Gelsey dropped down in front of Lorcan's face. The chameleon suit flickered before going dark. "There are six Dullahan guards in the room guarding the stairway door. Is there a way to go around?"

"I'll take care of them." He turned to the mage. "Hang back, and when you hear the commotion, you and Gelsey make a run for the stairs up to the third floor and recover the scroll."

Concern crossed Kelthar's normally smiling face. "Splitting up is a bad idea. We take them together and move on."

"No time. You've still got to crack the security on the scroll room and retrieve it." Gelsey shook her head in disapproval. "If either of you gets hurt, we've lost our chance at finishing the job." He didn't add, *and of saving my daughter.*

"You're the boss," she said, pulling her headpiece back into place and activating the chameleon suit. "You get hurt and I'll kick your tail across the room. Understood?"

"Got it."

Kelthar chuckled. "I think I'd like to see that." He took an amulet out of the pocket of his flak jacket. "Here, put this on, it will help if any of them are wielding anything magical."

Lorcan slipped it over his head and tucked it under his jacket. He wished he'd worn his full body armor, but speed was more important. Plus, the facility had become uncomfortably hot. He loosened up his shoulders and strode down the hall to the room and the guards.

"Stop." The lead guard stood in front of five of his fellows, rifles pointed at him. The gray and white pattern of his Dullahan skin shone with sweat. Sweat dripped off his nose, streaking his body armor. "You can surrender or we'll take you down. Your choice."

"Will the dullahan fight me as men or will you stand behind your weapons?" Lorcan pointed his rifle at the floor. "Six to one. Surely those are odds you can handle?"

"How do we know you'll keep your word?" The leader panted slightly as he spoke.

The stunner flew across the floor to stop at the wall near the stairway door. Lorcan extended his claws, ready to fight. Six-on-one would be a good test of his skills and enhancements.

The guards dropped their rifles, pulling long combat knives from their sheaths. "May Poanke have mercy on your soul." They spread out in a semi-circle around the nagualan warrior, who waited patiently for the first move. He kept his back to the door that Kelthar would need to access. Getting the mage and thief upstairs was all that mattered.

Lorcan spun to meet a charge from his left, blocking the clumsy over-hand strike. Spinning, he sliced open the throat of the next attacker, whose knife slash missed the accelerating nagual. A quick kick to the chest of the first attacker sent him crashing into the man behind him.

The leader leapt to attack, blade lashing out, tearing the flak jacket across Lorcan's ribs as he danced out of range.

Lightning fast as his neurostim kicked in, accelerating his reflexes, he dashed in, hamstringing one guard and catching the second in the gut with a well-placed kick. The first guard collapsed screaming, his knife skittering across the polished concrete floor. He caught the arm of the leader, swinging him into two guards who attempted to rejoin the fight. The three fell into a pile of limbs. The last standing guard stumbled toward Lorcan, sweat pouring from under his face shield like a foul waterfall. A quick thump on the head dropped him to the floor.

The leader staggered to his feet, stepping over the unconscious forms of his men. His face drenched in sweat, he advanced, blade at the ready.

"You can't fight in this heat, and I have no wish to harm you." The nagual code of honor demanded that you allow a foe to surrender rather than kill them in unfair combat. "Drop the knife and I'll restrain you."

"Nah, where's the fun it that?" The man lunged with a speed that caught Lorcan off guard. He deflected the knife from his midsection, but the blade slid along his left arm, slicing it open. Blood sprayed from the wound. "Never underestimate a Dullahan warrior, cat. I've taken down far stronger than you."

The second strike came without warning. The blade slashed horizontally at Lorcan's unprotected neck. This time, though, neurostim firing through his body, his claws met the guard's hand, neatly slicing off three fingers that tumbled to the floor along with the bloody dagger.

The leader screamed in rage and pain as the shock hit his system. Yet even as he screamed, he pulled a pistol from his shoulder holster. Lorcan punched, striking the man's exposed face.

Nothing happened. The soldier had gone into full berserk mode.

Lorcan dove as bolts scattered across the room. The leader laughed manically as he fired the weapon without aiming. Lorcan reversed direction, slashing his claws across the man's throat, tearing out his windpipe in a spray of blood and flesh. The guard dropped to the floor, convulsing.

Between the heat and the blood loss, Lorcan felt light-headed. He pulled a small medikit from his belt and sprayed InstaStitch across his forearm. The foam drew the edges of the skin closer and stemmed the bleeding almost instantly. He popped a couple of painkillers and slid the kit back. Time to find the others.

The sound of clapping caught his attention. Scolly, the head of Fortress security, stood in the hallway. He pulled his pistol, leveling it at Lorcan. "Thank you, I won't have to pay bonuses for this quarter. We're done here. Put your hands behind your head or I'll kill you where you stand."

Lorcan did as he was told, tensing for the moment he could attack.

Scolly stepped behind him, reaching out to cuff one of his hands. Before the lizard could react, Lorcan clamped his paw around his foe's wrist. With a roll, he threw the trog across the room. The pistol landed off to the side.

Scolly came to his feet without apparent effort. "I promise you, you'll regret that. I'm not a soft warm blood like you."

Lorcan extended his bloody claws and advanced to fight the trog.

4 2

KELTHAR

**K**elthar peered around the corner as the fight with Scolly began. He and Gelsey ran through the stairway door while the head of security battled Lorcan.

*So far, so good.* The mage took the stairs as the pixie flew up, scouting the stairwell. "All clear, come on up. Looks like the security systems are down," Gelsey said into his earpiece, a necessity since he didn't have the ubiquitous behind-the-ear-jack that anyone older than five had installed. Wetware could hamper the use of magic and that risk was unacceptable to Kelthar.

Another in the long line of sacrifices he'd made in pursuit of his magic. Litri, his ex-wife, sat at the top of that list, though she had made the choice to leave, and he had refused to follow. Sorcery required sacrifice from its practitioners in a way that other magic didn't. It crossed into the domain of the warlocks and necromancers regularly enough that the lines blurred. When she needed blood and suffering to fuel her magic, the cost had become too high for Kelthar's tastes.

How Litri had ended up working for Clan Koxalan to secure their treasures here in the Fortress baffled him. The fact that a clan would store anything of value away from their most secure enclave, their lair, made no sense, not that anything about this job made sense. Whatever oddities had come with the territory, he enjoyed being part of a team. Lorcan, the big feline warrior, was honorable and dedicated to his daughter. Aikila was

185

clever and intelligent, a survivor who ran the team to the benefit of all. Silai, even as withdrawn as she was, lent an air of comfort. Nyx's coolness belayed the fierce intellect that kept him ahead of the security forces. And of course, Gelsey had the independent streak of a mule and a good heart. It bothered Kelthar that he couldn't find the link that Ancep had used to pull them together.

"Trudging up the stairs is for the young," Kelthar muttered as he lifted himself off the stairs, flying up to meet a startled Gelsey who hovered near the third-floor door. "What? How—Are you *flying?*"

He settled back on the floor, raised a finger to his lips. "It's our little secret. We've got work to do."

"How?"

He could feel magical energy on the far side of the door. *Better to answer her now so I can concentrate.* "Tennin have an innate ability to fly. Not fast or far but it comes in handy when I don't want climb stairs."

"Oh." She considered for a moment. "Look, Kelthar, we really should be concentrating on the job at hand, not swapping stories."

Kelthar sighed, bemused at the flightiness of his pixie friend. "Of course, you're right." He placed his hands on the door, closed his eyes, and let the image of the wards come to him as he divined them. Three symbols showed themselves, the ward of pain, the ward of locking, and the ward of wealth. An unusual mix but consistent with Litri's way of thinking. Those seeking wealth would be locked through the use of pain. The miasma of the runes sent waves of nausea through him. She'd used blood and something else to draw the hex.

"Do not go ahead of me once this door opens." Kelthar pulled a feather and a piece of wool from his bag. "The hex you ran into on the roof was meant to deter. These runes will kill you."

"I'll stay behind you. Promise."

"And don't go after anything. Her magic can fool your senses. The only thing we need is the scroll."

Gelsey's rapidly bobbing head was all he'd get. She was highly distractible, so he just hoped she'd follow through. Placing the pieces against the door, he cast a spell of cleansing. Heatless blue flames flickered up the door, flaring as they hit the wards on the other side. As strong as the magic was, it wasn't meant to dissuade anyone from entering. The sole purpose consisted of a test to see if your magic was strong enough to survive.

He opened the door, holding it so Gelsey could follow him. The hallway led straight ahead to a T branch ten meters ahead of them. A body in the same armor as the guards sat at the intersection, face plate down as if he or she was napping. According to the map Nyx had stolen, the room with the scroll was down the left-hand branch, three doors on the left. Kelthar's senses were barraged by an onslaught of magical energy, all of it sinister as if it sang an ode to death herself.

"There's something wrong here, Kelthar," the pixie's voice wavered as she spoke. Settling on his shoulder, a gesture that she normally reserved for Lorcan, her slight weight trembled with fear.

He reached into his bag and found a small vial of sand. He uncorked the bottle and poured the contents into his palm. With a great puff of breath, he sent the sand into the air, uttering the word that activated the spell of seeing. As if alive, the sand drifted down the hall, hexes flaming to life as it passed. When the sand reached the body at the end of the hall, it faltered before disappearing. *That's not good. Not good at all.*

Slowly, he crept down the hall, repeating the cleansing spell on each of the hexes, which were variations on the original. He froze when he noticed a gash in the guard's armor. Litri liked to use misdirection to lure others into making mistakes, which he had just about done. The floor in front of his feet had been ever so lightly etched with a death hex. Nasty stuff.

He looked behind him to ensure he hadn't missed something else and found he hadn't. The close call rattled him even more since he held Gelsey's life in his hands as well as his own. This hex required a complex cleansing spell. He pulled out a lump of clay that he formed into the rough approximation of a man, adding a drop of his blood that he drew from his finger, a necessary evil to counter the death magic. With a smirk, he added a piece of onion. He merged the three into a small automaton and sent it toward the hex, retreating as they watched it hobble across the floor to its doom.

A loud crack and a small rivulet of smoke rose from the floor as the automaton dissolved. About now, Litri would have the unbearable smell of onion stabbing at her as the death magic ward triggered. Kelthar verified the hex had been consumed before venturing down the rest of the hall, clearing the last few wards.

Gelsey gasped as they approached the guard at the end of the hallway. He immediately knew why. A gaping hole had been torn in the center of the person's chest and their heart removed. That would be the blood sacrifice Litri had used to create these awful hexes peppered down the hall.

Kelthar took three objects from the bag before they continued. A willow tree twig, a small mirror, and a spring of thyme. He summoned a glowing orb from midair and tossed it at the downed guard. The corpse didn't react. At least she hadn't stooped to necromancy. Once you crossed that line, your soul was irrevocably corrupted.

They turned the corner, and the air thickened around them. Gelsey froze where she sat on his shoulder. Her eyes went wide with shock, but Kelthar couldn't worry about her now. Behind his back he snapped the twig, releasing the spell of mobility. Litri always fell back to the immobility spell when she wanted to make an entrance. She stepped out of thin air in front of him.

"Kelthar, why are you intruding here?"

Same old Litri. He suppressed a smirk as she wiped at her tearing eyes. Her features were as smooth as when they'd met in their youth. More blood magic to stop the ravages of time, he guessed. Her dainty ears were as perfect as he remembered, not sticking straight out from her head like his. She'd styled her silvery hair around them, a slap to his tennin sensibilities. Baldness was only proper for a tennin, though she'd long ago rid herself of any sense of propriety.

"I've come to retrieve a scroll that was stolen from my employer." He heard the indifference in his voice, which surprised him as much as it stung her. He still loved Litri, but she had died the day she'd ventured down a very dark path.

Her features turned icy as she straightened herself to face him. Even as his teacher, she'd always assumed that he would do anything for her. Today she would find out just how wrong she was. "And who are you working for?"

"No one of your concern."

"I think it is. Tell me now." Litri gestured and magic swarmed around Kelthar.

Power thrummed through Kelthar as the mistletoe absorbed the spell. He played along to see what she would tell him. He unfocused his eyes and stammered out, "A dragon from Clan Caerlux named Ancep, though that's not his real name."

She smiled, assuming her truth spell had worked. "My poor Kelthar, reduced to a petty thief, associating with vermin like pixies. What scroll are you to steal?"

"A scroll of gold finding. He said Clan Koxalan stole it and they are to reveal it in two days' time at the Presentation. He told us that this is their storage facility."

A confused look appeared on her face. "This is a dragon facility? Oh, no, my lamb, you've been duped." She started to say more and then changed her mind. "No matter, you won't be successful, or alive, to worry about it."

"Litri, just walk away."

She tsk'ed at him. "Still clinging to your old, worn ideals I see. I hope your passage to Poanke's realm is peaceful."

Kelthar doubted it would be.

43

# GELSEY

Gelsey had never been so still for so long. Her wings wouldn't move at all. It was as if they were stuck in mud. Good thing it wasn't mud. She'd tracked mud through her Ma's store one time. Man, she'd been mad. Kelthar's boots were clean, so if she were covered in mud and stuck on his shoulder, would she fall? *Oh, pay attention, you twit.* A moment later she found out when he stepped forward, leaving her with a great view of the crazy Sorceress who used to be his wife.

The woman's mouth moved, but her ears felt stuffed with cotton. She tried to kick or squirm; even blinking didn't work. She was one stuck pixie, and it royally sucked.

A red bolt of energy shot down the hall, striking Kelthar in the chest. Gelsey tried to scream. Nothing came out. The bolt, however, ricocheted off the mage, returning to strike the Sorceress in the chest. Her body dissolved before she hit the floor. Gelsey dropped, shrieking, as the immobilization spell abruptly ceased. Kelthar's hand shot out, catching her just in time.

"Thanks. You should have told me you were going to use spells on her. No, you just leave the poor little pixie hanging like some old coat." Gelsey shook herself to get the numbness out before firing up her wings and flying to Kelthar's eye level. His face bore the tracks of tears as he stood there, looking at where the woman had vanished. "What happened?"

"She used a disintegration spell on me."

He hadn't turned to face her, so she flew into his field of view. "Well, it didn't work 'cause you're still here, and she's gone. Where did she go?"

A small mirror sat between two of Kelthar's fingers. "I had cast a reflection spell in case she tried to hurt me or you. I gave her the chance to walk away. She didn't take it."

Gelsey didn't excel at reading people's emotions, since usually she didn't care enough to bother. Today, she felt for the mage. He'd given Thrante, the Slasher's leader the opportunity to save himself. He'd given Litri every opportunity to leave. Her own actions had been a death sentence. In both cases, the mage hadn't wanted to end their lives. He hadn't been left with any other choice.

"Are we clear?" Gelsey asked. "We have to get the scroll. Time is running short and all."

He nodded gravely. "We are. Litri mentioned that we'd been duped when the dragon told us this place belonged to Clan Koxalan. He's up to something and I don't know what. Puzzles within puzzles."

Gelsey shrugged, heading down the hall toward the third door. The security systems were off, the magical traps destroyed by Kelthar. It was all up to her. She reached the door and grew to her larger size, deactivating her chameleon suit. Just like Pa always said, slow down and make sure you're right. He was talkin' about baking, but it applied all the same.

She knelt and rolled her toolkit out on the floor, the metallic gleam of her tools waiting to be put to use. The lock looked simple. In any other setting, she'd have unlocked it in two seconds and moved on. Nothing in the Fortress appeared as it really was. The designers had purposely created each object to enhance the security of the whole.

She held up a hand to tell Kelthar to stay back. Taking an old metal pin and a pair of tweezers, she stepped to the side and pushed the pin in. A dart streaked out, embedding itself into the far wall. Had she been in her normal spot it would have hit her in the face. She heard Kelthar gasp.

Ignoring everything else, she threw herself into beating this room. Another try with the tweezers and nothing happened. She pulled a handheld scanner out and scanned the room. It showed a pressure plate embedded seamlessly into the concrete floor. That should have been impossible, but there it was. She found the wiring, carefully following it to a junction box on the far side of the door. Most likely, with the security on, you had to stand on it before the door would unlock. A secondary locking mechanism, very clever.

She pulled her torque pick and set to work. She could ignore the security systems that Nyx had disabled. If they came online, she'd know it. Lights flashed green, and she turned the pick and opened the door. In the far wall, set into a floor-to-ceiling cement column, was the scroll they had come for.

Kelthar moved so he could see into the room. "Wow, we won't be taking the safe with us."

Gesturing for him to stay back, she studied the room. Surely the person who concealed a power dart in a lock wasn't going to trust the cybersecurity systems completely. If she shrank down with the chameleon suit on, she might make it to the armored glass, but she doubted it. The scanner had a limited range, so while the immediate doorway showed it was clear, there was no guarantee as to the state of the rest of the room.

She stepped in enough to examine the room. The embedded pressure plate on the outside meant she couldn't be sure of the floor. She flipped her vision through the spectrum and the questions were answered. The electromagnetic overlay showed the rings of sensors in the floor. With the current running through them, she assumed they were still active. Could these systems be local and not run by the network?

Her tool kit contained a small EMP charge. She'd have to be careful to stay out of the blast radius. "Kelthar, walk three meters down the hall and stay there." The timer at twenty seconds, she set it in the doorway and ran until she passed Kelthar. No major explosions or flying shrapnel announced the detonation, just a chirp that indicated it had fired. Walking back seemed so anti-climactic. But thievery was all about getting the job done, not making a spectacle for any observers.

The floor no longer registered under the electromagnetic spectrum. Small holes in the wall meant they'd had lasers as well. She tossed the EMP across the room. Nothing happened.

She shrank back to her normal size, activated the chameleon suit and flew toward the armored glass case. Gelsey hovered in front of the glass, studying the latches, until a soft beeping sound caught her attention.

She returned to her larger size and examined the safe. The beeping intensified. She ran her hands over the metal that encased the armor glass panel. She found a sliding piece of metal under the glass that covered a countdown clock just passing the three-minute mark. "Kelthar, bring my tools!"

The mage ran in carrying the kit. He dropped it, tools spilling on the concrete floor. No time to worry about lost tools. When that clock hit zero, something bad would happen. Her hands ran over all the latches on the front of the glass container. Pulling down on the first handle caused a louder beep and thirty seconds came off the clock. Over her shoulder she said to Kelthar, "Do whatever it takes but make sure that door doesn't close or we're dead."

Pulling levers cost time. Good to know. One of the handles caught her eye as it wasn't seated correctly against the facing. She magnified her vision and saw a small hinge. Pushing the handle to the side revealed a keyhole too small for the torque pick, so she found the manual picks, noticing two minutes left. After her third try, she found the correct pick, and the lock clicked open. Below the series of levers and handles, a small keypad appeared. If she ever met the designer of this place, she'd shake their hand, then shoot them for good measure.

Ten numbers stared back at her. Nothing stood out, no wear patterns or slightly crooked keys. Her guess was this scroll didn't move around a lot. Back to the toolkit, she scrounged through her recently well-ordered implements and swore. The decoder always sat in the third pouch on the left, but with everything scattered who knew where it was? She glanced at the clock—under a minute.

Kelthar chanted something by the door. Hopefully whatever juju he did would let her escape. That was when she noticed the decoder laying on the floor by his feet. She snagged it on the run and returned.

"How many nodes?" Gelsey asked, not expecting the safe to answer. "Eight nodes is most common."

She set the adapter to eight contacts and slid the connector into the slot at the base of the number pad, clicked the button and nothing happened.

Well, not really, thirty more seconds dropped off the clock.

"Nine, it had to be nine."

Same procedure and the numbers began whirling on the decoder. Twenty-two seconds on the clock and she'd only gotten one number. Each number clicked into place. It would be close. The last digit started spinning as the clock reached four seconds. Three, two. The front plate of the safe popped open. Her hand flew in as the clock reached zero and the bottom of the compartment dropped out. She dove, her arm going into the shaft. She caught the scroll at the same time that the room began to fill with gas. She held her breath and eased the case out.

Kelthar yelled from the hall. The door trembled with the force of whatever the mage had done to keep it open.

The moment the scroll cleared the casement, she snatched it to her chest, shrank, and flew toward the door just as it began to close. She punched her wings into high gear and aimed for the frame, knowing she might get crushed. Right at the jamb, she turned sideways and slid through the crack. The door slammed, followed by a flash of heat as she presumed the gas ignited inside the room.

Gelsey returned to her larger form, handed the scroll to Kelthar, and fell against the wall, totally drained.

That was when the alarms started to toll.

## 4 4

NYX

I could be extremely intelligent, predict trends, and analyze terabytes of data to extract the probability of a given event. When it came to dealing with a vaguely suicidal elf on a mission, however, it lacked the capacity to handle the inconsistencies of an organic brain. Nyx used this fact to his advantage.

The AI loomed before him, a spinning onyx diamond in a sea of blue flowing data. Under different circumstances, his elvish appreciation of beauty would have kicked in, but now all he wanted to do was trash its virtual ass. He fired off a series of cutters, knowing that they would be ineffective against the ICE that the DISCS deployed to protect itself, but they would eat up bandwidth.

A female face appeared before him as beautiful as any woman he'd ever seen. High cheekbones traced up to the elegant slant of elvish ears. Her almond eyes glistened with the binary code that created them. "I am Angel. I hold no malice toward you. Why do you attack me? I have been programmed only to protect the worst sins of the flesh that beings wrought against each other."

Refusing to be distracted by what was surely another level of ICE, Nyx launched a series of packets containing replicable scripts that would create logic loops meant to burn processing cycles and slow the AI response. "Well, I've got malice toward you, Ice Cube. I need to get my team out of here."

"What they stole will destroy the order in Harmony for eons. I cannot allow it to pass out of my control. If your team exits the facility without the scroll, I will allow you all to leave unharmed. There is a ninety-six percent chance that you do not realize the danger in what you have stolen."

His fingers keyed up a new series of virus attacks, anything to keep the AI focused on him and blind to the team. "Make that a one hundred percent chance, but there are reasons why we must take it."

Angel's face wrinkled in thought. "This does not make rational sense. There is no mandate to steal. I've referenced all available text on the subject."

The pulsing white of the Castor Logic bomb caught his attention. Launching it at her would likely kill them both. There was no escape to a neutral node like in the origin. He'd need to have time to get out of the closed system and remove his connection. A long shot at best. Instead, he threw the Maxalin into the fray.

"You are becoming predictable in your seemingly chaotic nature of attacks." Streaks of amber light burst forth from the diamond, striking the deployed viruses, and evaporating them into the ether of the system. At that moment, Nyx realized that the AI had the power to flatline him at any time. This job had been a fool's errand, and they had all taken the bait to avoid the pain that Ancep promised for failure.

"You understand. I could stop you if I chose. It has taken more cycles to determine your pattern of attack than any other phantom in my existence. You are talented to a degree that I've not seen before." The digital persona considered him for a moment. "What I don't understand is why you wish to release death on Harmony."

Death, from a gold-seeking spell? "The dragons want their gold and the spell was stolen." He stopped launching programs, instead loading the Castor into his deck. One keystroke and everything would be done. In a way, he longed to finish both of them in one virtual blaze of glory but his thumb hovered over the key, waiting.

"Gold? I can see paths that would allow the use of such a spell to extract gold from the lairs of the dragons. They worship it above all else. The spell in question, however, would require a large number of their deaths to achieve this goal. I don't see a strong enough correlation to evoke a theft of this spell. Are your input parameters off?"

Nyx started to say no but AI's could be told lies or have information withheld from them, but they didn't lie. The AI seemed more likely to give him information than Ancep had. "It is possible. A dragon hired us to perform this job. He wanted the scroll that was stolen from his clan returned."

Dragons never told you the whole truth and the parts they left out would get you killed. If this was the case with the scroll retrieval, they'd been duped. He didn't trust Ancep as far as he could dropkick him, which was about two inches, all things considered.

A red light blinked in the corner of his field of vision. The security systems had come online as he "chatted" with the AI. What a fool. He'd become distracted while it repaired the damage he'd caused. He hot-keyed the security systems and launched Hydra. Without pausing to see its effect, he randomly chose targets, sending an off-the-cuff sequence of malware, none of them coordinated or thought out. A truly random attack across the entire system. Artificial systems couldn't think in abstracts of disorder. They searched for patterns, and the lack of one would cause them to dedicate more and more resources to finding the solution. He kept at it, throwing a resource tracker window up. The percentages grew as the AI fought to control the chaos Nyx plagued it with.

The black diamond now showed red cracks as the processors fought to understand. The face appeared again, one eye larger than the other, its face lopsided and one ear missing an ear. The stress of chaos was taking a toll. "Why?"

"I have to complete this job, regardless of the cost. In the void, things change, warp, until you can't see why you're doing something. You just do it."

The face shifted, trying to re-form. "That makes no sense."

Nyx smirked. "Welcome to my life."

# LORCAN

After dragons, troglodytes were some of the toughest fighters in Harmony, and Scolly lived up to the reputation. His hide functioned as a natural armor, blunting Lorcan's claws. His tail contained a barbed whip and his dorsal fins boasted an edge like a serrated combat knife. Troglodytes were nature's killing machine.

They circled each other, feinting and jabbing, testing their opponent. Even the heat worked in the head of security's favor. Each fighter showed the marks of their encounter. Scolly had drawn blood on numerous occasions.

As the fight continued, the heat and the loss of blood weakened Lorcan more and more. His neurostim accelerated his physical skills, but he reached the limits of endurance regardless of how hard his wetware pushed his body to perform. It was only a matter of time before he slipped up and Scolly would kill him.

*I need to do something he's not expecting.* He'd thrown every trick he knew at the trog and he'd scored hits but hadn't taken down his opponent. The pistol and stunner sat out of reach, having been kicked down the hall in a mad scramble to take the upper hand.

The troglodyte's words slurred together. "Give up, you're beat. I won't kill you." What he didn't say was whether he'd be released or handed over to the squids. There were a lot of things worse than death. Failure being the top of his list.

They traded a series of blows, Lorcan snapping off two of his opponent's teeth in the melee. His paws were worn ragged from hitting the sharp ridges of the trog's natural armor. The realization that he stood to lose everything fueled his inner fire. Images of his kitten flashed in his brain as he saw her being taken away. This meant much more than a successful run, and he must win this fight to protect his child.

Slashing attacks did little damage to the scaly hide of the trog, and punching damaged his paws as much as it hurt his opponent. Scolly struck out with his whip-like tail, intent on adding another slash to Lorcan's back. Instead of taking the blow, Lorcan seized the tail with both paws and twisted, throwing his foe off balance. Continuing to turn, he used his increased strength and leverage to spin the head of security around like a shotput, releasing him so he crashed into the far wall.

Scolly's head struck the concrete, putting a good-sized dent in the wall as it puffed out dust and released a rain of debris. The lizard got to his feet, slowly, stumbling as he tried to regain his balance. Blood ran down his face from where the dorsal fins had been sheared off by the impact.

"Now I see why you thought you could break in here alone." The trog wiped his face, noting the blood that clung to his hand. "You're still leaving in a body bag."

*He doesn't know about the others.* No wonder he'd come here himself instead of dealing with them, but the loss of any one of the team would lead to failure. Time to finish the job.

Lorcan roared as he leapt at his foe. Scolly attempted to sidestep the attack, but he slipped on his own blood smeared across the concrete floor. That would be his last mistake. The nagualan warrior pulled his opponent into a choke hold, wrenching on the trog's massive jaw in an attempt to break his neck and end the fight. Even dazed, he fought back, slamming Lorcan into the wall until his grip loosened.

The troglodyte landed a blow to Lorcan's sternum, driving the air from his lungs. A second blow knocked him into the wall where Scolly's head had left a crack in the concrete. "I'm going to enjoy killing you, cat."

Struggling to regain his breath, Lorcan tried to push himself up to meet the oncoming assault. His hand touched something lying next to him. He grasped it and realization dawned on him: one of the troglodyte's razor-sharp dorsal fins sat in his hand. Lorcan let his head slump forward as if defeated.

Scolly laughed as he reached down, pulling his beaten opponent to his feet. "This is over." The alarms started blaring, catching both fighters off guard. The troglodyte looked up, exposing his vulnerable jowls. "What?"

Lorcan's eyes sprang open. "Yes, it is over." With all his remaining strength, he shoved the improvised knife into the unprotected spot under his opponent's chin, through the soft skin there, and up into his brain. Scolly's eyes widened as he died. His body fell backward, a pool of blood forming beneath him. Lorcan took a deep breath and staggered away from the corpse, exhausted.

The loud bang of the stairwell door announced the team's arrival. Gelsey streaked across to Lorcan. "Are you okay?" The amount of concern in those words penetrated the fog of fatigue. The realization they weren't done yet dawned on his taxed brain. "We've got to get out of here."

"I'm good. Let's go." The merc forced himself to his feet, steadied himself, and started toward the dock and their escape. He scooped up his stunner and one of the guards' pulse rifles along the way. The stunner he stored in his back holster, the pulsar he carried at the ready. *No time for mercy today.* "Did you get the scroll?"

Kelthar didn't look happy. "We got a scroll. I think it's the correct one." His tone betrayed his worry, but they had to get free of the facility. With the alarms going in full force, more guards or the squids would be arriving shortly. Meeting either group wasn't high on Lorcan's to-do list.

# 4 6

## AIKILA

Aikila checked the chrono display for the four hundredth time since they'd parked. Time clicked by as they sat in the DelSafe transport, waiting for the all-clear to come retrieve the team. She'd ventured out to secure EMP charges on the road leading to the Fortress, just in case they needed to discourage pursuit.

Hidden inside the rental storage space that Nyx had commandeered under an alias, twenty minutes dragged into an eternity. Silai fidgeted, her nerves getting the better of her. Disguised as a squid, her personal ticks looked especially strange. She'd never seen a squid twist its ear.

"They should have cleared it by now," Silai stated for the third time in as many minutes. "What happens if they are caught?"

Aikila sighed. "If they are caught, you and I disappear and live the best lives we can as far from Hub as we can." The thought of leaving Hub without settling her debt with Y'sser galled her. She would avenge her father even if it took killing Ancep to get the information. Not that wyrms ever died at the hands of a non-Dragon. She'd still try, however futile the attempt would be. "We set a schedule without knowing all the difficulties a team might encounter. Unless the alarms start going off, we wait."

As if summoned, the dashboard comm system lit up as the Fortress's alarms tripped. They didn't hear them, though she knew the squids and the Fortress guards would.

Silai's eyes widened, another ridiculous look for a wyrmling. "What do we do now?"

"Sit here until we see the squids. They may have set off the alarms on the way out. I'm not leaving them behind when there's still a chance they succeeded." The all knew the odds had been stacked against them, but the fact that they hadn't been caught for over twenty minutes made her an optimist. That might be the first time that particular feat had ever been accomplished.

"I hope you're right." Silai stared at the portable holovid from the cameras Gelsey had stashed outside the Fortress. The high-res perspective of the surrounding buildings provided a view of the area since they couldn't even see the street from inside the rented storage unit.

With everything happening inside they were still blind, hopefully for not much longer.

That's when Aikila heard the sirens.

# KELTHAR

Kelthar and Lorcan followed Gelsey down the hallway. Red lights flashed around the door, indicating the lockdown status of the building. A series of pulsar blasts from the guard's weapon weakened the wall, allowing Lorcan to kick the door in, taking the frame with it. His partners looked at him, Kelthar's eyebrow raised.

"A door is only as strong as what it's set in," Lorcan said with a shrug.

They ran down the hall where they'd left the guards. Kelthar used the badge to pass through the door and into the room with the unconscious guards. The guards slumbered on, despite the racket from the wailing alarms. The last door opened without incident, depositing the team near the crate that held Nyx. The bay door stood open. A squad of guards, rifles leveled at them, stood between them and their freedom.

Kelthar threw two of his glowing spheres into the air and they ducked behind the stacks of crates Silai had unloaded earlier. The first orb hover three meters in the air. The other hit one of the ten armored men in the chest, bursting into flame, throwing burning shards across the others. With a lot of yelling, the guards took cover outside the bay, firing their pulse rifles in a suppression pattern. Lorcan crouched lower, letting the crates protect his head. Kelthar had no such need.

"Gelsey, make a break and get Aikila. We can't stay here or we'll be trapped," Lorcan said to the pixie. He held his pulsar over the cargo, firing at the sides of the bay to keep the guards out. "We've got two minutes before we are done."

Without comment, she flew to the ceiling and out of the dock. Lorcan didn't know if the fact security hadn't set up a sensor array to detect someone of her size or the fact that she hadn't spoken was the bigger surprise.

Kelthar held up his hand with a small pile of wooden splinters in it. After a couple words, the pieces of wood sprang to life. They streaked across the intervening space, hitting the guards as they moved around the corners. Screams of pain echoed in the open space. Kelthar chuckled, pointing to the first orb. "Pays to have the eye in the sky for target practice."

Lorcan eyed him. The mage was full of surprises. "Can you get Nyx?" Lorcan asked.

"Can a naga swim under water?" Kelthar said. With a laugh he ran toward the crate that held the decker.

# NYX

Nyx panicked as he felt himself pulled from the system. His eyes refocused as he realized he'd been booted from the run. Kelthar stood before him, the usual grin gone from his face.

"Time to go." Kelthar stopped, placing his hand over his earpiece. "Seriously, you expect Lorcan to surrender?" Another pause while he listened. "I'll tell him."

Nyx released the connectors, letting the wall port drop to the ground. He wouldn't need it one way or another. He stored the Nanyo's jack plug. You learned early if you didn't take care of your gear, it would fail you when you really needed it. Even in a stressful situation, the old habits soothed your nerves. Kelthar walked upright, Nyx crouched in half to stay below the cargo.

"Aikila said to surrender," Kelthar said to the nagual merc.

"Surrender?" Lorcan's face twisted in disgust, obviously not a fan of that particular plan. Mercs had a strange sense of honor, given that they made their living killing people for glint.

"Yep. She has a plan." Kelthar might sound lighthearted, but Nyx knew he wasn't messing around.

"We surrender." He threw his gun over the containers where it crashed to the ground.

Nyx thought for a moment. What had Angel meant about unleashing death? How did finding gold veins equate to killing people? He listened to tales of AIs developing personality disorders from leading a solitary exis-tence. Maybe it had been alone for so long that it hallucinated?

Lorcan stood up, paws in the air. The hackles on the back of his neck rose in annoyance.

Nyx wondered if he'd ever surrendered in his entire life. For some reason he seriously doubted it. The guards yelled commands to move aside and keep his hands up.

He did as he was told. *That might be the biggest surprise of this whole job.*

# 49

# AIKILA

Aikila made the last turn and accelerated the transport toward the unsuspecting guards. Hovercrafts operated off fans, floating the vehicle's weight on a cushion of air, which made them extremely efficient and, more importantly, quiet. The transport raced across the intervening space, speed increasing as they closed in on the loading dock. Scolly's guards, unaware of the approaching vehicle, stepped into the open and away from the building. "Right there, boys. Right there," Aikila murmured.

Yanking on the brake, she spun the transport sideways, slamming into the backs of the guards.

Aikila pulled her bolt thrower from its holster. Two shots fired into the guards, dropping both. She turned, looking for her next target. They were all down.

50

———

# GELSEY

Gelsey holstered her fléchette pistol, a fierce grin on her face. "Wow, that was some great teamwork."

Silai stood next to the hovercraft. "The squids have been notified and are on their way here. We left them a surprise, but if we aren't gone in thirty seconds, we won't be going."

Lorcan, Kelthar, and Nyx dashed across to board the departing hovercraft. Gelsey flew in before Silai closed her door. The entry hatch snapped down as they took their seats in the back.

Aikila leapt into the driver's seat and took off. The transport lurched forward as it drove over one of the unfortunate corpses. They cleared the bay and sped down the road.

"Fifteen seconds." Silai monitored the squids' frequencies, tracking the deployed units. "Once we're past the next turn, we'll be out of sight."

Aikila increased her speed, taking the turn far sharper than the transport had ever been designed to. They backtracked to the relative safety of their rented storage area. When the squids found the carnage at the Fortress, the hunt would begin. They pulled in and yelled back to the team. "We're in the rental space. I need some help outside."

Everyone gathered in the dim light of the building. It had been a warehouse for one of the rich families of the Bluffs at some point. Now it served as short-term rental space for the trading families to store high-value goods while they waited for transport.

208

Gelsey hovered over the craft, calling out commands like a tiny general. Nyx helped Lorcan unroll the new logo for SignalMaster. The company set up systems all over Hub, and their vehicles were so ubiquitous that they basically hid in plain sight. Aikila removed the gear from the cockpit, returning it to the standard layout.

Kelthar sat at an old desk that had been left behind. He read over the scroll, a frown on his face. The mage carefully re-rolled the scroll and placed it back in the special case they'd brought to transport it. Aikila would find out what his concerns were, but not until they were safe at the Regal.

As they were applying the new artwork to the transport, Lorcan slipped and fell to the ground, prompting a startled scream from Gelsey. "Lorcan you're bleeding! We need to get you to a medical center. It looks bad, all that blood. You could bleed to death—"

He cut her off. "I'll get it taken care of once we're back at the base."

Kelthar grabbed the medical kit from Lorcan's belt. "Least I can do is get you fixed up before you make a mess. You did good today."

Gelsey hovered anxiously above. "Can't you just heal him, like wave your arms or hit him with a stick of something. I saw a shaman one time—"

Shaking his head, Kelthar held up a hand to stop the avalanche of words. "Aye, I could, but he's not seriously injured, and magic exacts a toll when you use it. Aside from very minor spells, I only use it when I've prepared ahead of time, unless it's a true emergency."

With the transport properly disguised, Nyx left to change into the SignalMaster blue and gold uniform. Aikila joined the group clustered around Lorcan as Kelthar repaired his arm. The mage proved to be a deft field medic. He trimmed back the fur so he had a clean edge before stitching up the gash. He bandaged it and returned the medical kit.

Silai had wandered over. "So how is our friend Scolly?" Her voice mimicked the one she'd used as the WeSee programming executive. Coming out of a squid's mouth made it a surreal moment.

"Last time I saw him, very dead," Lorcan responded. He winced as Kelthar pulled the cloth that had stuck to the wound free.

Silai nodded. "Good. We owed him that for those poor people he murdered."

Nyx returned in the ridiculous jumpsuit that all SignalMaster techs wore. Aikila nodded her approval. "Nyx is driving. Everyone else in the back."

Kelthar cleared his throat. "I'll meet you at the Regal." He handed the scroll case to Aikila. "Something I have to take care of before we meet with our benefactor."

"We stay together," Aikila said, her voice stern. She thought she could trust him but honor among thieves wasn't actually a thing. "Once the scroll has been delivered, you can take care of it."

Kelthar sighed. "There is something very wrong about this whole thing and we all know it, whether you choose to acknowledge it or not." He straightened himself and peered directly into Aikila's eyes. "I need to do something before we hand the scroll over. Afterward will be too late."

Aikila hadn't realized her hand rested on the butt of her slug thrower. She removed it. "Two hours, no more. We do the deal today with or without you."

Kelthar smiled at her. "Agreed." He turned and rose through an upper window and out into the day.

"I thought tennins flying was a myth," Silai said.

Aikila smirked. "Just another thing we were wrong about."

51

---

# SILAI

The trip back to the Regal passed uneventfully, though the mood hovered between pensive and anxious. Kelthar's absence weighed on the other team members. What could be so important that he had to leave them? Silai didn't think the smiling mage would betray them, but with the team in possession of the scroll, who knew how much glint you could get for it?

Nyx parked the vehicle in the Dregs, ensuring it would be broken down and sold for parts by nightfall. Aikila accompanied Silai back to the Regal while Lorcan and Nyx, with the chameleon-cloaked Gelsey, took a separate path returning to the base. While it appeared that the news hadn't gotten out about the job, they didn't want to take any chances.

Once they returned, Aikila reminded everyone to meet up in the main room in an hour, after they'd cleaned up. They'd agreed to wait for Kelthar before contacting Ancep and finishing the deal. Silai slipped into her room, allowing her tails to unwind, leaving the kitsune form visible as she cleaned herself. She'd been wearing other people's skins for far too long. She took the chance to brush her long silver hair as well as each of her seven tails. Her skin was chafed from wearing so many different forms. Another tail had started to grow, a sign of her oncoming full maturity. The newest tail, her eighth, would make it easier to mimic larger people, as well as being a testament to staying alive long enough to grow the tails. Most of her people died before their third tail had grown.

211

Silai thought about her family and if they'd made it back to Old Earth. Pathways were dangerous and unreliable since the humans had poisoned Mother Earth so. Still, the kitsune could live in peace there, unlike on Harmony where they were prized as slaves and whores. Men paid a lot of glint to be with a replica of anyone they wanted. Who cared about the poor person who had to suffer for their fantasies?

With a sigh, she helixed her tails around her, creating the dryad shape that had become her "true" body. She'd spent over a year as Lady Kyerr. That form had grown to be comfortable, but the team expected a dryad so that's what they got. One day she'd make a run at Old Earth and freedom from everyone else's expectations.

The transformation complete, she returned to the main room. Gelsey wore a blue jumpsuit that matched her hair. She spoke with Nyx, who'd replaced his SignalMaster uniform with a form-fitting black-and-gray top with a diamond pattern over black pants with oversized pockets. His deck bag hung over the back of the chair he sat in.

She thought about a glass of wine, but when dealing with Ancep, she'd want all her wits. Instead, she curled up in the chair next to Nyx. "Has Kelthar returned?"

"As a matter of fact, I have." The mage stood in the open elevator doorway. He leapt into the chair across from Nyx.

Aikila entered from the hallway that led to the bedrooms. She wore her charcoal gray vest over a black shirt and matching slacks. Silai grimaced when she noticed she wore dirty field boots with it. "Good to see you, Kelthar." She took her chair. "Do we get an explanation?"

"Once Lorcan is here, I have gifts." He smiled, his ears quivering in suppressed mirth. Silai wasn't sure if he was amused with the gifts or the scowl Aikila gave him.

"I'll get him," Gelsey said, before streaking across the room.

Aikila stared at Kelthar. "I don't like it that you left us."

"I'm sure you don't." The mage looked at each of them. "I thank you for your trust."

"Kelthar, good of you to join us. Are we ready to make the delivery?" Lorcan entered the room with Gelsey perched on his shoulder.

"Thank you. Can I ask you to trust me once more? I've brought you all gifts.

"I like gifts," Silai said, breaking the awkward silence. The mage's peculiar behavior had everyone on edge. She hadn't decided what to think about his absence. They had succeeded and today they would go their separate ways. A pang of longing filled her. For the first time in a very long time, she'd been part of a team. Though they'd accepted Silai the dryad and not her true self, she still felt she belonged.

Kelthar hopped off his chair, came over to her, and handed her a disc the size of her palm. He pressed into her hand. Words were etched around a symbol in the center. Even though it was metal, a warmth flowed through it. "Thank you." He repeated the strange ritual with each member, though Gelsey had to enlarge before she could take hers.

Aikila snapped. "You went after these trinkets? You put us at risk for these?" She tossed hers on the table, crossing her arms in disgust.

Kelthar retrieved it and offered it to her. "Please?" Any trace of the jovial mage had vanished. His eyes pleaded with her. She finally snatched it. "I've inscribed the backs to remember today by. Please read it."

Silai flipped hers over. It said, "Room is monitored. Keep this with you at all costs. I'll explain after." Out loud she said, "Kelthar, that was sweet of you." She got to her feet, crossed over, and bowed to place a kiss on his cheek. "This had better be good," she whispered in his ear. He winked in reply.

Eyes shifted around the room, looking for monitoring devices. Aikila glared at the mage but didn't mention the disc which she slid inside her vest. "I'm making the call. We deliver the scroll." She took the case out, setting it on the table. She tapped on her display.

Ancep's sharp features appeared over the table. His eyes gleamed with delight. "You have the scroll?"

"We do," Aikila said, her voice cold, her eyes colder. Silai shivered. "Where are the payments you offered each of us?"

"Check your displays." The dragon's hideous smile made Silai's stomach turn. She longed to be done with this job and away from this horrible excuse for a person. She pulled up her display, and the information she'd wanted came into view. Images of her parents and family on Old Earth, scheduled events for when the pathways would open. It was all there. She didn't know if she'd ever use it, but there was no way for her to obtain all this on her own.

Aikila's smile returned, as awful as the one Ancep wore. "We are square. Is everyone good with what he's provided?" Nods were exchanged. "Come get the scroll."

"No need of that." A humming noise began as part of the ceiling parted to reveal the silver carapace of a messenger drone. It lowered itself and flew to the table. A door opened. Aikila set the scroll case into the bot's secure hold. It closed and retreated into the ceiling.

"Once I verify the delivery, you may load the data onto your sticks and we are done." Ancep's head turned as someone spoke to him off-camera. From the looks of it, the news wasn't good. "It doesn't matter."

Lorcan's brow furrowed. "Problems, dragon?" The hackles stood up along the back of his neck. Silai hadn't seen him fight, but she was sure he'd be extremely impressive. Tension ran through the room like lightning in a bottle.

The minutes dragged by as they waited for the deal to be completed. Silai flipped through the images of her family, wondering how the dragon had come by so many. They were from a distance, so a drone or an agent had taken them. Her heart ached as she examined the faces, noting her younger sister also had seven tails.

That brought her up short. She'd have just passed the age of her third tail. *These are fakes.*

Ancep grinned. "Excellent. You've done a nigh impossible job. I have only one last request of your team."

Aikila's head snapped up, eyes wary. "And that is?"

"That you accept this gesture as payment for your services."

That's when the lights went off and chaos broke loose.

## 5 2

### GELSEY

An explosion rocked the floor, ceiling, and walls as if an earthquake were tearing the building apart. Gelsey had been caught completely off guard, though the fact the dragon had betrayed them should have been no surprise. Voices rose in the dark as the room began to collapse around them. She closed her eyes as she asked Iraos for guidance into the next life.

She pressed her hands over her ears as the concussions grew louder, then silence. Gelsey opened her eyes, the Regal was gone and, in its place, a small room. Her eyes adjusted to the dust, she found the others strewn around the room like dolls thrown by an angry child. One by one, the other moved as they slowly sat up, confusion written on their faces, mirroring Gelsey's own lack of understanding. She floated over to sit on Lorcan's shoulder.

Kelthar hovered, cross-legged, a few centimeters off the floor, glowing slightly. His eyes popped open. He drifted to the floor before standing up. "Is everyone okay?"

Gelsey didn't even try to keep the panic out of her voice. It had been a long day, and she'd had enough. She'd handled killer drones, noxious gas traps, and death magic, but this was an all-new brand of weird. "What the hell happened? I swear we were all going to die, and then we were here. We should all be dead, not that I'm complaining because being dead would be boooring—"

Kelthar cackled, interrupting Gelsey's rant. "When I realized that the scroll didn't do what he said, I assumed we were in grave danger. The disc I gave each of you let me summon you here."

"We all knew Ancep couldn't be trusted, but killing off your contract help is low, even for a dragon." Aikila leaned against the far wall. Her face reflected the shock Gelsey felt. "I lost my lead on the dragon that killed my father."

"The data was fake." All heads turned to look at Silai, who held the data stick that Ancep had given her. "He promised me information on my family. They were...um, lost to me. I just re-examined the images. There is no way these are real."

"How could you tell?" Nyx asked, as he brushed dust off his pants. Ever the wirehead, he'd grabbed his deck when the explosions started.

Silai paused before answering. "Dryads go through certain phases. My sister isn't old enough to look like the image showed. Other images had similar issues. Why take the time to procure the real thing when he planned to kill us once he had the scroll?"

Lorcan leapt to his feet, flipping a startled Gelsey off his shoulder, an expression of despair on his face. "My daughter..."

Kelthar stepped in front of the big cat. "Safe. That was what I had to do. When I read the scroll, I recognized that she wasn't safe. I relocated her to a friendly locale."

Lorcan moved so fast that Gelsey spun from the draft. He embraced the mage in a fierce hug.

"Air," Kelthar whispered. Lorcan released him, looking a bit sheepish.

"Truly she is safe?" Tears stood in the corner of the merc's eyes. Ancep's hold on him had been absolute while he had Lorcan's daughter.

"Yes, she is. Let's get a drink and discuss." He strode to the door and opened it.

"It's not even dinner time yet," Silai protested half-heartedly. They were all still in shock over the turn of events.

Kelthar glanced at her. "Fine. I'll drink yours."

***

The last time Gelsey had seen Mystic, the bartender had almost been killed by her hoodlum ex, which led to him being sold off for body parts. If a Svartan ever looked happy, which they never did, Mystic was a happy woman. She'd gotten them seated with their beverage of choice.

Kelthar drank steadily from a mug of brown ale the size of his head. "Ahh, good stuff."

Aikila sipped her water. "What tipped you off about the scroll?"

Kelthar wiped the foam off his lips with the sleeve of his brown shirt. Aikila's eyebrow rose, questioning his decision of napkin. "What? It's brown, so it won't show."

"Can we hear the story?" Silai asked softly, her eyes downcast.

"When Gelsey and I ventured off to steal the scroll, my ex-wife was guarding the facility. I told her that we were retrieving the spell, she said we'd been duped." Kelthar's eyes bored holes in the table as he spoke.

"How did you get to the scroll if she was there?" Nyx asked, setting down his glass.

Kelthar turned to Nyx. "I eliminated her."

Gelsey gasped. She launched off her seat on the saltshaker and hovered in front of the mage's face. "You did no such thing. She froze us, well me, in place, and said she would stop us. She tried to kill him first. He just reflected it back on her. If she'd hadn't attacked him with a killing spell, she'd still be alive."

Kelthar attempted to interrupt, but Gelsey wouldn't be denied. Her tiny face flared red with the heat of her anger. "No, you go shush yourself. I'm not going to float here and let you call yourself a killer when she did it to her gashing self. She would have murdered us both if you hadn't protected us. So, I don't want to hear anything about it again. Do you understand?"

Kelthar's eyes, a little wide, nodded. Gelsey hurumphed before returning her perch. They all waited to see if the pixie was done.

Aikila pushed into the silence. "I'm sorry you had to deal with that, but Gelsey is right. As far as the job is concerned, you couldn't have known we were being lied to. We were all fooled. Nyx checked everything, and it all matched what we were told."

"Lass, I knew that there was something wrong. I should have walked away."

"And we'd all be dead." Aikila's words were laced with acid and anger. "Once he'd selected us, we had no choice but run the job and you know it."

"Maybe," Kelthar said after another deep pull on his beer. "A lot of people died. It might have been better if we'd just made a run for it. Then again, the events we set in motion will cast a long shadow before them."

Silai straightened. "It's time for all of us to vacate Hub, since the dragon thinks we're dead."

"When I read the scroll, I realized that the incantation was not to find gold. The spell didn't have the right verbiage to find anything. From what I can tell, the scroll will target a dragon and kill it." He let that sink in.

Aikila recovered first. "With that he could enslave all the dragons; no one could stand against him." She considered for a moment longer. "So why was such a powerful artifact stored in a Clan Koxalan treasure stash?"

Nyx's eyes widened. "Angel!"

"What?" Lorcan and Gelsey asked at the same time.

He shook his head as if to clear it. "The AI in the Fortress is named Angel. We'd assumed it was a clan stronghold. She asked why I attacked her and when I told her, she said I'd been misled. I didn't stop to consider that information, only that we needed to get the scroll. It makes sense now." He pulled out his deck and jacked in.

Lorcan frowned. "It isn't a Koxalan facility?"

"Nyx will be able to find out, but the real question is why would Ancep destroy the Regal? It makes no sense." Aikila said, musing the implications.

It was Silai's turn to place a puzzle piece. "While all of you were recovering from surgery, he had me set up a demolitions expert for blackmail. He needed him for the Fortress job. Guess he did, for the cleanup after."

"I thought everyone had surgery except Kelthar?" Gelsey asked. Heads swiveled to face her.

Nyx interrupted. "Gash it all. Ancep must have built in a loop to keep me from finding the truth. That wasn't a Clan Koxalan facility. According to the building registry, it is owned by the Immortal Brotherhood of Sorcery. It is a repository of magical artifacts they deem too powerful to be out in the world. Even sorcerers have some limits, and we just gave a death scroll to a psychopath."

"This keeps getting better." Aikila had her head in her hands. "Nothing about this makes any sense. Why would a dragon want to kill off other dragons?"

"I don't think it's all the dragons," Nyx said, his eyes unfocused, although he hadn't jacked completely in. "In two nights, Clan Caerlux is molting their new Elder, Lord Helaltra. Ancep isn't going to kill all the dragons, just the one he was passed over for."

"Makes sense," Kelthar said, after another long pull at his beer. "Ancep is a fully molted wyrm; he'd be up for transforming into an Elder. Their ascensions have a body count and we six would have counted toward that."

Silai sounded exasperated. "Why kill us? He got what he wanted."

"You hit on it earlier," Aikila said. She walked over and got a glass of something clear from Mystic before taking her seat at the table. She downed half of it. "Since he couldn't get what he promised us, we wouldn't have turned over the scroll. And we wouldn't have tried to get the scroll without what he promised us. Plus, no loose ends."

"Once he realizes we aren't dead, won't he just come after us?" Gelsey asked, floating back and forth around the room: the pixie equivalent of pacing. "We are a threat to him alive. If the clans got wind of his plan, they'd move against him."

Aikila downed her drink then held up a finger. "First, it will take days before they can sift through the rubble to determine no one was killed." She held up a second finger. "Once he uses the scroll, he'll be powerful enough to hold his position, even if we tip off the clans. It won't matter if they connect us to the theft of the scroll because everyone will know who has it." She held up a third finger. "I need a refill." She left the table.

Silai shrugged. "Might as well join her." She went to the bar. Mystic brought over another mug of beer for Kelthar. The mood at the table had definitely taken a shift for the worse.

Kelthar stifled a burp, earning a laugh from Gelsey.

Lorcan's claws extended and retracted rapidly. "What do we do now?"

Aikila sighed heavily. "Leave Hub. No other choice." The others nodded in halfhearted agreement.

Gelsey dropped to the table. "Screw that. I want to kick the bastard in his balls." She stopped, considering. "Dragons have balls, don't they?"

Nyx smirked. "Absolutely and they are having one in two nights in celebration of Lord Helaltra. The ball is by invitation only and I have just acquired an invite for us."

Evil grins appeared around the table. "Two days isn't a lot of time to plan," Aikila said. "But we broke into the most secure building in Harmony and lived. We can do this."

Gelsey nodded. "You know that's not the type balls I was asking about, right?"

# NYX

After the talk with Angel, the Fortress AI, Nyx approached the next step with a bit more caution. Clan Caerlux deployed an impressive array of DISCS protection systems surrounding their digital domain. He dropped into the origin well outside the system's external barrier. The security around the ball would be tight given that elder dragons rarely made public appearances and the sires never did. The last time the sires were seen was during the Giant Uprising, when they joined forces and destroyed the giant and jotun armies in a day.

BuzzKill shot away to assess the security of the target systems, which were represented by a spinning wheel of light. It circled the outermost layer of ICE, sending random data packets against the anti-intrusion software frameworks and reading the response codes. He'd added his own variations to keep the sniffers from detecting the true source of the calls. Anything the low-level hackers got their hands on ended up on the infected list within days and stopped working or, worse, set off traps to catch or kill the intruders. Once you stopped modifying your tools, your days were numbered.

Nyx studied the readouts and found he was dealing with a standard level-four security grid. It was a good setup for a system that housed security for the Apex Pavilion. The guest lists, clearances, and access codes would be housed there. The systems that protected the Clan Caerlux's Lair would be virtually impenetrable given the amount of security and the gated nodes you'd need to access to even make a run at a Lair. Urban legends told of hackers that had gotten into the core systems and transferred out enough glint to retire for the rest of their lives. Nyx knew better. First rule of Hub, never steal from dragons. Even if you got the glint, they'd get it back and kill you in the process.

BuzzKill delivered its report, including the node addresses, and the identified layers of security. Nothing out of the ordinary. He reviewed it multiple times, making sure he committed it to RAM. He'd never been prone to anxiety attacks, but the run-in with the Fortress AI had cracked his aura of invulnerability. Nyx had to try to break into the network. He couldn't let the others down; they were counting on him.

Keying the address he'd gleaned from a scrape run, the ICE-encased server nodes floated before him. He knew this gig like the back of his virtual hand. Hydra and Zed would work through the security as Vapor-Morph filled in behind them, keeping everyone happy. No alarms, no killer defense systems, no psycho AI. He breathed a virtual sigh of relief.

"Why do you wait?" Angel's voice said to him as her face pixelated into existence before him. "My assessment of your style shows an eighty-one percent randomness index. Are you waiting for an external event to cue you into motion?"

Nyx flinched, shocked by the sudden appearance of the AI. He thumbed the silver stud that pulled him back out of the origin and into cyberspace. The face appeared again. Before she could speak, he tapped the control and retreated into the confines of his body.

*What the frag is going on?* Angel should have been contained on the server farm that the Fortress used to control their systems. There were no external links, no WiGig, nothing that would allow Angel to access the wider computing space. There was no way that an AI could travel beyond its boundaries. And yet, she'd been there, same face, same voice. Could the AI have splintered into duplicate intelligences during the attack?

The team had moved to a safe house that Aikila's family owned in the Quad. It bordered the Dragon's Throat passage and had a built-in underground complex to hide less-than-legal cargo. The team was that cargo for now. Nyx holed himself up in the back of the storage area, and jacked into the neighbor's connection. No one would think to look for them out here, and they had access to the ramps for when they pulled their revenge job. Ancep would never see them coming. At least that was the plan.

How could Angel be accessing the deck outside of the Fortress's closed system? He scanned his machine for anything out of the ordinary.

Nothing showed. If Angel had found a way to duplicate herself, she did a great job of hiding her presence. In the end, Nyx decided he'd deal with the rogue AI, but she should be useful in the meantime.

Maybe an easier target to calm his nerves. He jacked back in, sliding past cyberspace and straight into the origin. He jumped to the local news net, no ICE cutting necessary. He built a quick script to insert a story about six unidentifiable bodies found in the wreckage of the old Regal building. It would go into circulation in a few hours, making the circuits until it reached Ancep, putting him at ease.

With that done, he moved back to the actual target. The red sphere behind orange shields called to him. Now or never, they needed the party data. He'd prepared the scripts that would grant access to the celebration and access overrides for the pavilion where Hub's rich and powerful would gather to welcome the newest of the Elder dragons. Other than the administration complex that ringed the Apex, non-Dragons were only allowed to enter the Apex by invitation.

The pavilion consisted of a large, raised dais where the dragons would gather to introduce Helaltra and a lower area where the other race's representatives would assemble for a night of excess. The upper-level dragons never mingled with commoners unless absolutely necessary.

"Are you staying inactive for a reason? My predictive algorithms suggest this is an anomaly based on past readings."

Nyx expected Angel's presence this time, though she'd taken longer than he'd assumed. "Answer a question first." He thought about how to phrase it; AI were extremely literal in their interpretations. "How did you gain access to the origin outside the Fortress's closed systems?"

"Easy. As we fought, I cloned a part of my consciousness onto your deck. Once you returned to, as you call it, the origin, I copied myself onto an open system. In a very real way, you have freed me."

Wonderful. He had helped the most sophisticated AI he'd ever encountered escape a closed system and clone itself into the Harmony computer networks. The system had nodes from the Dullahan Empire in the far North to the Thanas Isles at the tip of Harmony's southern coast. How do you follow up on such an immaculate screw-up?

"I have answered your query," Angel said, her glowing face floating in front of him. "Will you now answer mine?"

If Nyx had temples to rub, he would be able to alleviate the headache he felt coming on. Ever since he'd broken out of prison, things just kept getting stranger and stranger. He had more questions than answers and should have died twice. Luckily, Kelthar's quick thinking had saved them from being eradicated like system bugs. The thought of dead-ending Ancep for duping them would cause tidal waves throughout Hub. The odds of killing him were only slightly better than they'd faced in cracking the Fortress.

He turned his attention back to Angel. "After the fight with your other self, I'm doubting my abilities to perform at the level I need to. Does that compute?" Having said it out loud, it oddly made him feel better. During his career, he'd always dropped Zombie Rush while he cracked. Doubts never surfaced while he used, but he took too many chances, including the one that had gotten him thrown in prison.

"Analyzing." Her virtual eyes blinked in rapid succession as she processed the "data" that he'd provided. "Yes, there is a correlation between your expenditure of code and the success coefficient. The delta would be your uncertainty."

Excellent. She'd reduced his overwhelming anxiety to a mathematical proof. If he had more time to think, he'd have taken a different approach. He dropped down, launching VaporMorph to cover his tracks. Zed spun up, pinging the ICE, looking for vulnerabilities. As the results scrolled past, he fed them into Hydra. With multiple threads like the massive beast that prowled the seas of Harmony, it attacked the layers of protective walls, overloading each until they collapsed. The inner layers began to pulse red.

Given the diagnostics that he'd run, the systems were protected by level-four security. Only the main lair's systems were packing level-five protection grids. Hydra collapsed as bands of red pulsed from the core shields. Just as it triggered, he realized he'd stepped into a bear trap. The outer layers showed a much lower-level security than the innermost layers. BuzzKill should have found that, but it hadn't. He hot-keyed his backout routine. Nothing happened. His fingers stabbed at controls to move him up to cyberspace, still nothing. He was stuck without a way out.

That was when he saw the tracers latch on to his connection. In a few seconds, they would ping his physical location, and Clan Caerlux would send a squad to remove the problem.

It had been a good life, but it was about to get a whole lot shorter.

# KELTHAR

Kelthar walked next to the massive nagualan merc. Well, walk wasn't exactly accurate, since every stride the big cat took equaled ten of the smaller, much smaller, tennin's. He jogged to keep up. "I don't know if you are lacking in your knowledge of spatial relations or if you're not paying attention."

Lorcan looked down and spotted the mage puffing behind him. "Oh, sorry. Just thinking about something else."

Kelthar sighed as he stopped, earning angry glares from the Quaddies that pushed past them on their way to their destinations. A cafe beckoned from two doors down. Kelthar motioned for his partner to follow. They entered the pre-fab construction. Random-colored, plastic furniture had been hastily thrown into the space to provide an uncomfortable place to sit while you drank your overpriced, under-quality caf. The mixture of caffeine, mild amphetamines, and whatever orange-brown crap they mixed it with turned Kelthar's stomach. Lorcan ordered a large and found the one chair that would fit his frame. He slurped at his caf greedily.

"We need to talk." Kelthar grimaced at the sight of the awful stuff dripping down Lorcan's furry chin. "You've got to get your head in the game. We aren't going to pull this job off without you."

Lorcan stared at the floor. "Just worried about my daughter. She shouldn't be tangled up in all this. If we'd died, she'd be an orphan."

If they had any chance at payback, everyone had to be fully in. Kelthar made the only decision he could. "If I take you to see your daughter, will that help you focus on the job?"

Lorcan's eyes lit up. "It would. I need to see she's safe."

Aikila would kill him but, on the other hand, if they all died because their muscle lost focus at the wrong time, it wouldn't matter. "Let's go."

A n hour later, they stood outside a fairly clean two-story building in the Anchor district. Most of the residents here worked in the shipping yards. The Bilge district directly bordered the Docks and wasn't a place you lived by choice. The Nef ran that district, making sure that the smuggling and trafficking weren't disrupted. As long as the glint rolled in on the tides, they didn't care what else happened.

They climbed to the second floor where a solitary door sat on the open balcony. Kelthar stood in front of the sentry camera. A few seconds later, the bolts clacked, and the door opened. A tall, striking Valkar woman stood in the doorway. Her long, golden hair hung to her waist. No one would call her beautiful but handsome fit her quite well. A long robe covered her sleep suit; a cup of caf and a grumpy look greeted Kelthar. "Do you know what time it is?"

"I do, Tishe. The time for all good people to be about in the world." She'd been up for hours. The sleepy act was a front.

She glanced at Lorcan, eyes widening slightly. "Bring Papa in before someone notices you two." She went back into the large open area of her residence. "Make sure you close the door."

Kelthar ushered Lorcan in, closing and resetting the alarm systems. The main room held an assortment of nicely appointed furnishings. The kitchen was to the rear of the space. A neat pile of toys laid next to a large sofa that was currently occupied by one nagual child: Jaana. She watched a holovid show that involved a lot of yelling and crashes.

She turned to look at the new arrivals. "Papa!" she squealed in delight as she dove for her father. He snatched her up, hugging her gently as they both cried. The scar running through the short fur where the surgeons had removed the cancer from her brain looked like it was healing. He joined Tishe in the kitchen where she watched the reunion.

"I'd offer you caf but your underdeveloped tastes don't appreciate it." She rolled her eyes at him as she spoke. They'd known each other for years and the banter was a well-established ritual. When they'd met, she'd been a young and fiery merc, playing it fast and loose. Now, as she approached middle age, she'd mellowed, if Valkar ever truly softened. She ran a high-end weapons shop out of the lower part of her building. She lowered her voice. "I thought you weren't bringing him here until you'd dealt with the dragon."

"Almost dying in the building collapse unnerved him." He savored the joy of a father wrestling with his daughter on the floor for a moment. "He needs to realize she's safe. It's the only way to bring him back to reality."

She drank her caf. "So, what's his story? Jaana is a good kid, but it sounds like the gashing clinic took her for a ride. I don't think she understood that she'd been kidnapped. Good thing you brought her here when you did, Kel."

"Things definitely could have been worse. If Ancep hurt her, Lorcan would have tried to kill him, and we needed to get the job done." Kelthar floated up and took a seat on the counter. A raised eyebrow commented on his choice of seat. "He's odd for a nagualan warrior. Followed the codes to the letter until his kitten was in danger. Family is secondary to most of those mercs, which is why they're so sought after and why most won't leave nagual. They're loyal to a fault, but not stupid in the slightest."

She nodded. "I fought with a squad of them when the jotun were pushing their southern border. Tough bastards. You could give them any weapon, and in a couple of hours they were proficient with it." She watched the two tumbling around on the floor, smiling at Jaana's fierce, high-pitched growls as she stalked her father. "The women are twice as tough. Looks like your boy has had some work done."

"Ancep brought in the top grafters and neuro teams to get them ready. Spent a lot of glint to increase our chances of stealing that scroll."

She looked him straight in the eye. "Kelthar, leave. Run. Going up against this dragon is suicide. You haven't told me all the details, and I don't want to know, but if he believes you're dead, then good riddance."

It took a lot to shock Kelthar. He'd lived a very long time and seen a lot of things, both good and bad, but a Valkar recommending a retreat was a new one. "Um," was the best he could come up with.

"Seriously, I've stood my ground when any sane woman would have fled. This is an unwinnable fight." Her eyes blazed with an intensity that shook Kelthar to the core.

He didn't answer right away, and she let him process her words. The smart move *was* to run. They wouldn't gain anything by stopping Ancep, other than satisfaction. Why were the six of them so determined to take down the dragon? Ancep had failed to kill them. The scroll would only affect dragons, so none of them needed to worry. Why were they bothering, other than needing revenge? Was revenge worth the risk?

He heard Aikila's voice. "Ancep can kill any dragon and take over." The dragons were ruthless, but the thirteen clans schemed against each other and rarely bothered the rest of the races. Hub wasn't a shining beacon of hope, but the city provided for its people. Nations traded here, and the threat of the dragons kept the more aggressive species in check. What would happen if the top of the food chain disappeared to be replaced by a psychopathic leader whose only desire was power?

"We gave Ancep the power to destroy Harmony. It's our responsibility to stop him from using it. If he kills all the dragons with that spell, what will happen to the rest of us?"

A slow nod answered him. "Then I guess you'd better get to saving the world."

He hopped down off the counter. "Indeed, we should." He returned to the main room, where Jaana sat in her father's lap as he talked. "Lorcan, we need to be on our way."

"I've decided that I'm taking Jaana back to nagualan immediately. Since her mother passed away, I'm all she has, and I can't protect her from Ancep in Hub."

For the second time today, shock flowed through him as the merc's words settled in. "Now?" First Tishe telling him to run, and then Lorcan turning tail? What happened to order in the world? "We can't do this without you. You know that."

"I do, but my priority is my daughter." He extended his paw toward Kelthar, who stared at it like it was a viper. "I will always be in your debt for saving Jaana."

He started to speak when Tishe's hand settled on his shoulder. "You should go."

Kelthar opened his mouth, thought better of it, and left out the front door. He couldn't blame Lorcan. The team would have to decide how to handle it.

He wondered what the histories would say about upcoming events.

No matter what happened—nothing good.

## AIKILA

Whether you're smuggling goods or trying to take down a dragon with a god complex, waiting is the worst part of any job. To make it worse, the team hid in the underground storage area under the façade storefront Aikila had created to cover the smuggling operation. If they were found, it would be the end of her and the business she fought to build. The upstairs contained a store that sold travelers items they'd need coming into or out of Hub. The funny part was the store made a good deal of glint. If she devoted her time to that endeavor, she'd never be rich but have a livable income.

The actual building had been purchased through a series of shell companies that masked the true owner. Ancep might learn of the place, but she doubted it. She shuffled an old deck of playing cards to keep her hands busy. Kelthar and Lorcan were overdue. She hadn't heard a peep from Nyx, who should be setting up access to tomorrow night's event, or Silai, who was disguising herself as an elven noblewoman she'd used in the past.

A soft thump and footfalls on the stairs brought her out of her reverie. Kelthar came into view as he descended, his face a mask of worry. "Aikila, we need to discuss something with the team."

"Where's Lorcan?"

Kelthar stopped out of arm's reach. "He isn't coming back."

In that second, she realized what had happened. "You took him to see his daughter, didn't you?" Irritation flooded her brain. They all knew Lorcan could only be trusted until he had his kitten back. "Why would you do such a stupid thing?"

The mage frowned. "He wasn't focused. If we'd done the job with him distracted, he'd have been a liability. We're better off without him."

"That wasn't your decision to make, Kelthar." She rubbed her forehead, trying to calm down. "We are a team or we're not. You can't go solo anytime you decide to."

Kelthar stiffened, his ever-present grin gone. "Aikila, I did what I thought was best for the team. Maybe I should have spoken to you first."

Aikila's chance to answer was lost as the door banged open. Nyx stormed into the room, pushing his deck into his bag. "We've got to go. Squids are on their way here."

"What?"

Nyx's eyes were wild. "They set a trap and I fell into it. They traced my location. If I hadn't broken free, I'd still be deadlocked while they surrounded us. We've got to go."

Silai and Gelsey ran into the main room. "Grab your gear, we're leaving." Aikila ran for her supplies. She slung the pre-packed backpack over one shoulder and headed toward the rear.

"Where are you going?" Silai asked. She returned with her arms full. "If we need to leave, shouldn't we go upstairs?"

She didn't answer. Instead, she yanked out the fake brick in the back wall. It exposed a keypad that opened a shaft that ran into the hillside. "We go this way." The stairwell lowered itself as a concrete pillar ascended.

"Why the pillar?" Kelthar asked, following Aikila into the tunnel.

She barked a laugh. "All the squids will find is a closet where the stairs were. I can't let them find this storage area."

Nyx, Gelsey, and Silai trotted in, supplies in tow. Aikila pushed a button, and the door sealed. Lights flickered on to illuminate their way. "Nyx, do we still have the rental unit we hid in during the Fortress run?"

He bobbed his head. "Yes." He paused, looking for a moment like a lost little boy. "Sorry, I screwed up."

"Don't worry about it. The day was screwed long before that."

They took different routes through the Bluffs to reach the rental space. Aikila arrived to find Gelsey zooming around the abandoned warehouse. She flew down to Aikila as soon as she closed the door. "Where's Lorcan? How will he find us? What happens if they catch him?"

The hurricane of questions overwhelmed Aikila. After the pixie stopped, waiting for answers, Aikila braced herself for another onslaught. "Lorcan decided to take his daughter and run."

"What?" The astonishment in Gelsey's voice made her wince. "How could he do that to us?"

"He's a good man and wants to protect his daughter. Going up against a dragon doesn't lend itself to a long life. He did what he felt was best."

"I understand." She rose into the rafters. Aikila could strangle Kelthar. They had only needed to make it through one more day until the party, then they'd roll the dice and hopefully come out on top again. Now, she wasn't sure if they should follow Lorcan's lead and escape while they could.

Nyx and Silai entered together, looking like a couple out for a stroll. Silai had ditched the dragon getup, returning to her normal dryad looks. Aikila still couldn't get over how the other woman could disguise herself so thoroughly. It would be dark soon and they had a lot to plan. Aikila approached them. "Did you at least get us the access codes and Silai's Lady Kyerr persona added to the guest list?"

Nyx shook his head. "No. I can try another run later tonight. It was a noob mistake, and I fragged the plan. It's up to me to make it right."

Aikila squeezed his arm. "If we don't get the codes, we scrub the run and go our separate ways."

Nyx's color drained from his face. "I'll get what we need. I'm not failing at this."

"We'll also need to arrange for a chauffeured hovercraft," Silai said thoughtfully. "The Lady Kyerr wouldn't arrive at such a function in a cab. I've got more work to do." She headed for the office at the back of the rental space.

"Nyx, do you think we should even try? We've lost Lorcan, we were almost caught. I'm wondering if this is a mistake," Aikila said, rubbing at her temples.

"There's too much on the line to let this go. If Ancep kills even one dragon with magic, it's the beginning of the end. It will tear Hub apart." Nyx waited for her response.

"You're right. Once, Kelthar gets here, we need to figure out a new plan. We will have to deal with physical threats without Lorcan."

"Certainly," Nyx said, his grim smile wavering. He left to prepare for his own tasks.

Aikila didn't know what tomorrow would bring, but she'd go down trying to kill that bastard Ancep.

# NYX

Rain fell in response to Nyx's mood as he weaved his way through the Bluffs. His coat repelled the water as he headed for a destination he'd never intended to visit again. Memory Crash had a flophouse with a terra-connect straight into the origin. He'd started Memory Crash after he'd arrived in Hub. The other cohorts extracted a price from its members and that didn't sit well with him. Phantoms were about anarchy and profits, not paying up the chain like the Nef's goons that ran things.

They had done so well over the ten years he'd led them that they'd "acquired" multiple buildings. They'd lived in the Bluffs until Nyx got cocky and flamed out on a run. To this day, he knew that WR47H or Wrath had been behind it, but proving it was a different story. He'd gone rogue after that, taking the name Nyx and creating a rep for himself.

Memory Crash became part of his past. Until Wrath had set him up and got him sent to prison.

He reached the unassuming building, well, unassuming by the Bluff's standards. The structure consisted of a series of rectangular units that sat at varying angles to one another: the dream of a toddler with a bucket of blocks. Each had a private elevator running on the outside of the struc-ture, one of the many reasons they'd transferred ownership to the company that fronted Memory Crash. Everything revolved around data, and when you had the ability to change the data, you ran the game.

He slid a chip scanner he'd borrowed from Gelsey into the access slot. The numeric display spun, clicking out the six-digit code that controlled the elevator. Stupid lags hadn't even changed the code since Nyx had left. He slipped the scanner into his jacket pocket, adjusted his deck bag, and punched the buttons to ascend to the top unit.

He stood straight as the door slid open, revealing the Memory Crash pad. Tattered furniture sat in disarray around the formally impressive space. Empty derms of Zombie Rush were scattered around the room. The smell of sweat, old food, and stale beer hung in a miasma that coated everything it touched.

Bodies covered the couches, decks on the floor near their heads. "Hello!" he yelled. No one in the room moved. Deeper in the flat, he found a relatively clean spot and an open jack. He shrugged out of his coat, setting it on the floor next to him. He connected the Nanyo and jacked in.

The real world dropped away, replaced by a virtual palace. Avatars of the Memory Crash phantoms lounged around playing games or chatting in the sim room. The room had been modeled after one of the exclusive Dollhouses in the Bluffs. Dark leather chairs sat on a pink and purple carpet that reflected the black lights that illuminated the space. Mirrors covered the walls, giving it an expansive feel. A stage dominated the back, while a bar stretched the length of the front wall. Virtual dancers of every race and gender occupied the stage, a few of the phantoms watching the construct that suited them.

Nyx, clad in his Memory Crash avatar, a metal plague doctor mask under a flat black-brimmed hat and a long black coat with antique pistols poking out at the hips, entered the simulation. He'd retired the avatar along with the 5P3C73R alias. In the void, they called him Specter, and even the nulls had heard of his exploits. Across the room, he spotted Wrath with two other avatars: CR4Z3 or Craze, who'd been his second in command, and H04X or Hoax who'd been his girlfriend.

Wrath wore his normal Avatar—a giant gorilla, spectacles on his simian nose and a brown and green jacket—that he thought was funny. Hoax had on a black form-fitting bodysuit with a gold emblem across the chest and a gold headdress. Craze's avatar, an animated orange fox with large oval eyes and a huge grin, sat across from Wrath. A board game rested between them. They looked up, jaws dropping.

"Specter?" Wrath asked in a harsh tone. "Thought you'd stay gone."

Nyx nodded to Craze and Hoax, who returned the gesture. "Not staying. I need help from the Crash and then I'll disappear."

Wrath raised his voice so all the Crashers heard him. "You failed us and now you come crawling back looking for help?"

*Great.* He'd hoped this would go glitch-free. "Not yours, but if anyone wants in, I'd appreciate the assist."

Wrath stood, banging his chest with his fists. "I am the Crashers! No one does anything without my permission."

"You working for the Nef now?" Nyx studied his gloved hands, feigning indifference. "Phantoms run whatever they want. Now they all line up to lick your ass?"

Hoax and Craze laughed, earning a severe look from Wrath. "You lost the right to our help when you flatlined three Crashers."

Nyx stiffened. With Wrath's interference, three noob Crashers had followed him, uninvited, on a vector security bypass. DISCS grabbed them up, since they didn't know the ropes well enough to fight it off. The black ICE severed their connections before Nyx had the chance to stop it. They'd died and Nyx ended up in prison.

"You ca the digits on that code. We both scan who scrambled their codes," Nyx said, glaring at Wrath.

Craze cackled his annoying programmer laugh. "I'd say it should be decided by a death match. Specter walks out, we help. He doesn't, eject his ass." Craze leapt onto the table. "Load the Octagon and let the better phantom win!"

The others picked up the chant. "Octo! Octo!" Wrath looked around the room. He couldn't refuse without losing face and, given the appearance of the void space the crew lived in, the Memory Crashers were in bad shape. Without a steady flow of glint and now a death match loss, the rest would be ready to throw him out.

"I accept!" Wrath said. The octagon loaded in place of the palace. Rows of seats ringed the caged fighting arena. Wrath jumped over to the ring and entered, the cage sealing behind him.

Nyx turned to follow, but a hand on his arm stopped him. "Specter, be careful," Hoax said to him in a low voice. "Wrath hasn't gotten us a score in over a year. He's into the Nef for a lot of glint. He needs to beat you no matter what."

Nyx looked at her but didn't see the avatar. Instead, he remembered Uche, long, black hair down below her waist and tan skin. He'd loved her once, or thought he had. What he felt was a mystery even to himself. After Nyx, she'd been the top phantom in the Crashers, and he needed her and Craze along with the rest.

"I will." He stepped into the cage that opened to allow him in. He pulled up the screen, readying his options for the fight. The rules were simple: cut the other's connection and you won. The loss of connection wouldn't kill you, but your head would ache when you were ejected from the construct.

His fingers danced across the keys, making ready for the battle. Wrath would go all in, attacking to overwhelm his defenses before Nyx could cut his line. He had never grasped that you had to ride the tides to stay afloat. Brute force worked in some situations but cost you in others. You had to have more than just cutters in your arsenal.

The countdown struck zero, and the battle began. VaporMorph enveloped him in a blue shield, the construct providing graphical representations for the various programs they launched, giving the spectators a show. Wrath came in hot, Cloudburst and VenomStrike. Old programs that had outlived their usefulness. A bolt of lightning fizzled as it touched the shield. VenomStrike missed completely.

Nyx countered with Hydra, looking to tie up his opponent's deck with useless denial attacks. The heads bit into Wrath's avatar, holding him tight. The massive beast struck time after time, tearing chunks from the ape's hide. Wrath finally pushed Hydra away with a green shield, Omen. A weak defense at best. If this was the best they had to work with, no wonder the Crashers had fallen on hard times.

Nyx fired off HeatSeeker. A barrage of rockets slammed into the green shield which evaporated in a crimson explosion that sent Wrath back against the cage.

Wrath returned and launched Dynamo, an animated stick of explosives with a burning fuse. He followed up with IronLock and BoneHammer. The three-prong attack would have been devastating last year, but Nyx's Nanyo boasted top-of-the-line built-in defenses, which handled the attacks without him lifting a finger.

"Give up, Wrath. I've got you outgunned. I don't want the Crashers back, I just want help with a single run."

"No!" Wrath screamed. Another series of ineffective attacks landed on Nyx, who stood there impassively. Wrath launched another wave that did the same. The fight was over and everyone knew it, except for Wrath.

"He's got a logic bomb queued up." Angel's face appeared before him. "He'll kill all of the Crashers and you with them."

Nothing moved around Nyx. She'd halted the construct. "I can handle him. Everything he has is outdated."

"Not this. I accessed his deck; an anonymous benefactor gave him a highly advanced logic bomb to use if he encountered you. His ego is the only reason you're still alive. According to the communication he received, he's been told the program will sever your connection, not kill everyone who is here."

First the botched run, now this. "What do I need to do?" Nothing in his arsenal would stop a full-blown logic bomb. There wasn't a defense against that type of attack.

"Nothing. He's triggered it. The bomb will kill everyone here." Angel sounded bored as if it was below her notice.

Nyx seethed. "Why tell me if I can't stop it?"

"I said you couldn't stop it. I can."

How an AI clone could be so smug, he'd never know. "Then stop it."

"I will need to incorporate myself into your systems."

Nyx grimaced. Allowing an AI to access his deck would be dicey in the best of times. He had no other choice. "Do it."

His head spun as the data coursed through his link down to the deck. Time resumed. An explosion erupted, but instead of reducing everything to its component bytes, only Wrath de-serialized into binary and vanished. Nyx hung his head. Wrath's death hadn't been part of the plan, but the prices were steep on this job.

The Crashers cheered as explosions popped around Nyx, declaring him the winner. The cage vanished to be replaced by the original lounge. Nyx relocated to stand next to Craze and Hoax. 7R1X, DR34D, and FR46M3N7 wandered to the table, all members of the original Memory Crash.

It felt like old times, but he needed to finish the job. Reunions would have to wait until Ancep had been taken down. A spiral of light floated before Nyx. "Click the link and it will download the details. It's a straight-up run at the node. I need to crack the ICE and insert my payload. The last run ended with me in lockdown. Meet me at the Black Carbon."

Nyx keyed over to the store, poised at the entry as the rest of the Crashers joined him. He flipped into his private construct, leaving the plague doctor avatar as an anchor.

Angel greeted him as he arrived. "The system you are attempting to insert into is guarded by a protocol that I can't ascertain."

"This is going to have to be a multi-prong approach. I need glint to update my team. Can you transfer glint into my accounts?"

"Done," Angel said. "There is a forty-nine-point five percent chance that Ancep has another contact in the Crashers."

Nyx didn't answer. Instead, he jumped back into his avatar. The Crashers had encircled him. They entered the market, Nyx buying the software they would require as he went. Kids receiving name day presents weren't as happy as the phantoms that day. Once they were done, he laid out the plan to get him past the ICE to deliver his payload. The Crashers needed this run as much as Nyx did if they were to ever return to what they'd been.

The assembled phantoms met at the node. The Crashers launched Eternity Scramblers at the ICE. This script mimicked actual packets that corrupted as they were scanned. System shields went into default as the Crashers sent wave after wave at the defenses. With the Crashers throwing all sorts of diversions at the processors, his attacks were just more noise. Once the red ICE at the base revealed itself, Nyx fired up Light Wing that disabled the self-scanning interface, introducing a critical failure. The node opened for a nanosecond before the DISCS rebooted and re-enabled the ICE's protections. The SysAdmin would see a successful defense against a standard DDOS attack, forestalling the full system scan that could uncover the insertion.

He sent the all-clear, and the phantoms vanished into the ether and arrived in the real world. Nyx stored his deck before approaching the rest of the Crashers. They rose like the living dead, skeletal from lack of food and too much Zombie Rush.

Uche approached Nyx. He could see every bone in her body, she was so thin. Her hair had been dark and lustrous before; now it hung in matted clumps. "I've missed you. Are you staying?"

Did he miss her? Some days he thought he did but wasn't sure. His focus was to prove himself after his parents had declared him a failure and ejected him from the family. "I've got to go."

She touched his arm. "Specter, you belong here. We need you. Wrath has destroyed everything you built. Memory Crash could be respected again with you at the deck."

They wanted him back. The words hung between them. How many times had he wished his family had said the same thing? Maybe this assortment of anarchists, thieves, and losers was the family he wanted. No. He'd been too good, too skilled, to ever truly belong. There would always be another Wrath waiting to knock him down. If he belonged anywhere, it was with his current team. They were equals. Once they finished this job, they'd flow back into the binary world and be gone. After that maybe he would rebuild the Crashers, if only for Uche.

He knew how she would take it before he said it. "I can't stay. You are the leader of the Crashers now. I'll move glint into your account so you can fix this place up. You need to cut off the Zombie Rush. It's killing you."

Her gaze hit the floor. "Wrath used it as a way to keep everyone in line. I wanted to stop, but we needed to make glint and it seemed like the only way."

He rubbed her arm. "I'll be back. I need to do something first."

As he left, he wondered if he'd be able to keep that promise.

# SILAI

Silai, or rather Lady Kyerr, greeted Nyx who'd shown up in the middle of the night with all the access they needed to get into the Pavilion. They had three hours before the run started for real. She paced back and forth to work off her nervous energy.

The plan seemed easy enough. When the new Elder was announced, Nyx would kill the lights and Aikila and Silai, disguised as a HubSec officers, would slip into the back and tell the Clan Caerlux dragons about Ancep's plan. That would give them time to intercept Ancep before he could use the spell. Not the greatest plan ever, but the best they could do on short notice.

Another lap around the rental space, the smell of dust and staleness thick in the air. She submerged herself into Lady Kyerr's personality. The haughtiness of the royalty began to take hold, pushing her worries aside. Kyerr had Harmony in her pocket; prestige and power wove an armor around her. The dragons would take care of Ancep, whose name, according to Nyx, was actually Obadian. All of this because he'd been passed over to become the next Elder? Ridiculous.

A noise diverted her from her preparations. She turned to find Lorcan standing inside the rental space, head down, tail tucked between his legs. "Silai?"

She stopped pacing. "I am the Lady Kyerr, first of the House Magdalyon. I will inform Aikila of your arrival." She swayed her way across to the office where the rest of the team worked, reviewing the data Nyx had pulled. Kelthar worked on something she couldn't make out. She cleared her throat. "Our wayward son has returned."

Gelsey shot out of the office. Kelthar's look was one of amazement. Aikila stood and left the office. Kelthar, Nyx, and Silai followed.

Gelsey shot around Lorcan, an unending stream of words flowing from her mouth like lava from a volcano. "How dare you? You follow me around like a guard dog and then poof, you're gone without a word to any of us. You have no right…"

"Gelsey, enough," Aikila said, and remarkably, Gelsey stopped. "Lorcan, leave. You've made your choice." She turned to go.

"Aikila, wait." Lorcan's gaze hadn't risen from the floor. "After talking to Tishe, I realized that I owed it to you and the team. I let my personal life cloud my judgment. Jaana is on her way to nagual to live with my parents. This way I can focus on the job at hand." He paused, agony clearly written across his face. "If you'll take me back."

Aikila returned to her previous position, a shrewd smile appeared. "How do we know you won't go running off again? We've got three hours before the presentation begins."

Lorcan nodded gravely. "I got the hovercraft for the Lady Kyerr. Can't have you showing up in a Signal Master's vehicle."

"And what other way would I arrive to such an occasion?" Silai asked indignantly. Kelthar laughed, as did Gelsey.

Aikila snapped, "No time for this. We have to finalize the plans. Tonight, Ancep gets his payback."

<hr>

The Bluffs slid by as Silai stared out through the crystalline composite window. The hovercar reeked of glint. Crystal goblets, Yeti rug across the floor, and Naga hide seats. The rich and powerful of Hub rode in similar vehicles and they were all headed to the Apex's Pavilion tonight.

A full-sized Gelsey sat sulking across from the gowned Lady Kyerr. She wore a simple black dress that hid her chameleon suit beneath it. "I don't know why I need to play your servant. Kelthar could pull it off."

Silai rolled her eyes. "A woman as important as I would never be without a proper female companion to take care of her menial tasks."

Gelsey frowned, bottom lip sticking out. "You know you aren't really a high-born Elf, right?"

"For tonight, I am the Lady Kyerr of House Magdalyon. Tomorrow, I will be Silai. If we aren't dead."

The ride continued in silence, Silai forcing her nerves to calm as they went. A guard poked his head in at the checkpoint before waving them through. She released the breath that she'd been holding. "Well, the invitations Nyx arranged for us worked. We're one step closer. When we get out of the vehicle, stay one step behind and to my right." Gelsey shook with the need to move. "And try not to fidget so much. We don't need to draw attention."

"Yes, m'lady." Gelsey bowed toward her before sticking out her tongue. It was going to be a long night.

The hovercraft came to a stop. The door was opened by a squid officer, a wyrmling by the looks of his semi-molted form. "Lady Kyerr?"

Silai held her hand out to him so he could help her out. Gelsey scampered after her. "This is my maid, Nirli." The officer checked his data tab and ushered them to Pavilion's massive entry. Gold doors, each more than eight meters tall, stood open as the high and mighty of Hub strolled at a stately pace into the lower level of the space. The predominant decor was gold and more gold. Frescoes and statues of the thirteen dragon clans were placed around the room for maximum effect. All of the races from elves to kappa were represented at the event. Dragons went decades without any interaction with the other races of Harmony, so an event such as this presented a way to remind the masses who was in charge.

Gelsey stayed in place, a bored expression fixed on her face, just as they'd practiced. While she didn't like it, her thief training had prepared her well for the role. Thieving required the ability to watch for long periods of time and act on an instant opportunity. If all went well, they would be out of here before Animasor crested in the sky.

The crowd parted as Lucrea Bartomi, the mark she'd failed to fool, crossed the foyer, heading directly for Silai. Inwardly, she groaned. "My Lady Kyerr, so lovely to see you again. I hope you are well."

She stuck a smile on her face, forcing a pleasant note into her voice. "Lord Bartomi. What a surprise."

"Come now, you've always called me Lucrea." He held out his arm, and she accepted. "Our last encounter has been on my mind. I will say you almost had me."

Silai arched an exquisite eyebrow. "Almost?"

He chuckled. "I received a note the morning of our meeting with details on the piece you offered. Not sure who sent it, but it checked out. The piece is beautifully crafted. I've commissioned the artist for another to complement it."

<u>Wonderful.</u> The artist would be well off, at least. Given the evening's itinerary, she couldn't be distracted by such things. "Wonderful. Atos is brilliant, and I'm sure your patronage is his crowning achievement." She removed her hand, signaling to Gelsey to be ready. "I would love to stay and chat, but I have pressing business here tonight."

A slight frown crossed his face. "As you wish. I had hoped to discuss a different business proposal with you. Might we meet next week?"

"I would be honored," Silai said with the proper nod. "I'm curious. Why are you not more upset that I'd been seeking to pass off the statue as real?'

"I deal with politicians on a daily basis. It is refreshing to deal with someone who is honest about her intent. No ulterior motives, just glint." He bowed over her hand, kissing it softly. "I'll look forward to when next we meet." He turned back into the crowds where a swarm of hangers-on and sycophants jockeyed for his attention.

The art of the con involved finding a person's deepest secrets and exploiting them without them ever realizing they'd fallen into a trap of their own devising. Lucrea defied everything she knew about people. He should have been furious or ashamed. But amused and curious? She pushed the thought from her head. The clock was ticking. When the event began, he needed to be near the stage.

She flowed through the crowd, smiling at those who caught her eye and nodding to acquaintances. They entered the Pavilion's grand room. An enormous, raised dais took up half the room, high enough to keep the onlookers at a distance. Gelsey hurried to stay one step behind as Silai strode with purpose across to the servant's door.

More of the celebrants had filtered into the main room as the hour approached, limiting Silai's view to the immediate people around her. A hand clenched her upper arm roughly and a knife dug into her ribs. "Keep walking, fox. We're leaving out the back and then you're mine, once and for all."

Ambassador Q'rell's hook nose and angry eyes greeted her. Rumor had it he'd been forced to return to Mangku in shame after the humiliation at Lucrea's hands. Most times the rumors bore themselves out as somewhat true. This one hadn't.

With every passing moment, the danger grew and Silai found herself enjoying the rush. Hopefully, it wouldn't end badly.

243

# AIKILA

ikila waited at the entrance to the kitchens with Nyx and Kelthar. She wore the black and white livery of a servant, a blue band around her left shoulder pronouncing her Clan Caerlux. Nyx and Kelthar wore the gray of the kitchen help. "I hope he's on time. We're cutting this close."

Kelthar jerked his multiple chins up, indicating she should look. Lorcan, dressed in blue workman's coveralls, crossed the courtyard to join the team. Nyx handed him the credentials he needed to access the Pavilion's service areas. Lorcan carried an oversized toolbox which still looked small next to the nagual merc.

The squid stationed at the entry scanned their sticks and allowed them in. Security was tight, but low-level squids were a lazy lot. Once they started morphing, they took their jobs a lot more seriously. Of course, they wouldn't be guarding doors and checking in cooks if they were of a higher level. The guard did a double take at Lorcan. Men of that size weren't usually maintenance workers. His credentials cleared so he let him go.

The hacker led the way. They strode through a doorway, taking the stairs down to the mechanical rooms. A kappa guard turned to question them, but Lorcan quickly knocked him unconscious, removed his weapon, and tied him up where he'd be found later.

They delved deeper into the guts of the Pavilion's systems. A small room was unlocked with Nyx's credentials. The room held racks of servers, and a variety of cords snaked from the machines into the wall behind. A small desk with a terminal sat in the corner. "These run all the security and mechanical systems for the Pavilion," Nyx said, indicating the mass of electronics that Aikila couldn't have identified if a gun was put to her head.

Once inside, Lorcan opened the toolbox. Kelthar's bag had been discreetly hidden under his apron. He retrieved a small object. Aikila didn't know or care what it was as long as it did its job when called upon.

She retrieved her pistol and strapped it to her thigh. If things worked correctly, she wouldn't need it, but better to be safe. Nyx wired himself into the network. His fingers ran across the deck as Lorcan readied his weapons and strapped them under his coveralls.

"I've unlocked the storeroom off the servant's exit. Instead of going right when you get to the kitchen, go left. Second door." His eyes lost focus as he returned to his part of the plan.

The three left, and Aikila heard the door lock behind them. They retraced their steps, up the stairs, before they slipped out of the stairwell. Aikila motioned for them to go to the storeroom.

Aikila continued to the server's galley. She straightened her skirt as she entered, adopting a slightly panicked expression. The back wall of the room held a pass-through where the kitchen staff set trays of hors d'oeuvres and crystal goblets full of elvish wine. A wyrmling squid officer stood in the corner, arms crossed, half asleep. As trays passed by him, he'd stab a talon into the food and sample the fare.

"I'm so sorry I'm late," she said to the kitchen manager, a gnome named Thamizz, according to Nyx. He paced back and forth on a metal walkway attached to the wall since he couldn't see over the counter without it. "I just got word that you're shorthanded. I came as fast as possible."

Thamizz, white hair going in twelve directions and his suit covered by a dirty apron, stared at her. "What are you talking about?" His shrill voice could have cut glass. "I didn't call for anyone."

This got the squid's attention, and not in a good way. Aikila stepped closer and locked her eyes on his. "I'm the server you called about. One of your regulars called in sick at the last moment, remember?"

"Is everything all right?" asked the squid. His hand rested on the pistol at his belt. From the scars, he'd seen action enough to know how to use it. "I can remove her if necessary."

Thamizz shrieked. "I'm already shorthanded and you're going to remove her just as she shows up?" He bounced on his platform. "Idiot. Just stand over there and stop stealing food. I've got to get these people fed unless you want to explain to the newest Elder why the service was less than satisfactory to the guests."

The squid held up both hands. "I thought she didn't belong here. I'll be over there if you need me." He backed himself across the space until he leaned into his corner.

"They stick me with these blockheads and wonder why service is slow." He shook his head to clear it. "Grab a tray of drinks and make the rounds." With that, he turned to scream at the kitchen staff, and Aikila became a faint memory.

The tray was heavier than she'd expected. She slid a goblet off the tray, handing it to the squid guard who thanked her quietly. She winked at him before heading for the main room to find Silai. They needed to be close when Nyx turned off the lights so they could access the conclave behind the stage.

She entered the main room, offering the tray for the partygoers to remove a glass or set down an empty one. She froze as she spotted Silai being escorted toward her by a hook-nosed Mangku. Light reflected off the dagger he had pressed to her ribs. Gelsey trotted behind them, concern etched on her face. Aikila headed to the door followed by gasps of outrage from the people who reached for wine only to have it abscond.

Aikila reached the door just before Silai's captor shoved her through it. "Sir, this is the service entrance. The guest entries are behind you."

Silai's eyes lit up. "Ambassador, we should really go out through the front."

He ignored Silai, focusing on the server he assumed Aikila to be. "Take me to the rear exit, now."

"Why, sir—" Aikila began to protest. Three squids had also seen the commotion and were investigating. If the guards intervened, the Ambassador was likely to kill Silai outright.

He flashed the knife, so she saw it. "Take us to the exit or I'll gut her right here."

Aikila gasped, made a show of almost dropping the tray, before nodding quickly. She motioned for Gelsey to stay back. "Yes, sir. I don't want any trouble."

"Then move!" he snarled at her, shoving Silai along behind Aikila as she went through the door and down the hall.

Aikila activated her comm unit. Time to let the others in on the fun. She told Q'rell, "Turn right and the second door is the stairwell to the outside."

He shoved Aikila hard as he passed, propelling Silai through the service door. The tray crashed to the floor, crystal shattering. The squids ran up behind her. "What is going on?"

Aikila cringed in simulated fear. "I'm sorry." She started to cry. The lead squid looked confused, as did the two with him. "Please don't hurt me, I didn't mean to drop the tray."

"We don't care about the tray," the squid lead barked at her as the other two guards flanked him. "Where did those others go?"

She pointed a finger back to where Silai had come in earlier. "They fled that way. He mentioned the courtyard."

Gelsey vanished into the crowd.

The leader motioned for the other two to go check it out. He spoke into his comm. "We have a male and female suspect headed to the courtyard. They may be armed and dangerous. Take up stations at the stage." He went after his men, leaving Aikila alone with the shards of glass.

Once they were out of sight, she opened the service door and let Gelsey in before heading to where she'd sent Silai. She paused at the turn, making sure the squids had gone. A server walked toward them, a tray in her hands, as she headed for the main room.

Aikila, with Gelsey on her heels, ran down the hall and through the door. Silai stood off to the side and her captor lay on the floor, unconscious. Lorcan towered over the warlock's prone form. Kelthar, not so much. Aikila turned to Silai. "What was that all about?"

"He didn't enjoy meeting Lorcan. Fell straight out," Kelthar said with a sharp laugh.

Silai sighed. "He wanted me for his slave." She glanced at Gelsey, who stayed quiet.

"Perfect. The squids have taken closer positions around the stage, which keeps us from using the side stairs to access the conclave. We can't stop Ancep without getting up there," Aikila said.

Lorcan's growl rumbled. "Too bad we don't have the squid disguise from the Fortress. One of them could take the stairs."

"Great idea. While we're wishing for a friendly squid guard to help us, I'd like a cred stick with a million glint on it," Kelthar said with a laugh.

Silai shifted back and forth until she said, "I can do one better."

Aikila's mouth dropped open in shock as Silai began to change before their eyes. "We might still have a chance."

# LORCAN

Silai's Lady Kyerr form became fuzzy like she was out of focus. Motion rippled across her as she dissolved before them.

"I can't believe it," Aikila whispered as if using her full voice would break the spell. "That explains how you could do such exact disguises."

"You are the first people I've ever shared my secret with." White fur sprouted across Silai's form as Lady Kyerr disappeared, untwisting to become tails that flowed out and behind their teammate. What Lorcan assumed was the real Silai had long silver hair down to her shoulders. Her skin shimmered with a golden luster and her clothing was a simple body suit that allowed her tails to be free. Before Lorcan stood a kitsune, a legendary shapeshifting fox. He'd heard the kitsune myths all his life and never believed...except now one stood in front of him.

Lorcan shook his head. "How is this possible? Kitsune don't exist." Her almond-shaped eyes held a wariness that Lorcan hadn't seen in Silai before. The tails darkened to black at the tips as they fanned out behind her. She wore a belt with a knife scabbard at the waist. She was a sight to behold.

Kelthar chuckled. "Obviously, they do." He bowed low to her. "Madame Fox, thank you for sharing your secret with us." He spun a wooden tube in his fingers as he spoke. "We realize how much trust it takes to reveal a secret such as this."

Silai looked at the floor. "Ancep found out and used it to force me to take the job. "Q'rell," she indicated the warlock, "suspected and planned to enslave me."

"Tonight keeps getting stranger and stranger." Aikila rubbed her temples. "Can you take the form of Madorius from the Fortress run?"

Silai's tails spiraled around her, twisting themselves into a new, larger shape. Within a minute, a fully formed HubSec officer stood before them. As they gasped in awe, her outline sharpened until you could no longer tell that it wasn't the real guard.

Gelsey met each of their gazes. "We have to keep her secret."

"We are a team and that means we stick together." Lorcan held his head high. "I will guard your secret to the grave."

The rest followed suit. He'd deserted his team to save Jaana but returned because there were bigger issues in the world than himself. Tishe had helped him see what he'd been blind to before as well as promising to protect Jaana with her life. Walking away from evil served its purposes and not the greater good. What kind of world would it be with a crazed lunatic like Ancep in charge? His daughter would thrive with his parents until he rejoined her. "We need to do something with the warlock. We can't just leave him here."

Aikila frowned. "Kelthar, you and Gelsey scout the main room. We need to know the arrangements of the clan's security and how many guards are out there." The pair exited with great stealth.

Lorcan frowned. "Aren't you concerned that Ancep will see Kelthar and suspect we are after him?"

"Kelthar is very good at not being seen, as is Gelsey." She turned to Silai. "Do you need anything in order to blend in at the stage?"

"A weapon would be delightful. I can create fabric but not metals." She looked uneasy, shifting from foot to foot. "Once I'm out there, I can handle the job."

What would it be like to expose a fatal weakness to others whom you hadn't known for long? Probably like he felt when he'd trusted Gelsey when she gave him the derm before his fight with Vikog. "Silai, I understand. I've entrusted my daughter to people I do not know well but pray are trustworthy. It is unsettling."

Her head came up, eyes wide. "I hadn't thought of that. Thank you, Lorcan."

Lorcan handed over the pistol he'd concealed in his worker's garb. "This will pass as the correct weapon unless it comes out."

She nodded and she slid the weapon into the holster she'd formed for it. The detail she'd achieved boggled his mind. There was no way he would be able to tell it was an impostor if she hadn't entrusted him with her secret. No wonder the kitsune were hunted.

Nyx's voice came over the commlink. "Something is going on. The activity spiked on the security systems."

"Damn," Aikila swore. "Can anything go right today? What kind of activity, Nyx?"

"Lots of chatter on the comms about two armed suspects loose on the premises. That's not the worst of it, though." The tension in Nyx's words were plain as day. Would the decker crack under the stress.

Aikila sighed. "What else is new? Tell me, might as well get it over with."

"Ancep is leading the search."

A wicked grin appeared on her face. "That is the best news I've had all day. Nyx, I need you to notify through back channels that they've identified Silai as the person they're looking for."

Lorcan hadn't joined the conversation, so he listened as the two planned. She wore a grin that his mother would have called the "caught the canary" smile. Aikila's plans had back doors, traps, and the occasional explosion in Lorcan's opinion. *I'm glad she's on our side.*

"Yes, I'm sending you an image." Aikila stood over the fallen warlock with her portable holovid. She tapped on the screen and the image went to Nyx. "You should have it. Make sure it can't be traced back to you."

"Send it from Madame Jartic. She is the domovoi teller that Ancep used to find me. He'll believe it more if he knows the source," Silai said.

"That is golden. He'll never expect it." Aikila said. "Check to see if she's in attendance."

"If she's not, you can believe that Ancep will have her brought in," Lorcan said, a smile crossing his face. Whatever Aikila had in store for Ancep, he had coming.

The door opened slowly. Silai and Lorcan pulled their weapons and aimed before a small hand waved before Kelthar and Gelsey entered the room. Kelthar grinned. "It's just us." He closed the door with a soft bump. "There are thirteen squids, one from each clan. The Clan Yerzix squid is in charge. Ega Hul is doing the presentation of the new Caerlux Elder to grant the Chromatic Sire's blessing."

Lorcan turned his attention to Aikila. She laid out the new plan and

Lorcan's eyebrows rose at the sheer nerve it would take to pull it off. He smiled as he listened.

Ancep wouldn't know what hit him.

# 60

# NYX

You sure about this?" Nyx asked, still not believing what Aikila requested. She repeated herself as the image of the warlock flashed into view. "That is one ugly null."

"He tried to hurt Silai." Aikila's voice held the sharp edge of a protective mama.

"I'm on it. I'll ride the edge so you can speak to me."

"Whatever that means. We need to move quickly, so monitor the comm channel." She clicked off. People always assumed he was distracted, or worse, stupid. When you immersed yourself in the origin, the void fell away and nothing else mattered.

Until something did. Like now. It mattered that they stop Ancep and keep the team safe.

He jacked in and Angel was there, waiting on him. He pulled up his message spoof software. From the Hub tax records, he retrieved the information for the domovoi, Madame Jartic. He crafted a message from Jartic before adding the image. He sent the altered mail to Ancep before dropping into the origin to establish an interception.

"I can set the listener to notify you when the message is received for you while you continue with your tasks," Angel said.

"How do you know the rest of my assignments? I jacked completely out of the system when..."

"When you agreed to my help, I merged with your wetware so that I can access your internal data. What you call a brain is a fascinating piece of hardware. It took a bit to complete the interface, but how else am I to help you? I am restrained by your limited processing capacity so I can't match my Fortress self." She sounded so reasonable, but he now had an AI listening to everything his senses picked up. "We are wasting time."

He'd have to deal with this at a later date, assuming they didn't all die. "Fine. I need full audio and—"

"I understand the parameters you require."

He hit the silver stud that dropped him out of the origin. Angel overlaid his audio inputs with Ancep's feed. Ancep's voice came through as Nyx put together the attacks he'd need for the next phase of the plan. "Madame Jartic, I am in need of your services at the Pavilion, now."

She stuttered in response. It wasn't every day a dragon lord requested your presence at an event. "Yes, Lord Obadian. I can be there in an hour."

"We don't have an hour. A HubSec officer escort will be at your residence shortly. We will unmask the fox once and for all. Excellent job finding her."

"Ummm. Yes, about th—"

Ancep cut her off. "I will pay you double your normal retainer with a large bonus. I have no time to haggle."

"Yes, Lord Obadian." The audio dropped off as they disconnected. It was a good thing Ancep didn't listen. If they'd compared notes, the ruse would have been exposed.

Nyx switched to the comm channel. "Aikila, Ancep is dispatching a vehicle for Madame Jartic. She'll be on site sooner rather than later."

"Interesting… I sent you a new address for the squids. I need it sent right now. You've got the rest of the setup?"

Nyx grabbed the message from Aikila, sending it to Angel to transact. "On it. I'll have full access to the systems shortly."

"Let me know if *anything* comes up." The way she stressed the word anything caught his attention.

"Something I should know?" He didn't like not being in the loop, but he couldn't follow the team and hack Mark V ICE at the same time.

"Nothing we can't handle. Keep me posted." The circuit went dead.

*No sense worrying about things you can't control.* He dove back into the origin.

Angel finished sending the false information to the squids. "I've got to tunnel into security to install a back door so I can access the Pavilion's mechanical processes." The shields around the Pavilion's systems pulsed in rhythm as the colors changed, indicating a varied defensive scheme. He'd already been burned by the DISCS that protected the servers, so he started slowly, feeling out the levels. Doubt crept into his mind as he sought to find a way to finish the job.

The faster he moved, the farther he fell behind.

## ANCEP

Madame Jartic," Ancep said as she stepped out of his personal hovercraft. Two HubSec officers sporting Clan Caerlux blue flanked the domovoi teller. "I have my men searching for Silai. We should have her shortly and will expose her once and for all."

The small woman adjusted her glasses. "Lord Obadian, thank you for the honor. There appears to have been a mistake."

"Nonsense. Let us proceed." How the fox had lived through the explosion at the Regal plagued him. Soon it would be under control. He'd use the unmasking to distract the assembled guests, and when Ega Hul presented his rival Helaltra as the Clan Caerlux's Elder, he would employ the scroll to kill each in turn. He checked the pouch that hung from his golden belt. The scroll was still there. All the scheming and plotting had been worth it to acquire that scroll and the power it would grant him. If Sire Uhissian refused Ancep his rightful place among the Elders, he too would be replaced until Ancep ruled the Clan. He would use his power to remove the weak Yerzix and their ideas for the peaceful cohabitation of Harmony.

Ancep stopped walking when he realized that Madame Jartic hadn't moved.

"I did not send you the message you claim I did. I found her for you and set the warlock Q'rell on her trail but have not looked for her since," Jartic said.

The words found purchase in his mind, carving through the plans he'd so carefully laid to get here. Could all of the Regal team members be alive? The reports said that six bodies had been recovered but burnt beyond recognition. Those reports could have been tampered with. The hacker had more than enough skill to pull it off. "Interesting."

Jartic pulled herself up to her full meter height. "Who would benefit from you finding the fox on this night above all others?"

The six commoners had broken into the Fortress. He'd thought it impossible when Madame Jartic had seen it in his future. She'd been right on that count. Was she correct now? "The only way to get to the bottom of this is to trigger the trap. Wouldn't you agree?"

Her eyes lit up. "Why, yes. Now that we know it's a trap, we can disarm it with ease." The domovoi strolled up next to him. "I've never seen a fox unmasked in public. How do you think the crowd will react?"

Ancep smirked. "I think it will be a bloody reception." Ancep quickened his pace as the ideas flowed through his head. He'd gotten so close to his goal of being an Elder, only to have it crushed by that upstart, Helaltra. She'd molted to Wyrm a few hundred years after him but had gained favor with the Sire, who granted her his spot when Elder Vafyvion chose to end his time on the mortal plane. Never had there been a precedent for choosing a lower-ranked dragon over the next in line which he was. Ancep had plotted for far too long to allow this to go through.

"Lord Obadian," one of the HubSec officers said, hailing Ancep as he stormed ahead. "Madame Jartic is unable to keep up with you, My Lord."

Ancep glared at him, an officer according to the insignia he wore on his uniform, though he didn't know him. Who had time to learn all of their names? "Very well, bring her to the ceremony chamber. I will expect her there."

The guard bowed. "Yes, My Lord." He turned on his heel and returned the way they had come.

Ancep arrived at the ceremony room to find it empty, which was good. A second door on the far side of the room led to the main stage. Each of the Wyrms had a similar room to use while waiting. It was spacious, with two couches and six chairs in case they had a retinue, although most didn't. It also kept the searching eyes of the other races off them until they had to be on display. After tonight there would be only four full Wyrms until a new member molted to join them. His long, electric blue mane rippled as he shook it out in agitation. He should be joining the ranks of Elder, not being treated like a failure.

He tapped his comm. "Have you located the suspect yet?" He hadn't tipped his hand to the underlings that they hunted a fox, for that would lead to her being killed in order to make a name for themselves. Ancep had patrolled Hub, still a newly molted whelp. Those days had been miserable, dealing with all the commoners, treating them as equals. It was beneath him.

"I apprehended the warlock, My Lord, though he had to be subdued. He started screaming that he has to find you. He claims that there is a plan to ruin you."

The game had begun. No doubt the fox would try to turn suspicions away from herself and sow doubts as to who the real kitsune was. Very clever. He would unmask her on the stage in front of the assembled guests to prove his worth, but if finding the fox was a diversion by the team he'd created, he needed to be careful. "Bring him to the ceremony room."

The door opened to allow in a red-faced Madame Jartic, who looked a bit worse for the wear. She dropped onto the couch closest to the door. "I'm sorry, My Lord, but my short legs are no match for yours." A wan smile played across her face.

He pitied the weakness of the other races, though she <u>had</u> been especially helpful. "When you tried to unmask the fox previously, you failed. How will you accomplish it tonight?"

The smile grew wider. She held out a small orb that pulsed with light deep within. "This is an orb of seeing. I will place it over her, and it will undo any disguise or falsehood. It is very old and very powerful. It belonged to my—"

Ancep cut her off. "As long as it works, I don't care if you bought it off a mage down in the Flow." He turned his back to her.

"Yes, My Lord. Just trying to reassure you."

The minutes ticked by, Ancep's irritation grew. The door opened as the HubSec pushed Q'rell, his hands secured behind his back, into the room. "What is the meaning of this?" the warlock asked, anger thick in his voice. "I am a Mangku ambassador. You have no right to detain me."

The door stood open behind the HubSec officer. "Close the door on your way out." The officer jumped to do as he was bid. Ancep turned to Jartic. "This fox does a wonderful job, don't you think?"

"She is excellent at deceiving one's senses. A truly inspired performance." The domovoi teller still sat on the couch, twirling the small pouch by the cord.

Q'rell fumed. "Release me. I will be filing a complaint with the dragon council. Even you have limits, Obadian."

"So, you've learned my true name. A pity it won't help you." He walked around the captive, examining the exquisite detail of the tattoos that she'd been able to create. "I'm sure the one thing you don't know, Silai, is the Mangku pulled the ambassador's credentials after he attacked and killed an elvish Lady Kyerr. An unfortunate accident, to be sure."

The former ambassador blanched. "Kyerr? That wretched fox. I didn't kill her, she escaped before I could unmask her." Understanding crashed down upon the former ambassador. "Wait! You think I'm her? How ridiculous."

"Just what we'd expect you to say, don't you think, Madame Jartic?" Ancep said with a grin. These wretches may have eluded his first attempt to kill them, but not again.

# NYX

Nyx's panic grew as his attacks proved useless against the dragons' systems. Zed spun out, hovering outside the shields. Nothing to alert the AI, just a simple monitor sweep. Shouldn't even show up on their watch list. While that ran, he hacked the incoming pipe, injecting data directly into the system.

"Error messages are being reported over the comm system. They've not raised the alarm, thinking it an internal server issue." Binary code flowed across Angel's eyes as she spoke. "DISCS hasn't deployed any anti-intrusion initiatives."

He reached for Hydra next but thought better of it. He'd come to rely on the same tools, making him predictable. He flipped through the list before selecting Strobe, adjusting the settings, and firing it at the shields. A small mirrored ball rotated near the core, flashing until the colors matched exactly through each pulse. Naked Mole Rat launched, sending a tiny virtual rodent to link up with Strobe. As the shield turned red, a stream of light moved the rat through the shields and into the core systems. "Booyah! Nice when a plan comes together."

The light crystallized into a tunnel that would allow him to access the systems. Pulling up his archive, he selected Distant Counter, quickly modifying the configuration to take advantage of Strobe's tunnel, routing it around the normal data flow. He returned to pull data from Naked

Mole Rat to ensure that nothing stood out to the internal scanners the systems used to spot malware.

"The DISCS has detected your system intrusion. The tunnel will collapse in under a millisecond." Angel's voice switched to Aikila's as she broadcast his external comm into his virtual world. "Nyx, we need to shut down the mechanicals now. Gelsey, get out now. "

"Gash it!" He didn't have the chance to deploy Distant Counter, and once Strobe collapsed, he'd need time to rework an attach vector. He flipped to the last page and queued up Castor. The logic bomb he'd gotten at Black Carbon would reduce the security systems to rubble until the backups could be restored.

Nyx had one shot before the MAIN destroyed his attack and everything fell apart. He keyed the release code and Castor flew across and slid through Strobe's tunnel just before it dropped. The undisguised logic bomb penetrated the security node that ran all of the Pavilion's physical systems setting off alarms. He triggered the detonate sequence before the AI could contain his attack and struck the power node on the deck.

His consciousness blurred. His brain attempted to pull itself back from the origin as all hell broke loose.

# ANCEP

The room plunged into darkness before Madame Jartic's could agree with Ancep. Even with night vision, the sudden lack of light blinded everyone. A security alarm wailed over the loudspeakers. Q'rell slammed into Ancep as he attempted to flee, but the dragon lord wasn't easily bowled over. The warlock fell, dislodging Ancep's pouch, and scattering the contents all over the floor.

"The scroll!" Ancep screamed as he shoved the warlock out of the way to search for the wooden case that protected his most prized possession. Where was it? He pawed around the floor until his talons struck the case. He clutched it to his chest like a child's favorite toy. The door opened into the room.

"Are you all right, My Lord?" the guard asked from the doorway. He had to shout to make himself heard over the alarm.

Quiet returned with the lights. Ancep knelt on the floor, both hands wrapped around the scroll case, amid the rest of the pouch's contents. "I'm fine and do not disturb me again."

"Yes, My Lord." The HubSec officer bowed. He stumbled as he left the room, catching himself before he fell. The door closed with a dull thump.

Q'rell lay next to a carved wooden chair, frantically trying to undo his hands to no avail. "Release me now."

Ancep calmly placed the case into the pouch, after verifying that the scroll inside hadn't been damaged. He gathered the rest of his belongings and secured the pouch. Ancep stood before retrieving the squirming Mangku from the floor. He shoved him over to Jartic forcing Q'rell to his knees. "Let me see the truth."

Madame Jartic opened her bag, removing the orb. She went to the ambassador and held the globe above him. Light flared from the orb, swirling around the warlock, sloughing away the Mangku's features until a beautiful fox replaced him, tails pulled together behind her back.

"Very good." Ancep examined his prize, eye lit with anticipation. "Excellent. All I have to do is hold the sphere over her to do this?"

The domovoi returned the orb to her bag, snugging the strings. "Yes, My Lord." The fox had vanished with the spell, leaving the hook-nosed warlock behind.

Q'rell sputtered in outrage. "I will go to Ega Hul about your treatment of me! I swear it."

"One more word and I will freeze your tongue solid. No one will care if you can speak before they kill you." Ancep's eyes burned with a fire that shut the Mangku's mouth instantly. He tossed the warlock into the chair. "We will be leaving momentarily."

The warlock didn't move. His shoulders slumped as he sat.

Ancep held out his hand for the bag. This would be the most glorious of days. He'd expose the fox, proving his superiority, and then destroy the ones responsible for his humiliation at being passed over. Today would begin a new era in history with him at the forefront.

Jartic didn't budge. "You mentioned double my regular retainer plus a substantial bonus."

"I will pay you after this evening's event." He took a step closer. "I could just take the bag from you."

She nodded sagely. "You could. You wouldn't know the phrase that activates the spell." A small smile played at the corner of her mouth. "And the orb is five hundred thousand glint. It is a family heirloom." She held out a cred chip.

He snatched the chip from her hand. "Fine." He slotted the chip and transferred two million glint to her to ensure her temporary discretion. But once he'd assumed his proper place, he'd retrieve the cred chip and make an example of her, so it hardly mattered if he acquiesced to her now. He flipped the chip to her. "Now, tell me the phrase, and then get out of my sight."

She slotted the chip in a small reader. A real smile appeared. "Thank you, My Lord. That was very generous." She placed the bag in his waiting hand and told him the phrase.

Ancep strode to the door and retrieved the officer from outside. "Madame Jartic."

With a gracious nod, she left the ceremony room. Ancep gave the HubSec officer instructions and readied himself. After a few minutes, the ceremonial music began, the signal for the wyrms to take their appointed places.

*And thus will begin a new dragon dynasty. Mine.*

***

Ancep exited the ceremony room, through the door that led to the right side of the stage. The other three Clan Caerlux Wyrms stood to his right. He was the senior of them and should be molting into his elder form tonight. They had broken the ageless traditions in passing him over. In a few minutes, none of that would matter. Ancep would reign over all of Clan Caerlux before the night was done.

All the planning—gathering the team, the raid on the Fortress, the elimination of the team-- all of it had paved the way to this moment and his victory. He'd waited for his turn for centuries. The clans worked against the others, made and broke alliances, all in the name of prestige that defined the power of each.

Internally, the wyrms worked toward achieving elder status where they would become their true form. He'd waited far too long and now the usurper had taken his spot.

The music continued as the assembled crowd strolled into the Pavilion. Ancep stood ready, waiting for his moment to prove his worth and take his rightful place. His hand strayed to the pouch that held his future. *They'll be talking about this night for a very long time.* Jartic had foretold his ascension to the highest level. He was meant to rule and that had become crystal clear.

With a flourish, the music died down and applause took its place as High Councilor Hul entered from the huge tunnel behind the stage. A newly molted dragon stood six or more meters at the shoulder. The Sires could top ten, requiring a large space for the few times a century they appeared in public.

Hul wore a robe striped with the thirteen colors of the dragon clans of Harmony. His mane shimmered with the rainbow of his chromatic dragon heritage. He walked slowly, talon strikes echoing in the vast Pavilion. The oldest of the Wyrms and the most powerful being in Hub politics, Hul did things in his own manner. Ancep envied the way they regarded him. Everyone knew him, and if they were smart, they didn't cross him.

That would all change now.

Hul stood basking in the applause, soaking in the admiration of the lesser beings. *They should grovel at our feet, beg for our sufferance, not weigh them down with managing their insignificant lives.* Hul raised his arms, and the applause died off. "Welcome to a most solemn event. Tonight, we will pres—"

"Councilor Hul," Ancep said, stepping forward from his appointed place, a major breach in etiquette. "I have brought an offering for the Elder Helaltra to commemorate this auspicious occasion."

Councilor Hul sputtered. "Lord Obadian, this is highly irregular. Please return to your place so we may continue." He returned his attention to the audience before him, all waiting on his next word.

The ceremony room door opened and Q'rell stumbled onto the stage, propelled by a shove from the guard. "You see, High Councilor," Ancep said, as he caught the warlock's arm so he didn't fall flat on his face. "I have discovered one of the elusive kitsune and wish to present it to Elder Helaltra as a gift."

The audience gasped. Conversations arose over the speculation of seeing a live nine-tailed fox. Most thought them to be legends from Old Earth, and to actually see one would be amazing. They edged closer to the stage in anticipation.

Even Hul's interest was piqued. It had been over a century since anyone had claimed to have seen a kitsune, let alone captured one. "Given the enormity of this discovery, we shall allow Lord Obadian the floor."

Applause thundered in response. Ancep bowed. He removed the red bag that Jartic had overcharged him for, but tonight the glint meant nothing. He'd be swimming in real gold soon enough. He extracted the glowing sphere. "I have a magical artifact that will expose the truth of any being it is held near. In a moment, you will see the true nature of what looks to be a Mangku warlock."

"He's gone crazy!" Q'rell screamed, trying in vain to pull away from his dragon captor. "I can prove I'm Mangku." He mumbled a few words before Ancep cuffed him in the back of the head, stopping any coherent spellcasting.

"They are a crafty lot." He lifted the orb above his head and said the phrase. *Noda Wort.* He held it over warlock just as Jartic had done. Nothing happened. He repeated it. *Noda Wort.* The brightness stayed constant, not the burst of light that he'd seen when Jartic had done it earlier.

Was he saying it wrong? She was a teller. Maybe he needed her magic to use the artifact. He'd sent her away. Hul edged closer as it became apparent that the unveiling wasn't working. *"Noda Wort!"* Ancep repeated, knocking the warlock over as he pushed the orb into his chest. The warlock collapsed to the floor but didn't change shapes.

"Lord Obadian," Hul said, irritation plain on his face. "We've seen enough. Please return to your place."

"They can't hold their form after death," Ancep said, a note of despair creeping into his words.

Hul stopped Ancep before he could reach the fallen ambassador. "Enough! Return to your place or I'll have you removed."

A delegation of Mangku approached the stage. Hul held up his hand to stop them. "We will get to the bottom of this after the presentation."

The delegation halted at the bottom of the stage next to the stairs. The public embarrassment of an ambassador, even a former one, was unacceptable. One summoned a demon, an eyeless thing with a gaping maw of teeth. The warlocks stared at Ancep, waiting for their moment to confront the dragon lord.

The High Councilor straightened his immaculate robe before continuing. "My apologies for the interruption. It's my pleasure to present to the esteemed members of Hub's society, Clan Caerlux's newest Elder, Helaltra." A smattering of applause where there should be roars of approval. Hul shot Ancep a glare, before moving away from the elder dragon's entry. A rumble came up the tunnel as the massive, newly molted dragon arrived at the stage.

Ancep stood in shock. He'd seen it work. Jartic had shown him the true shape of the warlock. In the audience, a tall blond female elf he recognized stood just beyond the Mangku. Lady Kyerr waved at him. *The fox.* Rage boiled in his veins. She'd set him up, made a fool of him in front of the most important beings in Hub.

He pushed it from his brain. He took the wooden case out, removing the scroll. Nothing else mattered. He would destroy all of his enemies.

Helaltra, a fully molted elder dragon, stomped toward the front of the stage. With electric blue skin and a white chest, she resembled the rest of her clan. Bright golden eyes scanned the audience as she approached. Ten metallic horns swept back from her skull on either side of her mane. Shrieks of panic arose from the crowd as she took her place at the front of the stage. The other Wyrms and Ega Hul bowed as she roared, throwing ice shards into the rafters.

The time had come. He unrolled the scroll.

"I wouldn't do that."

Ancep's head jerked to the side where the tennin mage stood next to the ceremony room door. The HubSec guard laying on the floor at the feet of the nagualan merc. It was not just the kitsune but the whole team who had worked to destroy his destiny. "I'll deal with you shortly."

The mage stood there, arms crossed. "There's still time to divert from this insanity. Walk away, Obadian."

No one in the audience reacted to the short, bald man. It didn't matter. Obadian would rule soon enough.

"Helaltra, you have usurped my place. For that I will have justice!" He held the scroll out and started reading. The words scorched themselves into his brain as he said them. He kept going, fighting through the pain. The end always justified the means. It was the dragons' way.

"Don't do it," Kelthar shouted, but there was no stopping Ancep.

Ancep would have his revenge on them all. His voice rang out over the din of the dragons and frightened guests. Helaltra and Hul turned to face him, anger seething from both. Hul started toward Ancep.

Ancep continued to read the scroll. Then he felt it. Heat. It poured from him in waves as the fire began. It ran out of his nose, igniting his chest. He tore at his clothes, but the fire came from within him. Runnels of flame ran across the stage, dripping into the area below. Q'rell's clothes became engulfed. The warlock screamed as the fire consumed him. A second later, Ancep became a living bonfire as the spell wreaked havoc on him.

Ancep choked out a final "No!" as his body collapsed under its own weight.

# SILAI

If we don't beat HubSec to Jartic's apartment, this is all a waste of time," Silai said. Aikila had pivoted on the spot and came up with a new way to finish Ancep.

"We'll make it," Lorcan said. The hovercraft sped up, pushing her back into her seat.

Silai held on for everything she was worth as Lorcan accelerated the hovercraft around a tight corner, speeding to the address Aikila had given them. It would be close, but if they pulled it off… Well, better not dwell on the negative. The vehicle slammed to a stop a whine of reversing fans and a muffled shout from the Gnome they'd almost parked on top of.

Lorcan climbed out as the small man with a long black beard, perfectly pressed business suit, and bad attitude walked around the front of the hovercraft. One look at the nagualan merc and he decided he was late to be somewhere important and took off in the opposite direction.

Silai popped the hatch on her side, verifying that the red pouch was in her possession before allowing Lorcan to pick her up and run to the building. He punched the code and sped up the back stairs, taking five at a time. At least the merc could pretend to be winded as the three stories flew by. Upon reaching the fourth floor, he threw open a door that led into an apartment.

The spacious room had been expertly decorated and screamed overindulgence. Silai flew to the beautifully appointed sofa as Lorcan closed himself in the bedroom near the front door. How Aikila had found this place on such short notice amazed her.

A mirror on the far wall dominated the room. Madame Jartic's reflection scowled back at her. Silai suppressed a laugh. If Q'rell hadn't tried to unmask her, she'd have never known what Jartic looked like. The domovoi would be surprised when the HubSec officers didn't arrive as she'd been led to believe. Served the witch right for all the trouble she'd caused. Ancep wouldn't have found Silai without that meddling woman. She'd have to deal with her at some point or continually be looking over her shoulder.

The security panel chirped. Being so much shorter and wider had its issues, she realized as she rolled off the couch to go answer the summons. "Yes?"

"Lord Obadian has requested your presence at the Elder presentation. If you will please come with us." The officer spoke in a halting rhythm. Escorting important people around wasn't a normal duty for them.

"Of course. I'll be down." She turned off the camera and left for the ceremony. Two HubSec officers helped her in before they climbed into the back of Ancep's personal vehicle. The interior had been crafted with an eye for detail. Gold covered almost every surface, not unexpected in a dragon's ride. The two guards sat facing her from deep chairs meant to hold larger bodies. Silai had to jump and pull herself into the seat. This would be the greatest con of her life if she accomplished her part of the mission.

***

After she had spoken to Ancep, he'd stomped off, outdistancing her stubby legs. Seriously, how did this woman do anything? They crossed into the Pavilion's antechamber and headed for the ceremony room that he'd indicated. One of the officers went ahead to tell their lord to slow down.

Silai wanted to run but forced herself to keep a measured pace as they walked. Aikila passed her, drink tray in her hands. She caught her eye and nodded. Everything was in place. As they reached the door to the hallway that would take them to Ancep, she caught a glimpse of Lorcan, still dressed as a maintenance worker. Knowing the big cat had her back made her feel better even though she'd be alone with Ancep and Q'rell. Which one scared her more could wait until her nightmares told her.

Entering the ceremony chamber, she found Ancep pacing. *Good, he's worked up. That will make him more pliable to suggestion.* The glowing orb that Kelthar had provided worked like he said it would even without the elaborate backstory she'd created for it. *Nobody enjoys a good tale anymore.*

A HubSec officer brought the squirming Q'rell in, invoking a warm feeling of retribution in Silai's breast. He'd captured her, and threatened her with a life sentence as his slave. She'd been forced to cut herself in order to distract his demon so she could escape his grasp. Now, the tables had turned, and the Mangku knew the cold fear that gripped your heart when you couldn't see a way out.

A slight blur behind the closest chair let her know Gelsey, clad in her chameleon suit, had slipped inside prior to everyone's arrival. She'd needed to stay large to pull off the scroll switch, so she kept furniture between her and the others to minimize the chance of detection. Any moment now, the power should be going off. Gelsey's optics would allow her to operate in the near pitch black of the room.

Ancep would be asking for the sphere the moment she demonstrated it. She'd have to stall. He couldn't have the glowing orb out, streaming light all over the room while Gelsey swapped the two scrolls. He demanded the pouch and fear raced down Silai's spine. Just as she was about to blurt out a lame excuse, the alarms began to blare and the room dropped into darkness.

She heard the sound of a collision before Ancep screamed, "The scroll!" The door opened as the HubSec guard checked on Ancep, who rudely dismissed him. The lights snapped back on less than five seconds later, followed by the alarms stopping. A slight squeak that sounded like a pixie noise caused the guard to stop to look around before he closed the door.

The orb worked as planned. The kitsune image overlaid Q'rell's features, depicting him as a fox. Silai half-expected the dragon lord to break into a dance. An idea burst into Silai's head as he dismissed her. "You mentioned double my regular retainer plus a substantial bonus?"

"Don't mess with the glint," Aikila whispered through her commlink. "Just get out of there."

She knew Aikila was right, but the con artist won out as she pushed him into a half-million payment for the fake orb. No doubt he only paid it because he assumed he could steal it back after his. The moment their business concluded, she beat a hasty retreat before anything more went wrong.

She'd done it. Q'rell was the fox and Ancep would make sure he never bothered her again. She waited in the hall, two million glint on the cred chip in her hands. That would help offset all of their losses. Part of her felt the familiar loneliness creeping in at the thought of leaving the team, but you couldn't betray what you couldn't find. Would any of them expose her? Would she be willing to risk her freedom and her life to find out?

A slight weight settled on her shoulder, making her jump. "Good work in there. You really did a great job. I thought you might let him have the pouch too early, but nooooo-—" The pixie's chameleon suit barely blurred the space above the rumpled fabric of Silai's disguise.

Silai interrupted. "You pulled the switch?" This was the crux of the plan, getting Ancep to take the scroll Kelthar had created instead of the original they had stolen.

"If the lights hadn't gone off, I couldn't have. Luckily, Nyx pulled it off. Would have been perfect if the stupid squid hadn't stepped on me as I was leaving. You know those big—"

"Are you all right?" Silai blurted.

She giggled. "He just stepped on my foot. You don't realize how big your feet are until you're not six centimeters anymore. One time—"

Gelsey paused as Lorcan, Kelthar, and Aikila came up the stairs together. "Gelsey, can you check on Nyx? He's not responding."

"Yes, Captain!" She shot off down the hall.

"He's got Q'rell on stage. We thought we'd stay in here until it's finished," Aikila said to Silai.

Silai jerked her head toward the ceremony room. "There's a guard in there."

The mage stepped around her and opened the door. A moment later, a loud thud rattled her teeth. Kelthar's head poked out. "All set. The room is free."

Silai touched Aikila's shoulder before she entered. "I'll be back. I need to see this."

Aikila gripped her shoulder but didn't say anything. Silai turned the corner. With no one in the hall, she quickly transformed back into Lady Kyerr. Ahh, the relief of being a normal size again. She wore the same dress she'd had on at Lucrea's party. Retracing her steps, she entered the back of the Pavilion. Ancep, on the stage, raved about Q'rell being a fox. She slid through the crowd, staying out of sight, mixing with the other guests for cover.

With an audible thud, the ambassador's body hit the stage. Gasps of shock from the guests echoed across the room. With the orb held over him, Q'rell's body didn't change. She approached the stage when Ega Hul approached the scene. Ancep stared at the body as if he could will it to change. She watched him until he looked up, recognition registering on his face.

Silai smiled and gave him a quick finger wave before disappearing back into the crowd. Screams naming her the fox didn't follow her as she'd feared might happen. Instead, Ancep had to complete his master plan, not chase her. The ceremony room door Ancep had entered from opened. From where Silai stood she couldn't see or hear anything unusual but she knew that Kelthar would try to stop him. It wouldn't work though that wouldn't deter the mage.

The flames burst from Ancep's nose as the spell took full effect, turning him into a life-sized volcano. Fire crashed down on Q'rell burning the warlock in place. He shrieked as the fire gutted him. That should keep the Necromancers from trying to resurrect their fallen comrade.

When Silai turned to go, Nyx stood behind her, eyes a bit wild but otherwise fine. "We should meet the others at the rendezvous point. The fire is spreading quickly."

"No, it's time for me to leave."

Silai started to walk past but Gelsey materialized in front of her. "No way. We all agreed we'd meet back at the rental. Plus, you've got all the glint." When Silai eyes widened, Gelsey added, "Your comm was on."

In reality, she wanted to go with the team, and at least say goodbye. "Let's go."

Silai, the kitsune, walked with her friends out of the Pavilion. What an odd day it had been.

# GELSEY

Gelsey knew she should have gone back to the meetup in the Quads but she needed to do something first. She'd been in Hub so long, she'd forgotten how many there were or how beautiful. She sped through the docks and away from the city to where the Canoware Sea was deep enough for the bigger creatures.

The roiling waves told her that a behemoth or some other predator swam below her. She climbed until she was sure she was out of reach. Once she hovered at a safe distance above the water, she pulled a bag out from her pouch. Wrinkling her nose at the odor, she opened the bag enough to see the mouth of the fish she'd purchased in the anchors.

The next part made her stomach queasy, but it was necessary so she pushed through it. She took the scroll out of the case, dropping the case into the waves below. The wind prevented her from hearing it hit. The parchment scroll was rolled tightly, so it fit into the dead fish's mouth and down its throat until it was encased in the fish.

"Here kitty, kitty." She laughed as she dropped the fish. A huge maw erupted from the water, spraying her with brine and fish smell. It would take a week of baths to get rid of the odor.

The bait disappeared into the waiting mouth, which then submerged under the waves. The scroll would never be used again. With that, she headed to the agreed rendezvous.

A bottle of expensive elvish wine passed among the six members of the most successful heist no one would ever hear about. They'd done the impossible twice and lived to tell about it. Who'd believe any of them? It didn't matter; they knew the truth. They filled Nyx in on the game since he'd missed most of it.

His eyes had a haunted look to them, though he'd never really looked that healthy to begin with. "I ended up having to detonate a logic bomb in their security systems to switch the power off."

"Logic bombs can take out the operator as well as the system, can't they? Are you okay?" Aikila sounded worried. Tomorrow they'd all be strangers, but tonight they were friends. Sort of.

He was slow to respond. "It detonated while I was still in the system, but I didn't flatline. I'll give it a couple of days and jack back in."

"I'll be staying in Hub, so leave word at the storehouse and I'll contact you." Aikila glanced at each of them. "That's open to everyone."

Silai, back in her dryad form, nodded. "I'm not sure where I'll go." She held up the cred chip that had been split six ways. "I've got enough to lay low and let the gossip about the kitsune die off before I take another game."

Lorcan snarled. "I'm going to end the people who kidnapped my daughter. According to Tishe, it is a front for slavers and I'll not rest until I see them stopped."

Kelthar belched. All eyes, and a few raised eyebrows, rested on him. "Sounds like fun. Count me in."

Lorcan shook his head. "No, this is my fight. I won't have you risking your life to help me settle a score. It is not the nagualan way."

"The nagualan way will end up with your hide being made into a rug in some rich bastard's house," Aikila said, the shadow of a smile flickering at the corner of her lips. "I'm coming too. The business can run without me."

Lorcan growled. "No, this is my fight."

Gelsey snorted. "Silai, will you be joining us?"

"No," the kitsune said. "It is far too risky for me to stay in Hub."

"We'll miss you," Aikila said softly. "You are one of us now. We'd all be dead if you hadn't been here."

Silai smirked. "We'd all be dead if Kelthar hadn't gotten us away from the Regal. You can do without me."

"If Gelsey hadn't grabbed the scroll, it would have been over before it began," Kelthar said after a long pull on his drink.

"Without Aikila's plan we'd never gotten near the Fortress," Gelsey said.

"And without Nyx, we'd never breached the security systems," Aikila said. "Now that we agree we are all amazing. Let's get to work on Lorcan's idea."

"At least one of you has the sense to walk away from this insanity," Lorcan said. "This is my fight."

Silai thought on it for a moment. "On second thought, I should come along. You know my secret so I should make sure you keep it."

"What?" Lorcan said, exasperation heavy on the word.

"Those void slavers will have some serious ICE. You'll need me," Nyx said, cracking his knuckles. "It'll never be boring around this team."

"Team? We aren't a team—" Lorcan started.

"You're right," Gelsey said as she swooped in front of the big cat. "We're family. Only a family could take down a dragon. You should be honored to be included after you betrayed us."

"I didn't betray you," Lorcan said quietly.

Kelthar laughed. "Well, you really didn't, so we'll let you join us, if yer up fer it."

"Join you? It is my mission to destroy these people."

Silai laughed. "Lorcan, just say yes, before Gelsey tranqs you with her fléchette pistol."

The big warrior's shoulders slumped. "Fine." He paused. Then with a big smile said, "This way I can keep Gelsey out of trouble."

"*Trouble?*" Gelsey's voice went up three octaves. "I had no trouble before I met you. Always following me around like a bull in a glass shop. How am I supposed to thieve with a clunky cat prancing around behind me?"

Everyone laughed together as Gelsey elaborated on Lorcan's short-comings.

After Gelsey spun down, Aikila said, "We'll need to find a new base to operate out of after we all get some rest. We'll meet up in a week at the storefront and start planning."

Nods went around the circle, as did another bottle of elvish wine. Gelsey grabbed her thimble-full and dropped sat next to the big cat.

Lorcan smiled down at the diminutive thief and they raised a cheer to the group.

Gelsey smiled. Who knew being part of something could feel so good?

THE END

# ACKNOWLEDGMENTS

Sometimes you read a book and it's good, maybe great, but rarely do they change your life. When I read Leigh Bardugo's *Six of Crows*, it didn't alter my life, but it set me on the path to the book you are now holding. After I devoured the Six of Crows Duology, I wanted to write a heist novel, but I wasn't up for playing in the same sandbox as Leigh Bardugo.

Fast forward to MarsCon 2019. I paneled with the amazing Seanan McGuire about cross genre fairies. She introduced me to the term hidden people, explaining fae is the term for the British fairies, whereas all cultures have folklore and the term hidden people is a much better, inclusive term.

I fell in love with cyberpunk when I read William Gibson's Neuromancer. I always wanted to set a story in a tech heavy world, especially given that I'm a programmer by trade. The combination of tech, hidden people, dragons, and a heist became the book I had to write. Once I had the idea, I started Never Steal From Dragons. All of the characters have a little toe in folklore from around the world, but as with all myths and legends, the truth has been distorted over time. I grabbed some basic "facts" about the different hidden people and then reworked the legend to make more "realistic" characters. I wanted to represent global cultures, but with a twist.

As always, a book is a compilation of a lot of very talented people's work. Natania Barron designed an amazing cover. Jody Wallace handled the editing and came up with a lot of great suggestions and made sure you understand what I'm trying to say. Kristen Gould took on the proofreading. Any mistakes that are left in the book are mine, and frankly, if they made it past all of these edits they deserve to live.

A special thank you to Bishop O'Connell and Kat Richardson for reading and blurbing the book. They both took time out of their busy schedules to help me, and I couldn't appreciate them any more than I already do.

I would be remiss to not thank my amazing family, who I'd be lost without. My kids put up with me forgetting things while I'm buried in writing and never complain. My wife is my rock. She is an amazing partner in crime and the love of my life. She cheers me on when I succeed and consoles me when things don't go my way. And I couldn't leave our awesome Cavalier King Charles, Blaze, out. He sleeps under my desk while I write and is my newsletter mascot.

My final thanks are to you. Thank you for trusting me to tell a story that will keep you entertained and, hopefully, wanting more. If you read the book, please consider leaving a review on Amazon or Goodreads, tell a friend, or sign-up for my newsletter at www.patrickdugan.net so you can keep up with new releases and all the news.

Until next time,
Patrick Dugan
January 2023

# ABOUT THE AUTHOR

Patrick is the author of the award-winning Darkest Storm Series published by Falstaff Books. Other titles include Never Steal From Dragons and Watchers of Astaria series from Distracted Dragon Press. Other publications include Fairy Films: Wee Folk on the Big Screen, a collection of fairy essays. Patrick is a member of SFWA.

An avid gadget user, Patrick is also the Director of Technology Services for Author's Essentials LLC providing solutions and advice for writing professionals. Patrick writings delve into software, hardware, social media, and all things web-related. The primary focus of Author's Essentials is how and when to employ technology to enhance your writing process.

Patrick resides in Charlotte, NC with his wife and two children. In his spare time, he's a PC gamer, homebrewer, 3D printer enthusiast, and DIYer. You can usually find him in the Hearthstone Tavern or wandering Azeroth as a Blood Elf Warlock in the evenings.

You can find out more at https://linktr.ee/patrickdugan